MUSHROOM IN THE SAND

FARSHEED FERDOWSI

WingSpan Press

First Edition

10 9 8 7 6 5 4 3 2 1

Printed in the United States of America

Published by WingSpan Press
Livermore, CA
www.wingspanpress.com

The WingSpan name, logo and colophon are the trademarks of
WingSpan Publishing.

Ferdowsi, Farsheed.
Mushroom in the sand / Farsheed Ferdowsi.
p. cm.
ISBN: 978-1-59594-360-6 (pbk.)
ISBN: 978-1-59594-344-6 (hardcover)
1. Nuclear physicists–Fiction. 2. Nuclear weapons—Fiction.
3. Iranian Americans—Fiction.   I. Title.
PS3606 E72 2010
813—dc22
2009941902

MUSHROOM IN THE SAND

For
Aram, Kimia, and Donesh

Acknowledgments

Many wonderful individuals played valuable roles in making *Mushroom in the Sand* a reality. The lion's share of my gratitude goes to my writing consultant, Michael Wells, Ph.D. Without his support, encouragement, and guidance this story would not have been told.

Joyce Jackson provided the first round of edits. Stephanee Killen, senior editor at Integrative Ink, performed the final review. Daniel Middleton of Scribe Freelance completed the layout for the cover based on the original concept proposed by Brian Ruscio. Allen Clark's keen eyes composed the author's photograph. Skeeo Creative designed the web site. Jeremy Gossett brought his promotional and marketing skills to bear. More than a dozen friends and family members read the early drafts of the manuscript and provided valuable feedback. And finally, David Collins of Wingspan Press brought it all together.

I am grateful to all of you.

1

LYING ON HIS SIDE WITH HIS LEFT ARM OVER A LARGE PILLOW, Ross stared at the amber glow of the alarm clock as the digits declared 2:47 AM. It had been a sleepless night. At times, he felt angry at the clock for not moving faster. *Maybe it's stuck.* The thought had occurred to him more than once. Then, as if the device could sense his desperation, it would dole out another minute, causing him to rejoice. But his relief would be short-lived, as the agony of waiting would quickly return. The appointed hour was inching closer.

Oksana was fast asleep on her side of the king-size bed. Surrounded by pillows, wearing an eye mask, and drowning all ambient noise in the whooshing sound of her noisemaker, she was dead to the world. He had listened to that machine for so long that it somehow sounded natural to him.

2:55 AM—it was time to go.

Ross quietly rose and sat on the edge of the bed. He felt exhausted. As he arched his back to stretch, his glance fell on Oksana. Her silhouette, in a long satin nightgown, was barely visible in the starlight. For a moment, he felt guilty. Danger loomed near, but she was in the dark. He had weighed the pros and cons of confiding in her time and again. And on every occasion, he had arrived at the same conclusion: it was better this way—at least for now.

I wonder if they can see us in the bedroom, he thought. *With these people, anything's possible.*

For twenty-five eventful years, Oksana had stood by his side. Her love for him was unconditional, as was his for her. Together they had weathered many storms, raised a beautiful family, and managed to develop stellar careers despite the obstacles that are part and parcel of being foreign-born citizens living in America. They had made it.

At seventeen, their daughter Marina was a delightful and serious teenager, methodically narrowing her list of university options. She was named after Oksana's grandmother, who had been a seamstress in the court of the last Russian Tsar, Nicolas II. A cross between her Caucasian mother and her Middle Eastern father, Marina was a stunning beauty and, like most daughters, she had a mystical grip on Ross' emotions that he could not explain.

Victor, fourteen, was a dashing young man with features that favored Ross more than Oksana. This pleased Ross greatly. To him, watching Victor grow up held a twinge of déjà vu. He loved to tinker and build model airplanes, much as Ross had in his teens. As a scientist, Ross saw in his son the continuation of his own life: an engineer in the making. And in spite of his sarcastic accusations to the contrary, Ross loved Victor no less than he did Marina.

They framed his existence.

Ross peered out of his second-floor bedroom window. The house on the other side of Gordon Street was completely dark. The Millers used to leave their porch light burning all night, but not the new tenants. *Why did the Millers leave so abruptly?* Ross wondered. *And why rent a fully furnished house to three single men? The Millers didn't know these people nor did they need the money. It makes no sense. How were they talked into this?* He shook his head. *They must have been made an "offer they couldn't refuse."*

Oksana was mystified by the three men; they were secretive and clearly out of place in a family neighborhood. Not Ross. He suspected who they were: Iranian agents, sent by MOIS—the Ministry of Intelligence and Security—to watch him.

Are they training invisible laser beams at our windowpanes to eavesdrop on our conversations? Ross thought. *Are they using heat sensors to monitor our movements inside our home? Maybe they're using old-fashioned binoculars, bugs, and wiretaps?* Ross had no way of knowing, but he assumed the worst. He felt their presence like one does a nagging rash. And it angered him.

3:02 AM—he put on his black jogging suit and stepped into a pair of loafers. Careful not to make any sound, he picked up his Oakland Raiders cap from the nightstand and tiptoed out of the bedroom.

He donned the cap as he crept down the stairs. Passing Victor's bedroom, Ross sneaked a peek. The boy was asleep on his stomach hugging a stuffed blue rabbit. Ross smiled, thinking, *Habits are hard to break.*

Standing in the middle of the kitchen tilting his head, Romeo greeted him with an inquisitive stare. Ross was never more grateful for the Shih Tzu being one of the quietest breed of dogs than he was at that moment. When he knelt to scratch Romeo's head, he laid on his back waving his paws in the air, begging him to rub his belly.

To buy his continued silence, Ross obliged.

FEAR WAS ALL THAT ROSS HAD KNOWN SINCE THE "MESSAGE" HAD been delivered to him three days earlier. The horror it induced into his core was such that it rendered his many attempts at distraction useless.

Men are creatures of habit, and Ross was no exception. His Saturday routine began at dawn when he would drive across the Golden Gate Bridge, park on West Crissy, and set out for a five-mile run on the promenade. He usually finished the course in about forty-five minutes.

During his last jog, the morning chill felt particularly exhilarating to Ross. He loved the Bay Area, especially San Francisco. He found the scenery breathtaking. While he ran, he took in the reflection of the first light on Alcatraz as it glowed majestically against the white of the morning fog. It was poor visibility. When he approached the end of the pier, he noticed the silhouette of a burly man leaning against the rails. He seemed to be taking in the view like most people who showed up on the promenade that early. But when Ross got closer, the man turned to face him, as if he'd anticipated his arrival. Suddenly, Ross recognized him—it was Kazem, a man he had first met two weeks ago in Las Vegas. Seeing him now surprised him. *What the hell is he doing here?* he thought.

"What a glorious morning, my friend," Kazem called out.

"What is this?" Ross asked. "Are you stalking me now?"

He stopped in front of Kazem and bent over, panting to catch his breath. Without any attempt at disguising his contempt, he said, "Didn't I tell you...to leave me the hell...alone?"

"No, my good friend, I'm not a stalker," Kazem said. "I'm simply carrying a message."

"Okay...deliver it and...get lost."

"Your rejection of our invitation to visit Iran has angered powerful individuals."

Pushy people were as annoying to Ross as stupid ones. At that moment, he thought Kazem was insisting on being both. Less winded, Ross said, "First of all, I seriously considered the invitation and was willing to come to Iran." Ross paused to wipe the sweat off his face with a small towel. "But, as I clearly explained to what's his name, the Chairman?"

"Dr. Hakim," Kazem said, jogging Ross' memory, "the Chairman of the Physics Department at Shiraz University."

"Yes, Dr. Hakim. I explained to him that my position in the United States is somewhat sensitive, and it prevented me from accepting his invitation. I regret it, but that's the way it is." Ross then got into Kazem's face, staring into his eyes. "Second, I don't give a rat's ass who's pissed off in Iran. As far as I'm concerned, they can all go to hell."

"Ross," Kazem said calmly, "I'm your friend. Please reconsider. You must come. It's in your best interest."

"I told you, I can't."

With that, Kazem became quiet. Resting his arms on the guardrail, he turned to take in the view. Ross did the same. After a moment's pause, Kazem reached into his coat pocket and retrieved a manila envelope. He handed it to Ross without breaking his gaze.

"What's this?" Ross said.

"It's the message."

Ross ripped the seal open and impatiently pulled out its contents, which seemed to be photographs—glossy four by sixes. Suddenly, he felt nauseous. One was a close-up of Victor playing with Romeo in their front yard. The other was of Oksana and Marina carrying shopping bags at the mall.

"You son-of-a-bitch! Are you threatening me?"

"Take it as you wish. I'd rather call it motivation."

Ross grabbed Kazem by the collar. "Do you know what I can do to you?"

Kazem stood motionless.

"One phone call to my friends at the FBI and your fat ass will be in jail for an eternity."

"Do not shoot the messenger, my friend," Kazem said coolly. "I know you have powerful friends. I know you can go to the authorities and have me arrested. But, will that help you? Will that protect your family?" He paused to let Ross process what he had just heard. "You can't be that naïve. If I am arrested, they would simply send someone else, someone who may not be as friendly as I am, and someone who might be a bit impatient."

Ross let go. Kazem's lips continued to move, but Ross didn't hear anything else he said. The not-so-subtle threat was at once ambiguous and ominous.

What if I just broke his neck and threw him into the Bay? Ross thought. One glance at the prison island in the backdrop quickly dismissed the delicious notion.

Ross warily placed the photos back in the manila envelope, tapped it a few times, and then rolled the envelope into a baton. Without saying another word, he took a few steps back, turned, and took off running. The thought of his wife and children being harmed was revolting. Especially because he knew full well that this was not an empty threat. He had firsthand knowledge of their capabilities. He had witnessed their handiwork before.

As he ran, clutching the rolled manila envelope, for an instant he wished there was someone to whom he could pass this burden, as a relay runner would a baton. But he knew there was no one else. This cross was his to bear—his alone.

Ross hid the envelope in the trunk of his Lexus before getting behind the wheel. He was scared. So much so that he felt dizzy and nauseous. When he reached for the ignition key, he began to throw up. They were dry heaves.

ROMEO HAD FALLEN ASLEEP, SNORING. ROSS ROSE AND PROCEEDED TO the den. Passing Marina's bedroom, he carefully opened the adjacent door that led to the garage.

The stairway was pitch black and cold. It felt as if it led to a medieval dungeon. He grabbed the emergency flashlight from the stairway wall and pointed the beam to his wristwatch as he went down. *3:08 AM.*

At the bottom of the stairs, he tiptoed to the trunk of his vehicle to retrieve the manila envelope—Kazem's "message." The rear entrance to the garage opened to Oksana's rose garden, her small, private haven. He laid the flashlight on top of a storage shelf, opened the door, and stepped outside. He felt confident that he had eluded *their* prying eyes— but he couldn't be certain.

All was quiet.

Even in June it was nippy at that hour of the morning. Ross always thought San Francisco should be called the Windy City, not Chicago. But the suburb of Mill Valley had been home for the past fifteen years, and he loved it.

He crouched as he walked briskly toward Roy Sullivan's house. Their backyards faced each other. Roy and Alice had moved into the neighborhood from Birmingham a year before Ross and Oksana did. Roy worked for the FBI, swiftly ascending the career ladder. He was the Special Agent in charge of the anti-terrorism task force in the Bureau's San Francisco office.

To Ross, the memory of his first encounter with Roy remained vivid. Ross and Oksana were moving in and by noon, they were dog tired. Roy, muscular and broad-shouldered, walked straight over into their backyard and invited them to lunch, urging them to take a break from the move. That simple gesture of kindness sealed their friendship.

It was ironic that the same people who made Ross and Oksana feel so welcome had received no such reception when they had moved into the neighborhood. Roy and Alice were black, and subtle racism raged back then—even in California. The past fifteen years had only strengthened the bonds of friendship between them. To Ross, Roy was family, a surrogate for the brother he'd lost.

Roy had left one of his garage doors open. Ross made his way across the yard to the opening. Before entering, he paused and looked around. There was no sign of life but the chirping of the crickets. As soon as he walked inside, he sensed that he wasn't alone. He made out Roy's shadow as he stepped forward from the dark and manually closed the garage door behind them.

Roy turned on a pencil flashlight and pointed the beam to the closed door of his woodworking shop. "He's waiting for you," Roy whispered, motioning his head toward the door.

"Who did they send?"

"One of their top dogs."

"You're kidding."

Roy shook his head.

"Who?" Ross said.

"Colonel Timothy Nash...The Deputy Director for Operations." Roy doled out the words one-by-one, punctuating each with a pause for emphasis. "I knew you had people in high places, but the DDO of the CIA? Shit...I don't know if I should slap you or salute you."

Colonel Tim Nash. Ross knew the name. Its mention unleashed a torrent of long-forgotten memories. "Did he say anything about me?"

"Not a word, man," Roy said. "Spooks don't talk, they just listen."

"How long has he been here?"

"About an hour."

"Thanks for setting this up, bro." Ross squeezed Roy's left shoulder and headed for the door.

"I'll wait upstairs."

"Why don't you just go to bed?"

"I have to take him to the airport in two hours. His plane is waiting. He has to get back to Langley for dinner."

"His plane?"

"Yup. A big-ass military Gulfstream," Roy said. "The man sure knows how to travel."

Ross nodded, composing himself. The light from under the door summoned him. He approached the door, grabbed the knob, and paused. *This is it.* Then he entered the room. The well-oiled door didn't make a sound.

2

———————

H E SAT IN AN OLD, FADED ARMCHAIR FACING THE DOOR NEAR THE center of Roy's workshop. A dilapidated brass lamp on a long-discarded nightstand dimly lit his profile, as a makeshift ashtray, heaped with cigar dust, sat within easy reach. Using a round, wooden coffee table as his footrest, Colonel Nash sat comfortably reading something that seemed official. He looked up as Ross entered but said nothing.

"Hello Colonel," Ross said. His voice was emotionless as he closed the door.

"Dr. Ross Shaheen, it's been a long time."

"Twenty-five years to be exact."

"It went by fast."

"It sure did."

Nash tossed the report he was reading on the table. Ross noticed the large red classification stamp on its blue cover: TOP SECRET/ VLA.

As a physicist specializing in nuclear weapons research, Ross was no stranger to TOP SECRET documents. Plenty of them routinely crossed his desk, but he had never seen one with the VLA sub-classification. These were so rare and under such tight control that he had never even been in a room with one.

VERY LIMITED ACCESS materials were restricted to a few dozen people at the highest level of government. Numbered and hand-delivered, under the watchful care of armed couriers, VLA documents could not be removed from especially secured rooms. Ever! Yet, curiously, the "by-the-book" Colonel had taken such a file out of Langley.

What could be in that report? Ross thought.

"Sit down, take a load off." Nash motioned with guarded enthusiasm to the adjacent sofa, which like the rest of the furniture had seen better days.

Ross took a seat, positioned the manila envelope, the "message," to his side, and placed his cap on top of it. Then he turned and looked at Nash up close.

He had not changed all that much from their last encounter. Tanned and muscular, Colonel Nash still looked fit enough to lead a platoon of young Marines on a mission to Indochina, as he had done in the old days. Trading the uniform for the suit had not altered his commanding persona. His strong cheeks, piercing green eyes, and pointed jaw overshadowed the wrinkles. *Why has he shaved his head?* Ross thought. *Is it to mask balding or graying? Probably both.*

Ross said, "You've come a long way, Colonel—Deputy Director for Operations? I'm impressed."

"So have you, Ross. I understand they've named theorems, constants, and all kinds of crap after you. What's next? A federal building?"

"I've been lucky in the Lab, Colonel."

"Your modesty is insincere, Dr. Shaheen. We both know who you are and what you've achieved. You've served our country well."

How strange, Ross thought. *Last time we met—at the American Embassy in Moscow—he questioned my loyalty, shouting at the top of his lungs. And now, he's flattering me with platitudes. Things have surely changed.*

There was an awkward pause. Ross looked at the TOP SECRET folder on top of the coffee table while Nash stared at him with anticipation.

"Thank you for coming, Colonel," Ross said. "I didn't expect the CIA to send someone in your position."

"The Firm didn't send me. Your request for an urgent meeting was kicked up to me. When I saw your name, I decided to come myself—for old time's sake."

"I appreciate that."

"Besides," Nash said, shrugging, "consider this a professional courtesy to your father-in-law."

Ross smiled. "I see."

"How is the old bear anyway? Has he recovered from his by-pass surgery?"

"Colonel, you know the rules. You know I can't say anything about him. Why ask?"

"Times have changed, Ross. Despite Russia's saber rattling and their president's temper tantrums, we're no longer enemies. I speak to General Pugachov at least once a month. We're colleagues now, on the same side against Al-Qaeda." Nash leaned back in his chair, smiling. "Hell, I even sent the old bastard flowers when he got out of the hospital."

Ross chuckled. "I hope you remembered the Russian flower rules."

"You can bet your ass. Twenty one white gladiolas—by the book."

"You remembered."

"I think the Russians take their flower etiquette way too seriously."

"The General has recovered well," Ross offered. "Oksana calls him often. He loves the kids and gives them a hard time about their Russian."

Talking about his children was a painful reminder of why he was meeting in such secrecy with someone from the CIA. Ross placed his hand over the manila envelope.

"Do they speak Russian?" Nash asked, somewhat surprised.

"Oh yeah," Ross said. "But General Pugachov isn't satisfied. He expects his grandchildren to recite Pushkin and study Dostoevsky. They won't. They prefer rock and roll and Harry Potter."

"Kids will be kids," the Colonel said. Then he reached into his briefcase, retrieved a Cuban cigar, and proceeded to slice it with precision.

"I hope you don't mind," he mumbled, holding the cigar with his teeth.

"I don't, but Roy does."

The Colonel flicked a lighter on and sucked on the Cuban as he gave Ross an I-don't-give-a-damn look.

Some things never change.

Nash glanced at the wall clock. It was 3:35 AM. He fished out a small digital recorder from his briefcase, placed it on the coffee table, and pressed a button. The device sounded a short beep as a green light on its top came on—blinking. Without missing a beat, he leaned back, took another drag, and turned to Ross. "So, tell me. What's going on? What's so urgent? Why such secrecy?"

"Why are you recording me?"

"Cuz I'm too old to remember and too tired to take notes."

"I don't know where to begin."

"Start from the beginning, leaving out nothing."

Suddenly a thousand thoughts rushed into Ross' head. *Should I begin with my last encounter with Kazem? Or, start by telling Nash how desperately I need his help to protect my family? Maybe it would be more effective if I showed him the photos first.*

He picked up the manila envelope and reached in to retrieve the photos but hesitated and left them inside. *Maybe it's best to lay it all out from the beginning, "leaving out nothing." After all, details are the stuff of spy craft.* He returned the envelope to its place on the couch. Nash noticed the envelope but didn't ask about it.

Ross gazed at the green light on top of the recorder, which was blinking a lazy rhythm. He took a deep breath, paused to collect his thoughts, and began to speak.

MAY 30TH WAS MY FIFTY-THIRD BIRTHDAY. FOR THE FIRST TIME I FELT my age. To cheer up, Oksana and I went to Las Vegas for the weekend. The kids are old enough to stay behind, and Roy and Alice usually keep an eye on them when we travel. Vegas is our favorite getaway; we go there a few times a year. Oksana shops and spends long hours in the spa while I sit by the pool reading or when I feel lucky, shoot craps.

Obsessed to tame the cubed demons, I've tried every game strategy known to man. But the dice has always won. *Not this time,* I felt certain. After all, it was my birthday.

As soon as we checked in, Oksana went shopping, and I headed to the craps tables. It was a few minutes past five. I picked a half-crowded table and started to play. I was focused on the game and didn't notice the other players.

"New shooter," the stickman announced, as he shoved the dice toward me. I picked them up, paused to divine the outcome, and threw them across the table.

"Seven is the winner. Winner, seven," the dealer said. "Pay the line."

"That's a good start, let's make it last," I said to no one in particular. I threw the dice again; it came up seven.

"Bravo! Bravo!" a voice thundered from the opposite side.

His exuberance didn't mask his unmistakable accent. I looked up to acknowledge the cheer and confirmed my suspicion. He was Iranian. I've often wondered how I can pick out Iranians from a crowd. They look like any other Middle Easterner, but I can always tell the difference. I can't explain why. I guess it's intuitive.

Short, stocky, and boorishly flamboyant, which he made no attempt at hiding, he tossed hundred and five-hundred dollar chips on the table as if he were throwing crumbs at pigeons. The tailored black suit, maroon shirt, and the loud gold chain didn't make him look any younger. He seemed to be about sixty, and what was left of his balding curly hair had been dyed jet black. Basking in the attention that high-roller status afforded, he joked with dealers and flirted with the cocktail waitress who checked on him every five minutes.

The dice was pushed over to me again. I rolled another seven, followed by one more. Then came eleven, twice. I was on a roll. Suddenly, the table was crowded and the players went wild as I continued my winning streak. The adrenaline rush kicked in as I made the points time and again. The string of winning numbers seemed endless. I had never won that much in craps. Ever!

The biggest cheers came from the loud tenor across the table. "What a shooter!" he exclaimed repeatedly.

Next to him stood what I thought to be a rare example of nature's perfection. Slightly taller than him, her short blond hair framed her round, striking face. She wore little make up—none was necessary—and frequently allowed a warm smile. Large green eyes, a delicate nose, and fair skin spoke of her European origins. She looked sexy, yet sophisticated in her short red leather jacket over a black silk shirt, with more than a few buttons undone. She calmly placed small bets, saying little. On occasion, she leaned over the edge of the table and cradled her chin in her hands, revealing a red bra. The table blocked my view of the rest of her. The Iranian would occasionally place his arm around her waist and pull her close, claiming possession of her.

I couldn't help thinking, *Beauty and the Beast*.

All heads turned at her striking appearance. I picked up the Russian accent in her "Well done" cheers. More than once my eyes wandered over to her, and every time she looked back with a smile.

"What is your name?" the burly man asked from across the table.

"Ross."

"I am Kazem."

"You're bringing him good luck," I said to her in Russian, ignoring him.

"I can bring *you* good luck just the same," she replied.

"No Russian-speaking on this table," Kazem ordered.

"I'm sorry, love," she said.

Looking at her red jacket and stealing occasional peeks at her red bra, I suddenly realized why Russians used to use the same word, *Krasnaya* for "red" as they did for "beautiful."

Finally, I rolled seven. Seven, the cursed! My winning streak was over. I had held the dice for over thirty minutes, which is as rare as it is memorable. It was a happy birthday after all. I was up. Fifteen thousand dollars up, and it was time to walk away.

"Let us hear it for my new friend—Mr. Ross." Kazem burst into applause. He hooted with excitement, egging on the other players. They all cheered—except for the Russian doll. Grinning mischievously, she simply lifted her glass of wine and gestured a salute. *How seductive,* I thought, while acknowledging her with a nod.

In less than an hour, I had made up for over five years of gambling losses. I couldn't wait to tell Oksana, but I had to stop at the cashier cage first. Minutes later, I put a thick stack of crisp hundred-dollar bills in my side pocket with my hand guarding them. I had not walked twenty yards when I felt an iron grip on my right shoulder. It was Kazem with his trophy girl on his arm.

"Why don't we have a drink and celebrate?"

"Thank you. But I must go."

"I insist. And so does Natasha."

"I do," she said, leaning forward from the other side of Kazem.

"Okay. But I can't stay long."

"Great! How about the Fontana?" Kazem pointed and said, "Right over there."

"Sure."

The bar was not crowded at that hour of the afternoon. And the band was on break making the place conversation-friendly. We sat at a tiny round table in one of the alcoves. I could now see the rest of Natasha. She was, at most, twenty-five. With a matching short leather skirt, no stockings, and black, open-toe shoes, she looked flawless. She sat close to Kazem, facing me, and promptly crossed her long legs. I noticed that even her toenails were painted red. I strained not to stare.

"We have not been properly introduced," said Kazem, extending his hand. "I am Kazem Dowlat."

I squeezed his hand with a firm grip. "Ross Shaheen."

"This is Natasha."

"It's a pleasure," I said.

"You're Iranian?" Kazem asked.

"Yes—originally. I've lived here all of my adult life."

"Well, well. It's always great to meet a fellow *hamvatan*—countryman." Then he rose and gave me a bear hug. It was awkward.

"I was surprised you spoke Russian." Natasha smiled inquisitively. "How did you learn it?"

"I lived in Moscow for three years back in the eighties. My wife is also Russian."

"Oh how sweet." She clapped once, somewhat giddy. "What's her name?"

"Oksana. Oksana Pugachova."

"Is her family still in Russia?"

Apparently, Natasha didn't make the connection with General Viktor Pugachov. And I didn't care to tell her otherwise.

"Yes. They live in Moscow."

"Are they from Moscow?"

"No. They're from Tver. Her father was transferred to Moscow in the late sixties."

"Where do you live?"

"San Francisco."

"What are you drinking my friend?" Kazem asked, while waving to catch the waitress' attention.

"Just a soda. Ginger ale will do."

"Is that it?"

"Yes. I don't drink the hard stuff."

"What can I get you guys?" The waitress startled me from behind.

"Bring him ginger ale. She will have a glass of your best Merlot.

And for me, Jack Daniels on the rocks." Kazem, characteristic of his personality, ordered for all of us and then turned to me.

"Ross is not a Persian name. What is your real name?"

"Rostam." I grinned. "I've Americanized it to Ross."

"Clever." He nodded as he laughed approvingly. "That was quite a performance." Kazem motioned in the direction of the craps tables.

"Yes, it was amazing," I said. "That has never happened to me before. It was as if I could do no wrong. I think Miss Natasha brought us both luck." I flirted a little too obviously.

"Indeed. It must have been her." Kazem paused and then changed his expression. "Do you come to Las Vegas often?"

"Not that often, maybe once or twice a year."

"What line of work are you in?"

"I'm a scientist. I do basic research in physics at LBL and occasionally teach a graduate course or two at U.C. Berkeley."

"LBL?"

"Lawrence Berkeley Laboratories."

Natasha seemed impressed. "Wow!"

"What about you?" I decided to turn the table. "What brings you here?"

The waitress arrived with our drinks. Avoiding my question, Kazem raised his glass and proposed a toast: "To newfound friends." Natasha and I both followed.

"Cheers."

Kazem said, "Natasha, why don't you go up to the room, start the Jacuzzi, get comfortable, and wait for me?"

"Sure, love." She took a small sip of her Merlot and left the rest on the table. She rose and said, "It was nice to meet you, Ross."

"The pleasure was mine."

On her way out, she stopped behind me, gently placed her arms on my chest, and whispered in my ear, *"Pochemu bi vam ne prisoyedinitjsya k vam naverhu? Ya sdelayu tebye priyatno."* I could smell her perfume.

With that, she walked away, giggling as her hips swayed to the silent beat of an erotic drum. I was startled by what she said and laughed a nervous laugh.

"What did she say?" Kazem asked.

"Nothing."

"I am curious. Please, what did she say?"

"She invited me to join you two upstairs."

"Why not?" Kazem suggested with enthusiasm.

"No thanks. I'll pass."

"You don't know what you're missing, my friend." He lowered his voice. "She has the tongue of a serpent and a body to die for. Three grand a day—that's what she costs me. She never says no to anything."

"I can only imagine. But, I'm not into that."

"What do you mean you are not into that? Every man is *into that*. Who are you kidding?"

"Well, I'm married and wish to keep it that way. In fact, I must be going. Oksana is waiting."

"So, you are monogamous?"

"Yes. I have been for over twenty-five years."

"So am I." Kazem chuckled. "I'm sequentially monogamous—I sleep with them one at a time."

Loving his own joke, he burst into an even louder laugh mixed with a nasty cough. I just looked at him, amused. At the same time, I was somewhat thrilled about Natasha's offer but tried not to show it. However, my face felt warm and my heart was racing. Kazem must have sensed my excitement because he gave me this "who-are-you-kidding?" grin.

THE GREEN LIGHT ON THE RECORDER STOPPED BLINKING. IT TURNED solid red, accompanied by a muffled, short alarm.

"You're lucky you didn't fall for that bait," Colonel Nash muttered, chewing his cigar. Then he reached inside his briefcase searching for something.

"What do you mean, Colonel?"

"You would have been screwed twice—first in the Jacuzzi and then later when the video came out."

"You mean it was a setup?"

"Absolutely! It's the oldest trick in the book. And all intelligence services do it." Nash found a new battery pack and inserted it into the recorder.

"Did you think Natasha—or whatever her real name was—could actually be interested in you?" He placed the recorder back on the table. "I didn't know you to be vain, Dr. Shaheen…She was just doing her job, as she was told, to catch you in a honey trap."

Ross felt crushed. BEEP—the green light came back on, blinking its lazy rhythm. Ross continued…

⁕

KAZEM LIFTED HIS GLASS AND CHUGGED IT, SLURPING THE LAST DROPS of Jack Daniels from the ice cubes. Finally, he decided to answer my question. "To be perfectly honest, Dr. Shaheen, I am here to see you."

"What?" I snapped. "We don't know each other." A bit agitated, I continued. "How did you know to call me Doctor? Is this a scam?" I was upset. "Are you following me?"

"No. No. No. Please…calm down." Kazem came closer, placing his hand on my shoulder. "I will explain everything. Trust me, I'm your friend."

I managed to compose myself. "I'm listening."

"The fact is, your reputation precedes you." He leaned back and reached for Natasha's leftover wine. "We are very proud of you and your accomplishments."

"We?" I narrowed my eyes. "Who are we?"

"Yes, we. The Islamic Republic of Iran, your people. You are famous among Iranian scientists."

"I'm flattered. But you haven't answered my question."

"I work for the Iranian government and was eager to meet you in person. I was told you would be in Las Vegas this weekend. So, I took a chance and came here in the hope of running into you."

Responding to my puzzled look he said, "You see?"

"No, not at all." I made no secret of my suspicion. "Who told you I would be in Vegas? There are only a handful of people who knew I was coming here this weekend, and I know you didn't speak to any of them—I would have known if you had." I had nailed his ass to the wall, and he knew it. "So, how did you know to find me here?"

Kazem took a deep breath. "Ross…" He smiled ingratiatingly. "May I call you Ross?" He didn't wait for my response. "We're getting off on the wrong foot. I'm here simply to extend a formal invitation to you to visit Iran and possibly lecture at one of our fine universities." He paused to gauge my reaction. "You will find a lot has changed in Iran. How many years is it since you left?"

"Thirty-five years. But you probably knew that already."

"I knew it's been a long time."

"You're not going to tell me how you knew I would be here—are you?"

"That's not really relevant. But if you insist, I got a sheet of paper from MOIS telling me I could find you here at this time." He shrugged. "How they got the information is beyond me."

"MOIS?"

"Ministry of Information and Security."

I didn't like the sound of that, not one bit. Dozens of questions flooded my mind. *What did MOIS want from me? Were they spying on me? They must be. How else would they have known about my travel plans? After all these years, why would they send someone—from seven thousand miles away—to meet me in person? "Lecture at one of our fine universities." What a crock! How lame! Was Kazem himself an MOIS agent?* I sat there, dazed, processing these questions.

Kazem interrupted my thoughts. "What do you think, Ross?"

"I can't lecture in Farsi. I'm not fluent in the scientific terms."

"You can lecture in English at Shiraz University."

"Where's that?"

"In the city of Shiraz." He laughed. "You remember Shiraz. Don't you?"

"Is that the old Pahlavi University?"

"Yes. But we no longer call it that."

"Oh yeah. I forgot the former Shah's name was taboo in the new regime."

I assessed the situation quickly and decided it was best to buy a little time. "Will I be able to leave Iran after I am through?"

"Of course you can." Kazem appeared surprised by the question. "Why not?"

"I assume you know that my family was out of favor in Iran in the early eighties."

He stared with a poker face, waiting for me to finish.

"My father and brother were thrown in prison, our family assets confiscated, and ultimately my brother was executed—he had done nothing wrong. With this history, I'm not eager to go back home. I could wind up in a trap."

"That's silly." Kazem dismissed my fear with a wave of his large hand. "Certainly you will be free to leave—guaranteed! You will be the honored guest of the Islamic Republic. What happened to your family is most unfortunate. I know about your brother—you were twins. But, all that is in the past, ancient past." With a lowered voice, he became philosophical. "Believe me, Dr. Shaheen, the history of political revolutions throughout the world has been written with the red ink of martyrdom." He took a sip of wine. "In the early eighties, the beast of the Iranian revolution had a feeding frenzy. It turned on its own, spilling the blood of its finest. Many people lost their lives and countless others were imprisoned. They were mostly innocent. Your brother was more unlucky than he was guilty." He paused, looking down. "I am truly sorry about him."

"He has no gravestone, you know."

"Pardon?"

"There is just a number marking his grave. The government, your Islamic Republic, has never permitted a tombstone to be placed on his grave. This is the ultimate insult." I shook my head in disgust. "They even made my mother pay twenty tumans for the four bullets they used to kill him. And that, my friend, was the ultimate injury."

Kazem appeared sympathetic. "That is shameful," he said. Whether he was sincere or putting up an act, I'll never know. We sat there in awkward silence for a few minutes looking in different directions.

"I must be going," I finally said. We have dinner reservations at eight." It was 7:15 PM. "And, you've got someone waiting for you in the Jacuzzi."

"So, what's your answer? What do you think about the invitation?"

"I need to talk it over with my wife." I stood up to leave. "I'll get back to you later."

Kazem got up also and said, "How about dinner?" He added enthusiastically, "You and Mrs. Shaheen—of course."

"Thanks. But I don't think so." I stretched my hand and shook his goodbye. "I'm sure I'll bump into you at the craps tables."

"How about twelve noon, tomorrow, right here?"

"I'll see you then," I said, as I walked away.

WEARING A LONG, SLEEVELESS BLACK DRESS, OKSANA WAS READY AND waiting. Her light brown hair was drawn back. The emerald necklace and earrings complemented her green eyes. I've always thought Russian women were masters of creating visual poetry by combining their natural beauty with an impeccable ensemble of clothing.

"How do I look?"

"Breathtaking."

I hugged her and apologized for being late. While changing, I told her about my once-in-a-lifetime winning streak. She was thrilled.

Our dinner reservation was at Picasso, the famed French/Spanish restaurant at the Bellagio. The limousine ride was a rare treat and felt excessively lavish. But I didn't mind. After all, we were celebrating.

I must have been a bit quiet over dinner. Oksana sensed I had something on my mind but, confident that I kept no secrets from her, she just waited patiently for me to come out with it. Right after our salad plates were taken away, I said, "Something strange happened tonight."

"What?"

"I met an Iranian guy. I think he's an intelligence agent."

Oksana looked at me with concern. "Okay."

"He knew all about me and was sent here—to Vegas—specifically to see me."

"For what?"

"To invite me to go to Iran."

"Why?"

"As a guest speaker at one of their universities."

"That doesn't require a face-to-face invitation."

"Exactly."

"You didn't accept—did you?"

"No. Not without talking it over with you first."

Our entrées of filet mignon arrived. The waiter interrupted our conversation by offering fresh pepper and then refreshing our drinks.

Oksana returned to the subject as she calmly cut her filet. "What do you think about the invitation?"

"I'm uneasy." I put my fork down and looked at her. "First of all, after what happened to my brother, Sohrab, and my father, I feel nervous about going back—who knows what might happen to me the moment I set foot in Iran? Second, someone in my position with my level of security clearance and all the stuff I know can't just waltz out of LBL and into the 'Axis of Evil.'" I took a sip of my water. "If I did, the FBI, the CIA, DIA, DOE, and the rest of the alphabet soup of Federal agencies would want to know what the hell I was up to—or if had lost my frigging mind."

Oksana touched her lips with her finger, gesturing for me to lower my voice.

"As is, I already have to file a stupid 'Foreign Agent Contact Report,' which I hate to do."

"People are staring," Oksana whispered.

I turned my volume down and continued. "Third, of all the countless Iranian scientists in exile, why contact me?"

"So, what's the problem, honey? Just say no."

"It's not that simple. There's an upside."

Oksana looked puzzled.

"They would probably pay me a lot of money for a couple months of easy work. With Marina starting college next year, we sure could use the extra cash."

"That makes it more interesting, but you know how little I trust the Iranians." Oksana squeezed a lemon wedge into her water.

"Not any more than I."

"Then what're you going to do?"

"Tomorrow I'll give him a list of conditions to buy time. While they chew over my conditions back in Iran, I'll test the waters with Lance."

"Who's Lance?"

"Lance Vanderjack, the lab's general counsel."

"See what Roy thinks also."

"Good idea, he ought to know what these guys are up to."

"Okay, now forget about it." She came close, kissed me, and whispered, "Happy birthday, old man. I love you."

"Thank you. I love you, too. Do I get a present?"

"Yes you will…In the Jacuzzi."

"This old man can't wait." I smiled thinking, *I'm probably the only guy in all of America who was invited by two beautiful Russian women to join them in the hot tub in one night.*

IT WAS A FEW MINUTES BEFORE NOON THE NEXT DAY. I SAT ON THE same chair at the same table in the same deserted bar sipping ginger ale and waiting for Kazem. He showed up thirty minutes late. Obviously, he operated on Persian time, whereby being late is considered not rude but fashionable. Natasha dutifully accompanied him; she was dressed casually in a long white t-shirt and flip-flops. In bathing suit and sandals, Kazem was ready for the pool.

"Did you have a nice dinner last night?" Natasha asked.

"Yes. Memorable."

"You want to join us at the pool?" Kazem asked.

"Maybe another time." The man just didn't get the hint.

"So, did you think it over?"

"Yes." I handed him a folded sheet of paper. "Here's what I must have to even consider your invitation."

"Great!" He opened it and began to read aloud. *"Three thousand dollars per day for six weeks plus expenses.* That's about a hundred grand plus expenses—no problem." He continued. *"I'm an American citizen and insist on traveling with my American passport. I don't want any bullshit about having to obtain an Iranian passport because I was born in Iran.* This is tricky, but we can manage."

I thought, *Two down, three to go.*

Kazem continued reading my list aloud. *"I will be guaranteed safe passage and no hassles at the airport.* This I personally guarantee." He looked at me for added assurance. *"I can only travel during the summer months.* Of course." I waited anxiously for the last one. *"And most important of all, I will not meet nor interact under any circumstance with any clerics."*

Kazem hesitated. "Ross…you're being unkind. The clerics run the country. Iran is an Islamic Republic, a democratic theocracy. You're returning to Iran as a long-lost son, a world-renowned physicist. It would be insulting and scandalous if you didn't meet with any government officials—most of whom are *mullahs.*"

"I'm a scientist. I will visit Iran for scientific exchanges, not theological debates." I stood up. "The fact is, the *mullahs* ordered the cold-blooded murder of my brother—I can't stomach them."

Looking frustrated, Kazem sighed. "Okay, we can limit your interactions to the academic community. Done!" He reached out to shake my hand. Instead, I shoved my business card in it.

"Please ask the Chairman of the Physics department at the Shiraz University to e-mail me a formal invitation—with these five points spelled out—and suggest dates and topics of interest."

"I'll take care of the invitation, my friend. This is wonderful." Kazem turned around and walked away with Natasha on his arm. The girl looked back and blew me a kiss. I took a deep breath in a feeble attempt to quiet the butterflies in my stomach.

That was the last time I saw Kazem in Las Vegas. I looked for him and Natasha at the craps tables that evening, but they didn't show up. Curious, I called the hotel operator to see if he was still checked in. He was not.

SUNDAY WAS OUR LAST DAY. OKSANA WAS STILL ASLEEP WHEN I LEFT to get some coffee. The whooshing sound of her ever-present machine ensured her slumber as I dressed.

Sipping a café latte, I walked into the hotel's business center to check my e-mail. A few keystrokes later, I was connected to LBL's mail server. There were over a hundred e-mails waiting in my non-secure mailbox. Any classified messages would be encrypted and could only be accessed from the secure PC in my office.

I scanned the list for anything important. There were e-mails from the kids wishing me a Happy Birthday. I was pleased that they remembered.

Then I noticed it: s.hakim@shirazu.ac.ir. I was astonished. *How could it be? Kazem could not possibly have turned it around that fast.* I clicked on the e-mail hyperlink and sure enough, as I had requested, there was a formal invitation from the physics department at the Shiraz University. It was signed by the Department Chairman, Saeed Hakim, Ph.D. Attached to the invitation was a one pager titled, "Terms of Engagement." It meticulously listed my five demands, reworded for political correctness. He wanted me to arrive in Shiraz on the last Wednesday in June and be ready for work two days later on Saturday. I remembered that the workweek starts on Saturdays in Iran, as in all Islamic countries. I thought, *That's only three weeks away.*

My last day in Las Vegas usually feels strange. I am there but don't want to be. I generally don't feel like gambling or doing much of anything else. I just want to go home. So it was that Sunday. We checked out by noon, but our return flight wasn't until 4:00 PM. Walking around the Venetian's Canal shops, which surround the gaudy Disney-like gondola ride, was a good way to kill time.

I didn't tell Oksana about the e-mail without having any particular reason not to. But, it weighed heavy on my mind—it was all too strange. Oksana caught me talking to myself while I rehearsed the conversation I might have with Lance, the General Counsel at the Lab. At the same time, this whole episode made me feel privileged as never before—a privilege I didn't necessarily covet. All along, I sensed trouble brewing.

It was dusk when we pulled into our garage. Oksana ran inside. I followed her, carrying the bags. All was normal at home. Victor, playing a video game, looked up to greet us. Romeo went nuts and began running around the living room in circles. Marina, busy chatting with a dozen cyber-boyfriends, listened to her iPOD while typing at warp speed. She just smiled and waved hello.

Oksana hugged and kissed Victor and told him about our weekend. Leaving the cocoon of her headphones, Marina temporarily joined the brief reunion. They howled, hooted, and screamed, "Way to go, Dad!"

when they heard of my winning streak at the dice table. I just sat there on the couch, taking it all in, feeling that if there was a heaven this was it. *I must be the luckiest man alive,* I thought.

We ordered Chinese for dinner. Looking out the kitchen window at the Sullivan's house, I noticed that Roy and Alice were watching TV in their den. I decided to go over and tell Roy about my encounter with Kazem. Perhaps he would have advice.

When I arrived, Alice greeted me with a warm hug. Roy simply said, "'Sup man? Welcome home."

After some small talk, Alice sensed that I wanted to speak with Roy alone. So, she served us coffee with generous slices of homemade apple pie and left the room.

Roy listened to my story attentively while sipping coffee. Stingy with facial expressions, he had assumed the persona of the FBI Special Agent. He didn't say much until I was through. "What're you gonna do?"

"I don't know. What do you think I should do?"

"It stinks. I wouldn't touch it with a long stick."

"Why not?"

"Ross! Where's your head, man? Up your butt?" Roy sat on the edge of the sofa. "The bastards wanna lure your ass to Iran and pump you for information. Don't you see? They're all over the world buying technology shit for their nukes. I've busted a few of them right here myself. Besides, the Lab won't let you go—rest assured. They'll be on your case like white on rice. And your security clearance would be gone!" He snapped. "Just like that."

"Roy, you know I wouldn't give them anything."

"Yeah. You're big talking now. But you're gonna sing like a bird when they wire your nuts to electricity and light'em up like ornaments on a Christmas tree." He laughed heartily.

"I'm glad I provided you with some amusement," I said, cracking up. "You son-of-a-bitch."

"Seriously, man, forget about it. Don't go anywhere near it. You'll get burned."

"So, what do I say? Just decline their invitation?"

"Yup. Make up an excuse and say no."

"Okay." I stood up to leave. "Thanks for nothing."

Roy walked me to the door. "Later, man."

Leaving the house, I turned and said, "Roy, why don't you check your database? See if you can find out anything about Kazem. Kazem Dowlat."

"Will do. I'll see if he's on the Watch List."

⌇

THE FOLLOWING DAY, I FILLED OUT THE FOREIGN AGENT CONTACT Report, with sufficient detail, and set out to hand deliver it to Lance Vanderjack, the Lab's General Counsel.

Lance was rather eccentric. He had two Ph.D.'s—one from Stanford in theoretical physics and the other from Yale in computer science. But, he did not stop there; he went on to obtain a degree in corporate law from UC Berkeley and joined the Lab as Special Adviser to the Director. Within two years, he was named the General Counsel. At thirty-seven, he was known as the resident genius. Yet, the informal atmosphere of the Lab did not deter him from wearing bright red bow ties with starched shirts and tailored suits every day.

That Monday afternoon was no different. I walked into his dark-paneled corner office and handed him the report. Lance was not fond of small talk and spoke as if he was dictating a legal brief. Pacing back and forth in his office, I rushed through the story of my encounter with Kazem. With his feet propped on his antique desk, he listened and occasionally glanced at the report without reading it.

Afterwards, he asked a few questions, the last of which was, "How do you plan to respond, Dr. Shaheen?"

"I'll decline the invitation, of course."

"Excellent."

"Should I do anything else?"

"No, sir," Lance said. "I shall brief the Director. Please let me know how they react."

"I will."

⌇

Roy's basement workshop was filled with smoke, and Ross' eyes were watering. Colonel Nash had worked his Cuban down to a nub. Ross had been talking for over an hour, and the blinking recorder had not missed a beat—it was 4:45 AM.

"Did Kazem show up on the FBI Watch List?" Nash wondered.

"No. Roy didn't find anything."

"Did you take Roy's advice?"

"Sure did. Right after my meeting with Lance Vanderjack, I sent an e-mail to Dr. Hakim at the Shiraz University and politely declined the invitation."

"Did you give any particular reason?"

"I told him the truth. That I worked—indirectly—for the U.S. Government and therefore needed approval from my superiors as well as certain federal agencies to travel to Iran. And, in the present political climate, such approval was not granted."

"How did they take it?"

"Not well…Not well at all." Ross picked up the manila envelope and said, "Kazem personally delivered this 'message' to me last Saturday." Ross handed the envelope to the Colonel. "It was essentially, reconsider… or, else."

Nash retrieved the photos from the envelope and examined each one closely before moving to the next. He was deliberate, yet calm.

"I take it that these are snapshots of your children and Oksana."

"That's correct."

"Can I borrow these?" He waved the photos.

"Sure."

"Was there a note?"

"No. Just the subtle threat."

"There's nothing subtle about this. It's rather blatant—'You do what we say or else, harm will come to your family. And, we can readily get to them. The camera could have easily been a rifle.'" Nash spoke unemotionally. "That's what they're saying."

"I guess you now see the sense of urgency I felt when I requested this meeting and why such precautions for secrecy were necessary."

"I understand, Ross. Did you say this 'message' was delivered last Saturday?"

"Yes. Three days ago."

"Okay. Who knows about this?"

"Only Roy Sullivan."

"Has he filed a report?"

"No."

"Good, let's keep it that way. Now, let's see, what are you thinking? What are you planning to do?"

"I don't think I have a lot of practical choices." The scientist in Ross took over the evaluation of his options, checking them off one by one. "I could go to the FBI and have Kazem and his goons across the street arrested— they'll promptly send another crew with the order to kill us all."

"Goons? What goons?"

"Sorry. I left that part out. A few weeks ago, three Iranian grease balls moved in across the street from us. It's a strange coincidence. Roy is quietly investigating, but I think they work for MOIS."

"Let me know what he finds out."

"Okay. Where was I? I was reviewing my options. I could take an extended leave of absence and disappear to Russia for a year or two— we'll be safe there. But, I'd have to pull the kids out of school and sit on my ass in General Pugachov's dacha doing nothing. I'd die of boredom. I could do what they want: accept the invitation, take my chances, and go to Iran, defying every rule and regulation I've sworn to obey. I'd lose my job and security clearance. And I'd never recover from such a thing."

Nash reached over and turned the recorder off. "You'd lose more than your job and security clearance if you went to Iran." He took a puff from his cigar. "You might buy a bullet in the back of your head."

"How's that?" Ross asked. "If I do as they wish, why would they kill me? That doesn't make any sense."

"I didn't mean the Iranians."

"You lost me."

"The Mossad."

"The Mossad?" Ross said, with a trembling voice. "What about the Mossad?"

"What's your clearance level?"

"TOP SECRET. Ever since I was assigned to the NSA Advisory Board, I've also been cleared for UMBRA, CRYPTO, and GAMMA— the basic derivatives from Signal Intelligence." Pointing at Nash's file on the coffee table, Ross said, "Of course, I can't see VLA files."

"There are maybe twenty, twenty-five people in the entire government, all above my pay grade, who are VLA authorized," Colonel Nash said. "Hell, the only reason I get to see them is because I write half of them. It's all too complicated."

"Why are you interested in my clearance level?"

"I was wondering what I could tell you about the Mossad."

"Colonel, if the Mossad has got me in their crosshairs, I suppose I should know why. Don't you think? Damn the clearance, let's have it."

"Well…" He scratched his bald head. "I'll tell you. But, whatever I say will not leave this room." He stared intently at Ross. "If you repeat any of it, you won't have to worry about MOIS or the Mossad, I'll kill you myself, you understand?"

"Yes, sir."

With that blunt warning, Nash picked up the secret file and began to thumb through it.

Ross was anxious. He could feel his own heartbeat. Seconds felt like minutes as minutes seemed like hours. He could hardly bear it. *What the hell is he looking for?*

"Here it is." The Colonel pulled out a sheet of standard printer paper, folded it so that Ross could only see the top half, and laid it on the coffee table. "Check this out. Does it look familiar?"

The picture was a grainy black and white taken by a security camera. Ross came closer. It didn't take long for him to realize what he was looking at.

"This is Kazem and me in Vegas. The picture must have been snapped by the casino's eye in the sky." Ross pointed up.

"That's right."

"So?"

"This photo was part of a secret message we intercepted from the Mossad Station in DC to Tel Aviv…We're not supposed to spy on our friends, but we do. That's why this file is classified VLA."

"Is the Mossad following me?"

"No, they're tailing Kazem."

"Is the CIA shadowing him also?"

"No. The Mossad shares their intelligence about Kazem with us. And whatever they hold back, we get from intercepts—like this message about you."

"Who is Kazem? What's his angle?"

"Kazem Dowlat is a deal-maker. You could say he's a specialized purchasing agent. His cover is some made-up position at the Ministry of Mines and Natural Resources, but he spends eight months out of a year crisscrossing the world in search of equipment, technology, material, and expertise for the Atomic Energy Organization of Iran. And, apparently, he now fancies you."

"Okay, the Mossad has a photo of Kazem and me having a drink. So what? That doesn't mean anything."

"Ross, you're missing the big picture." Nash paused to collect his thoughts. "Hell, go ahead; look at the second half of the page. Read the damn text. I've already broken all the rules by letting you see this intercept. I might as well go all the way."

Ross unfolded the paper.

The text below the photo was all in caps, with every nonessential word and punctuation removed. It was a typical coded message. As part of his consulting work for the NSA, Ross had seen many such specimens before.

"MERCHANT MADE CONTACT NEW PERSON STOP." Ross began reading the message under his breath. Nash interrupted. "MERCHANT is Mossad's codename for Kazem." Ross continued reading the cryptic stream of words without acknowledging the helpful hint. "NEW CONTACT DR ROSS SHAHEEN RENOWNED PHYSICIST SENIOR OFFICER LBL SCIENCE ADVISOR NSA STOP STATION VIEWS DEVELOPMENT SIGNIFICANT SHAHEEN IRANIAN NATIONAL US CITIZEN WIFE DAUGHTER NATIONAL SECURITY ADVISOR RUSSIAN PRESIDENT STOP DETAILED PROFILE WILL FOLLOW END"

It was beginning to sink in. Ross slumped back and stared at the ceiling, thinking. His silence spoke plenty. After a few minutes, he said, "Has there been any more traffic about me?"

"Just one," Nash said, as he placed another sheet of paper on top of the old one. "EFFECTIVE IMMEDIATELY GO SILENT ABOUT DR SHAHEEN END"

"What does this mean?"

"It means the Mossad will have no further transmissions about you. No phone calls, no e-mails, and no letters—coded or clear. Nothing."

"Why?"

"The Mossad knows we're listening, and they don't want us to know what they're thinking about you. They're no dummies. They'll be using couriers instead."

"That's comforting," Ross said with sarcasm.

"You now have the unenviable privilege of appearing in the most secret files of our government as well as the Israelis." Nash grinned. "Congratulations, Ross!"

"How did I get here, Colonel? What did I do wrong?"

"You merely succeeded. You're a big fish in America, and that's a huge whale to the rest of the world. And now, friends and foes you didn't know you had want a piece of you. That's all."

"Let me see if I have this right. MOIS wants me to go to Iran, and the Mossad is nervous about me going. Is that about it?"

"It's much bigger than being nervous," Nash said. He then proceeded to paint the big picture for Ross.

⌒⅋⌒

IRAN HAS SOUGHT ENTRY INTO THE NUCLEAR CLUB FOR NEARLY thirty-five years. It all started with the Shah when he bought two reactors from the Germans. In 1974, Siemens, the contractor, began the construction of the 1200-megawatt reactors near the port city of Bushehr in southern Iran.

While they were being installed, the Shah sent thousands of students to America, Europe, and Russia to get the necessary training. To qualify for financial assistance, the students had to major in certain subjects such as physics, material science, thermodynamics, nuclear engineering, or a whole host of other specialties. In return, they would be guaranteed employment at the Atomic Energy Organization of Iran upon their return.

The reactors were eighty-five percent complete prior to the 1979 Islamic Revolution and were scheduled for completion in 1981. But after the Shah's fall, construction of both reactors was halted. The instability associated with the hostage crisis and the subsequent war with Iraq took Iran off the fast track to building its nuclear industry; yet the dream of the nuclear Iran lived on.

During the Iran-Iraq war, Iraqi warplanes struck the Bushehr reactors repeatedly. One of the reactors was severely damaged, with the structure sealed and the containment dome covered in sheet metal and subsequently mothballed. After the war, Iran sought to rebuild the Bushehr reactors, and asked the Germans to resume work on the facility. The Germans, however, under intense pressure from the United States, refused Iran's request to complete the project.

In January 1995, Russia and Iran signed an $800-million contract under which Russia would build a 1,000-megawatt reactor at Bushehr using the existing structures. The agreement also called for the spent fuel from the reactor to be shipped back to Russia for reprocessing. This clause was specifically put into the agreement to appease the United States. If the spent fuel were sent back to Russia, there would be no danger of it being converted and used for an Iranian nuclear weapons program. The CIA, however, had reason to believe that the Iranians were planning to renege and keep the spent fuel.

To guard against a surgical air strike by the Americans or the Israelis, the Iranians have bought a vast arsenal of surface-to-air missiles from Russia, which include Tor-M1s, and the deadly S-300s with a 48-mile range. To defend against a naval attack, they have purchased C-801 anti-ship cruise missiles from China.

"THE PLACE IS A DAMN FORTRESS," COLONEL NASH SAID. "So, THE Israelis will probably not attempt an air strike. Instead, they'll do everything in their power to prevent Iran's nuclear facilities from going operational."

"How?"

"Subversion, supply disruption, sabotage, anything other than overt military action," Nash said. "And this includes eliminating anyone who could provide them with technical assistance in perfecting their enrichment process or help them in building a bomb."

Ross looked at the floor as he processed what he had just heard.

"And that's you, Dr. Shaheen." Nash paused for emphasis. "That's why the Iranians want you alive, and that's why the Israelis would want you dead."

"What are my chances?"

"I'd place my bet on the Israelis—they never miss."

"Then why am I still alive?"

Nash said matter-of-factly, "Because you haven't yet bought your plane ticket to Iran."

"But I'm an American. The Mossad can't just whack me. Are they that stupid?"

"Listen son." Nash leaned forward. "As hard as it might be to imagine assassinating the son-in-law of the Russian National Security Adviser, and as farfetched as it might seem for the Israelis to harm an American scientist, I assure you the Mossad won't let you set foot in Tehran alive."

Ross became quiet. His fear had given way to anger. He didn't want any of this—who would? He was anxious and emotionally exhausted, yet determined to find a way out of the impasse in which he found himself. But he didn't know how. He looked at Nash and said, "How do I get out of this jam, Colonel?"

"The way I see it, you've got one choice, and only one choice."

"I'm listening."

"You go to Iran as a CIA informant," Nash said. "It's dangerous, but not as dangerous as your other options."

"What about LBL? What do we do about the Mossad?"

"I can tell the Lab to let you go. And I think I can talk the Mossad into getting off your back, at least for a little while."

"And, in return, I do what?"

"You go to Iran, do as they wish, look around, talk to their scientists, find out what they're up to, and assess their technical capabilities. The bottom line is we know they're after nukes; what we don't know is how close they are to building one."

"I'm not James Bond, Colonel," Ross quipped. "I'm a scientist. What the hell do I know about espionage? Being a science advisor to the NSA is one thing, but being a CIA agent? Even the thought of it is frightening. I have no training in your world—I can't do it. Even if I did, I have made a commitment to General Pugachov never to get mixed up in spy craft."

"Unusual circumstances require unusual action," Colonel Nash said. "Think of your family."

Ross became contemplative. After a minute of silence, he said, "Do I have to come to the Farm for training?"

"No. That's for Case Officers, not informants. You'll need minimal training and some communication equipment. I'll send someone to brief you in your office later this week."

"What about Oksana and the kids? Do I leave them behind with the MOIS goons across the street?" Ross asked. "They're not safe here."

"I'll have the FBI secretly cover them around the clock."

Ross sat there, statue-like, without the strength to move a muscle. *I'm in a trap,* he thought. *Nash is pointing the only way out, but what would his way lead to? Freedom or the gallows?* He closed his eyes and reluctantly whispered, "Okay. I'll do it."

Nash snapped back in his chair. "Now listen, and listen good." He got Ross' attention. "Like it or not, you're sucked into a deadly game of hide-and-seek where those who hide are often found dead; and those who seek are cold-blooded killers who usually find their mark."

Ross listened.

"You're hiding, Ross. And your only cover is a cloak of secrecy. Take everything we discussed tonight—I mean everything—put it in a box, nail it shut, and bury it six feet deep. No one needs to know, unless they have a need to know. That includes Roy Sullivan, your wife, your boss, and your mistress—if you have one."

"Not even Oksana?"

"Especially her. She may panic, call her father, and then all hell would break loose."

Ross said, "What would happen if General Pugachov found out?"

"Beats me." Nash shrugged. "You know him better. What would he do if Oksana and his grandchildren were in danger?"

"General Pugachov is a mean son-of-a-bitch when he's in a good mood, let alone when he's angry," Ross said. "And, he's crazy about Oksana. He still hasn't forgiven me for taking his 'little girl' away. No telling what he'd do. He'd do everything in his power to protect them—I have no doubt."

"Therefore, tell no one, including Oksana."

"What about LBL? How do I leave without permission?"

"Leave them to me," Colonel Nash said. "I'll take care of everything. You can travel to Iran with special permission from the State Department under the people-to-people or cultural exchange or some other bullshit program. Vanderjack or the Lab Director will get the necessary instructions from Washington as early as tomorrow."

It was 5:45 AM. The feeble rays of the morning light trickled into the room from a dusty porthole. The two men stood. With a firm grip, Nash shook Ross' hand. "Take care, Ross. And try to relax. I have your back."

Ross found his words comforting. All he could get out in response was, "I appreciate that, Colonel."

Goodbyes were not exchanged.

Ross picked up his Oakland Raiders cap. Wearing it loosely, he walked out of Roy's workshop into his garage and then onto their common backyard.

The cool morning breeze was refreshing after the stuffy basement. Ross inhaled the clean air as he walked toward his house. The neighborhood dogs were barking. Ross couldn't help being anxious about the road ahead. He was about to journey to the murky world of spies, a world he knew little about and understood even less. Yet, amidst the haze of his worried thoughts, he kept hearing the reassuring voice of Colonel Nash.

"Relax, I have your back."

3

IT WAS DAYBREAK. ROY SULLIVAN OPENED THE PASSENGER DOOR OF his silver Jeep Cherokee for Colonel Nash. He climbed in, fastened his seatbelt, and promptly started reading a thick briefing book. Awkward silence filled the air as they set out for the San Francisco International Airport.

Ten minutes into the drive, Roy couldn't take it anymore. Too many questions were swirling around in his head. Before merging east onto I-380, he said, "I didn't know you had a history with Ross."

"Yeah." Nash looked up without turning his head. "I knew him back in the 80s. I was the CIA Station Chief in Moscow and he was teaching physics at MSU—Moscow State University—in some cockamamie scientific exchange program....God, I hate those things."

Roy reduced his speed to stretch out the travel time. During their drive to his house earlier that morning, Nash had been quiet. Now he seemed to be more forthcoming, and Roy was eager to hear his story.

Nash continued with his recollections. "Ross was an amazing young man. Everyone told me he was a genius. But I didn't understand why and quite frankly, could have cared less. To me, he was a huge pain in the ass."

"That's where he met Oksana," Roy said. "At MSU, she was one of his students."

The Colonel looked at Roy. "I know. I was there."

Roy swerved around an empty bucket that had blown onto the road and said, "Sorry. Please go on."

"Genius or not, Ross was a strange bird. As a grad student at

Berkeley, he had developed a system for modeling nuclear fission using super computers." Nash turned to look at Roy. "Can you believe that shit? He was only a kid when he did this! He named his model, 'The Blind Scorpion.' Don't ask me why."

Nash paused to adjust his seat for more legroom. Then he continued. "Anyway, the moment LBL learned about it, they hired him, got him a Green Card, and fast tracked his citizenship so that he could get security clearance. You see, Ross couldn't work on his own project—the Blind Scorpion—without clearance. The Lab had grabbed it and classified it TOP SECRET."

Roy knew most of the story but listened closely for any new details. He merged onto US-101 going south.

"It might interest you to know," Colonel Nash said, pointing to Roy for emphasis, "that the techniques Ross pioneered in the Blind Scorpion were later used to simulate nuclear blasts, making underground explosions unnecessary. That's why we agreed to sign the Comprehensive Test Ban Treaty in 1996."

"I didn't know that," Roy said.

"Then, in the summer of 1980, Ross arrived in Moscow for a three-year teaching stint. The Russian intelligence services—both the KGB and GRU—immediately got major erections for what he knew," Nash said. "They tried every trick in the book to squeeze him for information. His apartment, his office, and his classroom were all bugged. They listened to his phone calls and read his mail. You name it, they did it. They even had a lip-reader watch him through binoculars while he walked around the campus talking to himself—as was his habit then—but they got nothing. You know why?"

Roy shook his head as he pulled down the sun visor.

"Because I was his babysitter. I had him come to the embassy every week for debriefing. Then I would tell him what to say and what not say, who to avoid, where to go, and what to watch for. As long as he listened, he had a shot at staying clear of the Russian spooks.

"Then, one day, I got word that Ross was dating a Russian girl—a total no-no in those years. As bad as that was, I soon discovered that she—that's Oksana—was the daughter of Viktor Pugachov, a senior KGB officer back then. I was petrified. I called Ross into my office and bore him a new asshole. I told him he was a security risk and that I had to revoke his clearance. I even called him unpatriotic. It got ugly, real ugly. After my tirade, he looked at me and said, 'Colonel, I love her and I love America. I assure you, I can love both without betraying either.' And, then, he walked out of my office...I'll never forget that day."

"When was that, Colonel?"

"Spring of 1982. After that blow up, I saw him at a few embassy functions, but we didn't speak to each other. Ross soon married Oksana and returned to California. As a condition for his consent to let Ross marry his daughter, Viktor Pugachov made him take an oath never to get involved in the intelligence business. And, as a rule, Ross has kept that promise."

Roy drove toward the San Francisco International Airport. Immediately before the domestic terminal, he turned right onto the access road that led to the protective chain link fence. He rolled to a stop in front of the gate and flashed his FBI badge at the guard. He waved them through. Slowly driving on the tarmac toward the "big-ass" military Gulfstream, Roy said, "Colonel, what did you and Ross decide this morning? How do we proceed from here? Is there something I can do to help?"

"Glad you asked." Nash proceeded to let Roy know the absolute minimum. "Here's what we're gonna do. Ross will go to Iran under some cultural exchange program. While he's gone, without alarming Oksana, you and the FBI will have to provide protection for his family twenty-four-seven."

"Will do."

"What do you know about the mystery men across the street?"

"They're Iranian nationals with Canadian citizenships claiming to be real estate investors. Aside from that, we know nothing. I suspect they are Iranian spies, but I can't prove it. We've asked for wiretap authorization, which hasn't yet been granted."

"I'll rattle some cages at the Justice Department when I get back to Washington," Nash said. "The Attorney General can authorize the wiretap by Executive Order for special circumstances, which this certainly is."

"That'll be great," Roy said. "We'll know a lot more when we get our ears and start listening."

Roy rolled the Jeep to a gentle stop in front of the stairway of the jet. The silhouette of the sleek fuselage, wet with the morning dew, shimmered in the feeble rays of the daybreak. The car was suddenly dwarfed by the imposing presence of the Gulfstream. Both men left the vehicle. Before climbing up, Colonel Nash told Roy, "Make damn sure the goons don't get wise that we're onto them. It's much safer that way."

Clasping his hand into the Colonel's, Roy nodded.

Nash was halfway up the stairs when Roy called him. "Colonel Nash?"

He stopped and turned.

"I'm just curious. What was Ross saying to himself as he walked around the campus? Back in Moscow."

"He recited poetry from some thirteen century mystic. I believe it was Rumi." The Colonel grinned and continued his climb.

Roy just shook his head.

4

AFTER BEING UP ALL NIGHT WITH COLONEL NASH, ROSS STAYED home the next day to catch up on his sleep. Oksana didn't suspect anything and let him stay in bed until noon. To wake him, she crawled in bed and gently placed her head on his chest. He began caressing her hair, thinking about how she made the ordinary feel enchanted. A cup of Russian tea, brewed on a samovar, with two sugar cubes on the side awaited him on the nightstand.

Ross sat up in bed, sipping his tea while holding a sugar cube in between his teeth, Persian style, delighting in the intoxicating aroma.

The sight of the Miller's house, with the curtains drawn cloaking its occupants, no longer evoked the same emotions. His fear and anger had surprisingly given way to a strange calm. Ross had crossed the Rubicon and was resigned to what lay ahead.

Oksana smiled. "Did you sleep well?"

"Yes. I needed that."

"Are you all right?"

"Yes, darling—I'm fine."

"Roy stopped by to see you."

"Oh yeah? I'll call him later."

But he didn't. Ross wasn't ready to rehash what had transpired between him and Colonel Nash. Besides, he needed time to determine how much he would tell Roy.

Later that afternoon, Ross drafted the e-mail he planned to send to Dr. Hakim at Shiraz University, reversing his previous message and accepting his invitation. However, he delayed sending it. First, he had to make sure that Colonel Nash had made the necessary arrangements with Lance Vanderjack at the Lab.

The next morning at dawn, before heading out to work, Ross took Romeo for his morning walk. It was Friday, and he looked forward to the weekend. He left for Berkeley before 7:00 AM to beat the traffic.

Ordinarily, he took the Richmond Bridge from San Rafael to Contra Costa and onto Berkeley. Traversing the five and a half mile span over water used to be awe-inspiring, but it was now routine. However, the view of the other two wonders, the Golden Gate and the Bay Bridge, was never routine. Ross loved them both.

The Golden Gate, with its towers rising high above the blue waters of the Bay, is a unique blend of beauty and grace whereas the Bay Bridge, over eight miles long, manifests raw power with dignity. Both structures look especially majestic as the sun rises or sets behind them. And, when the fog blankets the Bay, they are indescribably romantic.

Ross felt different that day—somewhat vulnerable. It had been a strange few days. The car seemed to drive itself while he was transported to another era on wings of vivid memories. He was thinking of his brother, Sohrab.

They had been inseparable. Ross recalled how they used to claim the landmark bridges as their own. The Golden Gate was Sohrab's and the Bay Bridge, his.

Andrea Bocelli sang on the car's CD player as Ross sped over the Bay, oblivious to the wind blowing through his hair. The prospect of returning to his birthplace evoked an odd feeling of melancholy, which he didn't want to explore. Recalling the carefree summer months of his youth in Iran and the precious college years he had spent with Sohrab here at Berkley were painful. Ross recalled how fearless and rich with promises they'd felt; the world was theirs to conquer. Who could have predicted how things would turn out for the two of them?

They had been born together—eight minutes apart—in the northern outskirts of Tehran. Here he was, fifty-three years later, on the other side of the planet, a well-known physicist, a high-ranking officer of one of the greatest research labs in the world, married with children, and living a picture-perfect life. There was Sohrab, buried unceremoniously in his blood-soaked clothes in an unmarked grave, only a few miles away from where they were born. The brutality of the way he died was only surpassed by the cruelty of dying at the age of twenty-seven.

Deep in thought, Ross continued to drive toward Berkeley. However, the melancholy lingered as Bocelli's voice soared.

Lawrence Berkeley Laboratory, named after its founder, Ernest Orlando Lawrence, is the oldest national laboratory in America. Even though it has a broad scope, it is best known as the Mecca of particle physics. Equally referred to as the "Berkeley Lab," "LBL," or simply, "the Lab," it is a sprawling campus of over one hundred buildings spread over a square mile, where nearly 4,000 employees and researchers toil in relentless pursuit of the most esoteric of nature's secrets. LBL is situated in Berkeley on the hillside directly above the campus of the University of California at Berkeley.

The meteoric rise of Ross' career from a promising graduate student in applied physics to the lead researcher on a TOP SECRET project was a tale that resembled fiction. Soon after receiving his doctorate, followed by a teaching stint in Moscow, he joined LBL and was catapulted onto the Lab's behemoth organization at a level that far surpassed his experience. Twenty-five years later, his journey had brought him to where he was today: the Director of Nuclear Science— merely two organizational levels below the Lab's Director. Ross was fond of saying, "Only in America could this happen to a foreign-born citizen, especially when the government ruling his native land is a sworn enemy of the state and part of the *Axis of Evil*."

The elevator door opened to the seventh floor lobby of Building 50 with a single ring of the bell.

"Morning, Ross." Pam Carlisle, his executive assistant for the past ten years, greeted him in her typical jovial manner. "I hope you're feeling better."

"I'm fine," Ross mumbled, as he walked by her desk toward his office. Not feeling particularly sociable, he said, "Cancel all my appointments for today."

He inserted a magnetic blue badge into the slot on the right side of the doorknob. The familiar green light flashed, and the door silently cracked open. The nameplate on his door simply read, *"R. Shaheen, Division Director."*

TOP SECRET clearance was a requirement for being elevated

to one of the seventeen Division Directors at the Lab. Working with sensitive technologies and serving on various government advisory boards, with access to classified information, mandated strict security precautions. This was especially true for Ross. He had only recently been appointed to the NSA—National Security Agency—Science Advisory Board. At the NSA, the greatest global information vacuum cleaner ever devised, secrecy is not merely an occupational necessity; it is an institutional obsession.

"Mr. Vanderjack wants you to call him as soon as possible," Pam said, as Ross entered his office.

What the hell does Vanderjack want this early in the morning? Ross thought. *He rarely calls me anyway. Surely it couldn't be because of Colonel Nash. The government never moves at this speed.*

Ross closed the door and flipped the light switch. He took a step toward the phone but stopped short when his feet touched something soft and unfamiliar. A Persian rug had appeared out of nowhere. He smiled. Oksana had tastefully redecorated his office, and the rug she had ordered—the last touch—had finally arrived. Ross paused to admire the overall effect now that everything was in place. To the left of the entrance, two suede couches, separated by a glass coffee table, faced each other. The oversized maroon Russian box on the table complemented the furniture. Panoramic windows spanned two adjacent sides of the corner office, resulting in a breathtaking view of the campus. Where the two walls of glass met stood a square granite conference table surrounded by eight black chairs.

Ross' workspace to the right of the entrance was rather elaborate. Two leather chairs, used informally by visitors, faced the large, cherry wood desk and side table. Two flat-screen monitors were carefully positioned—one on each corner of the desk—where they wouldn't obstruct his view of the guests across. The monitor to the left, connected to an ordinary PC, was for routine work and un-secure e-mail. It also connected Ross to the incomprehensible processing power of NERSC, the National Energy Research Scientific Computing Center. The Oakland-based NERSC operated some of the fastest computers and largest storage systems ever invented, and provided non-classified processing service to scientists around the world.

Unbeknownst to the public, NERSC also operated a clandestine supercomputer for the exclusive use of a select few. The IBM's Blue Glacier—codenamed, "Blind Scorpion," after a system Ross had originally developed in graduate school and had continuously enhanced ever since—was capable of processing 1,050 teraflops per second. The Blind Scorpion needed all that power to carry out its mission, to simulate the explosion of a nuclear device and calculate its yield.

Ross used the monitor to the right of his desk for classified work, secure e-mail, and most importantly, to access the Blind Scorpion. Connected to a diskless PC, the flat-screen recognized his face through the vigilant eyes of a tiny camera at the top corner. If the digitized image matched the sparse database of authorized users, a virtual corridor to the secret supercomputer would open and allow access—secure, encrypted, and immune from any hackers—otherwise, an armed guard would walk into the office within five minutes.

The Blind Scorpion had never been breached.

Ross walked to his desk, picked up the phone, and dialed a number.

"That's right, Dr. Shaheen," Lance Vanderjack explained. "Yesterday, the Director received a call from the Undersecretary of DOE green lighting your trip to Iran. It's my understanding that the State Department considers the invitation you've received as a positive gesture by the Iranians and doesn't wish to snub them. Any concern the Director and I may have regarding your security is secondary. So, it's up to you. If you want to go, you may."

"I plan to go," Ross said. "And, I expect to spend the entire summer there."

"Good luck, and be careful, Dr. Shaheen."

Colonel Nash had come through. Ross sat down and quickly retrieved the e-mail he had drafted to Dr. Hakim at the Shiraz University. He paused to read it over one last time before clicking SEND.

Then, he leaned back, staring at the ceiling.

5

THE CENTRAL INTELLIGENCE AGENCY (CIA) EXISTS, IN BROAD terms, to serve a single strategic customer: The President of the United States. True, dozens of other government agencies and countless officials benefit from the CIA's efforts. But its primary mission continues to be providing the Commander-in-Chief with the necessary intelligence and analysis to make informed decisions. The agency's Director—also known as the DCI—has a standing early morning appointment to brief the President every day of every week. The DCI controls untold secrets and enjoys unprecedented access to the President, which in Washington means only one thing: unparalleled power.

Established in 1947 by an act of Congress, the CIA, in its simplest form, is divided into two main divisions called Directorates. The Directorate of Intelligence (DI) is made up of thousands of analysts, experts in every conceivable discipline, who make sense of the flood of information that flows into the agency every day. The Directorate of Operations (DO) encompasses the information collectors, the worldwide network of spies and secret agents. Romanticized as mythical figures, these are the Case Officers, primarily stationed overseas, who gather information from local informants and human assets. As the Deputy Director of CIA for Operations (DDO), Colonel Timothy Nash was America's spymaster.

After September 11, the CIA has had more spies stealing more secrets in more places than any other time in its history. They go to the back alleys of hellholes in the far away corners of the world in search of forbidden and tightly guarded knowledge.

And Dr. Ross Shaheen was their latest recruit.

THE SIGN ON THE THIRD HANDBALL COURT READ, *RESERVED FOR DDO*, *7:00 – 10:00 AM, Saturday, June 16th*. The sprawling exercise and fitness complex was built on the CIA campus at Langley, Virginia for the exclusive use of agency personnel.

Colonel Nash, wearing a sleeveless military sweatshirt, khaki shorts, and white sneakers, was on the court thirty minutes early to stretch and warm up. After all these years, he still wore his dog tags. It was the Sabbath for his long-time friend, Evrom Rafael. Formerly a wing commander of the Israel Defense Forces, Evrom was now the Mossad's station chief in Washington, under the cover of IDF military attaché. Commander Rafael rarely broke Sabbath unless it was for an important reason. And the Colonel rarely called him otherwise.

Every square inch of the glass wall separating the gallery from the court was covered with sheets of opaque brown paper. Colonel Nash considered his ferocious handball duels with Rafael as private affairs, closed to spectators.

The door to the court opened promptly at seven, and Commander Rafael walked in. Dressed in black state-of-the-art gear and donning a pair of bright yellow goggles, he looked hip and half his age.

"Ready to get beat, old man?" Rafael gloated in his deep, Israeli accent.

"Sweet dreams."

"I believe it's your serve," Rafael said.

"Yes. I remember kicking your ass last time."

The irreverence was the only way they knew how to show affection. Nash was much more concerned about what he wanted to bring up with Rafael than he was with the game—not that beating Rafael wasn't important.

The old warriors, now spymasters, played handball according to their own simple rules. There were no sets. They counted points endlessly until one of them collapsed from exhaustion. Fight to the finish. Their legendary games used to take three hours or more to conclude. Nowadays, both in their sixties, they could barely manage into the second hour—although, like Nash, Rafael was athletic and remarkably fit. The two went at each other like Roman gladiators.

The quiet panting of the aging soldiers punctuated the shriek of the ball's ricochet. Toiling for the invisible spoil of conquest, which is pride, they only spoke to announce the score.

Shortly after nine o'clock, Nash and Rafael were both exhausted. At 177 to 181, they were neck and neck. Ten minutes later, Nash threw in the towel. Drenched in sweat, he leaned against the wall and slowly slid down it, his eyes closed. Rafael, barely audible through his heavy breathing, said, "You're slowing down, old man." He collapsed on the opposite side of the court. Nash shot him the bird without opening his eyes. For the next few minutes they just rested.

Finally, Nash cut to the chase. He lifted his sweatshirt to wipe the perspiration off his face and said, "Evrom...Ross Shaheen is clean, lay off of him."

Rafael got off the floor, squatted against the wall on the opposite side of the court, and shrugged. "I don't know what you're talking about, Colonel." Nonchalantly, he picked up the ball and began throwing it against the wall, catching it on the rebound.

"That's exactly what I expected you to say," Nash shot back. "We're done with the game, Evrom. Now let's get real." Nash turned up the volume. "Ross is going to Iran as a CIA informant. I want you to send an urgent message to Tel Aviv that he's got a pass from me." Nash jabbed his chest with his right thumb. "And hands off."

Rafael caught the ball and began to look at it closely while squeezing it in his right hand. After a short pause he said, "It's not that easy, Colonel."

"And why the hell not?"

Rafael looked back at Nash. "He's the missing link in their nuke program. If he sets foot in Iran, they'll squeeze him for bomb designs, for enrichment techniques, for neutron triggers, and God knows what else. They'll gain at least five years, Colonel. Besides, it's too late...the order has already been given."

Nash squinted. "What order?"

"How should I put it delicately?" Rafael threw the ball against the wall. "He's never to reach Iran alive."

"Rescind it for God's sake! I told you, he's mine."

Thinking, Rafael continued bouncing the ball against the wall. After a few rebounds he said, "I'll see what I can do."

"That's bullshit, Rafael. I want your personal assurance, here and now, that the Mossad will cross Dr. Shaheen from its hit list. Period!"

"And if we don't?"

"There'll be hell to pay." Nash focused his stare on Rafael like a bullet in flight. He didn't need to shout to make his point. "I swear, if any harm comes to Ross Shaheen, if he slips on a banana peel, if his plane crashes, if he so much as chokes on a damn fishbone—I'll blame the Mossad. And as God is my witness, I'll see to it that you pay. I don't mean 'an eye-for-eye,' Commander. That's your law. I'll take ten pairs of eyeballs for a single one. That's my law. Do we understand each other?"

"You're bluffing, Colonel."

"If I am, you can't afford to call it, Commander. And quit throwing that damn ball."

Rafael caught the ball and quickly pondered his options. He wasn't about to piss off the CIA and his old friend, Nash. Besides, he knew full well that the Mossad would ultimately back off from pulling the trigger on Pugachov's son-in-law. In the final analysis all people—and governments alike—act in their self-interest. Killing Dr. Shaheen would serve a lesser interest than being in the good graces of the CIA. Not to mention the second most powerful Russian alive, General Viktor Pugachov.

"All right. We'll stand down," Rafael said. "I trust the CIA will reciprocate by sharing any intelligence that Dr. Shaheen may provide."

"Haven't we always?"

After a long pause, Rafael said, "Colonel, I don't need to tell you that if the Iranians ever get their nukes, Tel Aviv and Haifa will be their targets, not Washington and New York."

"I know, Evrom...I know."

The two men grimly gazed at each other. The nightmare of an Iranian nuke heading for Israel on top of their Shahab III missile was one of the few scenarios that kept both men awake at nights.

"You know," Evrom said, "we might both burn for letting Dr. Shaheen go to Iran."

"We just might," Nash said, nodding. "But it's a risk worth taking to fill in any intelligence gap we have about their capabilities. All the same, I'll buy us an insurance policy."

Evrom nodded approval. He knew what Nash meant. "Buying an insurance policy," in spy lingo, means hiring a standby assassin.

6

A ROUND NOON, PAM CARLISLE WALKED INTO ROSS' OFFICE CARRYING a plate in one hand, a bottle of water in the other, and cheerfully announced, "Lunch time."

"What do we have?"

"Your usual: avocado, provolone, cucumbers, sprouts, and sour cream on rye bread. Happy?"

"What would I do without you, Pam?" he said, without looking away from what he was reading.

She placed the food in front of Ross. "You'd be lost." Then she said, "By the way, someone named Peter called and said he was in town and needed to see you. That the Colonel had sent him."

Ross looked up. Suddenly eager, he said, "Where is he?"

"I don't know." Pam shrugged. "I told him you were busy. Who's the Colonel anyway?"

"Someone from the Pentagon who wants me to look at a project," Ross said. "Did Peter leave a number?"

"Yes. His cell. I'll get it for you."

Within the hour, Pam ushered Peter into Ross' office and closed the door behind him. He was a small man carrying an oversized briefcase. About thirty, he barely stood taller than five feet. He wore blue jeans with an open-collar white shirt under a navy blue blazer. A pair of black-rimmed glasses sat on a large nose, which dominated his expressionless face. Other than looking nerdy, and a bit awkward, he was clean cut.

"Hi, I'm Peter." He stretched his hand a little too early as he walked toward Ross. "Colonel Nash sent me."

"Peter who?"

"Peter Erwin."

Ross suspected that wasn't his real name. It sounded too pedestrian. But he understood. After all, the man worked for the CIA, and they live in aliases. Ross stood and introduced himself. "What brings you here, Peter?"

"Colonel Nash sent me to brief you. I'm a regional analyst and mostly cover Iran."

They walked to the conference table and sat on adjacent sides. Peter placed his briefcase on the table and opened it. It was full of neatly organized files and papers with a few stamped CLASSIFIED in blue. Ross noticed the edge of a thick red envelope, which was visible from the inside pocket of the briefcase. *Red envelopes usually mean TOP SECRET,* he thought, but he couldn't be sure.

"How much time do you have, Dr. Shaheen?" Peter asked.

"As much as you need."

"I've briefed countless people on Iran, but never an Iranian. This is a first for me. I'm afraid you may already know a lot of what I'm about to tell you. So, I apologize in advance for any redundant information."

"Don't worry," Ross said. "I've been out of Iran and out of touch with its politics for so long that I might as well be a stranger."

Peter pulled out a small map and placed it on the table. It showed Iran and her surrounding neighbors. He also handed Ross a thick, spiral-bound book titled, *The Islamic Republic of Iran: Geo-Strategy, Internal Politics, and Markets.* "Read this at your leisure. It has a wealth of information. Nothing classified, but it should be treated as confidential. I wouldn't take it with you on your trip."

So he knows about my plans, Ross thought.

As Peter shuffled the files in his briefcase searching for something, Ross noticed a Yale ring on his pinkie. Finally, he produced a small yellow pad with a numbered, hand-written list on the front page and placed it before Ross. To his surprise, it contained entries in Farsi, the principal language spoken in Iran. Without looking at Ross, Peter said, "Let's take it from the top."

He waved his hand over the map. "The Middle East is arguably the most valuable real estate on the planet, and Iran is at its center. Two-thirds of the known oil reserves in the world are controlled by the countries surrounding the Persian Gulf." Peter pointed to the small body of water South of Iran. "This tiny Gulf, only 600 miles long, narrows to a trickle at the Strait of Hormuz, here." With his finger tapping the spot, Peter looked at Ross for added drama. "It's only thirty-four miles wide. And twenty-eight percent of the world's oil supply must pass through it. Obviously, it's in our national security interest for the Strait of Hormuz to remain open. But Iran is in a position to close it."

Peter continued. "Take a careful look at this map, Dr. Shaheen. The countries in the region are predominantly Arab states. All of them except Israel, Turkey, Afghanistan, Pakistan, and of course Iran. Now look, the only democracies—functioning or in name only—in the area are these non-Arab states." He looked at Ross. "Isn't that interesting?"

"Now that you mention it," Ross said, "it just dawned on me that no Arab country has ever produced a democracy."

Peter nodded. "Except for Lebanon and Iraq, and theirs was imposed by us."

"Do you consider Iran a democracy?" Ross asked.

"Yes. But Iran's democracy is unique and is more form than substance. Iranians vote. But as witnessed in the 2009 elections, their vote is not always counted properly. They elect their President and their representatives to the Majlis—the Iranian parliament—where a protracted power struggle between the conservatives and the reformists has raged for decades. And the reformists have been steadily losing ground."

Peter paused to make sure Ross was following him. "The problem with the Iranian democracy lies in their constitution. It doesn't give any real power to the elected President or the Majlis. They are, more or less, window dressings. The real power rests with the unelected Supreme Leader—the Grand Ayatollah of the time—whose consent is necessary for any decision of significance; and the appointed Council of Guardians, who has to approve candidates' Islamic credentials before they can run for office. The Supreme Leader and most members of the Council of Guardians are Muslim cleric hardliners. They preside over an entrenched religious establishment and enjoy the support of the conservative segment of the population—mostly the rural and the underclass. The clerical regime keeps a tight lid on the moderates and reformers through their security apparatus and other enforcers, such as the Revolutionary Guards, an independent paramilitary force, and the Basij, an army of young thugs who go around terrorizing people.

"The moderates and the reformers, in turn, have the support of some members of the Majlis, the underground and often exiled independent media, the women, the urban middle class, and the intellectual elite, including most university students—nearly a million strong. In the summer of 2009, this segment of Iranian society flexed its muscle after the presidential election seemed to have been rigged. The massive protest marches have permanently upset the byzantine structure of Iran's power structure.

"Any questions?" Peter added.

"No questions. But, what you're describing is a political tinderbox ready to explode."

"In light of their economic difficulties, that's the way we see it also. In fact, Iran is ripe for another revolution, and the 2009 protests were only a prelude. But, this time around, the people won't stand for a theocratic democracy. There's widespread disgust with the clerical regime—people blame them for making Iran a pariah nation in the world, worthy of the demeaning label, *Axis of Evil*. They demand, and will eventually get, separation of Mosque and State. The tectonic political forces at play in Iran are moving the country toward reform. All we need is time."

Ross knew most of this but was fascinated by Peter's account mostly because of his analysis. His encyclopedic knowledge of the region and spot-on pronunciation of Farsi words were impressive. Pondering what he had heard, Ross said, "It seems to me the leaders in Tehran have a lot on their plates internally. Why antagonize the world by pursuing nuclear weapons?"

"The appetite for nukes is simultaneously fed by insecurity and their burning desire to re-establish the Persian Empire, Dr. Shaheen."

"Are you suggesting that Iran feels insecure?"

"Very much so. Here is where their insecurities come from: The Iran-Iraq War was very bloody. It lasted eight long years and took nearly a million Iranian lives. The Iranians threw everything they had at Saddam Hussein, yet they couldn't beat him. Granted, we were secretly helping the Iraqis with battlefield intelligence and satellite imagery, but even without our support, Iran couldn't dominate Iraq. Then, three years later, Saddam's million-man army was decimated by the U.S.

military inside of forty-five days—flat. This shocked and scared the hell out of the Iranians. So, they concluded that an accelerated WMD program was the surest way to achieve security. During the last fifteen years, they've fully developed their chemical and biological weapons. After 9-11, they've intensified their uranium enrichment program and, we believe, nuclear weapons are now within their reach."

"How else does 9-11 figure into all of this?"

"Let's look at the map again. What happened to the region afterward? We cleared Afghanistan of the Taliban and the Al-Qaeda and installed a friendly government. We now have bases and a military presence in Afghanistan. And we're there to stay. In this effort, Pakistan threw its lot in with us as well. So, the Iranians stare at the U.S. forces and a U.S. ally when they look at their Eastern front. We have two aircraft carriers on permanent patrol in the waters to the south of Iran. Additionally, we have major bases in Oman, Qatar, Bahrain, and Saudi Arabia. Kuwait owes us big time after we saved it from the clutches of Saddam Hussein back in 1991. And tens of thousands of our troops are stationed there. In Iraq, the U.S. has a major military presence, which is expected to remain for the foreseeable future. Turkey, a NATO member and by default a U.S. ally, is located on their northwest border. To the north lie the tiny republics of the former USSR. Most of them have elected to side with us as a counterbalance against Russia and to fend off Iran's export of Islamic fundamentalism. This leaves Russia to the north as Iran's only ally and refuge."

"They're surrounded," Ross said.

"Yes. Directly or indirectly, by the U.S. or our allies, and they know it."

"So, they really view the U.S. as their enemy? It's not just hot rhetoric for the masses?"

"Yes, and that explains their support for Hezbollah, Hamas, and Al-Qaeda."

"It's war by proxy," Ross said.

Peter nodded. "Look, you're Persian and grew up in Iran. You know that there's no love lost between the Iranians and Arabs. They dislike Arabs! Their loathing is at the DNA level and dates back over a millennium. So why do they shed crocodile tears for the Palestinians? To stick it to Israel and by extension to the U.S. of A."

"All right," Ross said. "I understand their motivation for going after nuclear weapons. But how close are they?"

"Well, you're the expert, Dr. Shaheen; you tell me. The reactor in Bushehr will go live in a few months, and we believe their uranium enrichment plant in Natanz is already operational." With a red pen, Peter placed an X on the map. "As you well know, Natanz is a small city in central Iran." Peter looked at Ross. "So, how close are they to a bomb?"

"Very close," Ross said. If these facilities are all operational, they'll have what's necessary to make a nuke within a year or two. All they need is a bomb design that works."

"I believe that's exactly what makes you so interesting to them, Dr. Shaheen. You've spent a career perfecting nuclear bomb designs and fission technology. You can catapult their program five years ahead."

"I see." Peter was telling Ross what he didn't want to think about, yet it was a chilling fact. "Is there anything else?"

"Yes, sir. I've brought you a few special gadgets, communication gear, mostly."

Peter pulled out the red envelope from the inside pocket of his briefcase. As Ross had suspected, it was stamped TOP SECRET. Peter ripped open the seal, looked inside, and retrieved a small padded pouch wrapped in thick plastic. He tried to tear it open, first with his hands and then with his teeth. He couldn't. He asked for scissors, which Ross produced from the pencil drawer of his desk. Peter opened the pouch. To Ross' surprise, it contained an ordinary-looking Berkeley class ring—class of '77. He handed it to Ross and said, "Put this on."

"What is it?"

He allowed his first smile. "It's the class ring you never knew you had. But it's a whole lot more."

Ross took the ring and tried it on. It fit his right middle-finger, and that's where he left it. With its bright ruby stone, it looked at once gaudy and beautiful. They had intentionally soiled and scuffed it so that it wouldn't appear brand new.

Ross's curiosity was peaked. "So, what exactly does it do?"

"Underneath the stone, there's a small red tablet. You can get to it by prying it out. We call it the X-pill. It's a derivative of dioxin but fifty-thousand times more lethal than cyanide. It kills within seconds… Quick and clean."

"Am I supposed to kill someone, or is it for me?"

"Use it if you must, Dr. Shaheen." He raised an eyebrow. "Any way you see fit."

The intentional ambiguity didn't disguise his clear and cold message. Ross knew what he was being asked to do—if caught, kill yourself.

Peter continued. "The ring is also a micro-transmitter. It sends a signal once a minute that lets us pinpoint your location. The batteries will last over a year."

"Is it waterproof?"

"Of course."

Again, Ross glanced at the Yale ring on Peter's right hand but said nothing. Peter turned the thick red envelope upside down and shook it. Out fell an ordinary looking silver-colored cell phone—the kind that flips open—followed by a plastic bag containing a few Band-Aids. He picked up the cell phone, turned it on, and presented it to Ross.

"Here's your new cell phone, Dr. Shaheen. It's preprogrammed for your existing number."

Ross took the phone and quickly noticed that it was an exact copy of his present one. He was amazed. *How did they know the model and color of my cell phone?* He wondered aloud, "Okay, what's special about this phone?"

"This little jewel works anywhere in the world. From Sydney to Paris and from Johannesburg to New Delhi, if you dial any U.S. phone number, it will connect you. It links up with one of our military satellites. And we've got them all over the world."

"So, E.T. can phone home. How's that going to help me?"

"You can call Colonel Nash directly at any time, and from anywhere in the world." Peter looked at Ross for emphasis. "That's the real reason for giving you this capability. The number he wants you to use is, 900-TIM NASH. It is private and secure. And when you call him, the phone automatically goes into the encryption mode scrambling the signal. So no one can eavesdrop on your conversation. The rest of the time, it operates in the clear. It's important you don't part with these devices, Dr. Shaheen. Especially the cell phone—it's full of classified technology."

"I'll do my best."

"Now, the good stuff." Peter picked up the plastic bag of Band-Aids, opened it, and retrieved one. "This ordinary looking Band-Aid is a powerful eavesdropping device. It's a microphone, transmitter, and battery all in one. The circuitry is so miniaturized that it's not visible to the naked eye."

Ross took the specimen from Peter for a closer look. Impressed, he nodded, smiling. Peter continued. "It activates when you peel its cover open. You can simply stick it under a chair, behind a frame, or on top of a closet. Then you can listen to any conversations in the room, using your magic cell phone, up to a mile away. Simply press, STAR-STAR-FOUR-ONE-ONE and select the bug you want to listen to in the display area. They're numbered one through six."

"How long do their batteries last?"

"About a week."

Ross put the Band-Aid he was holding back into the plastic bag and zipped it shut.

7

SIGNALS SPECIALIST, ARMY SGT. EMMIT JAMES MANGRUM, affectionately called, "Jimbo" by his close friends, worked the graveyard shift in the palm-lined city of Larnaka on the Eastern shores of Cyprus. The hot humid summer days of June, in the middle of the Mediterranean, made the night shift highly desirable.

Jimbo was born and raised in Fairview, a suburb of Nashville, Tennessee. He often complained aloud, "What the hell am I doing on this God-forsaken island? I should be back home, taking out the johnboat, running a trout line and fishing with night crawlers. Instead, I'm sitting here with these big-ass headphones, turning dials and listening to gibberish." Jimbo worked for the super-secret NSA—the National Security Agency—and was assigned to serve a two-year tour at the crucial listening post in Cyprus.

The NSA, in partnership with the United Kingdom and other allies, has succeeded in creating the greatest eavesdropping and surveillance enterprise ever established. The global spy system, codenamed ECHELON, captures and analyzes virtually every phone call, fax, e-mail, and text message sent anywhere in the world. The basic design of ECHELON is mind numbing in scope, yet quite simple: position intercept-stations and listening posts throughout the world to capture *all* satellite, microwave, radio, cellular, and fiber-optic communications traffic. Then, sift through this ocean of data in real time, using a vast array of supercomputers, and look for keywords or phrases—present in the ECHELON "Dictionary." Any match, in one of 800 languages monitored, would prompt the computers to isolate the conversation or document for further review and analysis by intelligence officers.

The windowless two-story building sat atop a hill about ten miles south of Larnaka. It was surrounded by thirty acres of rocky land, festooned with hundreds of antennae. The grounds were cleared of all trees for maximum reception. The shadowy compound was protected by two rows of chain-link fence, complete with electrified razor wire coiled in between. Armed personnel, assisted by two dozen video cameras, guarded the compound in a manner to avoid attracting attention. Few Cypriots knew what the real purpose of the station was. Yet, most suspected it belonged to the Americans, and no one seemed bothered by it.

Inside, a platoon of operators manned their stations in the dim open space on the second floor. The air was filled with the chaotic bleeps, buzzes, whistles, and talk of frequencies and bandwidth. And Jimbo was in the middle of it. He was assigned, among other things, to monitor the UHF—Ultra High Frequency—signals originating from Iran, especially from MOIS, the dreaded Iranian Intelligence Service.

To counter electronic interception, MOIS had devised a clever technique for communicating with their foreign operatives. What they thought was foolproof. They would insert encrypted messages in the middle of innocent radio broadcasts in the form of microbursts, which sounded like occasional static to the ordinary listener. The secret agents abroad knew exactly when and where to tune in for their instructions. Their special receivers would pick up the illusive radio noise, isolate it, and convert it into an encrypted text, which would in turn, be decrypted on a laptop computer running the customized decoder software. As clever as this scheme was, it was hardly original.

The Romans used a similar method for their secret communications. They tattooed the Caesar's instructions, intended for one of his far-flung Legion Commanders, on the shaved head of a messenger. Once his hair had grown sufficiently to disguise the secret message, they would dispatch him to the recipient. If stopped by unfriendly forces, they could never discover the covert message buried under a full head of hair. At the destination, the messenger's head would be shaved in front of the Legion Commander who would read the dispatch. The Romans were as cunning as they were ruthless.

At three minutes before 2:00 AM, and after listening to the radio chatter of some Iranian field commanders stationed in the Bekka Valley in south Lebanon, Jimbo turned the dial to the designated UHF frequency and began to listen to the Iranian radio broadcast in progress. He understood Farsi fluently but had trouble speaking it. The southern drawl didn't mix well with the impossible sounds that anchored the ancient language. And, even though he was embarrassed to admit it, the Johnny Cash fan had developed a taste for Persian music.

At precisely 2:00 AM, Cyprus time, the radio broadcast was interrupted with a two second burst of static. The TOP SECRET equipment, built to NSA specifications, promptly detected and snatched the hidden message. The chorus of blinking red and green lights seemed to celebrate the successful intercept.

Jimbo dutifully logged the date, time, frequency, and duration of the intercept into a computer monitor and clicked on an icon labeled UNPACK. The text box on the monitor suddenly filled with what seemed to be a stream of random numbers, letters, and special characters.

fpZ23h8wCRVUbKwxEgCnqAJW8w9R1GNA3K7
NlJUQk2Q/zPUGzyrRllgOFSs3uO1O0LlU9FKgDM
s7G/O5yrL25QansZkIlfmIu2O2N0j2ykVLy1IwgTo
XTBhNlK7ydmH+wmleDNud/2s0l5q2nbOo5TqOgw

Following standard operating procedures, Jimbo clicked DECRYPT for a first glance at the secret communication. A minute later, the warning UNABLE TO DECRYPT, SENDING TO HQ FOR CRYPTANALYSIS blinked in red on the screen. MOIS had introduced a new encryption algorithm, a frequent practice.

Jimbo continued to listen as the Persian music played on. There were five hours left in the graveyard shift.

8

DEEP INSIDE THE GRAND PALACE, WITHIN THE TRIANGULAR, brick-walled fortress of the Kremlin, General Viktor Pugachov, the National Security Advisor to the President of the Russian Federation, was alone in his ornate office sipping his morning tea. He had just received the daily briefing from the Federal Security Service (FSB), formerly known as the KGB, and the Foreign Intelligence Service (SVR) about the latest domestic and foreign intelligence. The Military Intelligence Agency (GRU) briefed him separately, alone, in the evenings. He preferred it that way.

The heart of Russia, the symbol of her greatness for nearly nine centuries, has been and remains the Kremlin. It is at once the cultural, political, and ideological center of the ancient empire. Built on the north shore of the Moscow River, it is a unique example of European medieval fortifications. The Kremlin is surrounded by twenty feet wide brick walls that soar sixty feet high over the riverbank. The sixty-eight acres of enclosed space is filled with imposing palaces and gothic cathedrals.

Traversing on top of the three walls of the Kremlin, one may look down on the Red Square and the Lenin Mausoleum on the northeast, face the Moscow River on the south, and view the peaceful Aleksandrovsky Gardens on the northwest. From this same stronghold where the Tsars lived in brazen luxury, Lenin and then Stalin ruled the vast Soviet Union with an iron fist.

The Kremlin, the heart of Russia, is also her soul. However, not even the Kremlin could intimidate Viktor Pugachov. The General and the Kremlin were an integral part of each other. Graying and grave, yet, vigorous and larger than life, the heavyset powerhouse was a walking paradox. He instilled fear in others by speaking softly, in a deep baritone voice, while staring into their eyes and scarcely blinking. Yet, he tenderly doted on his only child, Oksana and his grandchildren, Marina and Victor, who didn't fear him in the least. During his long career at the KGB, countless people were sent to Siberia by a cold stroke of his pen. Yet, he raised homing pigeons, in an aviary that he had personally built at his palatial dacha. His encyclopedic knowledge of Russian history, born out of fierce nationalism, and his ability to recite Pushkin from memory for hours at a time were legendary. He expected and received flawless results from his subordinates who knew that anything less than perfection would not suffice. Few loved him; most respected him; and everyone feared his wrath.

Viktor Pugachov embodied his own favorite maxim: "One who has power must wield it, or else lose it altogether."

Sitting behind a massive antique desk in his stately office, generously decorated with red carpets, priceless furniture, and European masterpieces, the General mulled over how to prioritize the issues for the President. His standing 8:30 AM meeting with the Russian leader was only twenty minutes away.

The General usually wore dark blue suits and white shirts tailored for him in London. The small white, blue, and red Russian flag pinned to his left lapel matched the French red ties he donned. There were four old-style telephones, in different colors, on top of a massive credenza behind his chair. The bank of telephones enabled him to have instant and secure access to the various instruments of Russian power—except the white one.

The white phone was different. It wasn't secure. It was installed for a single purpose. And only one person in the world knew the number. At 8:15 AM Moscow time, the white phone rang. It was the 18th of June.

"*Da!*"

"*Papa, eto ya*—Papa, it's me."

"*Oy, Oksanochka, zdravstvuj, devochka!*—Oh, my Oksana, hello little daughter!"

It was 9:15 PM, the previous evening in San Francisco. Oksana had driven Ross to the airport early that morning as he set out on his long journey to Iran.

"Hello, Papa."

"How are you, little girl?"

"Not well, Papa."

"What's wrong?"

"Ross has gone to Iran."

"What?" the General thundered. "Has he lost his mind?"

"No, Papa. Don't be angry. He's gone there, by invitation, to lecture. He left this morning."

"I would've advised against it."

"I feel a bad premonition, Papa."

Despite his visceral reaction and the genuine concern he felt, General Pugachov skillfully removed any trace of apprehension from his voice. "It will be all right," he said confidently. "Don't think bad thoughts."

"I need a favor, Papa."

"Sure. Anything for you, darling."

"Since America doesn't have an embassy in Iran, could you ask the Russian embassy in Tehran to look out for him?"

"Of course! I'll send word immediately." Pugachov picked up his writing pen. "When will he arrive?"

"He'll arrive in Tehran on KLM flight 433 on the 18th. It gets in at midnight."

"That's tonight. Where will he stay?"

"At the Shams Grand Hotel. It's spelled: S-H-A-M-S."

General Pugachov took down the information and tried again, ever so awkwardly, to comfort Oksana. "Would you like me to send someone to stay with you?"

"No, Papa. That's not necessary. I've told you about our neighbors, the Sullivans."

"Yes. I remember…The FBI agent."

"I feel safe with them next door. Besides, Victor is a strong young man," Oksana said, laughing nervously. "He'll look after us."

"Okay, then. It's all set. I'm late for a meeting. Call me often, little girl. And hug the children on my behalf."

"I will, Papa."

The General stood and picked up the stack of TOP SECRET material from his desk. Then, he lifted the red phone on the credenza to his ear and waited.

"Yes, Comrade General," the Foreign Intelligence Service liaison officer answered from the 19th floor of the FIS building on Yasenevo Street. Ironically, he stood at attention while speaking with the General on the phone.

"I have some urgent instructions for our embassy in Tehran. Send someone to my office at 11:00 AM to pick them up."

AT THE NSA HEADQUARTERS IN FORT MEADE, MARYLAND, THE encrypted message intercepted by Jimbo in Cypress was unceremoniously received, along with tens of thousands of similar wordless babbles from around the world.

The vast NSA facility is a sprawling crypto city that knows how to keep its secrets. Not until recently did it even have a sign. Security guards in unmarked vans promptly stop hapless tourists who make the mistake of snapping distant pictures of the facility and confiscate their cameras. No questions, no answers, let alone arguments, are allowed. An old joke refers to the NSA as, No Such Agency. Another: Never Say Anything.

The jokes don't stray far from the truth.

Tucked away in a wooded corner of the secret city, nearly a mile's distance from the NSA operations complex, the Tordella Supercomputer Facility boasts the largest collection of supercomputers assembled in one place anywhere in the world. A Cray XT Jaguar, pumping out 1.64 quadrillion mathematical calculations per second, is but one of nearly 150 supercomputers the center operates. Its mammoth computer room is measured not in square feet but in acres. At last leak, the environmentally controlled palace of the giant number crunchers topped ten acres.

The supercomputers at the Tordella facility chew up high-grade ciphers of foreign governments and break them with uncanny ease.

In room A-301 of the operations complex, code-breaking Group M was busy assessing the previous night's catch. Dedicated to the analysis of electronic intelligence to and from the Islamic Republic of Iran, the sixty-person team of mathematicians, cryptographers, and linguists sifted through thousands of intercepts daily. The recorded voice conversations, marked by a supercomputer for containing words that matched the ECHELON's Dictionary, were reviewed by Farsi-speaking linguists. Others busily evaluated intercepted e-mails and fax messages. All encrypted text was sent through an underground fiber cable to the Tordella facility for deciphering.

Among them was the message from Cyprus.

Fariba Mehraban, the twenty-seven-year-old daughter of Iranian immigrants, was born and raised in Bethesda, Maryland and had joined the NSA after September 11. She had lost her best friend, a flight attendant, when American Airlines Flight 77 crashed into the Pentagon. Grief-stricken and stunned by the horror of that fateful day, Fariba had thought that her fluent command of Farsi, which, to her chagrin, was one of the prevalent languages of terror, could be useful to the NSA. She had reasoned that working for the secret agency might somehow avenge the cruel death of her close friend. So, she filled out the long application and, with much hesitation, sent it to the NSA. Little did she know that the agency was desperate to expand its Farsi-speaking personnel and would eagerly welcome her. After passing the grueling background screening, she was hired with TOP SECRET clearance and posted to Group M.

She was thrilled with her new job at the secret agency; it had spiced up her mundane life. The only downside was that she couldn't tell anyone what she did.

The slightly overweight and likable Fariba was glued to her computer monitor as she sat in one of the cubicles in the windowless expanse of room A-301. She had a habit of chewing bubblegum, often noisily, as she submitted the encrypted messages—which appeared in red on her screen—to the Tordella facility by clicking DECODE. Within seconds, the supercomputers would swallow the unintelligible gruel and spit back the dark secrets they contained. She would then read the plain text, which appeared in blue, and determine where to rout it for further analysis or action.

Just as the encrypted message from Cypress came up on her screen, Fariba left her station to join a few friends for lunch in the basement cafeteria.

9

Air turbulence didn't agree with Ross. It made him nauseous and tense. Fortunately, the United Flight 950 from San Francisco to Washington DC was comfortable and blissfully calm. He was relaxed and spent most of the time reading. The plane landed ahead of schedule at 3:35 PM, giving him a little more time to stretch his legs and make a few calls before crossing the Atlantic.

Ross used the CIA-issued phone to reach Oksana. The concern in her voice was palpable, and yet, she said nothing of her fears. Ross, however, knew what she was thinking—they had talked it to death. Once again, he tried to reassure her that he would be safe in Iran and there were no reasons for concern. Still, he wasn't certain if it made any difference.

He wandered to a nearby bookstore and purchased three magazines. As he waited in line for the cashier, he dialed 900-TIM-NASH.

"Hello, Ross. Welcome to Washington."

How does he know I'm here? Ross pictured a blinking dot flashing over a map on a huge flat-screen in Colonel Nash's office. "I guess the cell phone works."

"Yes, it does. And make sure you don't ever get separated from it."

"I'll try not to. Do you have any last words?"

"Not really," Nash replied casually. "Just keep your eyes open. Find out all you can. Never admit your connection with the CIA. And, get the hell out of Dodge as soon as your time's up."

"Am I still marked by the Mossad?" Ross whispered.

"No, sir. You're clear."

"What if I get into trouble? Who do I call?"

"Me."

"Any local assets I should contact?"

"They'll contact you."

"Do I need a code word or call sign?"

"No, Ross." The Colonel chuckled. "You've watched way too many James Bond movies."

Colonel Nash was right. Ross had seen them all.

"Okay. Wish me luck."

"Be careful, you'll do fine."

Ross noticed that he had lingered too long, and there was little time left before his flight. So, he picked up the pace and was out of breath when he arrived at the gate in the international terminal. As luck would have it, he was randomly selected—or purposely profiled—for additional security screening. While the inspectors thoroughly examined the contents of his pockets, Ross was concerned about the special CIA gear he was carrying, but the agents didn't seem to notice anything unusual. By the time he walked into the plane, most of the passengers were already buckled in. The Business Class flight attendant showed him to an aisle seat with much deference. There were only thirty-four seats in the front cabin.

As the colossus Airbus 330-300 taxied to the runway, the head stewardess welcomed the passengers to the North West Flight 8652 and informed them that they would arrive in Amsterdam at 7:15 AM, the next morning. Ross settled in for the long night over the Atlantic.

EARLIER THAT AFTERNOON, BACK IN SAN FRANCISCO, A BROWN windowless van arrived at Roy Sullivan's house, with Roy in the passenger seat. The van slowly backed into the garage. The moment he closed the garage door, the driver, an unusually tall man, left the van and opened the rear hatch. Two more agents in blue FBI windbreakers emerged from the cargo area carrying large metal suitcases. Without saying a word, Roy walked into his woodworking shop, turned on the lights, and called the men inside. "Here boys...You can set up in this room."

The Bureau's request for wiretap authorization had finally been granted. And Roy didn't waste any time. The special surveillance team from the CTT—Counter Terrorism Taskforce, Roy's own outfit in the FBI—was about to set up shop in his basement to electronically monitor the three suspicious Iranians living across the street from Ross and Oksana.

At six feet six, Special Agent Lem Konarski towered over his boss, Roy Sullivan. Lanky and quiet, the Polish American barely weighed 180 pounds, which is why most of his friends called him "the Broom." Agent Konarski was an authority in electronic surveillance, a skill he'd honed by fixing all sorts of gadgets as he grew up in the south side of Chicago. He joined the FBI in the eighties and soon found his niche—eavesdropping.

Tapping a phone was an easy task in the old days. All calls ran over copper wires that belonged to a monopoly—Ma Bell. To listen in, the FBI simply requested that the phone company isolate the suspect's wire and record any calls made or received. A single phone company that operated one network simply had to flip one switch.

That was another era.

Today, in addition to ordinary telephone and cellular communications, dozens of new technologies needed to be monitored, such as e-mail and text messaging. And thousands of new service providers were now in business. The most difficult communication method to intercept was VOIP, which stands for Voice Over Internet Protocol. The FBI's solution for monitoring voice or data traffic over the Internet was the CARNIVORE technology. It sucks up and filters all data traffic to and from the target address and delivers to investigators only packets, which they're specifically authorized to obtain.

The super-secret CARNIVORE was just one of the tricks that Agent Konarski had up his sleeves. Another device, even more hush-hush and sinister, was the TEMPEST.

Plenty of people fret about their online privacy. But, only a scant few know that someone may be eavesdropping on what they're typing into their PCs, even when it's offline. This could be accomplished with the magic of TEMPEST, the codename for technologies developed by the NSA to intercept and decipher the faint electromagnetic signals that all computers emit.

A few hours after their arrival, Roy, who had left the team alone to set up their equipment, returned to check on their progress. "Is there anything else you need, Broom?"

"Yes, Boss." Agent Konarski handed a small Plexiglas dish to Roy. "Could you take the TEMPEST antenna upstairs to one of the bedrooms and point it to the house? I can't get a good signal down here."

Roy obliged and positioned the antenna inside the guest bedroom on the second floor, pointing it through the shutters at the Miller's house. If the Iranians happen to use a PC, whatever appeared on their monitor would be captured, displayed, and recorded in Roy's basement. Alice looked on with puzzled amusement as her husband adjusted the tripod beneath the antenna.

"Dish is up, Broom," Roy announced eagerly. He peered at the monitor over Agent Konarski's shoulder. "Got anything?"

"Nothing yet, but we will," Agent Konarski said quietly, without looking back. "We're able to intercept whatever they use to communicate."

"What if they use pigeons?" Roy asked, snickering.

Not amused, Agent Konarski turned around and gave Roy a cold, have-you-got-nothing-better-to-do stare.

⌇

At the NSA, Fariba Mehraban was upset when she returned from lunch. She had spilled mustard on her new skirt, and had been unsuccessful in removing it with water. Now, she was left with an ugly yellow stain surrounded by a large wet patch. She spewed profanity in two languages at no one in particular.

She flung her purse on the side table, slumped into her swivel chair, and shook the left-handed mouse next to the keyboard. The monitor came alive. The encrypted message from Cypress was waiting in red on the top half of the screen. She clicked DECODE and again looked at her skirt with dismay. Still angry, she tried to rub off the stain with a wet handkerchief. It didn't work. Exasperated, she popped a piece of grape bubble gum into her mouth, chewing with ferocity.

Twenty seconds later, the plain text version of the scrambled message appeared, in blue, on the bottom-half of her monitor. She began to read.

JADOOGAR APPROACHING NEST STOP MAY NOT BE
HELPFUL STOP PREPARE HOSPITAL FOR PATIENTS
STOP STANDBY FOR GO FOX HUNT END

The plain text was written in coded language. Fariba was a triage specialist and still too inexperienced to assume the full responsibilities of intelligence analysis. But she had sorted through enough coded traffic to feel the menace in the latest message.

Ordinarily, after the Tordella facility deciphered a secret intercept, Fariba—or another member of the triage team—graded the message according to its importance. This was affected, among other factors, by its source and/or destination. It was then routed to the appropriate department for further analysis. In case of any ambiguities, Fariba could invoke the CODE TRACER software. This was a revolutionary tool that enabled her to instantly uncover patterns and hidden clues within each coded message by comparing every word and phrase with the colossus intelligence databases at the Tordella facility.

Fariba read the short message a second time. She hadn't seen JADOOGAR—meaning "the Wizard" in Farsi—used in any previous messages. She highlighted the word and clicked CODE TRACER. A window popped up and offered a number of suggestions, including the meaning of the word, which Fariba already knew; that it was probably a codeword for someone important; and that it had never been used before.

"Duh!" Fariba said to the computer. Curious and impatient, she used both these traits in her job. She proceeded with the rest of the message, one word at a time, like an archeologist unearthing a priceless find. But instead of a brush to remove layers of dust from a buried artifact, she used the CODE TRACER to peel off the cloak of secrecy from the message. CODE TRACER proved more helpful with the rest of the words.

Iranian intelligence services routinely used HOSPITAL in code-talk for prison and PATIENT for prisoner or hostage. FOX HUNT, according to the omniscient software, was likely the name of a preplanned operation assigned to a clandestine cell awaiting the GO order. The message was gradually beginning to make sense, but Fariba wasn't sure about the big picture. She highlighted the entire text and asked the computer to analyze the whole thing. In a matter of seconds, she read the assessment of the cyber guru: FOX HUNT IS A PLANNED KIDNAPPING OPERATION.

"But, where? It's a big world," Fariba mumbled. "What does JADOOGAR have to do with it? Who the hell is he?" She picked up a pencil and nervously tapped it on the edge of her desk, thinking. She blew a bubble—pop!—and without wasting any more time, she clicked ROUTING. A list of twenty or so departments and destinations appeared. She highlighted CTC—CIA's Counter Terrorism Center—marked it URGENT, and clicked SEND.

The next encrypted message—to or from Iran, intercepted somewhere in the world—appeared in red, on the top-half of her screen.

Pop!

10

SHORTLY AFTER TAKEOFF, A SUMPTUOUS DINNER OF FILET MIGNON and wild rice, complete with an assortment of French pastry, was served. The wine and champagne bottles kept coming; Ross drank his usual ginger ale.

It was pitch black outside. Across the aisle to his right, a familiar looking woman sat in the window seat. Once dinner trays were removed, she retrieved a sleek laptop computer from the empty seat to her left and began to work. She struck the keyboard too hard—as if she were angry—making a stream of click-clack noise at an amazing speed. Every now and then, she removed a pen from behind her ear and ticked off something on a yellow pad resting on the tray in front of the empty seat to her left. Wearing a loose, black v-neck blouse over faded blue jeans and white socks, she looked comfortable. Her sneakers were removed and neatly laid on the floor. She used a pair of sunglasses as a makeshift headband, keeping the dark brown hair out of her face.

Ross kept watching her and thought, *God, I know this woman... But from where?* He could only see her stunning profile, which in the absence of any glitz or glamour was even more alluring.

It was two hours into the flight when Ross noticed the nametag dangling from her laptop carrying case. *Oh my! She's Leila Conner, the CNN International reporter and superstar.*

Ross was a fan of the thirty-something beauty because of her extensive and accurate reporting on the Middle East and because her mother was Iranian, which made him especially proud. His pal, Roy Sullivan, on the other hand, was in love with her. He always spoke of how "fine" she was and that "She has it all going on." He made these remarks right in front of his wife, Alice, who took it in stride.

It's amazing how different she looks in person, Ross thought. "Excuse me, Ms. Conner; may I take a minute of your time?"

She looked at Ross and smiled. "Sure."

"Like you, I was born in Iran, and I want you to know that I'm really proud of your achievements."

"Thank you. And what do you do?"

"I'm a physicist—boring stuff." He handed her his business card. "I work at Lawrence Berkeley Laboratories."

"What a—"

The flight attendant interrupted by stopping the service cart in the aisle, blocking their line of sight. Ross strained to continue their conversation but couldn't see her. So, he rose, squeezed by the cart, and stood in the aisle facing Leila. "You were saying…"

Leila removed her things from the empty seat next to her, piled it on top of her laptop, and pointed. "Come sit over here."

Ross was pleasantly surprised by how friendly and approachable she was. He sat next to her and started by introducing himself. After a few minutes of small talk, he told her about Roy's infatuation with her and said, "May I ask you to write a note or something to Roy? I'll frame it and give it to him on his next birthday."

"I'll do better than that." She retrieved an eight by ten publicity photo from the side pocket of her laptop case and, with a thick red permanent marker, wrote in the margin: *To my dearest Roy, I miss your hugs-n-kisses! All my love, Leila.* She handed the photo to Ross and with a mischievous grin said, "This ought to light his fire."

Ross thanked her profusely. "I won't take up any more of your time. What are you working on anyway?"

"I'm going to Iran to do a documentary." Pointing to the yellow pad, she said, "The outline my producer wrote needs some work."

"What a pleasant coincidence. I'm going back to Iran also…for academic stuff. What's your documentary about—if I may ask?"

"It's about Iran's nuclear weapons program; a hot topic these days."

Ross didn't pursue the subject. He had already told her he was a physicist but hadn't hinted at his area of expertise. He decided to cut the conversation short.

"Perfect timing, Ms. Conner. I can't wait to see it. When will it air?" He stood up in the aisle way.

"It'll air in the fall." She handed Ross her business card. "Please e-mail me and let me know if you liked it."

"Be glad to. What will be the title of the program?"

"The working title is *Mushroom in the Sand.*"

Ross nodded approval. "That's really clever. Good luck to you." He returned to his seat, holding her autographed photo. He looked at it again, read the note, and smiled as he carefully placed it in his briefcase.

The click-clack sound of the keyboard resumed. Instead of watching the in-flight movie, Ross busied himself with reading the latest *Scientific American.* Even though Iran was still thousands of miles and a dozen hours away, he felt his level of anxiety steadily rising as the plane flew east. Reading helped him relax.

The movie was almost over when he felt a gentle tap on his shoulder. It was Leila Conner standing in the aisle.

"Excuse me, Dr. Shaheen. Could you help me with something?"

"Of course! And please, call me Ross."

"Come sit by me, will you?"

After they got situated, Ross said, "You're lucky to have an empty seat next to you."

"Luck has nothing to do with it. I always buy two seats when I travel so that I can spread out."

"I guess being a superstar has its perks."

"And its curses."

"I wouldn't know, I can only imagine."

She placed her yellow notepad on the tray in front of Ross and placed a pen over it. "You're a physicist. We've got four hours left on this flight and another five on the next. Could you explain to me, in plain English, how an atomic bomb is made? What makes it explode?"

"Well, that's not quite my area of expertise," Ross lied. "But I could review your briefing material and try to explain it, if you wish."

Leila handed him a one-inch-thick, spiral-bound book, which was stamped CONFIDENTIAL. "Here it is—mostly gibberish. Be my guest."

Ross thumbed through the material looking at the diagrams, reading chapter titles and section headings. He thought it was a fairly comprehensive manual of how to enrich uranium and make a crude nuclear bomb. Mostly available on the Internet, the material did not contain any secret information.

"CNN must have a good research department, Ms. Conner." Ross looked up after fifteen minutes of speed reading. "This is quite good."

"Call me, Leila," she said, smiling. "Yes, they're very competent, but they provide me with too much detail and use technical lingo, which is hard to digest and impossible to use on air." She pointed to the briefing book. "You see, I understand the politics of it but don't have a good grasp of the underlying science. And *this* is too much to master in a few days."

Ross hesitated. "That's a tall order."

"Please..." she pleaded, grabbing his arm.

Ross felt uneasy. Even though the information was public knowledge, the terms of his security clearance prevented him from discussing such topics openly. He turned, looking at the passengers behind them—an odd couple: a middle-aged woman who looked like a Hollywood socialite and a punk-looking young man with slick hair, wearing reflective shades. They seemed clueless. He leaned forward, eyeing the people sitting in front of them—elderly men, fast asleep. *Why not?* he thought. *No one can hear us. The material is harmless. It's a good way to break the monotony, and knowing a celebrity like Leila Conner could be useful in Iran. She will certainly interview senior Iranian officials, which might uncover some helpful information. Besides, how could I possibly refuse a stunning beauty like her?*

He picked up the pen and started sketching simple diagrams and writing notes as he spoke in a low voice. "How much physics do you know?"

She grinned. "Basic 101."

"Do you know what nuclear fission is?"

"Why are you whispering?"

"I'd rather not draw any attention to what we're talking about."

"Why not? This is all public knowledge."

"Trust me," Ross continued in a low voice. "Even though this information is public, it's very hard to come by. Besides, my clearance prevents me from discussing it. So, it's better not to draw anyone's attention."

Leila seemed impressed. "You have security clearance?"

"Well," Ross downplayed it, "at the Berkeley Lab, most scientists do."

"Okay," she said, nodding.

"Before we start, you must promise never to use my name."

"I assure you whatever you say will be off the record."

"All right, then. Where were we?"

"You asked about fission," Leila said. "That's where the nucleus of an atom splits, releasing energy."

"That's right. And fission is the basic principle behind nuclear reactors that produce electricity as well as nuclear bombs. In nuclear reactors, fission is controlled and occurs in an orderly manner to generate heat, which is used to boil water, which makes steam that runs turbines that produce electricity. In a bomb, the same fission is accelerated and allowed to happen in an uncontrolled manner, releasing enormous energy in a fraction of a second, which simply detonates."

"Can a nuclear power plant explode?"

"Never. They're not designed to explode. In case of a malfunction, where fission gets out of control, the core material overheats, causing a meltdown of the fuel, which releases radioactivity, wreaking havoc with the environment."

"Is that what happened at Three Mile Island?"

"More or less, which is one of the reasons why they build these giant concrete domes at nuclear power plants—to prevent any radioactivity from escaping."

"Okay, tell me about plutonium and uranium. What's the difference? Which one is used in a bomb and which one in a reactor?"

"Let's start from the top. Fission occurs best in two metals: uranium and plutonium. Like most other metals, uranium is mined. But plutonium does not exist naturally anywhere; it must be created."

She looked confused. "Created?"

"Yes. I guess I skipped a few steps." Ross turned to a clean sheet of paper. "Let me explain."

He drew a diagram to illustrate the benchmarks in the nuclear fuel cycle. "It all starts at a uranium mine where uranium ore is dug out of the ground."

"Does Iran have any uranium mines?"

Once more, Ross paused to look around, ensuring no one was

listening. He whispered, "Yes. Huge deposits were discovered in the Saghand mines in the Yazd province."

"Are they mining uranium?" Leila asked in a low voice, as she scribbled notes in a small reporter's notebook.

"I really don't know." In fact, Ross knew the answer, but couldn't reveal it to a civilian because it was highly classified. "That's a good piece of information for you to uncover."

"I thought their deal with Russia included the uranium fuel necessary to get the Bushehr reactor started."

"That's true, but the Iranians desperately want to be in full control of the entire fuel cycle and not depend on Russia. They have said as much publicly."

"Okay, we've got uranium ore out of the ground. Then what?"

"The ore is milled into fine dust and then leached with acid to separate out the uranium. It's actually uranium oxide."

"Is that what's called the yellow cake?"

Surprised that she knew the technical term, he said, "That's right. You seem to know more about this than you claim."

"Not really. Yellow cake was all over the news when Saddam Hussein allegedly tried to buy some from Nigeria. Remember?"

"Vaguely."

"Go on please. What next?"

"The uranium found in nature consists of two isotopes: U_{235} and U_{238}. The U_{235} variety is what is needed for fission and energy production. The heavier U_{238} is useless. The problem is, the uranium ore is less than one percent U_{235} and not usable unless its concentration is increased."

"Is that what you call 'enrichment'?"

"Exactly. We need mildly enriched uranium—where the U_{235} concentration is increased to about four or five percent—to power nuclear reactors. And highly enriched uranium—with ninety percent or more concentration of the lighter isotope—is necessary for atomic bombs."

"Tell me about enrichment. How's that done? What makes it so complicated?"

"Enrichment is the most difficult technological challenge in the nuclear fuel cycle. That's because the two isotopes have the exact same physical properties—you can't use any chemical procedures to separate them. The only difference between the two isotopes is their weight, where U_{235} is about one percent lighter than U_{238}, because it has three fewer neutrons in its nucleus."

Ross paused and looked at Leila to make sure she was following him. She nodded attentively as she took a sip from the glass of chardonnay she was nursing. Enchanted by his accidental VIP student, Ross continued the physics lesson.

"The most common method to enrich uranium is called Cascade Gaseous Centrifuge. Here's how it works: The uranium oxide—the yellow cake—is combined with fluoride and turned into a gas. This gas—uranium hexafluoride or UF6, commonly referred to as 'hex'—is fed into a series of vacuum tubes, each about six feet long and eight inches in diameter. At the center of each tube, there's a rotor. When the rotor is spun rapidly—at twice the speed of sound—the heavier gas molecules with U_{238} congregate toward the cylinder's outer edge. There's a corresponding migration of U_{235} gas molecules near the center. This enriched gas is siphoned off from the center and moved forward to the next centrifuge while the depleted gas is sucked out from the edge of the tube and sent back to the previous one. The process of moving the material from one centrifuge to the next and on to another is known as 'cascade.' At each stage, the hex is slightly enriched over the previous one. It takes about twenty stages to achieve four percent enrichment, which is suitable for nuclear power plants."

"What about weapon's grade?"

"The exact same process, if repeated over and over again, will produce ninety percent enriched uranium, which is ready for prime time."

"Can the Iranians enrich uranium?"

"There's an underground facility at Natanz, about four hours drive south of Tehran, which is suspected by the CIA to be a uranium enrichment plant. Not much is known about it; the Iranians have kept a tight lid over it until recently. I believe CNN first broke the story about its existence. That's where I first learned about it."

This was a lie.

Ross had known about the Natanz installation from the day the earthmovers began to excavate the site. As one of his first assignments on the NSA science advisory board, the agency had provided him with the plant's blueprints and satellite imagery for analysis. It was clearly a uranium enrichment plant based on standard Russian designs.

"Has anyone seen the inside of this plant?" Leila asked.

"Not that I'm aware. Maybe you'll be the first, Leila."

Intrigued by his suggestion, she said, "I'll try. They've promised me full access to all facilities."

Again, Ross wasn't quite truthful. He had seen photographs taken from the inside of the plant at Natanz. How these pictures were taken, he wasn't told. But they clearly showed at least one thousand centrifuge tubes installed with twice as many on the floor awaiting installation. The Iranians were preparing for high volume enrichment.

It must have been midway over the Atlantic when, suddenly, the plane began to vibrate and shake violently. Ross despised air turbulence; it made him feel unbearably helpless. The monotonous voice of the pilot came over the intercom asking the passengers to fasten their seatbelts. Ross dutifully obliged, then clenched the armrests and leaned back, silently praying for a quick end to his agony. Leila appeared relaxed and unbothered, but she noticed Ross' distress. After a few minutes of quiet endurance, she placed her left hand over his right and with a comforting voice said, "It'll be over soon."

Leila was right, but to Ross "soon" seemed like an eternity. Yet, he thought the kind gesture was at once comforting and awkward. When the plane passed through the rough air, Leila let go of his hand. "Are you all right?"

"Yes. Turbulence doesn't agree with me."

"Would you like to continue or take a break?"

"No." Ross unbuckled his seatbelt. "Let's proceed. Where were we?"

"We've enriched uranium to ninety percent purity in gas form. What's next?"

Ross quickly gathered his thoughts. "Then metallic uranium, which is now weapons' grade, is extracted from the gas and fabricated into bomb cores."

"So, a country in search of—" She made the double quotation mark with her fingers "—'the bomb' doesn't necessarily need a nuclear reactor. All they need is the uranium ore and the enrichment facility. Right?"

"Right."

"Then why has Iran paid a billion dollars to Russia to build one for them in Bushehr?"

"Two reasons: First, it offers their nuclear weapons program a 'peaceful use' cover and keeps the IAEA—International Atomic Energy Agency—off their backs. Second, they need a reactor to create plutonium, which makes even more powerful bombs."

"How does that work?"

"In a reactor, the fuel rods—filled with low-grade enriched uranium—are grouped in clusters and placed in an airtight water tank. The energy released by the controlled fission, inside the fuel rods, heats the water that eventually produces electricity. During the slow chain reaction, some of the uranium atoms absorb neutrons and transmute into plutonium. Once the fuel rods are depleted, they can be reprocessed to extract the plutonium, which is a relatively simple chemical process."

"Isn't that what the North Koreans are up to?"

"Exactly."

"How much of the stuff do you need to make a bomb?"

"You need to have enough fissionable material to sustain a rapid chain reaction."

Leila listened attentively.

Ross wrote the basic fission equation on the notepad. "Look here: when a neutron hits a uranium atom, the impact shatters the nucleus causing fission, which releases energy plus two or three new neutrons. If these extra neutrons find new atoms to shatter, a chain reaction will start. If not, they escape into the atmosphere and the process fizzles out. So, there's a minimum amount of fissionable material necessary to start a chain reaction, called the supercritical mass. It's about fifteen pounds of plutonium or thirty-five pounds of uranium—roughly the size of a large grapefruit."

"The size of a grapefruit?"

Ross nodded.

"How do you make such a huge bomb out of so little material?"

"The simplest bomb design, pioneered in the Manhattan Project during World War II and subsequently dropped on Hiroshima, consists of a gun type mechanism that fires one piece of U_{235} at another piece of U_{235}, instantly creating supercritical mass."

Ross sketched a long enclosed cylinder on the note pad. "In other words, suppose you take a grapefruit-size amount of enriched uranium, cut it in half, place each half in a tube about a foot apart, then place a hundred pounds of high explosives—such as C4 or Semtex—behind each half and then detonate them simultaneously. You'll have a crude nuclear explosive device."

Somewhat surprised, Leila said, "That's it?"

"Basically, yes. However, actually building it, making it detonate on demand, maximizing its yield and delivering it to the target, one and all, poses formidable technical challenges. For instance, once the two pieces of uranium are brought together, you need an 'initiator' to introduce a burst of neutrons to jump-start the chain reaction; sort of like a fuse. How do you protect the initiator from the violent initial explosion? A well-designed bomb assembles its supercritical mass extremely fast, and it shrouds that mass in a shell that prevents it from exploding until most of the atoms have had time to shatter—about a millisecond. What material do you use that has this much strength? A crude bomb like this is the size of a Volkswagen; how do you reduce its size so that you can put it on top of a missile? Bottom line: before it can actually work, there are countless engineering problems that need to be solved."

"Do the Iranians have the necessary know-how? Do you?"

"I don't really know what their capabilities are. The answers to most of these questions aren't readily available; most of them are closely held secrets. And I have no idea what they are."

He lied again.

Ross knew the answers perfectly well. In fact, he had solved some of the engineering puzzles himself. But, these were all TOP SECRET.

"That's all right." Leila shrugged. "I think I have enough material for now. Just one more question: how destructive are these weapons?"

"The smallest nuclear bomb yields about fifteen to thirty kilotons of TNT. That's equivalent to fifteen thousand tons of dynamite, at a minimum."

"From a grapefruit size of uranium to fifteen kilotons of TNT..." Leila was stunned. "How is that possible?"

"What's behind it is one of Einstein's basic laws of nature." Ross wrote: $E=MC^2$.

She nodded as she scribbled something in her notepad. Then she squeezed Ross' hand and said, "You have no idea how helpful you've been. I don't know how to thank you."

"Glad to help…you seem tired. Why don't I go back to my chair and let you take a nap?"

"Okay. See you in Amsterdam."

Soon after Ross returned to his seat, the turbulence started again. He wished he hadn't moved.

11

THE CIA'S IMMACULATE GROUNDS, ENCOMPASSING TWO HUNDRED and fifty-eight acres of fenced-in and impenetrable land, were originally envisioned to resemble a college campus. Fifty years in the making, the designer's vision had become reality. Strolling down the tree-lined pathways, one could not readily grasp the real purpose of the cloak-and-dagger campus—not unless one was privileged enough to roam the forbidden hallways of the imposing Headquarters Buildings.

The CIA compound was located near the city of Langley and was about eight miles from downtown Washington, DC. At the center sprawled the mammoth Headquarters Buildings. The complex of six-story structures boasted two and a half million square feet of secure office space swarming with an army of nameless people. Popular wisdom set the number of permanent staff at thirty thousand.

Etched into the wall of the central lobby was a biblical verse from the book of John. It read, *And ye shall know the truth and the truth shall make you free.*

Original works of art purchased or on loan from private collections were on display throughout the Headquarters Buildings. Oil portraits of each Director lined the walls of one hallway. At the end of this hallway was the suite of offices assigned to the Deputy Director of CIA for Operations—or DDO—the Agency's spymaster.

And now this position was occupied by Colonel Timothy Nash. As one approached his office, the palpable aura of power became conspicuous and the trappings of authority increasingly visible. The last one hundred feet of the hallway leading to his doorstep were covered with hardwood flooring, and the drab painted walls suddenly sported lavish wallpaper. Fluorescent ceiling lights gave way to recessed light fixtures, and staffers milling about were dressed more formally—either in dark business suits or military uniforms rather than business casual.

Colonel Nash expected it.

The grand mahogany double doors opened to the spacious lobby of the Director's suite. Tastefully decorated in shades of maroon and blue, the space was dominated by the large emblem of the Directorate of Operations, conspicuously inlaid into the floor.

A phalanx of seventy-five elite staffers supported Colonel Nash as he reigned supreme over the largest intelligence gathering and espionage operation in the world. A female marine sergeant in full regalia welcomed visitors, verified their appointments, and ushered them to their destinations. The select few who were privileged to have an audience with Colonel Nash sat on one of the navy blue couches while the marine sergeant announced their arrival to the Colonel's private secretary. Within minutes, Mira Cordoba, the Colonel's administrative assistant of Cuban ancestry, would appear from a side door to guide the guest to the inner sanctum. The Director's enormous office opened to a small, yet elegant, private lobby—at the center of which Mira's desk was situated.

Those who arrived late for an appointment with the Colonel—even five minutes, unless they were one of his few superiors—learned a bitter lesson: their appointment was abruptly cancelled. No one was ever late.

Inside his office, picture windows, specially designed to counter every known eavesdropping technique, provided a breathtaking view of the campus. A small conference table at one end of the room was separated from an antique desk on the other end by a set of leather couches. A wall-mounted flat-screen, next to the conference table, was used for secure videoconferences. On the side table adjacent to the desk sat a sleek black computer monitor.

Leaning back in his massive chair, Colonel Nash read a seven-page report, produced by the CTC, which had been hand delivered to him by special courier. The TOP SECRET/GAMMA classification required hand delivery of each numbered copy to each recipient. The report epitomized the institutional frustration of the intelligence community. It contained the plain text of raw intercepts, snatched during the previous twenty-four hours, that appeared menacing but couldn't be deciphered by the CTC. The enigmatic catalogue of code-talk comprised the dots that America demanded be connected together...somehow.

The message snatched by Jimbo in Cyprus, decrypted by Fariba at the NSA, and forwarded on to the CTC, was buried in the middle of page five.

Colonel Nash retrieved a Cuban cigar from a hand-painted Russian box, an old memento from his years of service in Moscow, and lit up. The strict nonsmoking rule of the CIA Headquarters Buildings was obviously unenforceable in his chambers. He occasionally circled or underlined a word as he patiently read the TOP SECRET report. *JADOOGAR* was one of the words that piqued his interest. As he circled it, Mira walked in and said, "I've got Pugachov's secretary on the phone. The General wants to speak with you. Are you available?"

"Yes, put him through."

After a few seconds of static, the instantly recognizable voice with the deep Russian accent came on line. "Colonel Nash?"

"Hello, General. What gives me the pleasure?"

Not used to the small talk foreplay, the General went right to the point. "Did you know Ross Shaheen was going to Iran?"

"Yes. I knew."

"And you did not stop him?"

"This is a free country, General. And he's a civilian. How could I stop him?"

"I am puzzled, Colonel. Your actions are confusing."

"How's that, General?"

"In each and every official meeting between our two governments, your side brings up American concerns about Russia's nuclear cooperation with Iran. Check your intelligence records, you will find that we have never sent a nuclear weapons expert to Iran. You, on the other hand, manage to send one of your top weapons researchers over there. I wonder why? Do you not find this odd?"

"With all due respect, General, your son-in-law is a respected scientist. I'm not aware of his areas of research." Skillfully avoiding any acknowledgement of what the General had alleged, Nash continued. "You probably know more about what he does than I do. All I can say is that his trip was by invitation from some university in Iran, and the

State Department approved the request. And he's on his way. I'm sure you're aware of our desire to improve diplomatic relations with Iran."

"And will he be safe?"

"We have no reason to think otherwise."

"Do you have your Mossad friends under control?"

Nash paused in order to formulate his response before answering. "They won't be a problem, General."

"I would appreciate any extra safety precautions you might think of, Colonel."

"I will certainly try, General."

"How about my daughter and grandchildren? Are they receiving any special consideration?"

Continuing the deception, Nash said, "To the best of my knowledge, they're not in any danger."

"Colonel Nash," Pugachov said. "Please permit me to be blunt: if any harm comes to my family, it will have an adverse impact on our bilateral relationship. I will see to that."

"So noted, General."

"Good day, Colonel."

It wasn't the best conversation they'd had, and it wasn't the worst either. Colonel Nash continued to study the TOP SECRET report, desperately looking for clues—any clues. He put out his cigar, picked up the phone, and said, "Call Evrom Rafael." The voice recognition system automatically found Commander Rafael's private number and dialed it. Seconds later, the top Israeli spook in Washington was on the phone.

"How about a game of handball, Evrom."

"Are you itching to get beat again, old man?"

"I need to run a few words by you."

"Saturday?"

"Saturday."

The Colonel was certain Evrom knew what he wanted. The two often exchanged information. Fortunately, such professional courtesy was commonplace among friendly intelligence services, above all between the CIA and the Mossad.

After Nash completed his review of the TOP SECRET report, he transferred the key words he had underlined or circled to a plain five-by-seven card, and placed it in the top drawer of his desk. He then walked to an innocuous-looking closet in the corner of his office and opened it to reveal a massive metal safe. To its right was a retina scanner. The Colonel placed his chin on the apparatus and stared into a dim blue light. Dual green laser beams vertically scanned both his retinas and immediately recognized him. The immense steel door automatically opened—the sound of the hydraulics barely audible—to reveal a space twice the size of a large, walk-in closet. Inside, shoulder-high beige filing cabinets covered the walls.

The Colonel entered the safe, filed the TOP SECRET report in one of the drawers, and walked out. The immense steel door automatically closed behind him.

The voice of General Pugachov still ringing in his head, he walked back to his desk, sat in his oddly modern chair, and picked up the phone. "Call Roy Sullivan."

Roy took the cell phone off his belt holster and looked at the Caller ID. It said, "Out of Area." Unwilling to interrupt his quiet dinner with his wife, Alice, he returned the phone to its holster and continued devouring the thick meatloaf. Two minutes later, it rang again. Once more, "Out of Area." This time he answered. "Roy Sullivan."

"Tim Nash here."

"Hello, Colonel." He rose from the kitchen table and walked out onto the balcony. Alice knew too well that it was FBI business.

Once outside, Roy said, "What can I do for you, sir?"

"Careful what you say. This is in the clear."

"Yes, sir."

"Have you picked up any gossip from the neighbors across the street?"

"No, sir. Nothing out of the ordinary. All we hear is real-estate talk."

"Have you got all the bases covered?"

"Yes, sir. They can't burp without us hearing them."

"That's good. Just got a call from the big grandpa, squeezing me for the safety of his daughter and grandkids."

"I understand, sir. We're looking after them."

"Have a couple of plainclothesmen quietly escort the kids to school."

"School is out, sir."

"Then to wherever they go. Tell your boss I requested the coverage."

"Will do, sir."

"If anything happens to them, my ass is grass. You follow?"

"Yes, sir."

"Give me a shout if you hear anything."

"Yes, sir."

Back inside, Roy looked at Alice with resignation and said, "Business." Then he walked past the kitchen table toward the door that led to the basement and muttered, "Gotta check on the boys." Roy barely noticed that Alice just kept eating in silence. After twenty-five years of being an FBI wife, she was numb to the interruptions.

Roy entered his dimly lit woodworking shop where Special Agent Konarski and his team were manning the state-of-the-art surveillance equipment. "Anything interesting?"

"Nothing." Agent Konarski removed his headphones. "Condos in Van Ness, property in San Jose, and soccer games."

"What about the Internet?"

"Escort services. And they're quite picky."

"Cell phone activity?"

"Routine shit."

"Has TEMPEST picked up anything?"

"Just an offer to buy some condos—three million for four of them. Can you believe this?"

"Stay with'em. Something's bound to turn up."

12

Ross wasn't thrilled about the nine-hour layover in Amsterdam. They arrived at 7:15 AM, local time, but his body clock read 9:15 PM San Francisco time. He was tired and would have kissed a pig for a comfortable bed.

As he aimlessly walked through the terminal looking for a quiet place to sit, he heard a familiar voice. "Hey stranger, you seem lost."

It was Leila Conner, ever so perky, pulling a suitcase with one hand and carrying her overstuffed laptop case with the other.

"Not lost, just looking for a spot to park."

"I'm going to the VIP lounge," Leila said. "Wanna come?"

Well, she's definitely interested, Ross thought. *If I don't watch it, she could get me into serious trouble with Oksana.* "Thanks, but I'm not a member."

"Come on, I can take a guest."

What the hell. She's inviting me to the VIP lounge, not her hotel room. "In that case, sure."

The lounge was a welcome refuge filled with amenities. Large comfortable armchairs, countless television sets, and complimentary drinks. Above all, it provided peace and quiet.

Once inside, Leila promptly went to a workstation, plugged in her laptop, and set up office. Ross wondered how she found the energy. He proceeded to a deserted alcove and quickly fell asleep on a sofa.

It was around noon when he woke up. He poured himself a cup of coffee and walked into the business center to mail Leila's autographed photo to his secretary, Pam, for safekeeping. Then he wandered over to where Leila was pounding away at the keyboard. "You're gonna break that computer."

"No worries," Leila said, without missing a beat. She turned to face Ross with a smile. "CNN buys me a new one every year."

"Aren't you tired?"

"I slept on the plane. Besides, I get hyper when I'm on a deadline."

"What're you working on now?"

"The intro to the fifth segment of my show. Check it out." She pushed back on her swivel chair, making room for Ross to see the screen. "What do you think?"

With one hand on the armrest of her chair, he leaned over and began to read.

Historically, Iran has a tradition, stretching over two and a half millennia, of being an independent powerhouse with projection capabilities. Iranians— known as Persians prior to 1935—have fought for centuries against the Babylonians, Greeks, Romans, Arabs, Byzantines, Monguls, Moguls, and Turks. In these wars, they conquered more frequently than they suffered defeat. And when vanquished, they still managed to preserve their cultural identity and ultimately subdued the invaders through perseverance and tenacity.

There was some jargon for blocking and camera angles in between paragraphs that made no sense to Ross. He skipped them and continued reading.

This regional dominance, severely diminished after the Islamic Revolution of 1979 and subsequently discredited due to its anti-Western policies and support of international terrorism, is what Iran hungers to restore. The Islamic Republic knows it can be destroyed in this power game—but only by the United States or Israel.

There was more video lingo and some reference to a wide-angle shot revealing the missile and her walking toward it.

Enter Iran's not-so-covert support of the Islamic Jihad, Hamas, and Hizbollah, which is nothing other than power projection against Israel as proxy for America. And add into the mix this missile—named, Shahab III with a thousand-mile range that can easily reach every major city in the Middle East including, Tel Aviv—and you will understand why Iran's nuclear cooperation with Russia is creating such alarm in Washington. And more ominously, in Tel Aviv.

"Well written," Ross said, standing up. "I'm impressed."

"You should've seen the trash my producer had written. It's amazing how ignorant, and worse, naïve, Americans are about the Middle East and its intricate nuances. Even the so-called professionals don't understand the half of it. The Brits, on the other hand, know the area and its intrigues quite well. They better—they created most of the mess."

As she packed up her laptop, she mentioned that she was ready for a break. They still had four hours before their flight to Tehran. Quite familiar with the airport, Leila suggested Café Amsterdam for lunch.

Over a plate of smoked salmon and goat cheese salad, she launched into a remarkable analysis of the geopolitics of the Middle East that would have made Dr. Kissinger proud. As they walked back to the VIP lounge, the conversation became more personal. She shared the anguish of her recent and very public divorce and child custody battle, the perils of living in a fish bowl, and told Ross about her future aspirations. Ross reminisced of the senseless execution of his twin brother, Sohrab, and what it meant to him. He told her about his work at the Berkeley Lab and about his wife and her very famous father, General Pugachov.

Her reaction to the revelation that Ross was the son-in-law of Viktor Pugachov was priceless—a Kodak moment. She stopped in her tracks, looked at him with her eyes opened twice the normal size, and with a startled voice said, "Pugachov is your father-in-law?"

"Yes," Ross said. "It's an open secret that my wife and I don't advertise."

"This is huge! I'd love to do a story on you and your family."

"I'm afraid I can't do that. I hope you understand."

She shook her head, grinning. "You're a waste of a great story, man."

KLM FLIGHT 433 LEFT AMSTERDAM FOR TEHRAN AT 4:10 PM. ON this leg of the journey, Ross had a window seat three rows behind Leila Conner and her customary extra seat. She didn't invite him to sit with her and, as pleasant as their conversations were thus far, Ross was tired of talking. He needed some time to himself to deal with the emotional turbulence he felt inside.

He was edgy. Twirling the CIA-issued Berkeley ring on his right middle-finger, he wondered if the satellites were able to track him while he was seven miles up in the air. There were no technical reasons why they couldn't, but he wondered anyway. He wished Oksana and his children, especially Victor, were with him. This was a trip he had always imagined taking with them. It would've been wonderful to play tour guide to his children around the country and city of his birth. He missed them already.

Dinner and a movie made the five-hour flight more bearable. Before he knew it, the giant Airbus A-300 began its descent to Tehran's Mehrabad International airport. Soon the ocean of flickering lights that was the metropolis of Tehran was spread out beneath him like an exquisite Persian rug.

As the plane approached the airport, the city lights grew brighter, revealing more detail. The marble-clad Shahyad Tower—renamed Azadi (freedom) Tower, after the Islamic revolution—was the only familiar landmark. Drowned in floodlights, the majestic gateway to Iran glowed like a precious ring stone.

It was a hard landing. The plane rolled to a stop about a quarter of a mile away from the main terminal. Ross noticed that the old building had changed a lot. It looked much bigger and had been totally renovated. So much so that he barely recognized it.

The airport was not equipped with skyways. Passengers had to walk down the stairs to the tarmac and then pile into large busses that would transport them to the main terminal.

As the travelers queued up in the aisles to exit the plane, Ross observed that Leila remained in her seat, looking back. She smiled and waved when they made eye contact. It took a while before he reached her row. She rose and said, "How does it feel, Ross?"

"Just fine," he lied. In fact, he felt nauseous. The butterflies in his stomach were dancing to a chorus of fear, anticipation, and melancholy.

Leila walked in front of Ross as they slowly made their way toward the exit. Watching her hourglass figure provided him with a fleeting distraction. When he stepped out of the plane and onto the landing, he felt as if the dry heat of the Tehran summer had slapped him in the face. Even after all these years, somehow, the air he was breathing felt familiar.

Ross was sizing up the three large busses that were lined up on the tarmac when he saw a black Mercedes with tinted windows slowly drive up and stop a few feet away to the right. He glanced at Leila. "Is that your ride?"

"No way," Leila said. "There must be some government heavyweight on board."

Ross and Leila started down the steps, side by side. Leila nonchalantly asked, "By the way, where are you staying?"

"Shams Grand."

"What a coincidence," she said, grinning. "Me too."

The butterflies in his stomach suddenly picked up their tempo. *This is great!* Ross thought. *I can see her again.* Then, he said, "Let's do lunch sometime." But he hesitated. *This is a slippery slope, man. Don't get too close.*

"That'll be wonderful," she said.

He took a deep breath.

Suddenly, Ross felt lost in the moment, as if he were in a trance. It was a month shy of thirty-five years since he and Sohrab had left Tehran as teenagers. Now, over fifty, he had returned alone. With each step, a fresh memory of his brother flashed in his memory.

As soon as he set foot on the pavement, the passenger door of the Mercedes flung open and a familiar face emerged. Walking toward Ross, with open arms as if expecting a hug, the man said in Farsi, "*Khosh amadeed!* Welcome, my friend! Welcome home."

It was Kazem.

Ross froze, loathing the sight of him.

Leila Conner tapped Ross on the shoulder and whispered, "I'm impressed, big shot."

He shrugged. "So am I."

"Find me at the hotel tomorrow," Leila insisted. "I want to hear all about this."

"If I make it to the hotel, I will."

Leila continued strolling toward the first bus with her head turned to watch the scene. Everyone stared. Kazem walked up to Ross and gave him a bear hug. Ross just stood there—speechless.

"Did you have a nice flight, Dr. Shaheen?"

"I didn't expect to see you here."

"Like it or not," Kazem pointed to the car, "I'm your host and this is your ride."

"No," Ross protested, trying not to make a scene. "I rather go with the others."

"But that's impossible." Kazem put his arm behind Ross, gently guiding him toward the car. "All the arrangements have already been made for you—the customs clearance, the transport to your hotel—everything is prearranged. Please come, this way." He then opened the door behind the driver and let Ross in.

Kazem sat in the passenger seat, barked an order to the driver, and tried to kiss up to Ross by heaping the exaggerated compliments which, combined with profuse pleasantries and half-hearted gestures of hospitality, constitute an ancient Persian custom known as *taarof.*

Ross ignored him.

From a side entrance, the Mercedes drove into the restricted area of terminal operations.

Ross looked around. Airport workers and baggage handlers were milling about doing their jobs. Uniformed guards carrying AK-47 Kalashnikovs were everywhere. They stared at the Mercedes but didn't seem to be bothered by it.

The driver stopped the car in front of an iron door, guarded by a soldier. Kazem turned to Ross. "May I have your passport?"

Ross handed it to him. He gave it a cursory look and left without saying anything. The soldier, obviously familiar with Kazem, opened the metal door, letting him through. Strangely, they didn't acknowledge each other.

Ross asked the driver. "How long will this take?"

"For Mr. Dowlat, fifteen minutes, max."

Using his Persian name, Ross introduced himself to the driver. "My name is Rostam Shaheen. What's your name?"

He hadn't spoken even one word so far, but he acknowledged Ross by making eye contact through the rearview mirror. "My name is Reza. I'm a chauffeur for the ministry."

"What ministry?"

"Ministry of Mines and Natural Resources."

"Is that where Kazem works?"

"Yes, sir."

As they engaged in small talk, Reza casually removed his hat, retrieved a small yellow piece of paper that was hidden inside, and handed it to Ross without looking back. Ross took the paper and glanced at him in the mirror. Reza gestured silence by placing his right index finger over his lips and continued talking about the intolerable gridlock on the streets of Tehran.

Ross opened the paper and was stunned to find a hand written note in Russian. *I work for your friends at the Russian embassy. Be careful what you say; this car is bugged. Your hotel room is also bugged. I will look out for you. Don't trust anyone.*

Without a pause, Reza continued to speak his nonsense. With his right hand, he reached over his shoulder and motioned for Ross to give the note back to him. He obliged. Reza then promptly stuffed the note in his mouth and—ever so calmly—started to chew.

Silence.

With a gleeful smile, Kazem emerged from the metal door and headed toward the car. This time he climbed into the back seat and instructed Reza to proceed to Shams Grand hotel. He then handed Ross' passport back to him. "It's all set, my friend."

"What about my luggage?"

"All taken care of."

As the Mercedes sped out of the operations building into an enormous access road filled with countless cars buzzing about, Ross remembered a line that CIA's legendary mole hunter, James Jesus Angleton, once said:

"Espionage is a wilderness of mirrors."

13

WITH A BURGEONING POPULATION APPROACHING TWELVE MILLION, Tehran, the capital of Iran, is one of the largest cities in the world. Its name means "warm slope," probably because it is situated on the southern foot of the Damavand Mountain, the highest peak in the Alburz range. And, since the sprawling metropolis is sandwiched between the snowcapped mountain to the north and an arid desert to the south, Tehran—except for a month or two in the winter—has a temperate climate.

Yet, it was a starless and oppressively hot night when Dr. Ross Shaheen, after an absence of thirty-five years, returned to his birthplace, the warm slope that was Tehran.

The black Mercedes snaked its way north through the chaotic traffic, which was heavy even at midnight. While the tinted windows of the car concealed the odd mix of passengers from the curious onlookers, an invisible veil of secrecy kept their true loyalties hidden from each other.

Kazem played tour guide to Ross. Extolling the virtues of the Islamic Republic, he enthusiastically pointed to the new buildings and elevated superhighways that had been constructed since the Revolution of 1979. Ross had trouble paying attention to what Kazem said. Preoccupied, he nodded to be polite while thinking about the yellow note that Reza had swallowed earlier. He felt uneasy about the listening devices in the car and the ones awaiting him at the hotel.

Reza negotiated the traffic in a determined manner and continued to head north on the Niyavaran highway while Kazem, like a bore at a cocktail party who doesn't know when to shut up, babbled on.

Meanwhile, Ross gazed into the distance, wondering what other secrets lay hidden in the darkness. He struggled to find recognizable landmarks but, other than the Azadi Tower, didn't find any. Nothing looked familiar, not even the street names—they had mostly been changed to either commemorate some Shaheed (Martyr) or a variety of mullahs (Muslim priests).

Oddly, it all seemed strange to him.

Fearing guilt by association after his twin brother's execution, Ross' immediate and extended family had emigrated abroad into voluntary exile. There was no one left to visit. His childhood friends and high school buddies had all vanished to North America, Europe, or Australia for their "pursuit of happiness." There was no one left to call.

Slowly, a cruel fact began to dawn on Ross: he had become an alien in his own land.

Kazem stopped talking when the car pulled into the portico of the Shams Grand hotel. He accompanied Ross into the lobby. "Please stay here while I get your room key. You are already registered."

Ross obliged without saying much and lingered in the lobby. Equally exhausted and anxious, he strolled around admiring the majestic space, the high ceilings, and the ornate chandeliers. The entire floor was white marble with inlaid brass, which created geometric patterns. In the center, a large blue Persian rug sprawled beneath a massive granite round table. Two enormous silk rugs—so exquisite, they appeared as if they were tapestries—adorned the walls on each side of the registration desk. Several sofas and loveseats, in stark blue leather, were positioned in various corners and alcoves of the lobby. At first glance, the five-star hotel lived up to its name: grand.

Reza entered the deserted hall carrying Ross' suitcase and stood a respectful few steps away. Ross approached him casually and whispered, "Can we talk here?"

Reza nodded.

"I'm free tomorrow." Ross looked back to see where Kazem was. "Can you take me around town in a car that has no ears?"

"I'll see what I can do," Reza said. "What time?"

"Late morning."

With nervous movements of his eyebrows, Reza signaled that Kazem was approaching.

"You have a penthouse suite, my friend," Kazem declared with obvious delight, dangling the key. "I had to pull a lot of strings to get this for you."

"Thanks," Ross said, thinking, *Yes, lots of strings along with a bunch of wire taps.*

"You must be tired, Dr. Shaheen. Let me show you to your room."

"Okay," Ross muttered. "After you."

Kazem entered the spacious suite on the ninth floor with Ross in tow. Reza followed, carrying the suitcase. Immediately, Kazem began to admire the room and the panoramic view from the spacious balcony. It was well past 1:00 AM. Ross kept yawning and couldn't wait to go to sleep. After a while, Kazem got the hint. On his way out, he went over Ross' schedule for the next few days and gave him his business card. "Call my mobile if you need anything."

Ross was mostly quiet until then. He took the card and said, "I don't know my way around Tehran. Can Reza drive me tomorrow? I mean later on this morning, and also on Friday?"

"Absolutely, my friend. He is at your service. Go around the city, Dr. Shaheen. See how much we've accomplished. Enjoy yourself. Get some rest and acclimate. And on Saturday, bright and early, your work will begin."

With that, Kazem and Reza left.

Alone and barely awake, Ross collapsed on the bed and dialed his home number in San Francisco. On the fourth ring, Oksana picked up. She was ecstatic to hear his voice. They chatted for a while, and Ross assured her that he was fine but exhausted. After a few minutes and with controlled excitement, Oksana said, "Guess what?"

"I'm too tired to guess. Tell me."

"We received a wire transfer today."

"From Iran?"

"Yes. Where else?"

"Great. They kept their promise."

"But, it's for ten times the amount you requested."

"You mean...a million!?"

"Yes."

"It's a trap! The bastards are trying to set me up."

"Set you up?" Oksana said. "What are you talking about?"

Ross caught himself. He had said too much. After all, Oksana was not aware of his true mission. "Nothing, honey. I'm just tired; don't mind me. It's obviously a mistake. Some idiot must have punched an extra zero into some computer. I'll look into it later."

It was a brief conversation. Ross tried to sound normal even though he felt awkward knowing that some grease ball was listening in. For a while, he wondered if besides the microphones, there were also hidden cameras in the room. But before long, he dismissed the thought and walked out onto the balcony for some fresh air. He leaned against the handrail staring at the ocean of flickering lights while twisting the Berkeley ring on his middle finger.

ON A GIANT FLAT-SCREEN, MOUNTED ON THE WALL OF A DIMLY LIT room one floor beneath Colonel Nash's office, a new bright green light was flashing. This was the Command Center of the Directorate of Operations of the CIA—the forbidden control room of America's worldwide spy network. There were eighteen such screens on the wall. Some two-dozen controllers, wearing headphones and mouthpieces, sat behind high-tech workstations and carefully monitored them. Hundreds of such green lights, blinking on every monitor, pinpointed the locations of CIA operatives in various regions of the world.

A unique codename appeared to the right of each light. And SPIKER was the word that marked the latest blinking dot over the map of Tehran. No one in the Command Center, not even the manager, knew who SPIKER was. In fact, the true identities of covert agents in the field were the most tightly held secret in the CIA. The information was so sensitive that a comprehensive list or database was never maintained in one place and, other than the Director of the CIA or his deputies, no one had access to the entire list.

At 4:35 PM, sixty-three hundred miles west of Tehran and nine time zones earlier, Colonel Nash was notified that SPIKER was in position. He knew who SPIKER was.

14

I T WAS MID-MORNING ON THURSDAY WHEN ROSS WOKE TO A HARD knock on the door. Thinking it was housekeeping, he moaned, "Come back later." But there was another knock. He dragged himself out of bed, put on a bathrobe, and opened the door until the chain link snagged. He looked out and saw Reza standing there ready to knock again.

"Oh, it's you."

"I tried to call from the lobby, but you would not answer."

Ross let Reza in and mumbled, "It's unplugged."

Once again, Reza gestured silence by placing his right index finger over his lips. "Where do you want to go today?"

Mindful of the hidden microphones, Ross said, "Just drive around the city, and visit some old spots. I feel like a tourist."

"I'll wait for you in the lobby. Wear something cool; it is a scorcher outside."

Ross stepped out of the elevator into the lobby where Reza was engaged in an animated discussion with one of the bellboys. When he saw Ross, he came over.

Ross said, "Let's get some lunch," and headed for the door without waiting for an answer. Reza dutifully followed him outside and led him to his car. It was his personal vehicle, an ancient white Paykan, assembled in Iran. He had made up an excuse for his boss at the ministry—that the official Mercedes was out of order.

Almost immediately after Reza drove out, Ross began to sweat profusely. The Paykan was not air conditioned, and the temperature was in the nineties. It was dry heat but still uncomfortable. Shams Grand

Hotel was located in the elite Niavaran neighborhood, north of Tehran. Reza drove south and then west toward the city center on the Hemmat highway. Moments later, he said calmly, "We're being followed."

Ross froze.

"Don't look back," Reza said, looking in the rearview mirror. "There's a red motorcycle with two riders behind us. They've been tailing us since we left the hotel."

"Who are they?"

"I don't know for sure. But I know the bike."

"How can you know the bike?"

"There are only two BMW motorcycles like this in the entire city. And they belong to two brothers—sons of a Jewish merchant."

Ross had heard enough; they must be Mossad agents. He looked in the side mirror to catch a glimpse. The driver was wearing a red helmet with a dark visor, obscuring his face, but the passenger wasn't wearing one. Ross easily recognized him; he was the punk kid with greased hair and reflective shades from the airplane. Ross felt nauseous. *The Mossad has been tailing me all the way from Washington. But why? Colonel Nash assured me that they had green-lighted this trip. So why the hell are they following me? Am I gonna take a bullet in the back of my head one of these nights?*

Reza interrupted his agony. "Don't mind them—they're harmless… Just keeping an eye on you. I wouldn't worry."

Ross didn't feel any less anxious by Reza's assurances, but there was little he could do. After all, he wasn't doing anything wrong—just sightseeing. So, he decided the best course of action was to heed Reza's advice and ignore them. Changing the subject, he asked Reza about his connection to the Russian Embassy and whether he worked for the Russian FSB—Federal Security Service.

"No, nothing like that. I'm just an occasional informant. Once in a while, I do special jobs for them."

"Do you speak Russian?"

"Yes. A little."

"Have you ever been to Russia?"

"Why all the questions about me, Dr. Shaheen?" Reza snapped. "I cooperate with the Russian Embassy. They've asked me to look after you and call them if you get yourself into any trouble. That's it. The rest is not important." After a short pause, he continued. "Instead of me, if I were you, I would worry about Kazem and what he has up his sleeve."

With that polite rebuke, Ross decided to change the subject once again. But he knew full well that Reza was a lot deeper than he pretended. If General Pugachov had instructed the Russian Embassy to look after his son-in-law, which he must have, then the Embassy would put their absolute best on the job—Pugachov wouldn't accept anything less.

Over a traditional lunch of rice and lamb kebab at the *Borj-e-Tala*—literally, golden tower—restaurant, Ross asked Reza about life under the Islamic Republic regime. Reza said, "Things could be worse. Just look to our east and west—Afghanistan and Iraq. Those people are reduced to living like animals. We're not. In Iran, no one is starving. We don't need handouts from the U.N. to stay alive. Most people have electricity, water, and some kind of housing. Our children go to school, and we have access to hospitals and clinics. We even have a metro for God's sake—probably the only one in the entire Middle East. So, as tough as it is economically, with inflation and unemployment at record highs, we still have the basics. And I, for one, am grateful for that."

Somewhat surprised by that answer, Ross said, "Then why all the unrest? Why the student marches in the streets?"

"We have everything but freedom. That's why."

The bikers came into the restaurant and sat at a corner table. The brothers closely resembled each other and didn't look particularly menacing. Ross pretended to ignore them and didn't interrupt as Reza continued. "In Iran, the entire system is designed to obscure the truth. There's always a scheme behind the façade of normalcy that often lines someone's pocket. The media create propaganda that the government, and more often, their patron cleric, wants put out. If you question anything, you risk being beaten up in the street or hauled away to jail. Even turn up dead. Of course, you know all this, Dr. Shaheen. Didn't they kill your brother because he published some article in a newspaper?"

Ross didn't expect Reza to know about his family history, but he was not surprised. After all, Reza was part of the community of spies, and spies usually know more than one might think.

"Yes," Ross said. "They killed him over a stupid article."

"What did he write?"

"It was during the indiscriminate purges that immediately followed the Revolution. My brother, Sohrab, was a journalist. Critical and humorous, he published an article that in essence said the principle achievement of the Islamic Revolution was trading one Crown with thousands of Turbans." Ross glanced at the bikers and continued. "That got him arrested, tortured, and finally executed."

Reza smiled. "That's clever, but the mullahs have no sense of humor. Be that as it may, I have to admit that things aren't as bad as they were in those years but we still have innocent people disappearing or mysteriously turning up dead."

"I'm sorry to hear that."

For the rest of the afternoon, Reza drove Ross around the city with the bikers in tow. A lot had changed, but he could still find a few things that had remained the same. They drove by his old house in the Shemiran district. Except for the marble facade looking gray from dirt and pollution, the house hadn't changed all that much. Ross had the strong urge to knock on the door and ask to look inside. He had lived the first eighteen years of his life in that house. But Reza convinced him otherwise. Instead, a lonely snapshot of the old house had to do.

They went by Ross' high school, which ushered in sweet memories of his youth. He was disappointed to see that the school had long been closed and converted into low-income housing, with each classroom accommodating a family. They were mostly widows and orphans of the Iran–Iraq war.

Traveling around the city, Reza often complained about the pollution, whined about the traffic, and bellyached about the overcrowding. But once in a while, he said something profound. Passing a huge picture of the Grand Ayatollah, he remarked, "In every society, the larger the size of the monuments of the leaders, the less freedom the subjects have."

It was nearly 5:00 PM when Ross mustered the emotional energy to ask Reza to take him to the cemetery where Sohrab was buried. Strangely enough, the place was called Kafarabad—literally, the abode of the infidels.

BEFORE SITTING DOWN FOR DINNER, ROY SULLIVAN CHECKED ON THE crew that had been holed up in his garage for the past few days. Agent Konarski, the Broom, was once again empty handed. As soon as Roy stepped into the woodworking shop, Broom waved his hands with frustration and said, "Nothing!"

"What do you mean, nothing? There must be some activity."

"They're having a party. Two Latino hookers and three horny Iranians. Here, have a listen."

Agent Konarski removed his headphones, placed them on his shoulders, and turned up the speakers. The TEMPEST, equally capable of picking up sound from vibration of windowpanes, played what went on inside the Miller's house. Spanish heavy-metal music boomed in the background, muffling the chorus of drunken laughter, moans, and rhythmic screams of, "Oh, yes!"

Roy gestured that he'd heard enough. "Cut the crap, Broom."

Disgusted, Agent Konarski muted the speakers. "These guys are either extremely good or awfully bad. They sure aren't ordinary spooks. Or, they might just be what they seem, regular businessmen having a good time."

"You're saying they're harmless?"

"That's what I'm speculating, boss."

"We need to stay with them a little while longer."

"How long?"

"A few more days, to complete a week."

With that, Roy went upstairs and joined Alice for dinner. He wasn't very talkative. His mind was wandering, trying to figure out the odds of these guys being civilians. *Nil to none.* He had to call Colonel Nash. After dinner, he went into the den, glanced at Alice loading the dishwasher, and dialed Colonel Nash's private number.

"What's up, Roy?" Nash eagerly asked.

Roy briefed him about the status of their surveillance effort and said, "I think we're wasting time on these clowns."

Nash said, "Stay with them a while longer," before unceremoniously hanging up.

From the kitchen, Alice called out, "Who's on the phone?"

"My CNN girlfriend."

"You wish."

15

In a cheesy motel in the back alleys of San Francisco's famed Fisherman's Wharf, two rough-looking Iranian men were eating a mushroom pizza for dinner. Propped up on one of the beds, Emad—a skinny man in his late twenties, with an emaciated stubbly face—took a huge bite out of a slice without moving his eyes off the TV. It was showing the movie *Alien*.

Next to the TV, on top of the dresser, there was a large metal suitcase with its lid open. At about the moment when Ripley was about to slay the seemingly indestructible beast, something inside the metal case beeped and then whistled. Emad glanced at the suitcase and quickly returned his attention to the movie. His roommate, Jaffar—an older and bearded man, naked to his waste and drinking Coke with a straw from a jumbo-sized cup—sat in a yoga position on the opposite bed. He looked at the metal suitcase and said, *"Bebeen Cheeyeh*—See what it is." He finished his Coke with a loud sucking sound while scratching the abundance of hair on his meaty chest.

Emad said, "I'll check it later," and reached for another slice of pizza.

"Do it now!" Jaffar barked.

Emad, wearing a tacky T-shirt over a pair of faded jeans, obediently stepped over to the suitcase. Inside, there was a short-wave radio, a black box with wires protruding out of its sides, and a laptop computer. The inner walls of the suitcase were lined with fine copper mesh designed to block all electromagnetic emissions, which rendered the powerful TEMPEST useless. Emad reached in and tilted the laptop screen. "You've got a message from above. It's coded. Come read it."

Jaffar rose and slowly walked over. He retrieved a laminated playing card-sized paper from his wallet. It contained a 7 x 31 table of six-digit numbers in fine print. Cross-referencing the day of the month with the day of the week, Jaffar typed the resulting six-digit code into the laptop. Seconds later, the stream of encrypted text transformed into readable secret instructions:

JADOOGAR APPROACHING NEST STOP MAY NOT BE HELPFUL STOP PREPARE HOSPITAL FOR PATIENTS STOP STANDBY FOR GO FOX HUNT END

Jaffar hunched over the suitcase, read the message carefully, and clicked DELETE & DESTROY without saying a word. Emad looked at his boss inquisitively as he slowly walked to his bed but didn't ask what their instructions were.

After getting situated, Jaffar said, "We must leave in the morning."

"Where to?"

"To the safe house. We must get it ready. I think the GO order may come at any moment."

Emad lit up a cigarette and offered one to Jaffar. They leaned back, puffing away and watching TV. Soon they were once again engrossed by the movie.

The coded message was the same transmission that Jimbo had intercepted in Cyprus, which Fariba had decoded at the NSA, and that would later be filed away in the secure vault inside Colonel Nash's office.

ABOUT THIRTEEN MILES NORTH OF FISHERMAN'S WHARF INSIDE ROSS' house, Marina was annoyed with her mother. Oksana didn't approve of her plans. Marina wanted to go to Pebble Beach with a group of friends. One of the girls had access to her uncle's condo and had invited Marina and others to join her for a long weekend of surfing.

"Please, Mom, can I go?"

"Absolutely not!" Oksana said.

"But why, Mom? Give me one good reason."

"Who else will be there?"

Marina rattled out eight names. Oksana knew the lot and started to feel a little better. But she was still against it.

"Are you sure Roberto won't show up?"

"Yes, Mom. He won't be there. I promise."

"You know how your father feels about him."

"I know, Mom," Marina said. "Roberto isn't even here. He's back in Venezuela for the summer. And, I don't understand why Dad hates him so much, anyway."

"Your dad doesn't hate him or anyone else. He's just suspicious of Roberto. That's all."

"He's suspicious of all my guy friends."

"That's how dads are. My father was suspicious of your dad just the same. Besides, the long hair and the tattoos don't help Roberto's image."

"So, can I go?"

Oksana vacillated. With Ross in Iran, she didn't want to worry about Marina in addition to him. *But,* she thought, *Marina is a young adult now and must be allowed to live her own life.* She took a deep breath and said, "You can go if you promise to call me every day and be very careful with the waves. I don't want any accidents."

Jumping with joy, Marina hugged her mother. "Thanks, Mom! It'll be so much fun. I can't wait."

Later that evening, Marina started to pack for the weekend trip while talking nonstop on her cell. Among the calls she made, there was a quiet one to Roberto. She tried on several bathing suits and modeled them for her mother, who approved every one. Young and beautiful, Marina looked good in anything she wore.

Tinkering with his latest model-plane project, Victor ignored the bikini show all together.

MOIS—Ministry of Intelligence and Security *(Vezarat-i Ettelaat va Amniyat-i Keshvar)*—was Iran's primary intelligence and security apparatus. The most secretive intelligence service in the world, MOIS remained one of the most ruthless. It was universally feared for its unconstrained power and its unsettling ability to quietly eliminate

Iranian dissidents, both at home and abroad. Few had firsthand knowledge of its internal organization, while its budget was known only to a handful at the pinnacle of the Iranian political hierarchy. As long as its actions advanced the aims of the regime, MOIS enjoyed absolute operational freedom. With nearly limitless resources at its disposal, the Ministry of Intelligence and Security was probably the most powerful of all ministries in the Islamic Republic of Iran.

MOIS secret agents, on assignment overseas, lived by a strict set of rules meant for their stealth and survival. They never stayed in one place more than three nights, unless it was in one of their countless safe houses. By paying cash for all purchases, these graduates of deception didn't leave any electronic trace behind. They drove ordinary vehicles at the legal speed limit; and by wearing everyday clothes, they remained inconspicuous in public. They avoided calling or writing home. Instead, they received instructions from Tehran in a variety of clandestine ways—imbedded messages in radio microbursts was the most tried and true method.

So Emad and Jaffar thought.

They loaded the metal case, two duffle bags containing their modest belongings, and a handbag filled with weapons and ammunition into the back of a blue Ford Taurus. It was 6:05 AM. The streets of Fisherman's Wharf were deserted. After a pancake breakfast at the IHOP on the corner of Powell and Beach, they headed north on the Coastal Highway 101. Their destination was a log cabin on the edge of the Six Rivers National Forest, near the city of Eureka in northern California. The rustic and secluded cabin was a recent acquisition by one of MOIS's front companies, to be used as a safe house.

They didn't seem to be in any hurry to reach their destination. Instead, they played tourist, took their time, and enjoyed the scenery. They traveled the 270-mile distance to Eureka in eight hours. Once they reached Eureka, they headed east on Highway 299 and, as their map indicated, took the Blair Road exit going north.

Perched on a hill and buried in the woods, the cabin wasn't easy to find. Since they had not seen this particular safe house before, they got lost a time or two before finding the place. It was totally isolated and perfect for the operation.

At the end of a long gravel driveway, Emad and Jaffar exited the

Taurus at the same time and stretched with loud grunts, as if they were synchronized swimmers. Jaffar looked around for a birdfeeder and found it hanging from a large walnut tree a few yards from the back porch. It was in the shape of a miniature house. He took it off the hook, turned it on its side, and shook it. A key fell out. Calmly, he picked it up, returned the birdfeeder to its place, and headed toward to the front door of the cabin. Emad followed.

Inside, they began to explore. The rustic A-frame was comfortably furnished. A large beige sectional sofa, in the shape of a horseshoe, was placed in the center of the living room facing a huge stone fireplace. A giant whitetail deer head was mounted above the mantle. On each side of the fireplace, French doors led to a wraparound balcony overlooking the national park and the mountains beyond. To the right of the front entrance was a well-equipped kitchen, open to the living space. Emad looked inside the kitchen cabinets, then the refrigerator. There was a loft bedroom above the kitchen, which overlooked the living room. To the left of the living area, there were four doors. One led to the master bedroom, the other to a powder room, the third was a closet, and the last one opened to a flight of stairs leading down.

Jaffar, with Emad in tow, trotted down the stairs. At the bottom, they found a short hallway leading to another door equipped with two strong padlocks, both open. A large ring with two brass keys was hanging from a rusty nail above the doorframe. Jaffar stepped inside. It was completely dark and felt cold. Emad flicked his cigarette lighter on, revealing a light bulb hanging from the ceiling. Jaffar pulled the string.

It was a wine cellar.

But there were no bottles on the racks. The damp room had been converted. There was a stainless steel cot in the far corner, equipped with a leg-shackle, which was chained to the wall. A small solitary window was loosely covered with a piece of cardboard. In the right corner of the room, a stainless steel sink and toilet were installed. Near the center, underneath the light bulb, there was a heavy metal chair with strong leather straps around the armrests and front legs, which were bolted to the ground. The concrete floor around the armchair faintly revealed several brown stains. Jaffar and Emad knew too well what the stains were: blood.

"This will do just fine," Jaffar said, as he removed the cardboard from the small window and opened it to let in fresh air. Then they left the cellar.

Upstairs, Emad took notes as Jaffar, shuffling around the kitchen, rattled off the grocery list. It filled two pages. On their way back from Safeway that evening, Jaffar stopped the Taurus in front of a FedEx Office store. He went inside and—ever so politely with his British accent—asked to use the Internet. He chose a secluded cubicle, went straight to AOL, produced a little black notebook from his coat pocket, and opened it to a page at random. It was filled with stolen username and password pairs.

He logged onto AOL with the first pair and promptly crossed them off from the list as a reminder never to use them again. He clicked on DISCUSSION GROUPS and selected the Persian Cuisine category. In the dialogue box, he typed, ALL SET FOR FOXHUNT. Then he quickly signed off.

It was pitch-black and deathly quiet as Jaffar and Emad unloaded the twenty or so grocery bags. Other than their footsteps on the gravel, the only sound they heard was the haunting song of the owls.

Before turning in for the night, Jaffar said, "We'll have to get back to San Francisco tomorrow morning."

Emad said, "As you wish."

<hr />

ONCE JAFFAR TYPED THE CLANDESTINE MESSAGE, ALL SET FOR FOXHUNT, into the special AOL chat room, it took only eighteen minutes for NSA's worldwide listening beast, the ECHELON, to pick it up. It had a match: FOXHUNT. The word had been added to its mammoth dictionary immediately after it first appeared in the decrypted message intercepted in Cyprus.

CIA's Counter Terrorism Center—CTC—was the main hub for all intelligence relating to the global war on terror. Armed with the latest ECHELON match, CTC's director, Mitch Cohen, entered Colonel Nash's office carrying a manila folder stamped TOP SECRET/VLA. With his feet propped on his desk and chewing on a cigar, Nash motioned for Mitch to take a seat while he finished his phone conversation.

"Senator, I'm fully aware of your concerns."

Colonel Nash closed his eyes and shook his head as he listened to the Chairman of the Senate Select Committee on Intelligence.

"Senator...Senator, I assure you the agency is doing everything possible to get to the bottom of this mess."

After a few quiet gestures of irritation, Nash closed the conversation. "Absolutely, sir. Rest assured, sir." He whispered, "Swine bastard," as he hung up the phone.

"What's up?" he asked Mitch tersely.

The balding, heavyset Mitch rose and said, "Colonel, you ought to see this." He approached Nash. The Colonel motioned for him to hurry up, so Mitch stood to one side of Nash's desk and placed the folder in front of him. Nash opened it. Inside, the message intercepted in Cyprus regarding FOXHUNT and the latest ECHELON snatch were stapled on the opposite sides of the folder. Mitch, a veteran of the Directorate of Intelligence, continued earnestly. "Sir, we believe there's an operation waiting a GO order from Tehran on the West Coast."

"What kind of an operation?"

"Its codename is FOXHUNT—most likely, a kidnapping operation."

"How do you know it's kidnapping?"

"CODE TRACER thinks so."

"How do we know it's on the West Coast?"

"ECHELON snatched the second message from AOL a few hours ago. We asked AOL where the message originated. They couldn't tell; over a billion messages go through their network each day. All they know is that the username that posted the message was verified by their NAME SERVER in Sacramento, which serves central and northern California."

"Who was the user?"

"The username was stolen, Colonel. It belongs to an eleven-year-old girl who lives in Sarasota."

Colonel Nash carefully studied the two messages, and without looking up, said, "I remember the reference to *JADOOGAR*." Then he leaned back, facing Mitch Cohen. "I'm checking sources in the liaison services. Maybe they can help us decode this."

"I hope so, Colonel. Without an ID for *JADOOGAR*, this is not actionable intelligence. It's worthless."

Staring out of the window, Nash said in a low voice, "I know."

As Mitch Cohen headed out of Nash's office, he said, "I'm starting to hate this job. The damn puzzle is always missing a piece or two."

16

THE HOUR-LONG DRIVE TO KAFARABAD—WHERE SOHRAB'S BULLET-ridden body had been unceremoniously buried—felt like an eternity. Reza, the driver, didn't say much, and Ross was equally quiet. They both found frivolous chatter disrespectful of the occasion. Ross felt anxious as they approached the cemetery. Once in sight, Reza turned off the radio.

The desolate cemetery was reserved for the victims of the Islamic Revolution. During the wholesale purges of the early eighties, political dissidents, religious misfits, and supporters of the former Shah were routinely tried in kangaroo courts, summarily executed, and buried there. This made Kafarabad—the "abode of the infidels"—an exclusive yet gruesome society.

The vast barren land was gated and walled in. Reza stayed in the car as Ross strolled solemnly toward the main entrance. His steps were slow; he felt as if he was wearing iron boots. Nothing could have prepared him for what he saw inside the walls of Kafarabad. Small, red brick squares marked the endless rows of graves for what seemed to be a mile in each direction. Only numbers were allowed on each marker. Gravestones and epitaphs, like trees and shrubbery, were luxuries denied such "infidels." The names and memories of the slaughtered could only live in the hearts and minds of the ones who loved them—those who were condemned to a life of sorrow, who would often visit this cathedral of the damned to grieve.

Ross knew Sohrab's number. It was 1482.

Walking the barren pathway in between rows of dirt plots,

something inside Ross began to hurt. He had long stopped thinking about the horror Sohrab must have suffered during his last months in prison while waiting his turn at the gallows. The torture, the beatings, and the humiliation he must have endured had haunted Ross for years. And now, all those thoughts were rushing back. He felt as if he was reliving his brother's experience.

Ross glanced at a marker—*1147.*

He remembered Sohrab. Acid-tongued and cynical, his writings were critical of the turbaned masters of the Islamic Republic. Eventually, his venom of ink bought him a one-way ticket to the notorious Evin prison, the regime's slaughterhouse. And in the winter of 1981, he vanished in thin air.

1293.

For weeks, his parents had searched hospitals and morgues looking for him in vain. Ross was in Moscow at the time and called home daily. He had even offered to return to Tehran to help search for Sohrab but was dissuaded by his mother.

1408.

Strolling down the dirt path, Ross noticed a backhoe, in the distance, digging fresh graves. It seemed the machinery of death had not stopped. He walked by a group of women in black *chadors*—a semi-circle sheet of loose cloth that covers the body from head to toe—wailing and sobbing around a fresh grave. An old man, in a gray suit and black tie, was crouched over the mound, quietly weeping in his hands. Ross could barely breathe. He felt the spasm of loathing for those who committed such atrocities.

1475.

He thought *this* must have been the scene when his parents were told of their son's fate in January of 1982. That Sohrab had been executed before a firing squad and was buried in Kafarabad at plot 1482. That the cost of the bullets used to kill him was twenty tumans—the price of a loaf of bread in those days. And, they better pay up.

1482.

Ross stopped. It was day's end, and the sun was hiding behind the haze of the city's smog as if it was ashamed of shedding its radiance upon such a grim sight. Ross had not been so close to his twin brother for nearly thirty years. He knelt on the dirt. There was no trace of

Sohrab; nothing but a piece of red clay with a cold serial number carved on it. Ross had thought about this moment for years, and now, he felt numb. Strangely, he couldn't even cry. It was a hollow reunion.

Staring at the number, he whispered, "I wish you'd stayed in Berkley and never came back here." Then, wiping a single tear from his left eye, he muttered, "What a waste."

Still kneeling, he gently ran his fingers through the grooves of the digits—one, four, eight, and two—over and over again, and reminisced. He thought of the Golden Gate Bridge, Sohrab's favorite landmark. He recalled their nights out, the parties, the arguments, and the many trips to Yosemite. He reflected on the years they were inseparable from each other and their separation since.

Time stood still.

Suddenly, Ross felt a hand on his shoulder. His thoughts interrupted, he looked up. It was Reza. "We must go. It's getting dark, and they'll close the gates soon."

Ross rose and shook the dirt off his pants. Then he looked at the red brick square one last time and whispered, "So long, brother. Someday you'll have a tombstone. I promise you that."

Reza and Ross walked away slowly, with their heads bowed. When they reached the gate, Ross turned and looked at Kafarabad one last time. He wanted to commit the scene to memory. With clenched fists, he looked up and whispered a prayer: "God, if vengeance is thine... grant that I might be Your instrument."

17

THE TEHRAN NIGHT FELL QUICKLY. ON THEIR WAY BACK TO THE Shams Grand, Ross was quiet. After visiting the cemetery, his mood had changed. He was emotionally drained and eager to return to his hotel. He had even lost interest in the bikers who had been shadowing them. He appeared to be someplace else.

Driving through the university district, they ran into a mass of student protesters. Nearly a thousand strong, they shouted slogans of democracy and chanted rhymes of liberty. The mob waved hand-printed placards and appeared peaceful from afar but menacing up close.

Ross broke the silence with quiet laughter. "If my brother was alive, he'd probably be in the middle of this crowd."

Reza said, *"Roohesh shad*—Delighted be his soul."

As they approached the commotion, Ross thought how brave it was for these students to risk their lives for what they believed in—freedom. This was doubly true in a society where the only good dissident was a dead dissident.

Out of the blue, a horde of thugs, driving cheap motorbikes, poured out of a side street. There must have been two hundred of them. To Ross' horror, the backseat riders wielded clubs, chains, and nightsticks.

"Here come the *Basij*," Reza said. "The hoodlums who enforce the will of the regime."

Moving at full speed toward the demonstrators, the motorized hooligans attacked the helpless students and started to beat them mercilessly.

Ross remembered learning about the *Basij* thugs from the CIA briefer, Peter Erwin. Describing their ruthlessness, he had said, "Doing evil is rather easy once you have a clear conscience. And getting orders from a man of God gives you that license." Watching the *Basij* in action, Ross understood what Peter Erwin really meant.

The beatings were ruthless; the kids were bleeding and running for their lives. Several lay motionless on the ground. Traffic was at a standstill. Reza looked as if he was concerned, which was enough to make Ross worried.

Suddenly, the mysterious bikers who had tailed them all day drove onto the sidewalk and waved at Reza to follow suit. Reza took the hint, drove up over the curb, and continued on the sidewalk. The mayhem was on the other side of the street, and the sidewalk was nearly deserted. Reza maneuvered his vehicle around the street vendors and even knocked down a handful of the stands, leaving the vendors screaming obscenities. After a few hundred yards, Reza turned right into an alley and away from the chaos. He was now following the bikers down the narrow pathway at top speed. Several blocks away, at a major intersection, Reza turned left, heading north, but the bikers turned right, heading south, and disappeared into the night traffic.

As Reza sped toward the hotel, Ross slumped in the passenger seat, breathing a sigh of relief. *The bikers were helpful*, he thought. *They're obviously not here to assassinate me. If they were, they could have done it many times over. Then who are they?*

Back in his suite, Ross took a long shower. The jet of hot water bursting over his scalp was soothing, so he stayed under it for nearly half an hour. Then he ordered room service while drying off. A couple of appetizers were all he cared to eat: Beef cutlet, yogurt, and cucumbers. He donned a thick, beige bathrobe and stepped out onto the balcony to ponder the day.

And what a day it had been.

Standing in the still darkness, gazing at the millions of flickering lights in the valley, he thought about how each light somehow represented a person, or a family. And how they all could tell their own unique tales of struggle and pain as compelling as his own while they endured the Islamic Republic's oppression. Was there anyone listening to these stories? Were they even being told? What epic accounts would future Persian scholars write about the experience of this generation?

After a while, he reached into his robe pocket, retrieved the CIA-issued cell, and punched 900-TIM-NASH. He hoped the secret microphones inside the room couldn't pick up his conversation out on the balcony.

He soon heard a familiar voice.

"Hello, Dr. Shaheen. How was the sightseeing?"

It never ceased to amaze Ross how much Nash knew. He seemed eerily omniscient. Ross said, "A lot has changed here, Colonel."

"How was the cemetery?"

"Worse than I expected." Ross shook his head in disbelief. "But it was something I had to do."

"Glad you got it out of your system."

It seemed the Berkeley class ring on Ross' middle finger worked its magic flawlessly.

"I just witnessed a violent demonstration near Tehran University. You wouldn't believe how bloody it was, Colonel. This place is ready to explode."

"We've known that for some time. But the mullahs have more than nine lives. You, however, only have one. And you'd better stay clear of their politics. Understand?"

"Of course," Ross said. "I don't even comprehend their politics and frankly, couldn't care less. I was just wondering if you guys had anything to do with these demonstrations."

Pause.

"You should know better than to ask a dumb ass question like that, Ross."

Colonel Nash had said enough. The pause gave it away. Ross had been on the periphery of the intelligence world long enough to know a few things about how they operated. Nothing is what it seems in their make-believe, parallel universe. Sociopolitical unrest, demonstrations, even civil wars—these don't happen on their own. Upheavals always occur when there is a sufficient quantity of combustible politics on the ground and someone manages to light a fuse. And almost always, that long fuse can be traced to the headquarters of one of the shadowy creatures in the jungle of espionage: the CIA, MI6, FSB, Mossad, MOIS, and God only knows who else.

"Sorry, Colonel," Ross muttered.

Nash changed the subject. "What's next?"

Ross wanted to inform the Colonel about Reza and his affiliation with the Russian Embassy but quickly changed his mind. It would be a betrayal of Reza's trust, and telling Nash would serve no purpose. "I'll go to work on Saturday."

"Where?"

"I'm supposed to lecture at the Shiraz University. But that's a few hundred miles away. I guess they'll fly me over to Shiraz in the morning."

"Don't bet on it."

"What do you mean?"

"I think they'll keep you close to Tehran."

"What about Shiraz?"

"Shiraz University was just a ploy to lure you back to Iran. Soon you'll discover their true intentions."

Silence.

"Colonel," Ross said, "I think Mossad operatives are following me."

"Doesn't surprise me. But don't mind them. I've been assured of your safety by their top dog. Relax."

"Oh, there's something else, Colonel. They've wired a million dollars into my account. I was promised one-tenth that amount."

"And?"

"Of course this can't be a mistake. They're obviously trying to frame or bribe me. But, since you seem to be the all knowing and the all wise, I don't want you or anyone else for that matter to get the wrong idea."

"I was wondering if you were going to tell me about the money."

Damn! Ross thought. *He already knew.* "Well of course I would, Colonel."

"Don't worry about it. It's part of their game. You'll find out what they have up their sleeves soon enough."

"All right, then. I'll call you when I have something to report, Colonel."

"Be careful."

⌇

THE MOIS AGENTS, EMAD AND JAFFAR, HAD CHECKED BACK INTO A motel in their favorite San Francisco neighborhood, the Fisherman's

Wharf. This was a different but equally inconspicuous place. It was Saturday night, and they were content spending it watching HBO while eating a bucket of KFC—extra crispy.

A few minutes before midnight, Jaffar poked Emad, who was dozing off, and said, "It's time to go." Instantly, Emad jumped to his feet, slipped into his loafers, and quietly followed Jaffar out of the room.

Fishermen's Wharf on San Francisco's north waterfront was one of the world's most popular attractions, yet the majority of San Franciscans loved to hate it. They complained of the tacky shops, the "novelty" museums, which were no longer novel, and busloads of tourists blocking the traffic. The locals preferred to avoid the Wharf all together. The busy waterfront, however, was an ideal place for shadowy people to hide and vanish into the crowds.

Walking shoulder to shoulder, Jaffar and Emad meandered through the thinning midnight crowd. It was windy, moonless, and cold. With hands in their pockets and cigarettes hanging from their lips, they blended in well; no one seemed to notice them. After a few minute's walk, they arrived where the famed sea lions congregate on the side of Pier 39. The animals outnumbered the people at that late hour.

Jaffar spotted the silhouette of a man wearing a windbreaker and donning a French beret. He was sitting on a bench toward the end of the pier. With his back to Jaffar and Emad, he was gazing into the darkness of the bay. As they approached the man, Jaffar pointed to a spot and told Emad, *"Inja kesheek vasta*—Stand watch here." Then he proceeded to the bench alone.

The end of the pier was dimly lit and completely deserted. Jaffar sat on the bench—an arm's length away from the man—lit up another cigarette, and whispered, *"Shomaie Mostafa*—Is that you, Mustafa?"

"Yes, Jaffar."

"We're all set in Eureka."

"Good."

"Did you bring what I asked for?"

Mustafa, the senior MOIS operative for the western seaboard of the United States, slowly slid an envelope over the bench toward Jaffar. "It's a white Avalon—its location and keys are in the envelope. You'll find eight grand in the glove compartment. That should last you a month or two."

Jaffar picked up the envelope and slid the car keys to their present vehicle—the Ford Taurus—toward Mustafa. Frequent car exchange was another MOIS tactic to maintain stealth for its agents. Placing the envelope in his coat pocket, Jaffar said, "The Taurus is parked in front of the motel."

"I'll have it picked up."

"Any word on our mission."

"Nothing yet."

"Who's the patient?"

"I don't know."

"How much longer do we have to wait?"

"I don't know."

"This is nerve-wracking, man. What the hell *do* you know?"

"Not much more than you, Jaffar."

Long pause.

"I've been here far too long," Jaffar said. "I'm tired, Mustafa. I'd like to go home and visit my family. My children are beginning to forget their father."

"How old are your children?"

"I have two daughters, sixteen and eighteen. It's a terrible age to be away from your father."

"I know, Jaffar. It's been two years for you. That's way too long to be away. But you know how it is. With all the added security after 9-11, it's hard to get our people in and out of America. Maybe after this assignment they'll send you home for a long stay."

"Yeah…If I'm still alive."

18

A MINUTE OR TWO BEFORE 8:00 AM ON SATURDAY, ROSS, SPORTING a khaki suit over a blue shirt with the top two buttons undone, entered the empty elevator on the penthouse floor. He pressed LOBBY. The elevator stopped after two floors and for an instant, he was annoyed. But that didn't last. To his delight, Leila Conner, the stunning CNN superstar, stepped in and flashed a warm smile.

"Did you forget about me?" she said.

"Who could possibly forget about you, Leila?" Ross said playfully.

"Apparently you." She laughed. "I thought we were going to hook up for lunch."

"I've been out for the past two days, and I'm sorry. How's it going for you, anyway?"

"I'm doing great. So far, I've interviewed two officials from the Atomic Energy Organization of Iran." Leila stepped closer and squeezed Ross' arm. "And thanks to you, I can speak their language."

Up close, the sweet scent of her floral perfume gave Ross the butterflies again. Conservatively dressed in a black pinstripe pantsuit, and with subtle makeup, she looked like the glamorous star that she was. Keeping his attraction for her in check, he gently patted her hand. "Glad I could be helpful."

The reflective steel doors slid open to the lobby. Always a gentleman, Ross gestured, "After you." Watching her as she walked away, he said, "Good luck."

Leila glanced back. "I'll be waiting for that lunch, Ross. I've got a bunch of new questions to ask you." She waved goodbye, then turned and strolled away in graceful strides toward the portico, where her crew had congregated.

Paradoxically, Ross was at once a straight-laced family man and one given to flirting. He was star struck by Leila and flattered by her obvious attention. Besides, he had never romanced an Iranian woman, and the curiosity was unbearable. He closed his eyes and took a deep breath before stepping out of the elevator.

Ross' official host, Kazem, was sitting on one of the couches in the lobby. When he spotted Ross, he came over and greeted him with fervor. "Have you had breakfast, my friend?"

Ross said, "Yes, room service," and proceeded toward the revolving door with Kazem on his heels. Once outside, Ross spotted Reza leaning against the passenger side of the official, brightly polished and thoroughly bugged ministry car. As soon as Reza noticed Ross, he opened the back door. Kazem went around the vehicle and let himself in.

When Reza drove the Mercedes out of the driveway, Ross asked Kazem nonchalantly, "Where are we headed?"

"Karaj."

"I thought I was supposed to report to Shiraz University today or tomorrow."

"There is a slight change of plans. Nothing major of course."

Ross listened closely as Kazem continued. "First you will spend a few days with the physics faculty and graduate students at the Nuclear Research Center in Karaj. Then, God willing, we will go to Shiraz."

Ross clenched his teeth and stared at Kazem, thinking, *This is exactly what Colonel Nash predicted last night. What does this mean? Why have they changed my itinerary? How should I react? I have no reason to object too strongly. But if I don't say anything, Kazem might think he can lead me by the nose.*

With a fake-sounding laugh, Kazem said, "We could not deprive our promising students and research staff at the NRC from your presence. Could we?"

Hushed tension filled the air as Ross turned and looked out the window.

The Nuclear Research Center, NRC, located in the outskirts of Karaj—twenty-five miles northwest of Tehran—was one of the largest research centers of the Atomic Energy Organization of Iran. Ross knew a good deal about the facility. Two years earlier, after reviewing TOP SECRET satellite images of the complex, he had recommended that the NSA ask the CIA to take a closer look at two new buildings in the compound, the construction of which had begun in 2000 under strict security. Now, a likely MOIS operative was personally accompanying Ross to the facility, where he was about to see the suspicious buildings firsthand and meet the scientists who toiled there. The irony was hard to ignore.

As Reza turned the Mercedes onto the Karaj highway heading west, Kazem asked, "Do you remember Karaj from the old days?"

Now a bit calmer, Ross said, "Yes. My father used to have a pomegranate orchard near the city. My brother and I spent quite a few summers there. What I remember of Karaj is a large village."

"That large village today has over a million inhabitants with high-rises, universities, and hospitals."

"That's hard to imagine." Ross turned back to see if they were being followed. Sure enough, he spotted the bikers riding the red BMW on their tail. He would give anything to find out what these guys were up to. Were they friend or foe? Were they the Mossad's triggermen or bodyguards? There were no answers. All he could do was wait.

Saturday is the first day of the week in Muslim countries, and the bustle of the morning traffic made the normally short trip to Karaj last over an hour. When the Mercedes pulled up to the front gate of the NRC, Ross noticed the heavy security around the facility. An outer ring of chain-link fence, topped with razor wires, prevented easy access to the fortress-like wall that surrounded the complex. This concrete barrier, some twenty yards inside the fence, seemed to be at least fifteen feet high, with guard towers at each corner.

When their car stopped at the first gate, a Kalashnikov-wielding guard, clad in a khaki uniform, peered inside with a stern expression. After examining an official piece of paper that Reza handed him, he waved them through. The guards at the second gate were equally gruff but more thorough. One of them collected Reza and Kazem's identification cards, along with Ross' passport, and went into a small guardhouse. The other asked to look inside the trunk and peeked underneath the vehicle with a mirrored contraption. In no time, the first man emerged from the guardhouse, handed three thick visitor badges to Reza, and said, *"In kard ha ra bayad hameeshe bepoosheed*—You must wear these badges at all times." Then he leaned down to address Kazem and Ross in the backseat. "These cards measure the level of radiation you might receive in case of a mishap." He stepped away from the vehicle. "You may proceed."

The NRC compound was a campus overcrowded with many buildings but devoid of any architectural theme. The multi-story brick structures were functional and well built. Yet the jumble of styles was proof positive that aesthetics was never considered in their scattered design. Strangely, there were neither trees nor shrubberies anywhere.

Ross had previously seen two-dimensional satellite images of the facility. But now, he was thrilled to view the compound in person. The physicist-turned-spy thought how Colonel Nash would kill to be in his shoes at that moment.

Reza dropped Ross and Kazem in front of a white four-story building and proceeded to the parking lot.

When they entered the building, a distinguished looking man cordially greeted them in the reception area. He had come down from his fourth floor office to receive them in person—a gracious sign of respect in Iran. Silver hair neatly surrounding a balding spot pegged his age at near fifty. Wearing an olive-colored silk suit befitting a tycoon, the tall, fit, and refined man was well-groomed and portrayed confidence.

With genuine delight, he said in fluent English, "Welcome, Dr. Shaheen." His smile revealed an upper gold tooth. While shaking Ross' hand, he repeated, "Welcome!"

"Thank you, Amir." Ross eked out a smile. "It's good to see you."

Nervously twirling a long string of prayer beads through his fingers, Amir said, "You remember me?"

"How could I forget?"

Kazem was taken aback. He said, "You two know each other?"

Amir said, "Oh yes, we go way back."

"Mr. Meshkin and I went to the same high school during our senior year," Ross explained. "We graduated the same year and went to America at about the same time. He went to Boston and I to Berkeley."

"What a small world!" Kazem said, as they walked toward the elevator. When Amir and Ross entered, Kazem prevented the door from closing and said, "Gentlemen, I have other business to attend to. I shall return in the afternoon around four to take Dr. Shaheen back to his hotel." Then he let the door close.

Amir Meshkin, one of the four deputy directors of the Atomic Energy Organization of Iran (AEOI), was an unwavering Islamist. By 1979, after six years at M.I.T., he had received both undergraduate and graduate degrees in nuclear engineering. Despite the wishes of his parents, he didn't pursue his studies any further, leaving the most prestigious engineering school in the world to join the Confederation of Iranian Students—a front organization for the anti-Shah forces throughout the world.

In those years, Ross had encountered Amir at various conferences and symposiums but had kept his distance because of Amir's virulent politics. Amir was vehemently against the crown and thought anyone other than the Shah would be better for Iran, a view that Ross didn't share. Not that there was any love lost between Ross and the repressive Shah. But he simply wanted to weigh the merits of any alternative regime before endorsing it.

Shortly after the Islamic Revolution of 1979, which deposed the Shah, Amir returned to Iran ready to serve the new regime and its theocratic masters. The potent mix of Islamism and ambition, combined with intelligence and nuclear expertise, made Amir's star a rising one. But he didn't go very far until he proved his mettle by getting his hands dirty and performing some odious deeds. During the purges of the early eighties, Amir was reduced to a brute enforcer, even serving a stint at the infamous Evin prison—the regime's slaughterhouse—doing the unthinkable.

Soon after the war with Iraq ended in 1988, Amir was named one of the deputy directors of the AEOI. He had a secret mandate: to make Iran's dream of becoming a nuclear power a reality. His dogged zeal and fierce nationalism propelled him like a guided missile toward achieving that goal. After twenty years of struggle and expenditure of countless billions, Amir was so close to achieving his mission that he could almost taste it.

But there was a missing piece.

Looking out of the expansive window of his office, Amir, standing next to Ross, pointed to the various buildings in the sprawling NRC compound and explained their functions.

"We've had several under construction lately. That one is almost ready. It will house a calutron—electromagnetic isotope separation system—we purchased from China." He glanced at Ross, gauging his reaction. "And that building houses our beam applications cyclotron."

"Where did you get the cyclotron?"

"Belgium."

Ross knew that these devices were innocent enough and used in routine research and development. He decided to push the envelope and test Amir's limits.

"Those two buildings in the far left." Ross pointed to the distant corner. "The ones with no windows…What are they for?"

"Those are redundant facilities for uranium enrichment," Amir said bluntly. "We figure if the Americans or the Israelis someday bomb Natanz, we will need another plant for uranium enrichment to fuel our reactor in Bushehr."

Ross was shocked. He wondered why Amir was so forthcoming. The information was probably highly confidential and likely TOP SECRET. Why would he risk his neck by revealing it? Thinking Colonel Nash would love to hear this gem, Ross muttered, "That's interesting."

Amir stopped twirling the prayer beads and turned to Ross. "In what way do you find this interesting, Dr. Shaheen?"

"Placing an enrichment plant in the middle of a population center… that's unheard of." Ross paused for effect. "And it demonstrates the extent of Iran's paranoia. As long as your nuclear program is peaceful, which has always been the official claim, no one will care. However, the moment it turns into a weapons program, you have every reason to worry."

"Worry?" Amir said. "Why?"

"Because in that case, someone will eventually take out all these facilities. Primary or redundant, it doesn't matter. And it won't be the United States."

"Israel?"

"That's logical," Ross said. "They've done it before."

"Yes. We all remember Iraq's reactor at Osiraq."

"And they've said as much."

"But America's actions in Iraq have stirred a raging suspicion around here," Amir said. "The U.S. has sinister designs on Iran—I am sure of it."

"I think you've walked in the shadows for so long, Amir, that you see secret plots everywhere. America has no more sinister designs on Iran than Russia does. Where does this nonsense come from?"

"I guess you see no harm in anything America does, Dr. Shaheen."

"And you see nothing but, my friend."

Fearing their dialogue was slipping into the hostile territory, they both became quiet and looked out the window. Amir took off his wire-rim spectacles and slowly began to clean them with a handkerchief. Silently gazing out, Ross was jolted by the loud ring of the phone. Amir sprinted to his desk, picked up the receiver, and proceeded to speak in Farsi with his back turned to Ross. Ever so coolly, Ross reached into his pocket and produced one of the ingenious CIA-issued band-aids. He carefully peeled it and swiftly turned around with his hands behind his back. His eyes were locked onto Amir like a hawk's on a squirrel, monitoring every move. Amir twirled the prayer beads in one hand while holding the phone in the other. Ross was petrified. Silently, he taped the band-aid underneath the edge of the windowsill, moved toward Amir, and slumped into a large chair.

He breathed a sigh of relief.

Ross was satisfied with himself, having successfully planted his first listening device. Soon, Amir finished his conversation and turned to face Ross. "Where were we?"

Ross shrugged. "What's on the agenda?"

"Round table Q&A with a group of graduate students and researchers."

"All day long?"

"All day long."

What is he really after? Ross thought. *Maybe the bug will answer the question. In the meantime, all I can do is play along.* "When do we start?"

"Right about now." Amir looked at his watch. "Let's go."

Ross rose to follow Amir out of his office. With his hand on the doorknob, Amir stopped and faced Ross. "By the way, did you receive your money?"

"Yes. But there seems to be a mistake—"

"There's no mistake, Ross." Amir opened the door. "We appreciate you being here."

Ross was stunned. He was now certain the money was a bribe, but for what?

It was approaching 10:00 AM when Ross, together with Amir, entered a spacious, high-tech conference room down the hall from Amir's office. Inside, tables and chairs were arranged in a horseshoe in the center of the room facing two enormous marker boards on the wall. The head table supported a half lectern. There were about a dozen so-called "students" and "faculty" in business-casual scattered around the room. Two were women with black scarves tightly covering their hair but not their faces.

As soon as Amir and Ross entered, the group promptly took their seats. There was a name card—bilingual in Farsi and English—in front of each participant.

Amir Meshkin stood at the lectern and introduced Dr. Ross Shaheen as one of the most preeminent physicists in the world and the undisputed best scientist Iran had ever produced. Ross was not used to this kind of hyperbole, but he knew the Iranian way and took the flattery in stride. Following the warm welcome, he proceeded to the podium and opened with a round of personal introductions. As they spoke about their education and background, Ross observed that these people were too old to be students and too young to be professors. Oddly enough, there was a Russian in the audience—introduced as a "researcher." He seemed to be in his sixties. Ross was convinced that the whole bunch were engineers working directly or indirectly for the AEOI. *Be careful what you say to this bunch,* he thought.

The scientific discussion that followed was stimulating. Comfortable in his professorial element, Ross was impressed with the level of physics being discussed. For the first hour or two, the questions were mostly theoretical and somewhat benign. After lunch, served buffet-style to the entire group, the questioning veered more and more toward the applied side of physics. On several occasions, the inquiries were about classified material. Ross had to either sidestep the question or plead ignorance, which made him feel uncomfortable. Throughout the day, Ross called on the participants by their full names in a subtle attempt at memorizing them. During the session, Amir Meshkin sat quietly in the back of the room.

The only other person who remained silent was the Russian—Sergey Saidayev. His first name was Russian enough, but Ross thought the last name, with obvious Islamic roots, was either Chechen or Azerbaijani. It stood to reason that he was a Muslim. But what was he doing here?

19

Peopled out and in need of some downtime, Ross decided to stay in for the evening. Earlier, he had called Oksana but had been unable to reach her. After leaving a message, he ordered room service and watched the Iranian evening news while enjoying his dinner of chelo-kebab—broiled filet of beef served with saffron rice. He was amused with the Iranian spin on their coverage of American affairs. *No wonder people hate us all over the Middle East*, he thought. *Listening to such a steady diet of broadcast venom, day in and day out, would even turn Oliver North against America, let alone the Iranian youth.* His train of thought was unexpectedly broken by a soft knock on the door.

Looking through the peephole, he was surprised to see Leila Conner standing in the hallway, holding something in her hand. As he fumbled with the chain lock, he couldn't help noticing that his heart had begun to race. He paused, closed his eyes, and took a few deep breaths before opening the door.

"It cost me twenty bucks to get your room number," Leila said, as she walked past him. The object in her hand was a tall glass of red wine.

"If you'd have called, I would've given you the number for free."

"I tried. They wouldn't connect my call." She inquisitively looked around the plush suite, then stepped out to the balcony, sank into a lounge chair, and continued. "My name wasn't on the list of 'authorized callers!' I wonder about you sometimes." She looked at Ross with a mischievous grin. "Who has an 'authorized callers' list? Who are you, really?"

Ross was tempted to say, *Bond, James Bond*, but he held his tongue, thinking that the moment of levity would not be worth increasing her suspicion.

He turned off the TV, walked to his laptop, and started *Les pecheurs de perles* of the many operas that were stored within. Then he joined Leila on the balcony and said, "That's strange. I didn't know anything about a callers list." He sat in the chair next to her. "And I'm exactly who I told you I was."

Though it was late, Leila looked as done up as she had in the morning when Ross encountered her in the elevator. But her outfit was more casual—an unbuttoned yellow shirt over a white t-shirt, one size too small, and matching white jeans. Leila got comfortable by taking off her shoes, revealing her perfect pedicure and deep red nail polish, and resting her feet on the chair. Ross noticed a small sore on the back of her right ankle, the kind women often get by walking in heels all day.

She took a sip of her merlot. "No matter how many times I come to Iran, they never cease to surprise me."

"How's that?"

"Oh, it's always something new: a fresh security measure, a different procedure, a new policy—now, an 'authorized callers list.' Whatever."

Ross stretched out as well in his own chair. "I suppose they want to control all access to me."

"But why?"

"Paranoia."

"That seems to be a national obsession," Leila quipped.

"No. It's a cultural norm. I bet the word xenophobia was invented for us Iranians."

Leila laughed. "That's funny. But I think it was first used for the Chinese."

"I guess they won the gold medal for xenophobia and we, the silver." After a moment's pause, Ross changed the subject. "By the way, how's your documentary...what's it called...*Mushroom in the Sand?* How is that coming along?"

"I can't complain, but it could be better. They're going out of their way to be forthcoming. To a point."

"Please elaborate."

"They answer lots of questions and then all of a sudden clam up. Then they lie. For example, I asked some deputy minister why Iran, with its vast oil and gas reserves, is spending billions of dollars on a nuclear reactor when it has enough energy supplies for the next two centuries."

"Great question!" Ross said. "How did he answer?"

"He gave me some cockamamie response like 'these estimates are unrealistic and the growing population and the expanding economy will require a lot of energy,' blah blah blah. Total bullshit."

"They think if they repeat a lie enough times, it somehow becomes truth."

She took a sip of merlot. "They've got their heads stuck in the sand and think the world cannot see their asses."

"That's a good one."

"I've asked to tour and film the nuclear facilities in Natanz."

"And?"

"They've agreed," she said nonchalantly.

"That's a coup!" Ross said. He sat straight up, staring at her. "Everyone in the nuclear field, all over the world, will watch your documentary. Lots of people have tried to peek inside Natanz. But few have succeeded, and none were allowed a camera crew."

"We'll see if they come through."

"When are you supposed to go there?"

"In a few days…I'm on standby."

"I hope they won't break their promise."

There was a comfortable pause in the conversation as the two Iranian-Americans, lounging barefoot on adjacent chairs, took in the nighttime view of Tehran. It was their common birthplace. Destiny had taken them away decades ago, and fate had placed them at an unlikely crossroad that evening.

Leila broke the silence. "You have one hell of a view, Ross. I should remember this suite when I negotiate my next contract with CNN."

"You should."

For a short while, they were lost in the beauty of the endless waves of shimmering lights. The cool, gentle breeze of the night was a welcome change from the searing heat of the day. Occasionally, Leila took a tiny sip of wine without turning her gaze from the panorama.

As the opera played on, Ross sensed that the comfortable pause in the conversation was slowly turning into an awkward silence. Alone in a far off land, he felt a palpable attraction for Leila, which somehow he knew to be mutual. Yet, he suspected that their feelings stemmed from different motives.

Leila was single, lonely, and looking for companionship away from the paparazzi. Any acceptable man would do. But in Tehran, safety was a paramount consideration. And not only did Ross appear safe but also his cerebral persona and natural charm made him irresistible.

Ross, on the other hand, was simply curious about this rare specimen of Persian beauty. He was feeling the butterflies again, which signaled that he was in danger of losing the inner battle of resisting the temptation. Besides, he couldn't easily extricate himself from the situation on the balcony—and wasn't sure if he wanted to.

At last, Leila turned to Ross with silent anticipation. Her gaze screamed, *It's now or never.* With pained hesitation, Ross slowly inched his head toward her as she closed her eyes. He gently placed his right hand on her left shoulder. Intoxicated by her perfume, he could sense his heart beating the adrenaline drum. Leila started to breathe a little faster. Just before his lips touched hers, the phone rang, jolting him as if someone had hit him with a baseball bat.

"I'm sorry." He jumped up. "I have to take this call." Noticing the hurt expression on Leila's face, he flashed an awkward smile, shrugged, and stepped inside the room.

It was Oksana.

"Hi, sweetie," he said, in a hurried voice. "How are you?"

Ross felt uncomfortable speaking to his wife within Leila's earshot. Therefore, he spoke softly so she couldn't hear him, which made Oksana sense there was something wrong. He assured her otherwise and proceeded to recount his day at the NRC in Karaj. As the conversation continued, Leila entered the room and mimed a request to use the bathroom. Ross nodded.

With Leila out of the way, Ross felt more at ease. He asked to speak with the children.

"They're not home."

"Where are they?"

"Victor is at a birthday party, and Marina has gone to the beach."

Ross suddenly felt terrified. He maintained careful control of his voice, though, to avoid scaring Oksana. "What beach?"

"She's gone to Pebble Beach with Valerie, Sandy, and some other girls."

Trying to sound casual, Ross said, "When did she go?"

"Earlier today."

"Where are they staying?"

"At Valerie's uncle's condo." Oksana paused. "Quit worrying yourself, darling. She'll be fine. There are six of them, and Valerie's older brother will also be there. So, relax."

"When is she coming back?"

"Wednesday…Or, maybe Thursday."

Pause.

"Are you all right, honey?"

"Yes." He continued quietly, "Just thinking."

"Something bothering you?"

"Have you told Roy?"

"Told Roy what?"

"About Marina's trip to the beach."

"No. Why would I tell Roy about Marina's plans?"

Now unable to hide his fear, he said, "Because I'm seven thousand miles away, and I don't like the kids being out of your sight! That's why." Ross paused a bit, getting control over his emotions. "And keeping Roy in the loop can't hurt; in fact, it will help."

"You've been out of town before—countless times. You've never acted this way…what's wrong? Are you keeping something from me?"

Remembering the hidden microphones, Ross changed his tone. "No, sweetie. I'm not hiding anything from you. I just want you to be careful. This is a long trip, and I don't want any accidents happening to you or the kids when I can't immediately rush home. That's all."

Oksana hesitated and then, after a brief pause, acquiesced. "Okay, honey. I'll tell Roy if it makes you feel better."

Thankful that she was not pressing the point any further, Ross said, "It will."

"All right."

For the next few minutes, Ross and Oksana chatted about the mundane minutia of their days. However, Oksana was as willing to talk as Ross was unwilling to listen. It wasn't that he didn't care to listen; he just wanted to be off the phone when Leila came out of the bathroom.

He didn't know what to expect. What if she came out naked? What would he do?

He felt embarrassed, having these thoughts while speaking to his unsuspecting wife, half a world away.

Finally, Oksana said, "Good night, my love."

Ross said with relief, "Good night, sweetie," and hung up.

Sitting on the edge of the bed, he ran his fingers through his hair, thinking, *What are you doing, Ross? Have you lost your mind? You've never cheated before...why start now?"*

At that moment, the bathroom door opened slowly. His heart in his throat, he turned to look. To his relief, and with a twinge of disappointment, Leila was fully dressed. Noticeably uncomfortable and seeming a bit embarrassed, she said, "It's getting late. I'd better get going."

"Yeah...sure," Ross said, as he rose to open the door. Facing her, while holding the doorknob, he said, "Listen...maybe it would be best if we did lunch next time."

Leila broke the tension with laughter. "I've heard that before." She walked out. Just before he closed the door, Leila pointed to her right ankle. "I borrowed one of your Band-Aids. I hope you don't mind."

She had covered the sore with one of the CIA-issued microphones.

Ross swallowed hard and said, "Sure, no problem."

20

IN THE COCOON OF HIS ORNATE OFFICE, GENERAL VIKTOR PUGACHOV slowly stirred sugar in a large glass of brewed Russian tea. At the usual time, 8:15 AM, the white phone on top of the enormous credenza rang with a muffled tone. His stern face was instantly transformed by a warm smile.

"Hello, Papa."

"How are you, little daughter?"

"I need a favor, Papa."

"Anything for you, my dear."

"Remember last time we spoke, you suggested to send someone to stay with me?"

"Yes, of course."

"Do so."

"Do you have any problems?"

"Not really, Papa. I spoke with Ross this morning, and he was so worried because of us. I don't know why it is, Papa, but I have a bad feeling."

"I understand," Pugachov said. "Somebody will arrive soon."

"Any news from Tehran?"

"This is not telephone talk. But all is well so far, and he seems to be all right."

"That's good, Papa. So, will you let me know when your person will arrive?"

"In the next twenty-four hours."

"I love you, Papa."

General Pugachov hung up the white phone and lifted the red. Without any pleasantries, he growled, "Get me Vasily Surikov." While waiting, he took a sip of the strong and sweet tea.

Vasily Surikov, the man in charge of all GRU—Military Intelligence Agency—operations in North America, promptly interrupted his conversation with his chief of staff. Hurriedly swiveling in his chair, he picked up the secure red phone on his end. "Good morning, Comrade General."

"Vasily, I need one of your female agents in America for some weeks."

"Yes, Comrade General," Vasily said dutifully. "What is the mission?"

"To stay with my daughter in San Francisco for extra protection."

"Does she have any problems?"

"It doesn't touch you, Surikov."

"Yes, Comrade General, forgive me." He paused, searching his mind. "I have the person you need. Natasha Galinova—the niece of Admiral Galinova. She is a good agent and is presently stationed in Las Vegas. When will you need her?"

"In the next twenty-four hours."

"Yes, Comrade General. I will send instructions immediately."

"Is she capable?"

"Yes, Comrade General. She has received advanced training in the GRU's Military-Diplomatic Academy."

Pugachov winced at this. He wasn't completely comfortable with some of the GRU training programs, and particularly with having one of its infamous "graduates" around his grandchildren. But he supposed the girl might be all right as long as she was limited to the capacity of a shrewd security guard for the family.

"How old is she?"

"Late twenties, or maybe thirty, Comrade General."

Pugachov sighed to himself. He could readily imagine what this girl looked like. He was damn glad Ross was away—any man, no matter how loyal or iron-willed, would be vulnerable to one of these GRU-trained…well, he should not think of them that way. It wasn't patriotic.

"How long has she been in America?"

"She was assigned to the U.N., as an intelligence officer, five or six years ago. We recently transferred her to Las Vegas to recruit military assets, especially from the Middle East."

"All right. You already have my daughter's information on file," Pugachov said. "Send the necessary instructions to Washington. I expect her to meet my Oksana for lunch tomorrow."

"Consider it done, Comrade General."

"Good day."

Taking another sip of tea, General Pugachov returned to the TOP SECRET material before him.

⌒∕∕⌒

IN A SPECTACULAR SETTING AT THE FOOT OF MT. TAMALPAIS, MILL Valley was known throughout the Bay Area for its natural beauty and cultural events. The charming village was situated north of San Francisco. Its residents loved the place because it uniquely combined privacy with tranquility and urban living.

It was a sunny Monday in June in that charming village. Wearing comfortable gardening clothes, complete with straw hat and sunglasses, Oksana Shaheen was in the backyard of her quaint house tending her rose bushes. Propped on top of a wooden lounge chair, a bright yellow boom box emanated soft classical music. A tall glass of fresh lemonade on ice, a few sips short of full, was on the ground beneath the chair.

"Hello," a voice called in Russian. "Anyone home?"

Oksana pressed PAUSE on the boom box and called out. "I'm back here. Use the sidewalk."

Before long, an eye-catching young woman dressed in a smart navy-blue pantsuit and crème satin shirt, emerged.

"My name is Natasha Galinova," she said, stretching out her hand. "I was sent here to stay with you for a few weeks."

Unable to mask her surprise, Oksana said, "You?" as they shook hands. "You work for the security services?"

"We don't all look rough." Natasha smiled knowingly. "Besides, beware of the fury of a woman." She gave a playful laugh.

"Welcome. I've been expecting you."

"Thank you. I'm glad to be of service."

"Let me show you to the guestroom." Oksana gestured toward the rear entrance of the house. "Are you hungry?"

"Yes. I left in a hurry. I was told to meet you for lunch today, and here I am." Looking at her watch, she added, "Only thirty minutes late."

Natasha Galinova, the youngest niece of Admiral Joseph Galinov, was an aspiring ballerina from the time she entered kindergarten. At age fifteen, she auditioned for the world famous Kirov Ballet Company in St. Petersburg, and was accepted. Three years later, an ankle injury interrupted her promising stage career. Depressed, rudderless, and untrusting of her alcoholic father, she asked her uncle, Admiral Galinov, for direction. The commander of the Russian Black Sea Fleet, the Admiral suggested a career in the GRU—Military Intelligence Agency—to his strikingly beautiful and ambitious niece.

The moment she nodded, she was in.

The former USSR pioneered one of the most sophisticated special services in the world, which trained female spies to seduce men. It was known as sex spying. FSB—formerly, KGB—as well as the GRU, recruited attractive girls and promised them countless privileges if they agreed to fulfill their civil duty by becoming sex agents. Their training progressed from basic to advanced spy craft, including martial arts, explosives, and weapons; even assassinations were taught. Afterwards, they were delivered from any shyness or shame by learning advanced sex techniques. These skills were honed by viewing pornographic videos, and then perfected through role-play exercises. Sex agents were supposed to be able to execute any sexual task. An orgy was one of the practical classes; teachers, both male and female, joined in. The whole event was filmed and then discussed in detail. Sex agents were told that they were soldiers in defense of the motherland, and that their most potent weapon was their body.

The objects of sexual attack were examined thoroughly beforehand, and their sexual preferences methodically researched. Once an incriminating video was produced, the blackmail began. The subjects had no other way out but to cooperate with the Russian intelligence.

Amusingly, the Mossad, as well as the British MI6, had followed suit, creating similar sex units, but the CIA had never been able to assemble one. The schizophrenic American value system, perfectly at ease with being the porn capital of the world and exploiting women for money, found such activity unbecoming in the genteel intelligence community.

Natasha took to the training like a duck to water. She was disgusted with her father, who had abused her mother, and didn't want any part of a "relationship" with his only daughter. She had a healthy hatred for men, which made her relish her work. After a three-year tour in London, she was assigned to Russia's United Nations Mission in New York, where she successfully recruited more than a dozen ambassadors or other high-ranking diplomats from target countries. After a few years, she received orders to move to Las Vegas, work as a high-priced escort, and pay special attention to Middle Eastern VIPs.

Out of professional courtesy, and possibly fear of reprisals, Natasha decided not to mention her chance encounter with Ross when she was working to recruit Kazem.

Taking Natasha's hand, Oksana walked her toward the house. Before entering the side door into the garage, she stopped and asked, "Is Natasha your real name or your cover?"

"It's my real name. I quit using an alias several years ago."

"Good to know. I wouldn't want to break your cover if I introduced you to someone."

"I'm glad you brought this up, Oksana. Even though Natasha is my real name, my mission here must remain a secret. You can't tell anyone, including the children."

"I understand. I'm sure you know who my father is," Oksana said matter-of-factly. "I grew up in the middle of the intelligence community and know the rules. I'll announce you as one of my cousins visiting from Tver."

"Perfect."

Oksana led Natasha up the flight of stairs and into the den. Inside, Natasha asked, "Are the children home?"

"Victor is riding his bicycle. He should be home any minute. Marina is on a trip."

"Where?"

"She's at the beach with a few friends."

"When do you expect her back?"

"Wednesday, or maybe Thursday. Why?"

Natasha approached Oksana, whispering in her ear, "I don't mean to be overbearing, but if I'm here for your protection, I'd like all of you close enough to keep an eye on you."

Oksana whispered back, "Why are you whispering?"

"Basic training," Natasha said. "Indoors, always assume someone's listening."

Now concerned, Oksana lowered her voice to match Natasha's. "Should I call her and tell her to return early?"

"No. It's only a few days. But please don't let her go on another trip until your husband returns."

Oksana, no longer whispering, said, "I'll get lunch started."

"I'll get my luggage."

21

An hour after Leila Conner left his suite, Ross walked onto the balcony to check in with Colonel Nash before calling it a night. It was a brief conversation. He told Nash about the trip to the NRC in Karaj and what he had discovered about the mysterious buildings. His encounter with Amir Meshkin, and the bug he had planted in his office, peaked Colonel Nash's interest. Ross concluded his summary by listing the names of all the so-called students and researchers he had met.

"Well done, Ross," Colonel Nash said. "You've taken to the spy craft rather quickly."

"As if I have much of a choice."

"I'll have these names cross-referenced and let you know if they're real or aliases and if we have anything on them."

"What about the Russian, Sergey Saidayev? He seemed out of place. What do you think his angle is?"

"I'll let you know tomorrow."

"Hang on, Colonel. The man didn't say a word all day, and I'd like to know something about him before facing him again. Why don't you look him up on INTELINK while I wait?"

"All right. Let's see if we have anything on this Sergey character."

Colonel Nash clicked on an icon and a Google-like page popped up on his monitor. The super-secret search engine had been created for the exclusive use of the entire intelligence community—all ninety agencies—for sharing information. Colonel Nash was authorized to access it with the highest level of security, known as INTELINK-P, a privilege reserved for the president, the vice president, and fewer than a dozen high-ranking officials.

He typed, "Sergey Saidayev" in the text box and clicked SEARCH. Instantly, dozens of hyperlinks, each prefixed with the acronym of the agency that was the intelligence source, appeared. Nash clicked on the first link, whose source was his own outfit: the CIA. The page opened, revealing Sergey's photograph and resume. Nash said, "Ugly-looking bastard," and started reading the highlights for Ross.

"Sergey Saidayev: Chechen, born in Grozny. Sixty-one years old, Muslim. Wife and son killed in a raid five years ago. Studied physics at Moscow State University—that's your Alma Mater, Ross—class of '67. Has had stints in several secret cities."

"Which ones?"

"Sarov, Snezhinsk, and, let me see…"

"I get the picture, Colonel. I know these cities. I've been to Sarov. It's not even on the frigging map. If he's had a tour in Sarov, he must be a nuclear weapons expert. I'm certain."

"No shit!" Nash said sarcastically.

Ross paused to gather his thoughts. "Colonel, I don't have a secure way of contacting Roy from here. Please call him and tell him to be extra vigilant with my family. Something's about to go down…I can sense it."

"They're safe, Ross. I've asked the FBI to cover them twenty-four, seven. Roy and his men are also on the lookout. He hasn't found any dirt on the goons across the street. But he's still monitoring them."

"Marina has gone to the beach, Colonel. I want a pair of agents to go and check out the place."

"I'll take care of it, Ross."

"I'll call you tomorrow, same time."

"Okay. Good night."

Ross stepped inside, collapsed into the bed, and began to stare at the ceiling. It had been another eventful day. He was exhausted. Before long, his thoughts drifted to Leila Conner. Wondering what she was up to, his imagination ran wild. Was she asleep? Was she alone? The idea occurred to him, but he decided that spying on her wouldn't be right.

He rose and entered the bathroom. As he brushed his teeth, he thought about Marina alone with a bunch of teenagers at the beach. He feared for her. She was in danger and didn't know it, while he was half a world away. But his mind, time and again, veered back to Leila Conner and the listening device on her ankle. And every time, he banished the notion.

Lights out.

He couldn't sleep. The curiosity was unbearable. He tossed and turned, suppressing the urge over and over again. Eventually, he gave into it. Reaching for the cell phone resting in its charger on the nightstand, he punched STAR-STAR-FOUR-ONE-ONE. With a tiny beep, the numbers one through six appeared in the display area. Numbers two and six were labeled ACTIVE and the rest were blank. Using the DOWN arrow, he highlighted number two, pressed SND, and listened.

Nothing.

That must have been the bug he'd planted in Amir Meshkin's office. His hands were now sweaty. Trembling, he highlighted number six, pressed SND, and listened.

Ross' whole body tensed when he heard the sounds. They were unmistakable. Leila Conner had found what she was looking for. Ross felt his face actually flush at the stark intimacy he was privy to, intimacy between two people who had no idea they were not completely alone. Ross listened to the erotic chorus for a few long seconds and then pressed OFF.

At first, it tortured him to know that she was with someone else. But, strangely, the sound of Leila's passion actually turned him off. Was it because she was with another man? No matter. His curiosity was satisfied, and he no longer felt the urge to eavesdrop. Turning over to sleep, he wondered what Roy's reaction would be to this story?

"He'll probably kick my ass," he muttered to himself.

ᴄᴍ

THE MORNING CAME SWIFTLY. IN SPITE OF THE ODDS TO THE CONTRARY, Ross hoped to run into Leila Conner in the elevator. In anticipation, he had splashed a generous handful of aftershave on his face. But it didn't happen. Instead, the burly Kazem, pacing in the lobby, greeted him with his usual fervor. It was just after 8:00 AM on Sunday. Ross wore the same khaki suit as the day before but with a black v-neck.

The trip to Karaj was uneventful. They traveled the distance in an hour and a half. To Ross, the traffic, the heat, and the bustle all felt routine. Even the mysterious duo tailing them on their red motorcycle seemed ordinary.

Inside the NRC compound, again Reza drove the Mercedes to the entrance of the white four-story building and let Ross out. However, this time, Kazem stayed in the car and waved him off.

Amir Meshkin, along with the supposed students and researchers, were already assembled in the fourth floor conference room when Ross entered. Everyone inside, including Amir Meshkin, followed Persian custom and rose to greet Ross with deference. That is, except for Sergey. He remained seated, nursing a cup of tea.

Having memorized everyone's name, Ross went around the room and greeted each of them in Farsi. "*Sobh beh kheyr*—Good morning." When he reached Sergey, to break the ice, he said in Russian, "*Dobroe utro*—Good morning." Sergey, the only person in the room wearing a necktie, greeted him politely in stiff Russian. Ross figured Sergey probably wasn't fluent in English or Farsi, which may have explained his silence the day before.

Without much delay, Ross continued from where he had left off, and the session started smoothly. Before long, one of the ladies asked him to talk about the origins of the "Shaheen Constant," and how it came about that it was named after him.

Having done so before on countless occasions across the world, Ross walked to one of the marker boards and started to fill it with diagrams and formulae. After the first board was out of space, he moved to the second and continued his explanation while writing an endless string of obscure equations. At the end, he underlined a number and said, "Therefore, this ratio remains constant at all temperatures…I'm flattered that it's been named after me."

"Bravo!" said Amir Meshkin. And the seemingly adoring audience surprised him with a standing ovation and enthusiastic applause. Ross felt pleased and sensed genuine warmth and appreciation. He thought, *These guys aren't so bad after all.* They were his countrymen and women, brilliant scientists who appeared to be truly proud of him. In spite of the odd alienation he had felt since his arrival in Iran, at that moment, he felt at home. The cultural divide, created after his thirty-five-year absence, was for the moment bridged by the wonder of science.

Ross flashed a smile and said, "Oh please! That's not necessary." He bowed, as a conductor would, to acknowledge and humor the cheering crowd. Curiously, as the commotion subsided, he noticed that Sergey was the only person in the room who was neither standing nor applauding. He sat statue-like, looking down—doodling in his notebook.

What's wrong with this guy? Ross wondered.

After quiet was restored, in broken and heavily accented English, Sergey said, "That is very impressive, Doktor Shaheen. But it is nothing new." Then he switched to Russian. "It has been published in textbooks for the past twenty years." Back to English, he said, "Tell us about more interesting things. Like the Scorpion...what do you call it? The Blind Scorpion?"

A moment of silence blanketed the room. With characteristic calm, Ross broke it. "What would you like to know about it?"

"Everything."

Even the existence of the Blind Scorpions was TOP SECRET until a few years ago when an anonymous leak, attributed to "a high-ranking official at the Berkeley Lab," made it a front-page story. Fortunately, the disclosure was somewhat benign and didn't reveal any technical details. It did, however, tell the world what its capabilities were—simulation of nuclear fission—as well as the name of its creator: Dr. Ross Shaheen.

A cold chill set in. So far, there had been no direct questions about fission, bomb making, or any other restricted subjects. Sergey's was the first, and he had made no attempt to be subtle. He wanted to know "everything" about one of the most forbidden of all American secrets. Aside from a select few researchers in the United States, only the British were allowed access to the Blind Scorpion—and even their privileges were limited and strictly supervised.

So, the Blind Scorpion is what they're after, Ross thought. *All the other stuff, the physics questions, the Shaheen Constant, and the rest were just window dressing. The bastards!*

He assumed, with a fairly high degree of certainty, that his host's knowledge of the Blind Scorpion was limited to the leaked material, which was scattered all over the Internet. Maybe they had some additional intelligence from other sources, but he couldn't be sure. Therefore, as long as he stayed within the scope of what was already in the public domain, he'd be safe.

Calmed by this logic, he began to speak. "The Blind Scorpion is a computerized model that simulates the three-dimensional dynamic progression of fission. That's basically all there is to it."

Amir said, "Is it true that the United States uses the Blind Scorpion to test its nuclear weapons? Sort of a virtual detonation?"

With a straight face, Ross said, "I really don't know. And if I did, I couldn't tell you." He sat down and continued in a matter-of-fact-way. "You see, everything about the Blind Scorpion is highly classified. And I really can't say much more about it. Sorry, ladies and gentlemen."

"Is it true that you wrote the first version?"

"I've played a minor role in its evolution. But even the scope of my involvement is privileged information."

Sergey said, "What kind of computer does it take to run it? Certainly you can tell us that much."

"A very fast one! Exactly how fast and what model is also classified."

One of the students said, "Does it use the finite element method for simulation?"

"I don't know."

Another asked, "Is it based on quantum physics or string theory?"

Now agitated, Ross said with a stern voice, "Guys! I told you, the subject is off the agenda. This item is *not* on the menu. Period. I can't talk about it. I'll wind up in prison if I do. Let the Blind Scorpion stay in his dark hole and let's move on to something else...please!"

Amir Meshkin ended the awkward silence that followed. "It's time for a fifteen-minute break." Looking at his watch, he added, "Make that twenty. We'll reassemble back at 11:00 AM."

One of the participants approached Ross to ask a question about the Shaheen Constant, while the rest bee-lined for the refreshment table. After the brief exchange, Ross noticed that Amir and Sergey had left the room. Nonchalantly, he asked someone, "Where's Mr. Saidayev?"

"In Mr. Meshkin's office."

Ross excused himself to use the restroom. Passing a man at a urinal to his left and another at the sink to his right, Ross entered the last stall and locked the door. He pulled his pants down to his ankles, sat on the toilet, and activated his cell phone. With trembling hands, he used the DOWN arrow and highlighted number two. For a second, he hesitated. What if he was caught? Surely he would meet the same fate as his slain brother. The last sight of the barren cemetery, which he had meticulously committed to memory, flashed before his eyes.

Undaunted, he pressed SND and listened.

Hearing Amir and Sergey sent a cold chill down his spine. The reception was perfect and the voice quality, crystal clear. For a fleeting second, he thought about the Band-Aid on Leila Conner's ankle. Then he tried to make sense of what he was hearing.

"...he would not fall for this...how you say? Charade," Sergey was saying. "He is too smart for it."

"I thought the indirect approach, the million dollars, and the classroom setting would be the best way to bring him out," Amir said. "I haven't given up yet. Maybe I'll try a private conversation with him."

"It is useless, I am telling you."

"Patience, my Chechen brother, patience. This was the first round. I have many hands I haven't played yet—winning hands."

"He is a tough nut," Sergey said. "He seems disciplined."

"Nah! He has lived in America too long. He's soft. His brother... now he was a tough nut. But, Ross? I'm not worried. He'll crack."

Ross felt as if a bucket of ice had been dumped on his head. Amir had mentioned his brother. But how did he know Sohrab? He must have. He referred to Sohrab as a "tough nut," which he certainly was. What was the connection between the two? He silenced his runaway brain and continued to listen. But suddenly the phone went dead.

He looked at the display with horror. It was ON, showing the numbers one through six with number two, labeled ACTIVE, highlighted. He hit the phone on his knee several times and then listened. Nothing. Now frantic, he powered the cell OFF and back ON again. Going through the startup procedure, he noticed he was breathing faster and his hands were moist with sweat. At last, he highlighted number two and pressed SND.

He listened.

"What next?" Sergey asked.

"We'll take him on a field trip after lunch."

Quiet.

It sounded like someone else had entered the room. "Yes, Mr. Meshkin?" It was a woman; she must have been his secretary.

"I'm taking Dr. Shaheen to the plant after lunch," Amir said.

"Yes, sir. I'll make the arrangements."

"It's time to go back," Amir said, a moment later.

"What is the use?" Sergey grumbled.

Wondering about the "field trip" that awaited him, Ross pressed OFF, flushed, and pulled up his pants.

22

EXOTIC, SOPHISTICATED, AND EXPENSIVE BEYOND THE REACH OF most people, laser eavesdropping systems were the exclusive province of intelligence agencies and the military. To listen in, an invisible high-energy beam was pointed at a window of the room where the target conversation was occurring. A specialized laser receiver then collected the reflection of the beam. Since the sound vibrates the surface of the window, it produces interference patterns in the reflected beam. The laser receiver converts these patterns to voltage fluctuations, which are reconstituted as high quality sound.

Behind the blinds of the second floor bedroom in the Miller's residence, six laser beams painted the windows of Ross' home. The sleek contraptions resting on steady tripods incorporated long and tapered laser guns and graphite-covered mini dish receivers. A jumble of black cables snaked from the high-tech gear across the floor to the walk-in closet. Copper wire mesh was tightly spun around the cables to provide the necessary electromagnetic shield against the indiscriminate TEMPEST.

Inside the closet, Farzad, a sharp-looking Iranian engineer, monitored an assortment of electronic gear. Multiple laptops connected to a bank of converters recorded the slightest sound inside Dr. Shaheen's residence. Once every three or four hours, Farzad would listen to the audio catch, discard the frivolity, save the relevant, and copy anything spoken in Russian on a disc for translation and analysis elsewhere. Sheets of fine copper wire mesh blanketed the small room—all four walls, floor, and ceiling were covered with it.

Farzad had joined MOIS shortly after 9-11, and the Iranian intelligence service found him especially useful because of his electronics expertise. His Canadian passport, which enabled him to enter America at will, enhanced the capabilities of MOIS' third tactical team. His cohorts, Mehdi and Bijan, both middle-aged veterans of the Iranian Special Forces, worked undercover as real estate investors. They were not as accomplished as Farzad and portrayed the worst Middle Eastern stereotypes. But they were proficient triggermen.

While Mehdi and Bijan practiced their samba downstairs with a couple of Brazilian escorts, Farzad was upstairs tinkering with the eavesdropping equipment. After donning a white t-shirt and stonewashed jeans, he began reviewing the archive of dialogue snippets between Oksana, Marina, and Victor. Unexpectedly, one particular exchange caught his attention. It had to do with Marina going away to Pebble Beach for a long weekend of surfing.

"Now, that's promising," Farzad muttered.

THE SELF-STYLED STUDENTS AND RESEARCHERS WERE SLOWLY warming up to Ross. The two-hour lunch break—filled with an endless variety of Ross' favorite Persian dishes served buffet style—was a good occasion for connecting with the group on a personal level. Sitting around the horseshoe table, they asked Ross myriad questions about life in America, its people and politics. The informal free-for-all covered the gamut from American foreign policy in general to its posture in the Middle East and the *Axis of Evil*—in particular. Even religion, culture, and crime were not spared the scrutiny of their probing minds.

Parvin, a beautiful, thirty-year-old woman, asked politely, "Tell me, Dr. Shaheen, why is America in Iraq? There are no weapons of mass destruction. Is it oil?" Ross was impressed with her command of English. He suspected she must have lived in America for several years to be able to speak the language with such ease.

Running the question through the filter of conspiracy talk, an Iranian pastime, Ross said, "It's not as simple as that. The concern for WMD's wasn't the only reason for America's attack. There were other motives, the least of which was to create a model of democracy in the Arab world."

"What about supporting Saddam Hussein in the war against Iran? Saddam was a puppet of America, you know. America told him to attack us in 1980," Parvin snapped. "If he was so bad, why did America side with him then?"

Ross felt as if he was being personally attacked for something in which he'd played no part. As irritating as this was, he thought that the woman was trying to show off her nationalism in front of her colleagues. So he remained calm.

"America also sided with Stalin against Hitler. And as we all know, Stalin was a terrible man—a butcher, worse than Hitler." Ross shrugged. "So what? America was acting in self interest when it sided with Stalin, and it was behaving in the same manner when it sided with Saddam."

Another researcher, a cerebral thirty-something with a three-day beard, chimed in with an indignant voice. "Are you comparing Iran with Nazi Germany?"

"Oh no! Not at all. All I'm saying is, in siding with Saddam, America practiced what we as Iranians have been preaching for thousands of years: the enemy of my enemy is my friend. In 1980, on the heels of the hostage crisis, America saw Iran as an enemy, and if Saddam was fighting Iran, then, by definition, Saddam was its friend."

Amir Meshkin, standing a few steps away but apparently listening to the conversation, walked over and interjected, "Which ultimately wound up biting America in the ass."

Ross nodded in agreement. "You could say that again."

"The same way Bin Laden, the rattlesnake America supported against the Russians in Afghanistan, wound up biting your ass."

Intrigued by the way everyone viewed him as an American, Ross said, "You won't get an argument from me on that mistake either."

Another student said, "First it was Afghanistan, then came Iraq. Do you believe Iran is next?"

"No," Ross said. "I don't."

"What makes you so sure?"

"Iran is bigger, it's more populous, and its military is infinitely stronger than Iraq's. Above all, its government doesn't pose a direct threat to America. Unless, of course, Iran tries to build a nuclear bomb; then, all bets are off."

Everyone became quiet. Ross' reference to the forbidden weapon hung in the air like the smell of garlic in a crowded bus.

Amir changed the subject and started talking about Europe and the strategic dangers associated with the expansion of NATO. As Amir went on, Ross became distracted by the lingering sound of helicopter blades whirring in the distance. He tried to ignore it and pay attention to Amir, but he couldn't. It became louder and louder until Ross was certain the helicopter was approaching the building. Soon, everyone looked up at the ceiling tiles, which visibly vibrated, but no one seemed troubled by it. The windows started to rattle. The sound became more intense until it was deafening. Then, with a loud thud, the noise faded away.

Thinking the helicopter had landed on the rooftop, Ross gave Amir an inquisitive look.

"Our ride is here, Dr. Shaheen," Amir said, flashing a big smile and revealing his golden tooth. "We're going on a field trip."

Ross had heard as much while eavesdropping on the conversation between Amir and Sergey. But he hadn't expected a helicopter.

The gravity of the situation quickly dawned on Ross. He knew that the moment he climbed into the helicopter, he would lose contact with his only protector: Reza the driver. *Should I make up an excuse and refuse to go?* He walked to the window. As he took in the sprawling campus, he considered his choices. Refusing to go would not be an option. After a few minutes, he decided the best course of action was to play it cool and deal with the events as they unfolded.

No one seemed in the mood to resume the physics discussion. Likewise, the political discourse was waning.

Amir excused himself to make a phone call. When he returned, he approached Ross. "I've asked Kazem to join us. He should be here around three."

"Where are we going?"

"To the plant."

"Which plant?"

"You'll see…It's a surprise and a treat rolled into one."

A PHALANX OF AIDES GENERALLY SURROUNDS THE DIRECTOR OF Central Intelligence and his deputies. Colonel Nash, however, preferred to wander around the building alone and come, as he put it, "eyeball-to-eyeball" with his troops. He frequently ate in the cafeteria, played handball in the in-house courts, and shunned the limousine to which he was entitled. Instead, he chose to get around sitting in the back of an armored SUV, with his security detail in the passenger seat.

Called to testify before the Senate Select Committee on Intelligence, Colonel Nash left the CIA compound two hours before his scheduled appearance to schmooze the Senators in advance. On his list of most despised activities, Congressional hearings ranked below a colonoscopy without Vaseline.

He was in a bad mood.

The short caravan of identical black SUVs with thick, tinted windows left the front gates of the CIA a few minutes after 7:00 AM. Colonel Nash rode in the middle car behind the lead vehicle, which was loaded with armed men. His staffers followed in the third SUV. The reason for the heavy security, besides the Terror Alert Level being elevated to Orange, was a specific tip from the Jordanian intelligence that HAMAS was planning to assassinate a high-ranking officer of the CIA.

As the convoy crossed the Chain Bridge, the ultra secure telephone, built into the middle-seat of Colonel Nash's vehicle, rang with three short beeps. The small display showed Mira Cordoba, the Colonel's administrative assistant.

"I have Commander Rafael on the line," she said. "You want him?"

"Put him through."

After a short pause, Commander Rafael with his signature accent said, "You owe me big, Colonel."

"What for?"

"I've cracked four of the code-words you gave me."

"Four out of twenty ain't bad, old man."

"Ain't bad, my ass," Rafael said. "I've impressed even myself."

"All right," Nash said, grinning. "Save it till Saturday. We'll play a game, if you're up to it."

"This can't wait till Saturday, Colonel. It's too hot. I need to see you as soon as you can spare a moment."

"I'm on my way to a damn hearing. It'll probably take all day. How about tomorrow morning?"

"Where?"

"Come up to my office. I'll buy you a cup of coffee."

"I'll be there."

Nash hung up without saying a word. He opened a leather-bound folder, which contained his opening statement, and began to read. Thinking of the hearing room, the dozen or so Senators as inquisitors, and the army of reporters, he muttered, "Swine bastards!"

23

THE HEAT WAS SCORCHING IN THE LATE AFTERNOON HOUR. AMIR
Meshkin led the procession of passengers from the staircase onto the
barren rooftop of the NRC administrative building. Feeling anxious,
Ross followed him while Kazem and Sergey, engaged in animated
conversation, straggled behind.

Out in the distance, Ross noticed a giant helicopter painted in desert
camouflage, its blades drooping low—so low, they nearly touched the
ground. He didn't know the exact make or model of the craft but was
almost certain it was Russian-made. Maybe because the massive bird,
functional yet devoid of all grace, just looked like something Russians
would make—rough and menacing.

Halfway toward the helicopter, Amir stopped, waiting for Ross to
catch up. As he approached, Amir said, "This is an Mi-28 Hind, made
in Russia. It's an assault helicopter, but also capable of transporting
passengers." When Ross caught up, they proceeded toward the chopper.
"They used it extensively in Afghanistan," Amir added.

Ross nodded. But he was afraid. Trying to calm his nerves, he
wondered why he felt so worried. Was it fear of the unknown? Or
leaving his only security blanket, Reza, the driver, behind? Maybe a
little of both; he wasn't sure. At the same time, there was eagerness
beneath the anxiety. He was intensely curious about where they were
taking him.

Sweat dripped down from Ross' armpits as he climbed into the
belly of the flying beast. The pungent cocktail of gasoline and body
odor slapped him in the face. Eight passenger seats in two rows of four

faced each other. From the austerity of the cabin, Ross concluded that the Hind was fitted as a troop transporter and not a passenger carrier. The two-member crew, buried in a cocoon of instruments behind the bulkhead, appeared occupied and ignored the passengers. Kazem and Sergey climbed in and sat across from Ross and Amir.

CLICK. Ross, as usual, buckled his seatbelt. He looked around; he was the only one who had.

The hydraulic doors shut and the engines began to rev up, rendering any conversation impossible. The rotors churned with a whipping hum, accelerating into a high-speed pitch. Seconds later, the helicopter lifted off, hovered, and banked sharply to the left. Ross welcomed the cool air that poured out of the vents. The vibrations on takeoff signaled that this would be a rough ride. Discreetly, he grabbed the edge of his seat. Amir produced his amber prayer beads and, looking out the window, started fingering them.

No one spoke.

The chopper gained altitude. With its nose pointing slightly downward, the craft tilted about thirty degrees to the left, giving Ross a panoramic view of the ground below. Reza, standing next to the Mercedes, was watching the helicopter while shading his eyes with his hand. *Does he know I'm inside this bird?* Ross wondered. *Probably. Would he report this to the Russian Embassy?* Ross hoped so. In the meantime, he knew for certain that the only passenger he could trust was himself.

Across the street from the main gate of the NRC compound, the bikers were sitting on a bench next to their red BMW. They, too, were staring at the helicopter. Even though Ross was still unsure of their purpose and who employed them, he wished they hadn't been left behind. It was strange, he knew, but under the circumstances, he preferred the security of the familiar.

Ross had never flown in a helicopter over Iran. For the moment, he decided to quiet his apprehension by soaking in the beauty of the terrain. Before long, Karaj was behind them and the commotion of the city had given way to the tranquility of lush farmland, sand-colored huts, and fenced-in orchards. The vista brought back bittersweet memories.

As teenagers, Ross and Sohrab would help their father pick persimmons and pomegranates in their family orchard, sweating together during the sun-baked days and then cooling off in the nearby stream in the afternoons. They would pass the evenings playing backgammon and sharing stories in the quaint cottage. Recalling the sights and sounds of yesteryears brought a sense of melancholy. He yearned for the warmth and simplicity of those years, wishing time had somehow stood still.

Within a short time, they were flying over the vast ocean of sand in central Iran known as the Dasht-e-Kevir—valley of desert—the largest wasteland in the country. An uninhabited wilderness, it was composed of mud and marshes covered with salt crusts and sand dunes. It reminded Ross of a recent vacation he had taken in Utah with Oksana and the kids. He quickly pushed that memory from his mind; this was no time to stir up his emotions. Still, he worried about them, especially for Marina, away at the beach.

The view of the afternoon sun over the reddish horizon was the first clue of the direction they were headed—south to southwest. Ross knew of several major cities on that track. *Could it be Shiraz? Or is it Isfahan?* He slowly turned the Berkeley ring around his middle finger, praying that the transponder inside was sending a strong signal.

Dusk was at hand when the helicopter began its slow descent. Ross glanced at his watch; they had been in the air for nearly ninety minutes. When he looked out, he instantly recognized the place: Natanz—Iran's renowned and equally controversial uranium enrichment plant.

In his capacity as a science advisor to the director of the NSA, Ross had seen high-resolution satellite images of the mammoth facility on numerous occasions. The plant construction had started years before the CIA knew of its existence. By the time the CIA's sister agency, NRO—the National Reconnaissance Office—had tasked one of its super-secret satellites to start aerial photography of the site, the bulk of the subterranean work was already complete. The spies in the sky could only see the tip of the clandestine iceberg. In a panic, the CIA was reduced to purchasing crude, 25-meter resolution images from commercial satellite companies in order to piece together the sequence of activities at Natanz. Moreover, because of the absence of an adequate network of well-placed informants in Iran, the intelligence community could not determine what exactly was hidden underneath the innocent looking buildings, let alone what was happening inside. Yet, judging from some of the photos he had seen, Ross suspected the CIA had a mole inside—a very high-value asset.

Aware of the gaps in what the NSA and the CIA knew about the enrichment facility, Ross felt a certain euphoria because of where he was about to set foot: Natanz, the most forbidden real estate in all of Iran. For the moment, fear gave way to elation. The helicopter put down on a concrete pad, marked by a giant X, inside the vast compound.

The facility was named after the city of Natanz, a dusty town of no other consequence on the edge of Dasht-e-Kevir and along the Kashan-Natanz highway. The sprawling compound, with buildings in various stages of completion, covered two square miles, and was completely surrounded by an imposing concrete wall. Toward the center, an above ground area, enclosed by an additional high-security fence, contained six large buildings. The white-roofed structures were clones of each other and, unlike most industrial buildings, were devoid of any windows, roof exits, or skylights. According to the IAEA—International Atomic Energy Agency—these buildings contained centrifuge assembly facilities and a centrifuge pilot plant that had recently become operational. Adjacent to this cluster of flat roofs, a large two-story, redbrick structure served as the main administrative building.

Ross knew all this, and much more.

The passengers boarded a stretch golf cart that awaited them near the landing pad. The young driver singled out Amir Meshkin with an effusive greeting and set out in the direction of the administration building. Two guards, with sub-machine guns flung over their shoulders, waved them through the security gate. Ross surveyed the intensive construction work around the site. It was a beehive of activity even at that late hour. A number of heavy trucks hauled dirt out of tunnels, which disappeared underground; countless hard-hats milled about as dozens of cement trucks poured concrete into wooden forms. The air smelled of dust, smoke, and diesel fuel.

"Welcome to Natanz, my pride and joy," Amir said, as the golf cart leisurely rolled toward the redbrick building a quarter mile away. "We started construction about ten years ago, and we have another year or two left before it's complete."

Ross nodded with interest. Amir wound the prayer beads around his right hand and pointed to the white buildings in a sweeping motion. "The purpose of this complex is to test and assemble gas centrifuges."

"Do you manufacture them here?" Ross asked.

"No," Amir replied. "The components are made at other sites by a network of private and government-owned contractors. The parts are shipped here for assembly in Building One, over there. It's a complicated process, as you know."

Ross nodded.

"Building Two—" Amir pointed to identify the structure, "— contains an assortment of equipment to test whole centrifuge tubes one by one. There's a pilot centrifuge plant in Building Three, which currently has four-hundred centrifuges operating in cascade." Amir turned to face Ross. "We're planning on expanding the pilot to one thousand tubes before winter."

From the backseat, Kazem bellowed, *"Aghayoon, khorsheedo bebeeneed*—Gentlemen, look at the sun!" Ross looked to his left; the gigantic crimson disc gently touched the horizon, glowing in luxurious orange. The view of the majestic sunset, unhindered by smog or pollution, was breathtaking. For a fleeting moment, Ross felt reconnected to the ancient land.

The cart pulled up under a brown awning in front of the administration building. Amir stepped off and the others followed. Ross was as curious as a child in Disneyland, committing every detail to memory. The accidental spook knew full well that if he ever got out of Iran alive, Colonel Nash's men would debrief him for days, recording even the minutest scrap of information he could recall.

As they entered the empty lobby, Kazem grabbed his cell from its holster and pressed a button. *"Baleh khanoom jaan*—Yes, dear lady?" He stepped away from the group.

Standing face to face with Ross, Amir continued with his guided tour. "The other three buildings are reserved for future expansion." Ross tried to listen in on Kazem's conversation, while soaking up every word that came out of Amir's mouth. It was difficult, but he managed. He surmised that it was Kazem's wife on the other end of the cell. Apparently, she was not happy with Kazem's sudden field trip.

Kazem pleaded, "No! I'm not going over to *her* house. I'm in Natanz." Pause. "I promise." Now pacing in a random pattern, he said, "Keep my dinner warm. I'll eat it later tonight or maybe tomorrow." He bobbed his head up and down, *"Khoda hafez*—Good bye."

Holstering his cell phone, he approached the trio. "Gentlemen, take it from me," he said earnestly. "Never take a second wife…It is hell."

"What is the matter?" Amir grinned. "You look like you've seen a ghost."

"My first wife expected me for dinner," Kazem said, with exaggerated animation. "When I did not show up, she immediately assumed I was going over to my second wife's house. I doubt if I convinced her otherwise…I tell you, it is hell."

Laughing aloud, Amir said, *"Khodat kardee ke laanat bar khodat baad*—" an idiom that Ross had not heard repeated in nearly thirty-five years of living overseas, "You did it to yourself, then damn yourself."

They all laughed heartily, even the Russian. At that moment, it would have been easy for Ross to delude himself into thinking that he was among friends; but he wasn't, and he didn't.

The spacious lobby of the administrative building was like any office foyer in America: an imposing entrance hall leading to an oversized reception area. Nearby, a few couches and chairs were arranged in a welcoming manner—all in government-issued earth tones. What was different was a gargantuan photo of the Supreme Leader, the bearded Ayatollah, wearing a black turban, a constant reminder of who called the shots.

With a stiff nod, Amir acknowledged the receptionist, a middle-aged man with grayish hair and neatly trimmed beard. Amir then proceeded toward the elevator while continuing his conversation with Ross.

Things seemed deceptively normal.

Inside the roomy elevator, Ross observed three buttons on the control panel labeled: G, 2, and B. There was also a keyhole and a magnetic card reader—like elevators in Las Vegas casinos. He figured the labels meant, Ground floor, Second floor, and Basement. He knew that the buildings at Natanz all had basements—plenty of them. But, would he get to sneak a peek?

Amir punched B, selected a brass key from his key chain, stuck it in the keyhole, and turned it a quarter to the right. Then he fished out a red magnetic card from his wallet and swiped it through the slot. The button labeled B lit up, and the elevator doors closed. Ross felt the floor give a slight jerk as the hydraulics beneath the elevator cab engaged, and they began a slow descent. Ross' belly gave a painful spasm, either in response to the downward motion, or to the excitement, anticipation, and fear that gnawed at his stomach lining. Probably the latter.

How deep is the basement? he wondered. The elevator kept moving for an unusually long time. It was obvious that *this* basement was much deeper than the standard fifteen or so feet in ordinary buildings.

After what felt like an eternity, the elevator stopped with a gentle bounce, and the stainless steel doors parted. Ross watchfully stepped out and looked around. "We are forty feet below ground, Dr. Shaheen," Amir said, continuing his guided tour.

They were standing in an austere, subterranean lobby about twenty-five feet square, but the high ceiling made the space feel larger than it really was. The lobby was entirely white—the walls, the floor, the three metal doors, one on each side, the ceiling...all painted white. Opposite the elevator, a uniformed security guard observed the men from behind a large glass window. Amir pointed to the guard. When he had the man's attention, he motioned to the steel door on the left wall.

With a short buzz, the door unlatched. "This is our gas centrifuge enrichment plant," Amir said, as he held the heavy door open. After they were all inside, he let the metal door automatically close behind them. Peering deep into the cavernous space, it took a while for Ross to believe what his eyes were taking in.

They had stepped onto an observation deck, overlooking a space the size of a football field. The concrete floor was another fifteen feet below where they stood. The guard watched them through another opening as they started down the metal staircase.

The greatest Egyptian pharaoh would be pleased with this as his tomb, Ross thought, as he set foot on the concrete floor. Observing the endless network of bright red and green pipes snaking overhead in unison, he was amazed at the scale of the project. On the far right, thousands of polished, stainless steel centrifuge tubes stood vertically in 4x4 clusters, daisy-chained together with brass pipes. Technicians, wearing white uniforms and white tennis shoes, milled about like gardeners tending a steel bamboo patch.

"We have ten-thousand centrifuge tubes up and running here," Amir said to Ross' astonishment, as they walked alongside the clusters.

Sergey chimed in, "Of course, we have only enriched uranium to five percent purity." Ross suspected otherwise. Judging by the amount of unused space left, he estimated that the underground plant could hold at least fifty thousand centrifuges.

As Amir spoke, Ross felt as if they were in a scene out of an old James Bond movie. With a backdrop of a gargantuan high-tech facility, the chief villain, plotting world domination, extolled the virtues of his evil design while caressing a Persian cat. It was eerie. And the cat was the only thing missing.

Amir continued. "Based on our current technology and the separation capacity of our centrifuges, once this plant is complete, it will be able to provide enough enriched uranium for the annual reloads of the Bushehr reactor."

Ross realized that what Amir had just said confirmed Washington's worst nightmare. If Iran ever decided to make weapons-grade uranium, it would be able to do so by simply recycling low-enriched uranium— five percent U_{235}—as "feed" back into the facility. Repeating this cycle could produce enough weapons-grade uranium for a nuclear weapon in just a few days. With 50,000 enrichment tubes, Natanz could produce about 500 kilograms of weapons-grade uranium annually. Ross calculated. *At 20 kilograms per weapon, that's enough for roughly 25 bombs per year.* At that rate, Iran would outrun Israel's nuclear arsenal in less than a decade. Not to mention Pakistan and India combined.

Ross was keenly interested in where Amir's outfit, AEOI, had first obtained its centrifuge technology. He hesitated to ask, thinking Amir would become suspicious if he appeared overly curious. Besides, Amir was blathering highly sensitive and secret information anyway. *It's best to wait*, Ross thought. *Sooner or later, he might just come out with it.*

The intelligence community had long suspected that Iran had received design assistance from Pakistan or from individual Pakistani scientists—specifically Dr. A.Q. Khan, the father of Pakistan's atom bomb. Supporting this theory was Iran's centrifuge design. It was eerily similar to the type that Pakistan had pilfered in the mid-1970s from the Urenco enrichment plant in the Netherlands, where Dr. Khan worked as a scientist. Rumor had it that Washington possessed hard evidence to prove this theory.

Amir waved down a golf cart, dismissed the driver with a backhand motion, and took the steering wheel. Ross climbed in next to him, leaving the back seats for Sergey and Kazem.

"There are two of these underground structures," Amir said, driving. "Each is one-hundred and ninety meters long and one-hundred and seventy meters wide, with a gross area of approximately thirty-two thousand square meters." Quietly, Ross calculated the area to be over 300,000 square feet or nearly eight acres. Each!

Amir buzzed by the endless rows of centrifuges and stopped in the middle of the open space. Pointing to the concrete walls, he said, "These are three meters thick." Looking up, he continued. "The ceiling is over five meters of reinforced concrete."

Kazem blurted out with a chuckle, "Advise your friends in Washington to tell their friends in Tel Aviv to forget about bombing this place. It's indestructible."

Amir quieted him with a cold stare, and drove to the far corner of the bunker toward a giant concrete opening. "That tunnel is the access road in and out of the plant. It allows eighteen-wheelers to pass through." Then he stopped in front of the mouth of the tunnel to allow Ross a closer view of the shape of the mammoth steel gate—which was half open—and the curved entrance ramp. There was no way a guided missile or even a glide bomb could penetrate it. Ross quickly concluded that only a nuclear bunker buster would be able to destroy the plant.

Is he using this guided tour to send a subtle message to Washington? Ross wondered. Given the adverse political ramifications of using nuclear weapons, which would be of epic proportions, neither Israel nor America would consider using such ordnance.

Kazem was right. Natanz was virtually indestructible.

"What about the Hex?" Ross inquired nonchalantly. "Where do you make it?"

"The Hex that feeds the centrifuges isn't produced here," Amir said, as he turned the cart around and sped toward the steel platform. "It's produced at the uranium conversion facility in Isfahan and shipped here in tankers."

The men climbed the stairs onto the platform. Before returning to the elevator lobby, Ross paused for another look at the forbidden grounds. The magnitude of what he had witnessed, the sheer size of the project, and the daunting task of completing it, incognito, was overwhelming.

He was quietly impressed.

Back in the all white atrium, once more, Amir pointed at the guard, demanding his attention. Then, with the prayer beads dangling from his right hand, he motioned to the door on the opposite wall. The magnetic lock released with a loud, buzzing sound.

"This is the nerve center of the entire operation," Amir said. He led the way into the spacious open office. The wall-to-wall blue carpet gave the vast, windowless area a warm feeling. The workplace, divided into hundreds of tinted glass cubicles, seemed well organized.

"This area is for our engineers," Amir explained, as he walked through the main hallway. "You've met two of them already—at the NRC."

Striding alongside Amir, Ross looked at him knowingly, wondering which two.

"Most of the engineers work regular shifts." This clarified why there were so few people around. "And they've closed up shop for the day."

Ross took it all in, committing every detail to memory.

Amir approached a glass wall at the far corner and waited for the others to join him. "That's the control room," Amir explained. "It's manned around the clock."

Inside, five technicians with their backs to the glass wall monitored an array of process control equipment. Hundreds of digital gauges and a dozen or so flat-screen displays were mounted on the wall in front of them. CISCO routers and firewalls, LUCENT switches, and FUJITSU servers were neatly organized in racks in the corner of the spacious control room. Ross said, under his breath, "So much for sanctions and export restrictions."

No one responded to the comment.

Amir led the way to a spacious private office off the main hallway. Expensive modern furniture, a late model computer workstation with two flat-screen monitors, and ultra comfortable seating betrayed that its occupant must be a senior manager. In the corner, an open door revealed a bed in the small anteroom. *The manager must be a hard-working man—he could practically live here,* Ross thought.

"This is my office, Dr. Shaheen. You'll be working here."

"Working?" Silencing his shock, Ross said, "Doing what?"

"Patience, my friend…patience." Amir grinned. "Follow me."

The procession retraced their steps and returned to the elevator lobby. "I want to show you something no outsider has ever seen," Amir said gleefully, pressing the elevator call button. "This is the treat I had promised you earlier."

Ross felt waves of anxiety grip his stomach.

Sergey approached Amir and in his throaty voice said, "Can I have a moment?"

Amir nodded and took him aside. Ross could not make out their hushed conversation but sensed the tension.

"Chechens are as animated as us Iranians," Kazem observed, as Sergey flailed his arms with excitement. Ross took the opportunity to sound out Kazem.

"What did Amir mean when he said I would be working out of his office?"

"Exactly that."

"How could I work here if I'm staying in Tehran?" Ross frowned. "As if two-hour commutes to the NRC weren't bad enough, now you expect me to suffer three-hour helicopter rides to and from Natanz every day?"

"I don't know what he has in mind. Just give him a chance to explain."

"What happened to the invitation from Shiraz University?"

"For the moment, it's on hold."

"I knew I shouldn't have trusted you."

"Relax, my friend. You have made a good bargain…You will see."

"No! This is not what we agreed to," Ross said, clenching his teeth. "I was supposed to lecture for six short weeks at Shiraz University. That's all! I've been here almost a week and haven't been anywhere near that city. 'It's on hold,' you say."

Kazem didn't respond.

Ross persisted. "What the hell am I doing down in this bunker anyway? Are you trying to suck me into your nuclear program? I want no part of it—none!"

"Please have patience, my friend."

"Patience my ass!" Ross' quiet rage, bottled up for days, was about to explode. But Amir had started shouting at Sergey and, for the moment, the distraction diffused Ross' anger.

"I will take *full* responsibility for taking him down below!" Amir said. He passed the prayer beads from one hand to the other and jabbed an index finger at Sergey's chest. "Dr. Shaheen needs to know everything and see it all…That's the only way!"

After that exchange, Amir abruptly returned to the waiting elevator and said, "Let's go."

Sergey followed sheepishly.

Ross' agitation caused him to enter the elevator ahead of the pack. He was sweating and could hear his own heartbeat. Leaning against the back wall, he avoided any eye contact with the others. He breathed in deep, thinking, *Calm down.* There was a repeat of the brass key and the magnetic card routine. But this time, Amir turned the key in the opposite direction without pressing any buttons. A section of the control panel swiveled, revealing a sophisticated hand scanner. Ross' interest was piqued. Amir placed the palm of his right hand on its surface. After a speedy verification, signaled by a green light, the elevator came to life and started to move. Down.

Ross was amazed. *How many underground layers does this place have?* At least one more, obviously, which reminded him of some of the Israeli tactics. They had several floors built underneath their main nuclear reactor facility at Demona where they reprocessed plutonium. Legend had it that there were seven secret floors under Demona—no one knew for sure. When American inspectors came calling, the Israelis bricked over certain elevators and staircases to hide their secret program. Ross found it ironic that the Iranians had borrowed a page from the nuclear playbook of their archenemy—Israel.

The elevator crept down for nearly one minute as if it was traveling to the bowels of hell. Then it stopped with a jolt. Ross thought they must be over one hundred feet below surface.

"We are fifty meters under ground," Amir said. "This floor is protected by five meters of reinforced concrete. Nothing, not even your deep penetration bunker busters, can reach this depth." Staring at Ross intently, he added, "Only a direct nuclear blast can take it out. And we don't think the U.S. or Israel would ever go that far."

Ross was speechless. The situation he was in seemed surreal. He was about to enter where no American had ever gone. *Does this mean I will never see the light of day? Will I ever see Oksana and the children again?*

The elevator door slid open into a small, grayish concrete lobby. Cool and a little damp, the subterranean hall was deserted but brightly illuminated with fluorescent lights. There were three metal doors—all shut. Amir headed straight toward the door facing the elevator. It was also equipped with a hand scanner. Recognizing Amir's palm print, it snapped open. He held the door for Ross to enter.

Inside, Ross' jaw dropped.

24

I N LANGLEY, THE MORNING FOG HAD BLANKETED THE IMMACULATE grounds of the CIA campus. From Colonel Nash's office, on the sixth floor of the Headquarters Buildings, only the treetops protruding above the billows were visible. The crimson rays of daybreak accenting the vista created a most tranquil landscape.

Reading the synopsis of the previous night's intelligence reports, Colonel Nash leisurely paced the floor of his office and occasionally stopped to take in the view.

One floor below, in the Command Center of the Directorate of Operations, the flashing green light with the codename SPIKER next to it had stopped blinking for the past 15 minutes. The now solid light, together with the codeword, had changed color and appeared in red.

Charles Rubin, the manager of the Command Center, followed standard operating procedures and performed the prescribed tests to ensure there were no malfunctions.

All systems checked out OK.

Rubin, a quiet CIA veteran and former field agent himself, knew too well that behind these codenames and blinking lights there were living, breathing professionals. They put their lives on the line every hour of every day in defense of America. Even though he didn't know their true identities, he considered them as family. And when their codenames turned red on the big screen, he felt a lump in his throat because it was usually bad news. He had to notify the officer in charge of the operative in trouble as soon as possible.

Rubin glided the mouse over the deep blue, CIA-monogrammed

mouse pad. He double clicked on SPIKER. To his surprise, Colonel Timothy Nash was listed as the officer in charge. Rubin raised his left eyebrow. *This is interesting...Nash rarely runs agents himself.* He stood up, staring at the screen. *SPIKER must be a big fish.*

Ignoring all protocol, Rubin dialed the Colonel's direct line.

"SPIKER has quit transmitting, sir."

"Since when?"

"It's been fifteen, twenty minutes."

"Hang on." Nash clicked a few icons and began to review the trajectory of Ross' movements on his computer monitor. Each stop, transposed over the map of Iran, was date and time stamped. "Have you traced him?"

"Yes, Colonel."

"I'm looking at it now. From Shams Grand hotel to the NRC in Karaj, then a straight shot to Natanz, and then...lights out."

"That's definitely a plane or a chopper, sir. It's moving too fast, and it doesn't follow any roads."

"I agree. What's your assessment, Rubin?"

"Either the transmission device is discovered and destroyed, or he's buried deep underground. Could be under water."

"There's no water in Natanz, Rubin. But there are all kinds of holes under ground."

"That much we know, sir."

"Keep your eyes on him. Let me know the moment he resumes transmission."

"Will do."

~

ROSS DID A POOR JOB OF HIDING HIS ASTONISHMENT. HE HAD NEVER witnessed anything like this. He had entered the most spacious underground laboratory he'd ever seen. It was the size of a modern superstore—a Wal-Mart or Home Depot. High vaulted ceiling, tiled floors, and brilliantly lit with industrial lights—all below ground, nearly fifteen floors under.

Amir said pompously, "You've entered Iran's Los Alamos, Dr.

Shaheen." Spanning the space with a hand motion, he proclaimed, "And this is my Manhattan Project."

Ross didn't need any translation. The Manhattan Project was the codename for America's ultra-secret program, established during World War II, to develop the first nuclear bomb. The idea of forming a research team to create a nuclear weapon was advanced by none other than Albert Einstein, in a letter to President Franklin Roosevelt, in 1939. Six years later, on July 6, 1945, the first atomic bomb was detonated at Los Alamos in a desert location, codenamed Trinity. The director of Los Alamos, Dr. Robert Oppenheimer, wrote in his journal upon witnessing the test of the first nuclear weapon: "Now, I am become Death, the destroyer of worlds," a verse from the ancient Hindu scripture, the *Bhagavad-Gita*. A month after Trinity, two nuclear weapons—one fueled with uranium and the other by plutonium—were exploded over Japan, at Hiroshima and Nagasaki, killing over 100,000 civilians.

Oppenheimer's cry of conscience had come to pass.

Everything was too clear. Ross had just entered the clandestine laboratory where Iran was building its own nuclear weapon—buried deep underground, beneath their "peaceful" enrichment plant. Ross knew how immeasurably dangerous the monstrous project was. It threatened the balance of power in the region and would undoubtedly trigger an arms race—if not Armageddon. Yet, other than quiet astonishment at the scope of the facility, he showed no emotions.

Again, Amir led the way on the VIP tour. To the right was an endless array of massive machines, meticulously lined up parallel to the wall. Like a proud father showing off his children's handiwork, Amir pointed to the assortment of equipment and said, "This is the most advanced metal forming equipment in the world. It's all computerized and laser controlled." He stopped and looked at Ross. "We can manufacture any part to a precision of two microns."

Ross nodded, noticing the plates on the equipment. The place looked like the exhibit hall of the machinists trade show. They were from all over the world. France, Germany, Russia, Japan, and even the United States were proudly represented. *Where did they get this stuff?* Ross' brain worked overtime. *Have they succeeded in evading all the intelligence services? Is the CIA aware of this place? What about the Mossad?*

Ross said, "I'd like to meet and congratulate your purchasing agent."

"You've already met him." Amir pointed over his shoulder to Kazem. "You can congratulate him later if you wish."

There's more to that thug than meets the eyes, Ross thought.

"How did you get this equipment down here?" Ross asked. "They certainly don't fit the elevator we took."

"There's a freight elevator, of course." Amir pointed to a huge set of doors on the opposite side.

"What about emergency exits? I don't see any."

"That's because there are none," Amir said, in a matter-of-fact manner. "This is a do or die work environment, Dr. Shaheen. If there's an emergency down here, we'll all die for the cause—gladly."

A dozen technicians, wearing lab coats and goggles, tended the machines. Two were studying a set of blueprints spread over a large table. Once they saw Amir, they stopped what they were doing to acknowledge him with reverence. One came over and shook his hand fervently, as if he were a celebrity.

The guided tour continued. Kazem and Sergey followed a dozen steps behind without uttering a word. Only Amir spoke. Cognizant of the weight of the moment, Ross asked questions sparingly.

Amir walked toward a set of glass double doors, opposite the main entrance. As they approached, the sliding doors—each conspicuously marked with the universal yellow sign for radioactivity—automatically opened with a suction sound. The space inside seemed like a high-tech, clean-room assembly area. In the middle, there were four industrial workbenches and highchairs neatly arranged in a cluster. A freestanding toolbox was positioned behind each workbench. At the center of the cluster, a metallic box, the size of a coffin, lay sideways on a stand. An extra large surgical light, hanging from the ceiling, illuminated it. Two technicians wearing white lab coats and masks hunched over the unit with their hands deep in its bowels, as if they were surgeons performing a heart bypass procedure.

Is that their nuclear device? Ross wondered. He noticed that his heart was racing. *Could it be their A-bomb?*

A number of offices surrounded the open area. On the far side, a large stainless steel door boasted an oversized radioactivity decal. It looked like the opening of a walk-in freezer. Amir said, "As you might imagine, there's a small team of dedicated scientists and engineers who work with me on this project—thirty-seven to be exact." He stopped and faced Ross. "They're the best engineers Iran has produced. You met a few of them in Karaj, Dr. Shaheen."

Ross was tempted to say, "I knew it," but he didn't.

Amir led the way into a modest, yet spacious, conference room. Pointing to a seat, he said, "Sit down, Dr. Shaheen." The round table in the center of the otherwise sparse room accommodated twelve chairs. "Will you guys leave us alone for a while?" Amir held the door open for Kazem and Sergey to leave. Then, he pulled up a chair and sat on the opposite side of the table—personal, yet distant.

Ross looked at his watch—7:45 PM. He usually called Oksana in the evenings. But somehow, he knew he wouldn't do so that night.

Amir retrieved the prayer beads from his pocket and began to handle them contemplatively. After a moment, he leaned over and said, "Dr. Shaheen, I've brought you where no outsider has ever come. You know why?"

Ross shook his head thinking, *Not exactly, but I have a pretty good idea, you scumbag.*

"Because you and I go back a long time...Hell, we've known each other from high school." Amir narrowed his eyes, looking at Ross intently. "And even though we chose different paths in life, deep down, I feel like I can trust you." Amir looked at his prayer beads for a brief moment and then looked up. "And I certainly hope you will do likewise."

Ross remained quiet.

"Can I—trust you?"

Ross nodded reluctantly, thinking, *Trust me? Like hell you can. You've sent your goons to threaten my children, forcing me to come here. And now you've practically kidnapped me. If you're foolish enough to want to trust me, have at it. But don't expect any reciprocity.*

Amir took Ross' hesitant nod as affirmation, and said, "Well, then...I need your assistance, Dr. Shaheen. No, let me restate what I just said: your motherland needs your assistance." Amir thumbed the beads nervously. "And I don't know how else to put it other than simply asking you directly. No sense beating around the bush."

Are you serious? Ross sat statue-like, staring at Amir. *Do you really think I'm going to help you in any way? How naive. As soon as I see the light of day, I'll be on the first plane out of Iran.*

Amir continued. "I guess by now it's clear to you what we're doing here."

Ross quipped, "I guess this makes you the Iranian Oppenheimer."

"With one major difference, Dr. Shaheen: Oppenheimer was plagued by self-doubt and the morality of the *Bhagavad-Gita*, whereas I act with complete self-assurance and the authority of the *Koran*."

Readily recognizing the sarcastic reference to Oppenheimer's entry into his journal, Ross said, "I see."

Amir continued. "We have produced enough highly enriched uranium for a number of bombs."

"How much uranium?"

"That's a state secret."

"Understood."

"We have a working design for a uranium bomb." Amir pointed his right thumb to the work area. "We've built a prototype. I'll show it to you later; it's a beauty."

"You're playing a dangerous game—"

"Save it, Dr. Shaheen," Amir said, cutting him off tersely. "As I said, I need something from you, but I don't need any lectures."

"You seem to have managed everything on your own—Bravo!" Ross shrugged. "What do you need from me?"

"Nothing major, Dr. Shaheen."

"Major or minor, makes no difference, Amir. I cannot help." Ross stood, leaned forward, and said, "You keep forgetting a tiny inconvenience. I'm an American citizen, which means I can't support your plans—in any way."

"Do you think a piece of paper and a little blue passport makes you any less of an Iranian?"

"No. But it makes me an American first, and an Iranian second." Ross turned up his volume. "And before they gave me that piece of paper, I swore an oath of allegiance to America. And I don't take it lightly."

Amir rolled his eyes. "We'll see about that."

"What do you want from me, anyway?"

"The Blind Scorpion," Amir said dismissively, as if it were a minor request.

Ross' chest tightened. Sitting down slowly, he recalled his first encounter with Kazem in Las Vegas, and their subsequent meeting on the pier. Kazem's not so veiled threat, the million dollars, and the interaction with the students at the NRC—it all made sense. He had finally figured out exactly why he had been lured to Iran. All the machinations, the lies and the intrigues, it had all been for the Scorpion.

"The Blind Scorpion?" Ross collected himself. "What the hell for?"

"Simple. I need to know if my nuclear device will go supercritical. And what it will yield. That's all."

"Dig a deep hole in the desert, stick the bomb in it, and push the damn button. You'll know if it blows."

"So will the entire planet," Amir snapped. "And there lies the problem."

"What?" Ross said, mocking him. "Are you embarrassed by your creation, Dr. Oppenheimer?"

"We want to keep our enemies guessing, Dr. Shaheen." Amir spun the string of beads around his index finger. "As it is, the world doesn't know for sure if we have a working nuclear bomb. At the same time, they can't be certain that we don't."

Ross leaned back and said knowingly, "Nuclear ambiguity—the Israelis invented that policy."

"It has worked for them brilliantly. Why not for us?"

"I won't do it, Amir. I don't want any part of your shenanigans."

"Please reconsider, Dr. Shaheen."

"Hell, even if I wanted to, I couldn't do it. The Blind Scorpion is in America, and I'm here."

"We'll discuss the logistics later. Let me first show you what we've built." He rose and said, "Come with me," and hurriedly exited the conference room.

Sergey and Kazem were lingering outside. Amir told Sergey, "Go over the device with Dr. Shaheen. Explain everything and answer all his questions."

"This way, Doctor," Sergey said grudgingly, as he headed toward the work area. Ross followed quietly. Amir and Kazem entered the conference room and closed the door.

Approaching the nuclear bomb, Ross felt the familiar blend of excitement and horror. He was about to examine what every intelligence service in the civilized world would have paid a ransom in blood to sneak a peek at. At the same time, he doubted he would ever be able to leave the place alive. *This is it,* he thought. *I've seen far too much. They'll certainly kill me. They have to. What will happen to Oksana? And the kids?*

Occupied by these worries, Ross approached the device and stood next to it. Sergey waved the technicians away and took the other side. He paused for a few seconds and said, *"Ne vozrajaesh' esli ya objasnju po-russki*—Do you mind if I explain in Russian?"

"Davai—Go ahead."

At first glance, Ross could readily tell that the design of the nuclear bomb was based on the rifle technique, where two sub-critical pieces of highly enriched uranium are shot against each other using conventional explosives. But, instead of a long cylinder, the "rifle" was in the shape of an hourglass—nearly six feet long and two feet wide at each base. It narrowed in the middle to a choke tunnel of about eight inches in diameter.

This is a novel approach, Ross thought. *If the narrow chamber stays intact, the fission would be more complete, increasing the bomb's yield.*

"To achieve maximum concentration of the fissile material in the shortest time, I have adopted this configuration," Sergey explained. "The combustion chamber narrows in the middle, achieving the greatest pressure possible."

Ross took note of Sergey's use of the pronoun, "I." He must have been the bomb's designer.

"Is the assembly made of steel?"

"All components are made of ultra-high-strength maraging steel. This material enables the fission chamber to withstand the heat and pressure of the initial explosion and still maintain its geometry."

"Have you tested that? I mean the explosives?"

"Off course."

"Where is the maraging steel from? It makes a difference, you know."

"England."

"What about the explosives?"

"Two hundred kilograms of Semtex—the best plastic explosive in the world—at each end."

"Courtesy of the Czech Republic, I presume."

Sergey did not respond.

"How much uranium?" Ross tapped the throat of the gadget. "What shape?" He looked up. "And what level of enrichment?"

"Eighteen kilograms in total. Each half is formed into a cylindrical disc, weighing in at nine kilos." Sergey demonstrated the shape with his hands. "We have achieved ninety-three percent enrichment so far. But we will improve on that."

I'll be damned...They've done it. Ross didn't need the Blind Scorpion to tell if the nuclear device before him would explode. Based on Sergey's description, and the quality of workmanship, he knew it would. What Ross could not predict was the yield—the kilotons of explosive power. For that, he needed his super-computer in Oakland.

Ross kept his initial assessment to himself. He proceeded to pepper Sergey with questions about the control mechanisms, how they ensured simultaneous detonation of the two Semtex volumes, the neutron initiators, and other design features.

Sergey answered Ross' questions with relish and seemed to have overcome his initial reluctance. His enthusiasm readily betrayed that the bomb was his baby. During his explanation, he let it slip that the device they were looking at was their second. They had already assembled the first bomb, and it was stored behind the freezer-looking door.

Surprised by the absence of any access controls, Ross said, "Security seems pretty lax around here. You've got bomb components and explosives lying about without anyone watching."

"It's impossible to enter this level without the highest level of security clearance," Sergey responded. "We assume anyone who has made it down here, belongs here. Any further restrictions become a hindrance."

The review of the nuclear bomb lasted thirty minutes. Afterward, Sergey and Ross returned to the conference room, interrupting Amir and Kazem's conversation.

Amir inquired impatiently, "Are you impressed?"

"You don't need any encouragement from me, but since you asked, it's good work, technically." Ross slumped into the same chair he had previously used. "But it's dreadful work, politically. And, from a military standpoint, it's suicidal."

Amir hesitated, and then motioned for Sergey and Kazem to leave the room. Once alone, he became quiet and started to manipulate his prayer beads. It seemed as if he was rehearsing what he wanted to say.

After a long minute, he looked up and calmly said, "You're entitled to your opinions about what we're doing here. But I must know, Dr. Shaheen. I must know, without detonation, if it works. And you and *your* Blind Scorpion will have to tell me."

"No way, Amir. I won't do it."

"I'm a reasonable man, Dr. Shaheen. Think of the million dollars as a down payment. You'll get another million when you run the test."

Ross shook his head. "No!"

"Holding out for more?" Amir snickered. "Okay, make it five million—in a numbered Swiss bank account. No one will ever know, my friend."

Masking his unease, Ross said calmly, "You're wasting your time, Amir." Then he shrugged. "I'm not for sale...or rent."

"Listen!" Amir said. "I don't wish to appear rude or inhospitable." He rose and approached Ross. "We can do this the easy way or the hard way. The easy way will bring out my appreciation." Then he bent low, so close to Ross' face that he could smell the cigarette on Amir's breath. "The hard way, my wrath. The choice is yours."

Frightened, all Ross could muster was, "Are you threatening me?"

Amir walked away and leaned against the wall. Fingering his prayer beads, he said, "I suggest you sleep on it tonight. We'll discuss it again in the morning. It's late. I have to return to Tehran."

"What about me?"

"You're spending the night here, Dr. Shaheen. You'll be comfortable in my suite upstairs. The kitchen has prepared dinner for you."

"Well, that's just great! I'm a damn prisoner now."

"Far from it, Dr. Shaheen. You are my honored guest. But you will stay here tonight."

Ross stood and kicked a chair across the room. "That's bullshit!"

Amir's eyes followed the chair's trajectory. Ignoring the outburst, he said, "Sergey will stay with you to go over the blueprints. Take your time. Use my computer, if you like, to examine the details of our design. It's all there. Tomorrow we'll feed the schematics to the Blind Scorpion."

"You're being delusional, Amir. We cannot hack into the Scorpion from here. No one has ever been able to breach it."

"You will."

Ross composed himself. "I need to call my wife. She'll get worried if I don't phone and may call the FBI. Then all hell will break loose."

Amir opened the door to exit. With the doorknob still in his hand, he turned and said, "That's a risk I'm willing to take, Dr. Shaheen. You think about a way to tap into the Blind Scorpion."

Silence.

"Good night, Dr. Shaheen."

25

IT WAS NEARLY MIDNIGHT WHEN THE HELICOPTER RETURNED AMIR and Kazem to Karaj. Lost in thought, the two men didn't speak during the flight. The engine noise made conversation nearly impossible anyway.

When the aircraft approached the compound, Kazem noticed that his driver, Reza, was still waiting in the parking lot. Walking on the rooftop toward the staircase, Amir said, "Come to my office for a drink. We need to talk."

Kazem looked at his watch. "Can it wait till tomorrow?"

"No. It's important."

In his office, Amir produced a bottle of Jack Daniels from behind a row of books and poured the whisky into teacups.

"*Salamati*—To your health."

"*Salamati*."

Amir chugged it, and poured himself another. Then he slumped into his chair, retrieved the ubiquitous prayer beads, and said, "What do you think, Kazem? Will he do it?"

Kazem nursed his drink, thinking. After a moment of quiet, he leaned against the bookshelf and said, "Without extra motivation, I doubt it."

"Why not? He's a smart man," Amir said. "By now, I'm sure he's figured out that if he wants to see the light of day again, he must cooperate."

"Why should he? He obviously doesn't care much about himself. If he did, he wouldn't have come here." Kazem took a small sip of the whisky. "Besides, he seems to be an idealist. He wants be a hero, even a martyr. So, threatening him personally will not be effective."

"He might be persuaded to help the Islamic Republic," Amir said. "After all, he's an Iranian. Nothing ever changes that, Kazem—it's in our genes."

"Too late for him. He switched loyalties a long time ago." Kazem sat down in a chair facing Amir. "Do you think the Americans would put him in the position he's in if they had any doubts about his loyalty? No way. I tell you, Amir, he'll never do it out of any love or sympathy for Iran. That's wishful thinking."

Amir wondered aloud, "You think because of his brother's death, he's holding a grudge."

"I don't think so. I know so."

"They're so much alike, Kazem, it's eerie. I remember Sohrab so well—as if it were yesterday. I was an interrogator at the Evin prison when they brought him in. I couldn't break him either; it's a shame he had to die."

"Well, let's not volunteer any information about his brother, okay?"

"All right." Amir poured another drink and continued. "I offered him more money, you know. Maybe the cash will persuade him."

Kazem shook his head. "I doubt it."

"Well, I'm all out of ideas."

"Let me remind you that the only reason he agreed to come to Iran in the first place was because of my veiled threat. I just showed him pictures of his kids. You should've seen the look on his face, Amir. He would have killed me if he could have—then and there."

"So, his weakness is his family."

"Right."

"Then that's how we'll get leverage."

"That might be premature," Kazem said. "Let's wait."

Amir pondered the situation for a few moments and said, "Wait for what? You know my philosophy: what you have to do eventually, do immediately." He opened a small black book on his desk and dialed a number. Holding the receiver to his ear, he stared at Kazem. There was no answer; he dialed again.

"Good evening, Saeed. I'm sorry for calling this late."

"In my business late and early are meaningless phrases."

"I guess the weather is nice enough for the FOXHUNT."

"I understand. When should we go?"

"As soon as possible."

"I'll take care of it right away."

"Good night."

Amir gulped what whiskey was left in his teacup. "I hope you're right, Kazem."

"We'll know soon enough. Won't we?"

Amir turned the lights off as they left his office. Walking out of the building, he said, "Are you coming to Natanz tomorrow?"

"I don't see any need. Do you want me there?"

"No. Not really."

It was a moonless night. Kazem approached Reza and climbed into the backseat of the Mercedes. When Reza inquired about Dr. Shaheen, Kazem said, "He's spending the night with some old friends."

Reza knew better.

THE SULTRY MEDITERRANEAN NIGHT, ON THE REMOTE ISLAND OF Cyprus, was filled with seduction. At his simple apartment in Larnaka, Army Sergeant Emmit James Mangrum—a.k.a. Jimbo—the Signal Specialist, dragged himself out of bed. The graveyard shift at the super-secret NSA listening post would start in an hour. Bella, his Italian girlfriend of two weeks, opened her sleepy eyes and mumbled, "Jimbo, do you have to go?"

Jimbo leaned over, gave her a long kiss, and said, "Don't want to, but I gotta."

"Will you call me later?"

"I've told you a million times, sugar plum, no calls in or out of work."

Bella sat up and said, "You're so mysterious, James." She lit a cigarette. "Like James Bond."

He snickered. "Oh yeah, baby. That's who I am: Bond, James Bond. Now, give us some love." He crawled back into bed.

Jimbo's apartment was twenty minutes away from the NSA listening post. Because of Bella, he was speeding down the winding shoreline highway. He knew that the commanding officer did not have a sense of humor when it came to his men being late. And recently Jimbo had been tardy too often—all because of Bella.

It was two minutes before midnight when Jimbo reached the parking lot. The armed gatekeepers waved him through. He ran uphill toward the nondescript, windowless building. Out of breath, he walked upstairs to the secure metal door; the guard buzzed him in.

It was midnight, on the dot.

Once inside, Jimbo paused to catch his breath. Then, he slowly walked through the dim, open space and approached his workstation— the ninth from the entrance door. As usual, the room buzzed with the hectic beeps, whistles, and crackle of frequencies. Jimbo sunk into his chair, put on his "big-ass headphones," and began turning the dials. Seconds later, he was listening to his favorite gibberish—the voice of the Islamic Republic of Iran.

The midnight news broadcast was routine. It fell into the *nothing to write home about* category, and the usual mind-numbing propaganda. He turned the dial to other targets of interest, as if casting a fishing line into cyberspace.

The fish weren't biting.

Five minutes before 2:00 AM, he turned the dial on his high-powered UHF—Ultra High Frequency—radio to a special channel originating from Iran, which was often used by MOIS. It was innocently broadcasting Persian music. Jimbo listened patiently and intently. The instant the digital clock on his instrument panel displayed 2:00 AM, he heard a two second burst of static. He knew it was another encrypted message from MOIS to one of its shadowy agents abroad. Was this an order to blow something up? Or assassinate someone? With the relations between Iran and the United States at a new low, the Signal Specialist could not help but wonder.

The TOP SECRET equipment in front of him swiftly intercepted the hidden message. Jimbo, following standard operating procedures, logged the particulars about the intercept in his computer and clicked UNPACK. The encrypted message appeared.

*fpZ23h8wCRVUbKwxEgCnqAJW8w9R1GNA3K7Nl
JUQk2Q/zPUGzyrRllgOFSs3uO1O0LlU9FKgDM*

Then he clicked DECRYPT to see if the encryption algorithm used by MOIS was one already broken by the NSA and loaded into his desktop computer. It was. Seconds later, the plaintext message appeared before him.

GO FOXHUNT REPEAT FOXHUNT IS GO END

FOXHUNT blinked in red, which meant the word was an entry in ECHELON's Dictionary. *This is an intercept NSA will want to know about immediately,* he thought. With a few mouse clicks, he transmitted the intercept to the NSA headquarters in Fort Meade, Maryland. "Hot digidee dawg," Jimbo whispered. "Go to Daddy."

Since the message contained a word that matched one from the Dictionary, he escalated it to the highest level of urgency, known as CRITIC.

Buoyed with his big catch, Jimbo turned the dial and found the chatter of a military pilot with the air traffic controller in Tehran. He listened while thinking about Bella.

HOLDING HANDS, MARINA AND ROBERTO STROLLED BAREFOOT ON the cool sand of Pebble Beach. It was the waning hours of their last day together. A gentle breeze wafted through her golden hair as they stopped to take in the sunset. A few minutes passed in silence. She looked at him expectantly. He kissed her. Then he held her close as they watched the sun melt into the ocean.

The rest of the girls were in various stages of packing for their return trip home. They had agreed to leave early so that Marina and Roberto could have some time alone together. It had been a delightful and fun-filled trip. Roberto had joined the group two days ago. The other girls were less than thrilled to have him around, but they knew Marina's situation—that her father didn't approve of him. So they did what teenagers do: they covered for her.

By 7:00 PM, Marina and Roberto had the place to themselves. In search of one last memory before separating for the summer, they stood on the beach, alone in a warm embrace, and watched the sunset.

26

Mira Cordoba, Colonel Nash's secretary, stuck her head in his office. "Commander Rafael is here to see you."

"Send him in. And get him some black coffee."

A minute later, Commander Evrom Rafael entered the spacious office. "Good morning, old man." In a tailored, black pinstripe suit, completely out of season in June, over a bright green shirt and matching Oakley sunglasses, he could have passed for a movie star.

Never surprised by Rafael's choice of attire, Nash said, "Come in, Evrom. Take a load off."

Commander Rafael took out a cigar from the Russian box on Nash's desk and drew it under his nose. "I thought Cuban smokes were banned in America." He slumped in the chair in front of the Director's desk. "Are you a lawbreaker, Colonel?"

"Look at the label, fool. They're Dominicans."

Mira walked in carrying a black mug emblazoned with the eagle-and-compass seal of the CIA. She placed the coffee on the small table next to Commander Rafael. With a seductive smile she said, "Just the way you like it, Commander—black and hot."

Evrom was quite fond of Mira, who teased him mercilessly but didn't return his affections. CIA rules did not permit employees to fraternize with foreign operatives. As she turned to leave, Evrom stared at the graceful shifting of her hips. Her toned and shapely figure filled out the beige pants and red blouse perfectly, revealing the contours of her undergarments. Evrom sighed. Once they were alone, he winked at Nash. "I like Cubans," he said, smelling the cigar again.

"Are you through? Can we get to work?"

"Okay, okay."

Evrom retrieved a handful of three by five cards from his jacket pocket. "Here are the four cover-words we've cracked so far." He tossed the first card on Nash's desk. "'Dark Prince' is Saudi Arabia's code for their Defense Minister, Sultan Mohammed. He's taking you guys for a ride, you know."

With a grin, Nash said, "So, the Dark Prince is Sultan Mohammed... the lying son of a bitch."

Evrom took a sip of coffee and tossed the second card on Nash's desk. "'Chinese Tango' is how the French refer to their upcoming trade talks with America."

"We shouldn't trade shit with the bastards," Nash said under his breath.

"They've got great wine."

"And, don't forget the prostitutes," Nash said.

"They're all whores if you ask me. Anti-Semite whores."

"All right, Evrom. Do I have to listen to your commentary?"

"The commentary is the price of the Mossad's cooperation, Colonel." He laughed. "It's mandatory."

"Come on. What else have you got?"

Out flew the third card. "The Egyptians use 'Pharaoh' to refer to your President."

"No shit!"

"And finally..." Commander Rafael rose and gently placed the fourth card, upside-down, before Nash. "I saved the best for last."

Nash reached for the card, but Evrom stopped him by placing his hand on top of his. "Do you know what the Iranian's codename for your boy, Dr. Shaheen, is?"

Nash shook his head.

Evrom removed his hand and as Nash turned the card, he said, "Jadoogar." Rafael chuckled. "It means *the Wizard!*"

Colonel Nash froze. He picked up the card and stared at it. After a lengthy pause, he said, "That he is."

He began to think.

Ross' story of his encounter with Kazem on the pier, the photos of his children, the ominous electronic intercepts about operation

FOXHUNT, Ross' whereabouts at that moment, General Pugachov's recent phone call warning Nash about the safety of his daughter and grandchildren—they flooded Colonel Nash's mind. He was clearly shaken—a rare occurrence for the ice-cold spymaster.

Commander Rafael sensed Nash's alarm but said nothing. He returned to his chair and continued to nurse his coffee.

Colonel Nash decided against letting his Mossad colleague in on the FOXHUNT secret. It wouldn't serve Ross' interest. If Commander Rafael discovered that the Iranians were squeezing Ross, he might panic and order Ross' execution. Just like that. The Colonel had to get rid of his guest as fast as he could.

Evrom held up the empty coffee mug. "Can I have a refill? Besides, I don't mind looking at your Cuban eye candy once again."

"I have to take a rain check, Evrom. And I really appreciate this info."

"Is that it? Love'm and leave'm?"

"Sorry, my friend," Nash stood. "I'm late for an ops meeting."

Taking the hint, Evrom said, "Goodbye, Colonel," with a firm handshake. Just before leaving, he opened the Russian box, retrieved one more cigar, and placed both of them in his coat pocket. "Thanks for the Cubans."

"They're Dominicans."

"Dominicans, my ass," Evrom said, as he approached the door. "You think I don't know you switch the labels?"

As soon as Evrom Rafael left, Nash stepped inside the secure vault in the corner of his office. A few minutes later, he emerged with the TOP SECRET/VLA file, which contained the FOXHUNT intercept.

He brought the file back to his desk and opened it. Suddenly, everything made sense. *Jadoogar*, being the cover word for Dr. Shaheen, was the Rosetta stone for cracking the coded message. He pressed a button on his phone without taking his eyes away from the file and barked at Mira, "Get Mitch. Now!"

Waiting for Mitch Cohen, Director of CIA's Counter Terrorism Center, Nash crossed out *Jadoogar* in the coded message and replaced it with Dr. Shaheen. Then he blackened the words "hospital," and "patient," and wrote "prison," and "hostages," instead. The dots successfully connected, the message now read:

> Dr. Shaheen *APPROACHING NEST STOP MAY NOT BE HELPFUL STOP PREPARE* Prison *FOR* Hostages *STOP STANDBY FOR FOXHUNT END*

"What is it, Colonel?" Mitch hurried into the room and stood next to Nash's desk.

"Here's a little assistance from Commander Rafael. He has cracked four of our riddles. The first three are inconsequential. The last is scary as hell."

"What is it?"

"Jadoogar…is Dr. Ross Shaheen."

"The physicist?"

"Yes," Nash said ominously. "Here, look at this intercept. It's crystal clear."

"They're going to kidnap him?"

"Not him. Someone in his family."

"How do you figure?"

"Because he's already there, genius!"

"Where?"

"Iran."

"Iran? How the hell did that happen?"

"Never mind."

"You don't understand, Colonel. We have a fresh intercept form MOIS." Mitch placed another manila folder, marked TOP SECRET/ VLA with a diagonal red line across the cover, on the desk.

"They've green-lighted FOXHUNT. And if the target is a member of his family, we need to alert them. And the FBI."

"Let me see this." Nash opened the folder and stared at the paper pasted inside. His eyes moved from left to right, scanning the short sentence. "GO FOXHUNT REPEAT FOXHUNT IS GO END."

It was unmistakable.

"When did this arrive?" he asked.

"A few hours ago. CRITIC, from the NSA."

"That'll be all, Mitch. I'll handle this myself."

"I'll inform the CTC to coordinate with the FBI."

In no uncertain tone, Nash said, "You will do no such thing, Mr. Cohen."

"But—"

"This is now a National Security matter. I'll ask the DCI to include it in the Presidential Daily Brief tomorrow. You see, Dr. Shaheen's wife is General Pugachov's daughter."

"You mean, P-Pugachov at the Kremlin?"

Colonel Nash nodded tensely.

"I'll be damned."

"We need to stop this from becoming an international incident. Pugachov will not mobilize the Red Army, but knowing him, he'll come awfully close."

"Should we alert Dr. Shaheen in Iran? Can we reach him?"

"Negative and no."

"What do you want me to do?"

"Open a separate compartment on FOXHUNT and keep the information contained. I want to be personally notified of any new intercepts."

"Understood, Colonel," Mitch said, as he headed for the door.

"And no leaks, Mitch. Period!"

Nash looked closely at the secret messages before him. The implications were ominous. The only conclusion he could draw was that Ross had resisted his Iranian hosts and had not divulged anything. The million-dollar money transfer must not have worked. Nor had their attempts to pump him for information in Karaj. And, now he had disappeared and they were after his family. Ross had refused the carrot, forcing the Iranians to reach for the stick.

Nash lit up a cigar, pressed the VOICE-DIAL button on his telephone set, and said, "Roy Sullivan."

27

Holding a half-empty bottle of Russian vodka by the neck, Sergey joined Ross in Amir's office, in the belly of the cavernous underground facility at Natanz. They were casually served a simple dinner of saffron rice and chicken kebob on the coffee table. With little appetite, Ross mostly picked at his food, his mind busy with all he had witnessed, how critically important the intelligence was, and how he might escape. *It's virtually impossible*, he thought.

Earlier, Amir and Kazem had returned to Karaj, leaving the two physicists behind. Sergey spoke mainly in Russian but would occasionally switch to English for effect. He reminisced about his life as a nuclear scientist in the Soviet Union—a "respectable and important career." Of how irrelevant his Chechen or Muslim heritage had been during the Communist era and how singularly significant it suddenly became afterward. Passionately, he described the struggle for Chechen independence and how the *Jihad* against the "Russian infidels" would never stop unless and until mother Russia would relent and let go of his homeland.

"Then why aren't you in Grozny, fighting?"

"After the breakup of the USSR, I lost my job." Sergey took a swallow from the tall glass of vodka in front of him. "I was a relic of the Cold War—obsolete. So, we packed up what little we had and moved to Grozny."

"We?"

"I had a family…wife and a son." Sergey said, with pain in his face. Then he dropped his head and became quiet. After a brief pause, he looked up, raised his bushy eyebrows, and continued. "Anyway, I took a job teaching physics in high school making 1,500 Rubles a month—that's about fifty dollars."

"I know."

"Grozny was a mess—a bloodbath. The freedom fighters attacked the Russians relentlessly, and they retaliated indiscriminately. One day, a stray missile leveled my house." He took another gulp of vodka. "And killed my wife and son…it was 1994, the worst winter of my life."

Ross shook his head. "Wars are horrible."

"I lost everything to the mistake of an operator—probably a kid, who punched the wrong coordinates into a computer somewhere."

There was another pause, this one longer, and Sergey broke it with a fake laugh. Holding the glass up, he said, "That's when vodka became my best friend."

Ross didn't want to be rude, but he was only half-listening to Sergey's story. His mind was elsewhere. *Maybe Sergey knows of another way out of this hole,* he thought. *But how can I make him tell me? Perhaps more vodka would do the trick.*

Ross topped off Sergey's glass. "What happened next?"

"The accident pushed me over the edge. I was angry. Hopeless. The only sensible thing to do was to join the freedom fighters. Bin Laden was spending millions supporting our cause. The Iranians supplied the weapons, while the Chechens eagerly produced the fighters." Sergey took a large swallow. "It was a killing field, and I was in the middle of it with a death wish." Squinting, he said in his raspy voice, "I must have personally dispatched at least a hundred of the bastards to hell."

"Do you feel that you've avenged the death of your wife, and your son?"

"No," Sergey said. "Not in the least."

Ross didn't respond, wondering, *What would motivate a man like him to work for the Iranian nuclear program?*

"Then, one day, Kazem showed up and offered me this job making a hundred times more money than I did before."

"So, is that why you're here? The money?"

"Partly, yes. But there's more to it. At the time, the Russians were on my trail and getting close. I had to leave Grozny or face death." The vodka was taking its toll on Sergey. He slurred, "I figured, I would take this job, live a while longer, and fight another day." Then he chuckled.

"Maybe I'll return to the battlefield with a big bomb." With his hands, he gestured an explosion, "Who knows?"

Stunned by the snide remark, Ross said, "Do you mean what I think you mean?"

Flashing a mischievous smile, Sergey shrugged and avoided answering. *Amazing*, Ross thought. The Iranian nuclear program was even more dangerous than he had previously imagined. It seemed that America and Israel were not the only potential targets; Russia was also in peril. Was Sergey promised a nuclear bomb in exchange for his services? Or, was he planning to steal one? Probably the former. Swiping a toothpick from this underground fortress would be a difficult job, let alone a refrigerator-size nuke. Were Iranians that reckless? Didn't they know that if one of their nukes exploded in Russia, the Red Army would level their country?

Ross shook his head in disbelief, thinking, *Nuts with nukes!*

"What about you, Dr. Shaheen?" Sergey said, in between hiccups. "Why are you here?"

Ross did not tell all, just as he was certain neither had Sergey. But he did speak of his tour in Moscow, and how he had met Oksana. Sergey listened intently, even though he seemed to be generally familiar with Ross' biography. Except that when Ross mentioned Oksana's father, Sergey froze as if he had seen a ghost. Nervously, he said, "You mean, General Viktor Pugachov is your father-in-law?"

With a blank stare, Ross nodded, thinking, *How could Sergey not have known this?*

Sergey put the half-full glass of vodka down. "No disrespect to you or your wife, Dr. Shaheen," he continued, struggling to concentrate. "But Pugachov is a pig and a butcher."

"No offense taken, Sergey. The General and I have an understanding. I don't ask about his work, and he doesn't tell. In fact, my relationship with him is an open secret. Everyone in government and most people in the academic circles know about it but, strangely, no one ever brings it up."

"It must be more than an 'open secret,' because I didn't know about it."

"Does that change anything?"

"No. It shouldn't." Sergey lit up a cigarette. "But you need to know that I hate your father-in-law." He offered one to Ross, which he refused.

"And hold him personally responsible for the death of my wife and son." He took a long drag. "Him, not you."

"If he's guilty, you have every right."

After a brief silence, Sergey changed the subject. "What do you think of the bomb?"

"It's a huge waste of money, and a runway to disaster."

"We both know it will go super-critical, Dr. Shaheen. But Amir wants proof positive that it will explode. Will you please confirm this?"

"No, Sergey. I've already made my position very clear to him. I can't take any part in this project."

"Dr. Shaheen, I tell you as a colleague, you must treat your situation seriously." Sergey leaned over and, staring into Ross' eyes, added in a low voice, "Amir is a dangerous and ruthless man. He has killed many people, and he won't hesitate adding your name to that list." He leaned back and put the cigarette to his lips. "You must cooperate."

"I prefer *my* death to that of millions."

"Yet by refusing, you're not stopping Amir. He will continue and get what he wants by other means."

"I don't doubt that. However, I will not make it any easier for him."

Frustrated, Sergey said tersely, "You're at once brilliant and stupid. Alive, you're a father, a husband, a scientist, and can make a difference. Dead, you'll be nothing. Worthless."

"That's a risk I'm willing to take."

Sergey stood. A bit woozy, he touched the wall for balance. "It's late, and we better turn in." He pointed to Amir's desk. "In case you decide to examine the schematics of our device, they're in that computer." He opened the door. "Just click on the icons."

Ross rested on a narrow bed, fully clothed except for his jacket and shoes, and stared at the ceiling. Unable to sleep, he had surveyed the small chamber for hours. The only ornaments on the walls were a framed map of Iran and a round clock. He felt it was ticking too slowly. Nearby stood a small shelf filled with physics books. Ross found it bizarre that a copy of every title he had authored was neatly arranged on the top shelf—all nine of them.

Unable to quiet his mind wondering how he could escape, he longed for the soothing sounds of opera. It was past 3:00 AM, and he felt exhausted. His body craved sleep, but his brain, tormented by the idea of the underground fortress becoming his mausoleum, repeatedly vetoed the request. He hadn't phoned Oksana that night and was concerned that she might be worrying about him. Eventually, he passed out from fatigue.

Four hours later, a gentle knock on the door awakened him. With a startled voice, he said, "Who is it?"

It was the butler. Placing a pot of tea on the desk, he said, *"Sobh-be-kheyr, Doktor Shaheen."*

Unable to see the man from the adjoining bedroom, Ross entered the office area yawning. "Good morning to you, too," he said.

"Here's some tea and cookies. I can make you eggs if you wish."

Ross slumped into Amir's chair and said, "That won't be necessary. This is fine."

The butler left, closing the door behind him. Ross looked at the blank screen, paused, and reluctantly moved the mouse. The monitor came to life, revealing a busy desktop. He poured tea from the *ghoori*—a small porcelain teapot—into a glass cup, clad in a silver holder. It looked similar to Russian *stakans,* which at once reminded him of Oksana.

He was worried about her. How would she manage without him? He had a million-dollar life insurance policy. That, plus the million-dollar payment already in their account, should be enough. *Would she remain in America or take the children back to Russia?* Ross felt increasingly disheartened. After a few moments of feeling sorry for himself, he shook off the downward spiral of emotions and regained his resolve. He took a sip of tea from the *stakan* and returned to the computer screen.

There were several folders of schematics, neatly organized into groups; their icons were labeled with letters of the alphabet. He clicked on SCHEMATICS-A and began to explore. The folder contained dozens of files with DXF or DWG extensions, which told Ross that AutoCAD—the powerful design software, popular among engineers of any stripe—had been used to create them. He double-clicked on the first file. One glance and he recognized the design—it was the trigger mechanism for the nuclear device. They were using Krytrons, small vacuum tubes found in ordinary copying machines, as electronic activators. Clever. He shook his head and moved to the next file.

He caught himself thinking that since the Blind Scorpion readily accepted AutoCAD files as input, his task would be simple if he ever decided to comply with Amir's wishes. Fighting back the impulse, he chastised himself for even allowing the thought.

All of a sudden, it dawned on him that the PC might be rigged with key-logging software, which would later inform Amir what he had been up to. With a few mouse clicks, he discovered his hunch to be true. Key-logging software was running stealthily on the computer. Thinking of Amir, he muttered, "You moron," and disabled the electronic spy. At one point, he tried to send e-mail, but Amir's computer was not connected to the Internet—Ross was not surprised.

The hot, bitter tea tasted sweet as it flowed over the sugar cube clenched between Ross' teeth. He continued to rummage through the rest of the drawings. There they were: the fruits of nearly thirty years of clandestine research by the best engineers Iran had produced, in search of the Holy Grail of nuclear weapons. *What a colossal waste of talent*, he thought.

In other folders, he discovered blueprints for the gas centrifuges. They looked strikingly similar to the Pakistani designs. *Oh man*, he thought, *wouldn't Nash love to see these?* There were also layouts of the underground plant. He committed as much to memory as was humanly possible.

Poking around further, he found the drawings for the secret underground bunkers. Indeed, there were only two levels, as he had witnessed during the VIP tour. Examining the designs, he took special notice of the freight elevators as well as the ventilation shafts. *Could I escape through one of these?* he wondered.

He refilled the *stakan*, placed another sugar cube in his mouth, and clicked SCHEMATICS-G.

28

SPECIAL AGENT ROY SULLIVAN HAD SET HIS CELL PHONE TO VIBRATE. As it went off, at the crack of dawn, it began to dance on top of the nightstand, sounding as if there were a giant wasp in the bedroom. Quickly reaching for it so as not to wake Alice, he muttered, "Roy Sullivan."

"This is Nash…did I wake you?"

Roy sat on the edge of the bed and whispered, "What's up, Colonel?"

Alice peeked from under the sheets and growled, "Who is it, Roy?"

"No one, honey. It's just business, go back to sleep." Speaking into the cell, he whispered, "Hang on. Let me go downstairs."

Standing in the middle of the kitchen, he said, "Now, what can I do for you, Colonel?"

"Can't say in the clear. Do you have access to a secure phone?"

"Yes. I've got an STU-3 here at home, but it's fibered to FBI-NET."

"CTC has a bridge into FBI-NET—courtesy of the Patriot Act," Nash said. "What's your extension?"

"Seventy-nine, forty-eight."

"Good. Standby, I'll call you in a few."

Craving caffeine, Roy popped open a can of Coke, entered his small study, and sat on the edge of his desk—waiting. *This better be good,* he thought.

Director Nash pressed VOICE-DIAL on his phone set and rattled, "Bridge to FBI-NET—dial, STU seven, nine, four, eight."

"Connecting," the VOICE-DIAL announced in a mechanical tone.

꧁

ROY STARED AT THE GRAY STU-3 ON HIS DESK. THE SECURE TELEPHONE Unit—affectionately called "Stew three"—was a special communication device widely used in the intelligence community. Likewise, the upper echelons of government used it for discussing classified information. To operate, one uses the STU-3, in non-secure mode, to place a call to another person who also has the device. After the connection is made, one party tells the other, "Go secure." Each side then inserts a Crypto-Ignition Key (CIK) into the phone terminal and presses the SECURE button. When the secure connection is activated, which usually takes about 15 seconds, the display screen on both units shows the highest classification level at which discussion is authorized. Eavesdroppers listening to STU-3 secure signals only hear noise, which cannot be decrypted even with giant supercomputers. To further enhance security, many government agencies operate private networks—such as FBI-NET, or Pentagon's MIL-NET—for their secret communications, which are isolated from the public phone systems.

Roy finished his Coke. He wanted another but was reluctant to walk away from the phone. After a couple minutes, it rang.

"I'm here, Colonel."

"Go secure."

Roy inserted the red CIK into the phone set and pressed the oval button labeled SECURE. The display showed his clearance: TOP SECRET, which was several notches beneath that of Colonel Nash; his was the highest possible. In fact, the codename for Colonel Nash's security level—PEARL—in and of itself was classified.

Roy confirmed, "Done."

After a short silence, without any attempt at disguising his disappointment, Nash said, "I see your clearance is only TOP SECRET, but what I want to discuss is CODEWORD classified—NSA material."

"Christ!"

"What the hell," Nash said. "I'm going to break the rules and pretend you've got the clearance—if you think you can handle it."

"I can handle it."

"All right then." Nash paused to take a deep breath and choose his words carefully. "I'm afraid I've got bad news, Sullivan."

Without hesitation, Roy said, "Lay it on me."

"Ross is trapped."

Roy's heart sank. "Trapped! Where?"

"If you hold your horses for a few, I'll tell you everything."

"Sorry, Colonel. Go ahead."

"Ross is in an underground bunker at Natanz. We've been tracking his movements, and that's where we lost him. He hasn't surfaced since."

"How long ago?"

"Almost forty-eight hours."

"Got a theory?"

"I'm piecing one together. My assumption is that they want something from him—maybe some technical assistance, or secret know-how. And we have reason to believe he's not cooperating."

"I could've told you that, Colonel. He won't give'm shit."

"Now, here comes the worse news."

"It gets worse?"

"Afraid so."

"I'm listening."

"We have signal intelligence that MOIS has ordered a body snatch of one or more of Ross' family members."

Roy froze. After a few seconds he whispered, "I'll be damned," while glancing at a framed picture of him shooting hoops with Victor Shaheen. "Are you sure, Colonel?"

"This is not speculation, Sullivan. I'm looking at the plaintext right in front of me."

"Last we spoke, I upped their security detail. There's a pair of agents shadowing Oksana and her son, Victor—24/7. Her daughter, Marina, is at the beach, and I've got a couple of my guys watching her as well."

"Good. But not good enough."

"What more do you suggest, Colonel?"

"First, put an end to this nonsense at the beach. She's out there in the open and under the circumstances, that's foolish. Bring her in."

"Done. What else?"

"Second, let Oksana know what's going on. Tell her to stay indoors for a while. Then post a dozen agents around the house. Nothing goes in or out, not even a cockroach."

"I can't do that, Colonel."

"Why the hell not?"

"I've got no authority to do so."

"You have no authority?" Annoyed, he shouted, "*I am* your authority, Agent Sullivan."

"No disrespect, Director Nash. But when I call the Bureau to request a dozen agents for security detail, the Chief will ask all kinds of questions: What's the Op? Who's the VIP? Who'll pay the overtime? Who authorized this? You know the drill, Colonel. Bureaucracy ain't pretty, nor is it fast."

"Ah…it can be hurried along. Before sundown, today, there will be an Executive Order from the Attorney General on your Chief's desk, giving you free run of the place."

Impressed with the pointed reminder of Nash's power, Roy said, "Will the Chief be briefed?"

"No. This is a national security matter now, TOP SECRET with Very Limited Access. The DCI is set to brief the President and the National Security Advisor tomorrow at 0700."

"The President?"

"Yes! We're faced with the disappearance of a top American scientist somewhere in Iran, and a plot by MOIS to kidnap the daughter and grandchildren of the Russian National Security Advisor on American soil. If that doesn't concern the President, I don't know what will."

"I understand, Colonel."

"And my worst nightmare is to see this mess on CNN. You catch my drift?"

"Yes, sir."

"We've got to play this close to the chest, until it blows over."

"Except, Oksana should know…I mean about the plot, right?"

"Yes. And for her own good, she should cooperate, play ball, and keep quiet."

"She has family visiting. What should we do about that?"

"What family?"

"Her cousin, Natasha. We hung out with them last night."

"Oksana has no cousins," Nash said. "General Pugachov's only family is Oksana. There are no brothers, no sisters, no nieces, and no nephews—only her, the kids, and his pigeons."

"Pigeons?"

"Never mind the damned pigeons. Natasha is no cousin of Oksana—guaranteed."

"Then who is she?" Roy wondered. "Why would Oksana lie to us?"

"She's probably an undercover agent—FSB or GRU, sent by Pugachov to look after his daughter."

"Okay Colonel, I'll take it from here."

"Before I let you go, what's the latest on the suspects across the street?"

"Nothing. We came up dry, and had to end the surveillance yesterday morning."

"I don't buy it, Sullivan. It's too strange a coincidence that a bunch of Iranian men land across the street from Ross exactly when all this shit hits the fan. It can't be."

"I agree, Colonel. It's very strange." Roy closed his eyes, rubbed his temples as if he had a migraine headache, and added, "Incidentally, yesterday, as we were loading our van, I noticed the three of them were packing their SUV. Looked like they were going on a road trip—with duffle bags and coolers."

After a brief pause, Colonel Nash said, "Sullivan...why don't you get over there and have a look for yourself?"

"I'm on it, Colonel."

"Let me know something good. And, Sullivan, watch your six."

"Will do."

ROY SAT THERE, IN WHITE BOXERS AND A SLEEVELESS SWEATSHIRT, gathering his thoughts and calmly planning his next move. The first light pouring through the shutters highlighted his broad, muscular shoulders. His best friend, Ross Shaheen, had disappeared in hostile territory—maybe kidnapped, maybe killed. The prospect that he might be lost forever was difficult to contemplate. Horrified, Roy even blamed himself. *Maybe I could've tried harder to dissuade him from going to Iran.*

Then he felt angry. "Goddamn it, Ross!" he muttered with agony. "Why did you have to do this, man?"

It took a while before Roy sorted out his emotions. Masking his anguish with bravado, he recalled the FBI's motto: "Fidelity, Bravery, Integrity" and thought, *I might not be able to help Ross at the moment, but I'll be damned if I let anything happen to his family.*

He got up.

It was time for action. He hastily put on his jogging pants, which were thrown on the couch. Then he pulled the top desk drawer open, revealing the FBI-issued Glock-22 and his personal weapon, a .357 Magnum.

Roy had grown to favor the Glock. He strapped on his shoulder holster, shoved a 15 round magazine into the gun, and placed two spare cartridges in his pocket—enough to kill half the neighborhood. He holstered the weapon and concealed it by pulling up the zipper of his blue windbreaker, the one with the giant FBI letters on the back. Unable to find any socks, he put his running shoes onto his bare feet.

He grabbed another Coke and chugged it while passing through the kitchen. Then he walked onto the porch, down the steps, and sprinted away.

Gordon Street was quiet. Roy made his way across the road and nonchalantly jogged in place in front of the Miller's house. He looked around to ensure no one was watching. Then he ran up the driveway, turned behind the house, and seconds later was standing on the back porch, looking into the den.

Aside from the unkempt appearance, there was nothing suspicious inside. He tried the French door, but it was locked, as were the windows. Then he checked the window directly above the kitchen sink. Bingo. He opened it with some hesitation. Entering the house without a search warrant could cost him his job. He thought about it and muttered, "What the hell," and climbed inside. Somehow, Colonel Nash's words, "*I am* your authority," felt reassuring.

The sink reeked from a few days worth of dirty dishes. As Roy crawled over it, his grip on the edge of the sink gave way, plunging his left hand into the smelly dishwater.

"Shit!"

Disgusted, he quickly recovered his balance. With a swift move, he heaved over the sink and landed on all fours inside the kitchen. He stood, drew his gun, and looked in every direction. With a CLICK, he loaded the chamber, pointing its muzzle slightly up.

He wiped his wet hand on his pants and began searching the house methodically. The ground floor seemed clear. With the Glock leading the way, he slowly climbed the stairs. During his long career at the FBI, Agent Sullivan had swept unfriendly places hundreds of times and was coolly proficient at it. Yet the adrenaline rush would make his heartbeat pound in his eardrums every time he had to do it. He was so focused that he even blinked sparingly.

The master bedroom was empty. There was nothing suspicious in the walk-in closet or the spacious bathroom. Then he searched the first guest room—it, too, was clear. As he crept along the hallway wall, the silence was abruptly broken by a voice coming from the master bedroom. Roy turned instinctively, crouched, and aimed his weapon in that direction; he was itching to waste someone. Breathing heavily, he quickly realized that it was the clock radio, which pissed him off even more.

The third bedroom door was locked. *That's odd*, Roy thought. *What are they hiding?* He twisted the handle, trying to force it open, but it wouldn't budge. He took a few steps back and rammed his massive shoulder into the wood. No help. "Damn!" he said, holding his throbbing upper arm. After a minute, he recovered. This time he kicked the door as hard as he could; it flung wide open.

Clasping the Glock with both hands, Roy entered the room cautiously. It was dark. When he flipped the light switch, he was astounded by what he saw: spy gear everywhere. The six laser guns and matching receivers on tripods, and the copper-shielded cables snaking toward the closet, were obviously not toys. He approached the window and opened one of the shades; the devices were pointing out at Ross' house.

"I'll be goddamned," Roy said.

The cables invited him to follow. What he found inside the closet— the state of the art equipment, the bank of laptops, and the cocoon of copper wire mesh—only increased his alarm and anger.

He picked up the cordless phone off the floor, which like the walls, was covered with the reddish copper net. He rapidly dialed a number.

Seconds later, he said tersely, "Broom, get your ass out of bed and over here immediately. I mean pronto!"

"What's the matter, boss?"

"And call your crew to bring the van back."

Agent Konarski seemed confused. "Why?" he asked.

"Listen. I'm inside the target house and am looking at a truckload of black-op equipment that the bastards were using to spy on the Shaheens." His volume rising, Roy continued. "While your lanky ass was sitting behind a million dollars worth of the most sophisticated hardware in the world and couldn't catch the bastards."

"That's impossible, we used the TEMPEST—"

"Well, I've got news for you, Broom: the camel jocks snookered the TEMPEST."

"Are you putting me on?"

Now wound up, Roy screamed, "Are you still in bed, Agent Konarski, or already driving? Because I called your sorry ass three minutes ago, and as far as I'm concerned, you should be in your punk ass car by now. Are you? You better be, or else I'll—"

"Be over there in fifteen minutes."

"Now you're talking. I'll call for backup; we need to exploit this dump."

"Hey chief, do you have a search warrant?"

"Yeah," Roy said sarcastically. "I've got your search warrant right here, asshole."

29

THE FOURTH MOIS TACTICAL TEAM, DEDICATED TO COVERT operations on the western seaboard of the United States, had been activated the previous day. All that was necessary was the GO order from Tehran, which had been issued.

Operation FOXHUNT was underway.

The first elements of the team to receive the order were Jaffar and Emad. Vegetating in another cheap motel somewhere near Fisherman's Wharf, they were bored and nervously waiting. The pair had spent countless hours watching old movies, chain-smoking two packs of filter-less Camels each day, and wolfing down fast food for breakfast, lunch, and dinner.

When the short, encrypted GO order arrived, they were as giddy as teenagers on prom night. Emad rubbed his hands together over the prospects of the impending action while Jaffar, the senior operative, savored the idea of returning home to his wife and children afterwards.

Upon receiving the order, Jaffar knew exactly what to do. From a nearby payphone, he dialed Mustafa's one-way numeric pager, which he had obtained under an assumed name. The two had devised a clever method for arranging meetings: Jaffar would page Mustafa with a fictitious callback number. Only the last two digits were meaningful; they referred to the pier where they would meet that evening—always at midnight.

At the tone, Jaffar entered 3124125541 and quickly hung up. Obsessed by the fear of being caught, he nervously looked around and started walking in the opposite direction of his motel. After a lengthy stroll, he returned to his room, where Emad had fallen asleep. There were eight long hours before midnight.

Jaffar was restless. He couldn't stand the wait or the company much longer. He looked at Emad, snoring, with disdain. Emad was an uneducated brute, devoid of the sophistication or social skills, which are necessary for acceptance in Iranian elite circles. The two had little in common and even less to talk about. Yet they had to spend weeks at a time together on assignments.

Jaffar had joined the Iranian intelligence service immediately after the Islamic Revolution of 1979. Fresh out of Tehran University, with a degree in political science, he had been more of a full-time protester than a student. *"Marg bar Shah—Death to Shah—Marg bar Emrika—Death to America"* had been his battle cry throughout the last two years of school. Frequent strikes had prevented him from completing the requirements for the Bachelor of Arts degree. Therefore, he was quite surprised when the university graduated him on time. He wondered if they just wanted to be rid of him.

With the victory of the Islamic Revolution, for the first time ever the people of Iran went to the polls in April 1979 and voted in favor of the establishment of the Islamic Republic. This was an unprecedented event in world history, with incalculable consequences—the clergy ruling a powerful state.

Jaffar was elated to cast his ballot in favor of the Islamic Republic along with 98 percent of his fellow countrymen. Little did he know at the time that, to Muslim clerics, democracy meant one man, one vote—once! It didn't take long before things changed, and mass euphoria gave way to universal despair as democracy turned into totalitarian theocracy.

Once established, as one of its first acts, the government disbanded SAVAK, the notorious and widely despised security apparatus of the former Shah. Formed in 1957, under the guidance of American and Israeli intelligence officers, SAVAK developed into an effective and ruthless secret agency. Over the years, SAVAK became a law unto itself, having legal authority to arrest and detain suspected persons indefinitely. It even operated its own prisons in Tehran, where its torture methods resembled those practiced by the SS during the Nazi reign. Consequently, it was no surprise that the hated SAVAK was singled out as the primary target for reprisals by the leaders of the new regime. Its headquarters were overrun, and its prominent leaders were tried and summarily executed.

SAVAK was finished.

Except totalitarian regimes cannot survive without secret services to keep them in power and keep any dissenters in check. Almost immediately, a new covert organization rose from the ashes of SAVAK. The new agency was at first known by its Persian acronym SAVAMA and charged with practically the same mission: to keep tabs on and eliminate domestic opposition. Later, in 1985, it was reorganized and renamed, Ministry of Information and Security—MOIS.

Without delay, MOIS assumed a much broader role. Following in the footsteps of SAVAK, it expanded its functions to include international spy operations, targeted killings of dissidents overseas, and support of the terrorist organizations that fought against Iran's perceived enemies: Israel and America.

To achieve its new expanded goals, former agents were recalled to bring back their specialized knowledge, while new recruits swelled the ranks of MOIS. SAVAK's global intelligence-gathering network was simply rolled over to MOIS. And as it grew larger and gained power, the shroud of secrecy surrounding it became more opaque.

Looking out of the window at the slow moving traffic, Jaffar remembered the day he signed up as if it had been yesterday. The Iran-Iraq war was raging, and he felt working for SAVAMA a patriotic duty. After basic spy training, he completed several missions inside Iraq and then was dispatched to London to work with the Iraqi dissidents. It was an easy assignment, which included clandestine meetings with the anti-Saddam activists, paying them off, and writing discussion memos for his station chief. To his amazement, some of the same characters were now running Iraq. He loved his job in those years, and serving the Islamic Republic filled him with pride.

Then one dreadful day, an order arrived—a TOP SECRET order—for his eyes only, directing him to eliminate a certain Iranian dissident. He had never killed before; but he did it anyway, in cold blood. He didn't know he could be so callous. Somehow, the assignment, and his successful completion of it, had introduced him to his true self, and he was not happy with what he saw. That was the first in a series of such missions over the next ten years. Soon he became known as the most proficient MOIS assassin in Europe.

In 1995, he put in for transfer to Canada. Once there, he sought a field assignment and subsequently joined the fourth tactical team. Five years later, he sneaked into America and had since been living a nomad's life up and down the west coast doing MOIS' bidding.

By now, after a quarter century of living in the shadows, Jaffar was sick and tired of it all.

Midnight could not have come soon enough. Thirty minutes after eleven, Jaffar and Emad set out to meet Mustafa.

Pier 41 was located on San Francisco's historic waterfront, immediately adjacent to Pier 39, the city's most popular attraction. It was only a few blocks away, and Jaffar decided to walk the distance. Even though the thinning tourist crowd was unlikely to notice them, they strolled nonchalantly through the Wharf so as not to attract unwanted attention. With cigarettes dangling from their lips, they both had their hands buried in the pockets of their dark windbreakers. In order to ensure they were not being followed, they would occasionally stop and pretend to be window-shopping.

The two arrived at the meeting place on time. As usual, the pier was empty at that hour; and unseasonably, a thick fog had set in. The wooden planks screeched as Jaffar and Emad approached. Jaffar noticed the silhouette of a man leaning against the handrails, away from the lamppost. Wearing a corduroy jacket and a French *chapeau*, he faced the darkness of the Bay while holding a cigarette peculiarly in between his left thumb and index finger.

It was Mustafa—the grand wizard of the MOIS fourth tactical team. Jaffar and Emad repeated the all too familiar routine: Emad stood watch a dozen steps away, while Jaffar moved toward Mustafa, stood an arm's length away, and lit up.

Smoke billowed from Jaffar's nostrils as it did from the corner of Mustafa's lips. The two stood there silently staring into the gloom of night. After a few minutes, Jaffar took one last drag from the Camel and flicked the cigarette butt overboard. Without turning to face Mustafa, he said, "I got the word."

"So did I."

"Nervous?"

"Yes."

"What's next?"

Mustafa edged closer. "The guys will do the snatch tomorrow. The hostage will be handed over to you on the beach at Half Moon Bay."

"There are three beaches in Half Moon Bay. Which one?"

"Venice Beach, at the end of Venice Boulevard."

"I know the place. But it's very crowded. How can we make the hand off?"

"It'll happen when the beach is closed. You'll drive there at midnight and look for a green California Fish and Wildlife van. It'll be unlocked. You'll find the keys and your instructions in the glove compartment."

"How many hostages will there be?"

"We hoped for two, but looks like it'll be only one."

"What then?"

"Drive north to the safe house. Stay low, and wait for further instructions."

"From you?"

"No. You'll hear directly from Tehran."

Jaffar lit up another cigarette. The operation seemed simple enough. Except, somehow, he felt uneasy. Something didn't feel right, but he didn't know why. After a short pause, he swallowed hard and said, "Mustafa…After this operation, I'm through."

"Through what?'

"I'm done. I'm tired of this life."

"You're burned out. I'll see to it that you're sent home after this. Maybe an office job for a while, perhaps as an analyst."

"No. I want out of the outfit. Totally out."

"Who do you think you are? A cashier at Seven-Eleven who can simply quit?"

"It's a job. Why not?"

"Because you know too much. This is a profession you choose for life. Like the song goes, 'You can check out any time you like, but you can never leave.'"

Jaffar didn't pursue the matter. He knew that he would leave MOIS regardless of the consequences. But pressing Mustafa further could buy him a bullet in some dark alley. At the right time, he would simply slip away and disappear. "I guess you're right. I need a desk job for a while."

"That can be arranged."

30

Farzad, the Iranian-Canadian electronics engineer, together with his team members, Mehdi and Bijan, received the coded GO order much the same way, and at the same time, as their colleagues at Fisherman's Wharf.

The annoying sound of the radio receiver startled Farzad as he monitored the eavesdropping equipment from inside the closet. Once the gadget-man decoded the secret message, he felt a tense rush, thinking, *Finally, the real action is about to begin.* He closed his eyes and took a deep breath to calm his nerves, then emerged from the cocoon of the copper mesh to notify his comrades.

He barged into the master bedroom. Mehdi was busy under the sheets with his latest Latina catch.

"*Chera dar nemeezani, olagh?*" Mehdi screamed. "Why don't you knock, jackass?"

"We gotta leave."

"Damn! I'll be down in fifteen minutes."

"Hurry up!"

Farzad rushed downstairs where he found Bijan, disheveled, wearing red polka dot boxers and nothing else, standing at the kitchen counter making an egg sandwich. "It's a GO," he said, with controlled excitement, gesturing thumbs up.

"Thank you, God!" Bijan looked at the ceiling and then at Farzad. "I thought we'd die of boredom in this God forsaken house."

Farzad pressed his index finger against his lips. He whispered, "Watch what you say out loud."

Bijan nodded.

"It stinks around here."

"It's the dishes." Bijan pointed to the sink. "It's Mehdi's turn to wash; you know what a pig he is."

Farzad shook his head with disgust as he walked away.

Mustafa's plan was at last coming together. Nearly two months earlier, he had secured the Miller's residence as the base camp for the operation. He had selected it from among four others on Gordon Street with direct views of Dr. Shaheen's house. The location was perfect. The retired couple lived alone, away from their grown children who had recently moved to San Diego. Through an intermediary, Mustafa had offered the couple $10,000 per month to rent their house with all the furnishings. Cash. No questions asked. And three months' rent paid in advance. The Millers jumped at the opportunity to make some easy money and spend a few months with their children.

And the fix was in. Mustafa then ordered Farzad and elements of the fourth MOIS tactical team, stationed in Canada, to move in and carefully observe Dr. Shaheen and his family. Within a month, Farzad had discovered everything about them. He had meticulously studied their daily routines and identified their friends—complete with charts and diagrams. Where they shopped, what they ate, and what they did for entertainment was recorded. When Oksana spoke in Russian, Farzad would record the conversation and send it out for translation. It was he who had taken the photographs that Kazem used to persuade Dr. Shaheen to return to Iran.

Receiving the GO order was welcome news—a morale booster. Farzad and his team had been ready for weeks and were becoming increasingly restless. They had practiced countless scenarios to kidnap one or more of the Shaheens and had staked out many grab points.

It was early in the afternoon when the order came, and the sleepy street was filled with the usual joggers, bikers, and neighbors tending their gardens. The three operatives casually loaded the red cooler, suitcases, and the pre-packed duffle bag, crammed with weapons and ammunition, into the Toyota 4Runner and climbed aboard. Farzad took the wheel. He knew where to find his prey and began to mentally check off Mustafa's meticulous instructions.

The duffle bag was in the passenger seat. As he entered Gordon

Street, he looked at his teammates in the rearview mirror. Bijan and Mehdi seemed somber. A serious look had suddenly appeared on their faces, as if they had been transformed into fierce combatants. The frivolity of words and the playfulness had given way to a stern focus. Farzad knew how tough this assignment was and what dangers lay ahead. *Could they pull it off?* he wondered. *With some luck, perhaps.*

Destination: Half Moon Bay.

From Mill Valley, it was a 40-mile haul through rush hour traffic and over the Golden Gate Bridge. Around 4:00 PM, the southbound traffic was no better than a crawl. Inching ahead on Highway 101, it took almost an hour to reach San Francisco and pick up I-80. Farzad took care not to draw any attention. He drove patiently and to mask his anxiety, he listened to the radio while looking at the scenery.

At 5:40 PM, they passed Daily City, merging onto Coastal Highway 1 and heading south. The traffic was now moving faster, and Half Moon Bay was not too far away. Trying to break the silent tension, Farzad looked at Mehdi in the rearview mirror and said, *"Begoo bebeenam, chetor bood?*—Say, how was she?"

"Mind your own damn business, pretty boy."

Bijan chimed in with, "Yeah, don't be stingy with details."

"Will you guys knock it off? I am trying to concentrate."

"Are you nervous?" Farzad asked, with a smirk.

"Yes, I am," Mehdi said seriously. He turned his face to look outside.

"Why?" Farzad asked.

"We don't know this country all that well. These Americans are overfed cowboys. They get vicious if you mess with them."

"Nah," Bijan muttered. "They're nothing but a bunch of pussies."

"I wouldn't say that," Farzad cut in. "The MOIS manual says the FBI is formidable. 'Ruthless.' I sure wouldn't want to pick a fight with those guys."

"Let's hope we won't have to," Mehdi said. He leaned over and tapped the duffle bag. "But if we do, I'm coming out blazing."

"We won't have to if we execute the plan," Farzad said. "Let's go over it once more."

Two miles before reaching Half Moon Bay, Farzad turned right onto Princeton Avenue, which seemed to stretch out into the ocean. "We're here, boys," he said. "Act natural, like we belong here."

Up a shallow hill and then down, he stopped in front of a large metal warehouse situated on the water's edge. On cue, Bijan jumped out to slide the massive door open. As Farzad drove inside, Bijan looked around the quiet street and closed the door behind them.

It was dark. Farzad turned the 4Runner's headlights on and started to walk toward a small tool shed on the left corner. Shortly after he stepped inside, the warehouse was brightly illuminated by two parallel rows of florescent lights hanging from the ceiling.

Farzad knew his way around. He had been here before. He disappeared into a suite of dilapidated offices, situated to the right of the entrance. Mehdi and Bijan walked around exploring the place. It was their first time in the warehouse. There was an assortment of vehicles parked in no particular order on the far side. Some seemed new while others were covered under a thick layer of dust. Mehdi pointed to a green, windowless van with "California Fish and Wildlife" written on its sides. "Look. There's our ride."

Along the opposite wall, several boats rested on metal rigs, as if they were being repaired or painted. At the far end of the warehouse, a large speedboat was suspended a few feet above a pool of water facing the sea-gate. Mesmerized by the size and the sleek shape of the vessel, Mehdi and Bijan were drawn to the boat like moths to a flame. "Check this out," Bijan called out. "Have you ever seen anything this beautiful?"

Pacing alongside the length of the speedboat, Mehdi said, "With this, I could have any woman I want."

Bijan nodded his head in agreement. "No doubt."

Totally awestruck, Mehdi wondered aloud, "How fast do you think she can go?"

"Don't know. Maybe thirty-five, forty miles."

"That's a twenty-seven footer," Farzad said proudly, as he approached. "It's called 'Victory,' which, God willing, is what we're going to have."

Mehdi echoed, "*Inshallah*—God willing."

"What's her top speed?" Bijan inquired.

"It's been clocked at sixty-five miles per hour. Better yet, it gets up there in less than twenty seconds."

"Range?"

"It has two four-hundred horsepower engines. They're gas guzzlers. So, it can travel about two-hundred-fifty miles before running

out. We've added an extra fuel tank in case we need to go further."
Farzad continued as a salesman would. "There's also a spacious cabin
underneath—sleeps four."

Staring at the boat, Bijan marveled, "That Mustafa is a genius."

"Yeah," Farzad said, "a genius with a blank check."

From the other side of the craft, Mehdi said, "She's perfect—just
perfect."

Excited, Bijan said, "Let's take her out for a spin."

"Hell, no!" Farzad said. "Are you out of your mind? We'll do this
by the book. You two will take off in the boat at the crack of dawn, as
planned. So let's settle in for the night."

"Does the 'book' mention anything about dinner?" Bijan asked
sarcastically.

"After dark, I'm going to Half Moon Bay to switch cars and touch
base with Mustafa. I'll pick up something to eat."

Farzad started to walk back to the offices. "Now, let's get the gear
and go to work."

∾✐∾

SPECIAL AGENT ROY SULLIVAN WAITED UNTIL AFTER 8:00 AM BEFORE
walking across the street to see Oksana Shaheen.

Agent Konarski, the Broom, and a swarm of FBI counterintelligence
specialists were busy searching every square inch of the Miller's residence.
Konarski, the Bureau's electronic surveillance expert, was inside the
closet pouring over the treasure-trove of gadgets and records Farzad
had left behind. Roy had alerted the San Francisco Police Department
(SFPD) requesting that they stop the 4Runner on sight and arrest the
Iranian spies. Impatiently waiting for Konarski to emerge from the
closet with something they could act on, Roy thought it was time to
bring Oksana into the loop.

He dreaded the moment. Like most tough guys, he was not
comfortable with emotional situations, and he knew that Oksana's
reaction to the horrifying news would be volcanic. Yet he thought it
would be best if she heard it from him rather than someone else.

He hesitated a moment before ringing the bell, then waited until

Natasha opened the door. The loose silk robe over the skimpy nightgown and her uncombed hair betrayed that she had just woken up. Startled to see him, she quickly wrapped the robe around her and tied it with a belt; but Roy had already seen more than he cared to acknowledge.

"Is Oksana up?"

"Yes. We're having breakfast. Would you like to join us?"

Roy walked into the kitchen and found Oksana sitting on a stool at the counter with a tall stack of *blinis*—pancakes in front of her. Russians love their pancakes, and unlike Americans who mostly eat them for breakfast, they might serve them at any meal.

"What a pleasant surprise, Roy…Welcome." Pointing her fork to the plate before her, she said, "Want some pancakes?"

"No, sweetheart. I'm afraid this is not a social call."

Throughout the years, Oksana had never seen the serious side of Roy. The jovial neighbor, always ready with a story to tell, or a new prank to try on the children, was the Roy Sullivan she had known and grown to love. "Not a social call," was an aberration. Intuitively, she felt there was something wrong. Besides, she could see the worry in his eyes. Her cheerful expression turned grim. She lowered her fork slowly and placed it on the side of the plate. Then she rose and, without breaking eye contact, calmly approached Roy. As she got closer, she ran the last few steps and embraced him. With her head on his broad shoulder and arms around his neck, she whimpered, "Is it Ross?" and began to cry before Roy had a chance to respond.

Holding her close, he tried to sound comforting. "He's all right, but in big trouble."

She looked up. "What trouble?"

"Let's sit down, and I'll tell you everything."

Oksana would not let go. He continued. "He'll be okay. Washington's on it…Even the President is involved. But there are things we must do—right away."

Oksana composed herself. They walked into the living room while she held on to his arm. Natasha, quiet and somber, followed a few steps behind. Roy sat on the ottoman in front of Oksana as she slumped into an oversized armchair. The morning sunlight creeping through the shutters barely illuminated the room. Natasha leaned against the wall with her arms crossed.

Roy plucked two tissues from the box on the coffee table and handed them over to Oksana. Then, ever so gently, he explained Ross' predicament. Always the professional, he left out the CIA connection and other classified information. Oksana listened intently, wiped her tears, and said softly, "I felt a bad feeling the day he left."

"There's more." Roy continued with the Iranian spies living across the street and the plot to kidnap her or the children to pressure Ross.

Oksana exploded. "What? Kidnap?" She began to sob. Natasha came forward and, sitting on the armrest, held her close. Oksana was inconsolable. Crying aloud she said, "Roy, Victor is upstairs...but Marina is at the beach."

"I know. I know. Relax, two of my guys have been watching her the whole time." Roy retrieved his cell phone from his pocket. "She's all right, but to be on the safe side, I'll have my men escort her home."

With bloodshot eyes, Oksana stared at him inquisitively. "Why have you been watching Marina?"

"Before he left, Ross asked me to look after you and the kids while he was out of the country." Roy was less than candid. "That's all."

"Bring her home, please—bring my baby home."

As he flipped his cell phone open, it started to ring; Agent Konarski was calling. Roy stood and approached the windows. Peering at the Miller's residence, he said, "What have you got, Broom?"

"It's Marina!" Agent Konarski yelled. "They've gone after her...in Pebble Beach."

"Are you sure?"

"Positive. I've hacked their computers—it's all here."

Roy started to bark orders. "I'll call Norm. Get the airborne SWAT team over there and have a chopper pick me up. Now!"

Oksana sensed a crisis was at hand. She ran to Roy. "What's happening?"

Rapidly punching numbers into his cell, Roy said, "It's Marina." He placed the cell to his ear and shouted at Natasha, "Get me another phone."

Oksana grabbed Roy by the collar and screamed, "Is she okay? Please tell me, Roy. Is she okay?"

Roy squeezed her wrists. "They know where she is and have gone after her. I'm trying to alert my men at the beach."

Trembling, Oksana was speechless and didn't know how to take in the news. She buried her face in her hands and knelt on the floor weeping. "Oh God! What am I going to do?" Natasha rushed forward and handed the cordless phone to Roy. She sat beside Oksana, quietly placing an arm around her shoulder. After a short while she whispered, "*Ya pozvonju v Moskvu*—I'll call Moscow."

"*Nyet. Poka ne nado*—No. Not yet."

As Roy walked away from the windows, he looked at his cell and shouted, "Answer the goddamn phone, Norm!" Then he dialed a number in the cordless and placed it to his other ear. Norm's voice mail answered. "You've reached Norman Tavish—" Roy cursed as he hung up the cell and pressed SEND to redial. Speaking into the cordless he said, "Dispatch—this is Roy Sullivan. I want the Hostage Rescue Team sent to Pebble Beach ASAP. Get the details from Konarski. Also send four guys to Dr. Shaheen's house immediately, and by the way," he shouted, "where the hell is my helicopter?"

Confused by the screaming and bedlam, Romeo ran around, uncharacteristically barking at no one in particular.

STEALTHILY, LIKE LIONS ON THE PROWL, FARZAD AND COMPANY KEPT a low profile and stayed out of sight. Except for a short trip to Half Moon Bay to switch the 4Runner with a nondescript black Chevy, which Mustafa had left in the underground parking garage of some hotel, the Iranian spies remained inside the metal warehouse. Sleeping on decrepit couches and cots was an annoying departure from the comfort they had enjoyed at the Miller's residence. Of the three, Mehdi whined the most about their accommodations. His teammates were used to his bellyaching and just ignored him.

At the crack of dawn, Farzad lowered the speedboat into the water. All he had to do was press the green button labeled DOWN, located in the control panel mounted on the wall, and the hydraulic lift did the rest.

Mehdi and Bijan took their time loading the duffle bag and the large cooler aboard the sleek, white and blue vessel. In long pants and golf shirts, they weren't properly dressed for boating, but the two didn't seem all that concerned about appearances; they had a job to do. Mehdi wore an earpiece wired to a cell phone, which was clipped to his belt. Farzad's miniature headset had an attached low-profile mouthpiece, and its wire snaked into the pocket of his Hawaiian shirt.

They'd decided long ago that cell phones were the safest means for clandestine communication. In the United States, privacy laws prohibited the intelligence community from eavesdropping on Americans without specific court orders. Even the NSA's colossus ECHELON, the global vacuum cleaner of signal intelligence, was programmed to ignore domestic communications unless otherwise ordered by a federal judge. By obtaining cell phones under aliases, the Iranian spooks could speak among themselves without fear of being caught. For extra precaution, they often used coded language and discarded the phones after each operation.

Farzad whispered into his mouthpiece, "Call Fisherman." Seconds later, Mehdi's phone began to vibrate. He squeezed a button on the wire hanging from his earpiece and said, "Hello. Hello…You're loud and clear, Boy Scout."

After the communication check was complete, Farzad and Mehdi read off coordinates displayed in the matching GPS devices they wore on their wrists to make sure they were synchronized. Then Farzad stepped to the wall and pressed the red button labeled GATE. The seagate groaned open. He waved them out excitedly, as Mehdi gunned the powerful engines and the speedboat roared away.

Before setting out in his new ride, the black Chevy, Farzad carefully examined his MOIS-issued sidearm and placed it in its holster, which was well hidden under his colorful shirt. A highly customized Colt M1911, his weapon was capable of holding ten rounds of .45 caliber bullets. For ammunition, he preferred the Silvertip Hollow Points— they exploded inside the body, killing the victim instantly. He shoved a magazine into the weapon and placed three extras in the glove compartment.

It was a few minutes after 7:00 AM when he slowly drove out of the warehouse, stepped out of the car to close the door behind him, and then took off. Pebble Beach was over 100 miles south of Half Moon Bay.

⸙

After a long walk in the cool morning hours, Marina and Roberto were sitting on the damp sand at the edge of the water. He had his arms around her. She rested her head on his shoulder. Her dark blond hair danced in the gentle breeze while they gazed at the endless blue of the Pacific Ocean. They spoke about how the water seemed so calm in the distance and so full of excitement near the shore. A flock of seagulls hovering above the waves were delightfully entertaining

Special Agent Norman (Norm) Tavish, formerly a street cop with the San Francisco Police Department, was new to the FBI. Following seventeen weeks of instruction at the FBI Academy in Quantico, Virginia, completing the grueling battery of investigative as well as physical training, and firing more than 5,000 rounds of ammunition to qualify with every weapon in use by the Bureau, he was ready to put it all to work. After two months on the job, Norm was peeved at his first field assignment: to protect some VIP's teenage daughter at the beach. *I'm no goddamn baby-sitter,* he thought at first. But, his boss, Roy Sullivan, had stressed that this was an important mission with hush-hush national security implications. So Norm and his partner saluted and dutifully reported to Pebble Beach.

Norm gave the pool attendant a dirty look when he asked for the twenty dollars rental for the cabana. Sitting in its shade, wearing sandals, shorts, and a white Pebble Beach golf shirt, Norm pretended to be reading the morning papers. The reflective sunglasses obscured his eyes to onlookers, while the beach-bag filled with towels, water bottles, and sunscreen lotion camouflaged his Glock-22 and spare clips. To avoid unwanted attention, he was not wearing his telecom device—a violation of the standard protocols for gumshoes in the field. Every now and then he would pick up a pair of powerful binoculars and look at Marina and her boyfriend, sitting on the sand, less than fifty yards away. Then he would scan the beach, to the right and to the left, looking for anything unusual before returning to the sports page.

Mehdi and Bijan found the hundred-mile ride aboard the Victory thrilling. Scheming how they would keep the boat after the mission and use it to lure women out to sea, they disguised their anxiety by laughing and cutting up. As planned, from Half Moon Bay they sped ten miles west before slowing down and turning south toward Pebble Beach. Mindful of the boat's 250-mile range at top speed, they saved fuel by traveling only at 50 miles per hour. They were not due to arrive in Pebble Beach before 9:00 AM anyway.

Around eight o'clock, driving south toward Monterey on State Highway 1, Farzad whispered into his mouthpiece, "Call Fisherman."

"Come in Boy Scout," Mehdi shouted over the roaring engines.

"I can barely hear you."

Mehdi pulled back on the throttles. "Can you hear me now?"

"Yes. Much better. What's your position?"

Mehdi looked at the miniature GPS strapped to his wrist. "We're halfway there."

"I'm closer, about thirty-five miles out."

"Anything else?"

"Nope."

"See you at the party."

"Over and out."

Roy Sullivan was pacing in the front yard of the Miller's house anxiously waiting for the FBI helicopter. He had tried to reach Norm Tavish on his cell at least a dozen times but had not succeeded. Apparently, Norm wasn't wearing his telecom device either, which infuriated Roy even more. Four additional agents had already arrived on the scene and were conspicuously guarding the Shaheen residence. Inside, flanked by Victor and Natasha, Oksana was sitting on the couch, quietly waiting. Rocking back and forth, she looked at her watch frequently, letting her silence speak of her torment. Alice Sullivan had also come over for moral support.

The exact number of airplanes and helicopters in use by the FBI was a closely held secret. The Washington grapevine pegged the total at about 100, with one-third being fixed-wing aircraft. But no one seemed to know for sure. The Bureau deployed these unmarked vehicles for myriad activities. From aerial surveillance and eavesdropping missions to tactical operations, the fleet was in constant use and in high demand. Piloted by FBI agents, most aircraft were civilian models, favored for their unobtrusive appearance. Given the geographic size of the country, when the fleet was spread among the 56 FBI field offices, and allowing for downtime for routine maintenance, there was not enough aircraft to go around.

The San Francisco Bureau had access to only one Cessna and two helicopters.

"Dispatch—I'm trying my level best to stay cool. I requested a damn chopper an hour ago." Unable to control his temper any longer, Roy yelled into his cell, "Do you have an ETA?"

"Sir, one bird is down and the other was on assignment in Napa Valley. We've called it back. It's refueling as we speak and will be on its way to you shortly."

"I asked for an ETA, not a frigging soap opera."

"Nine o'clock, sir."

"What about the HRT?"

"On its way to Pebble Beach. Should get there by ten."

"Airborne SWAT?"

"Assembling now. Should arrive with the HRT."

"Any word from Norm?"

"No, sir. His cell must be off, and he's not wearing his wire."

Roy mumbled, "If the Iranian grease balls don't kill that son-of-a-bitch, I'll kill him myself." Continuing with the dispatcher, he said, "How about his partner?"

"Sir, his partner had the night-watch and is now sleeping."

Gritting his teeth, Roy said, "Well, can we wake up the sleeping beauty?"

"I've tried, sir. I can't reach him either."

"Keep trying."

AT 8:47 AM, FARZAD PULLED INTO THE PARKING LOT OF THE EXCLUSIVE Oceanside Condominiums and Yacht Club at Pebble Beach. Driving around looking at the vehicles, he paused behind a yellow MINI

Cooper, and read the license plate—it was Marina's. He grinned as he parked a few spaces away.

The handsome spy placed a brown straw-hat loosely on his head, tilting it back. Then he grabbed a pair of binoculars and casually approached Building A. As he climbed the stairs to the third floor, he encountered an overly tanned, yet sophisticated looking older woman and greeted her politely. Except for a nod, she ignored him. He knocked on unit 31-A—there was no answer. Thinking the girls might be having breakfast, he proceeded down the stairs, strolled through the veranda, and into the luxurious poolside café. A handful of people were scattered around sipping coffee or reading the morning papers—none of them teenagers. He sat on a pool-chair overlooking the ocean and, peering through the binoculars, began to scan the beach.

It didn't take long before he spotted someone resembling Marina. Thinking, *Who's the guy?* he zoomed in. Instantly, he recognized the distinctive, dragon-shaped tattoo on Roberto's right arm. "Bad little girl," Farzad mumbled. "Momma doesn't know what you're up to." Then he thought, *Roberto could complicate things.*

Farzad looked at his watch, 9:05 AM, and then whispered, "Call Fisherman."

"Boy Scout, we're here."

"How far?"

"By the book—ten miles off."

Farzad quietly read the coordinates from his GPS into the mouthpiece. "Approach slowly and stand by at one mile." Then he stood, looked through the binoculars once again, and proceeded down the boardwalk toward the private beach.

BEFORE SPOTTING IT IN THE SKY, ROY HEARD THE SOUND OF THE helicopter approaching. Neighbors had sensed there was something strange unfolding. Many were standing in front of their houses, while others stood on their back porches, staring. No one dared approach the swarm of agents donning FBI windbreakers.

The helicopter, a midnight blue Bell 206, with yellow and white stripes, landed gracefully onto Gordon Street in between the Shaheen and Miller residences. Its 33-foot rotors continued to spin, wreaking havoc in the sleepy neighborhood, knocking trash containers and gas grills on their sides.

Agents Konarski and Morgan, both carrying sub-machine guns, flanked Roy Sullivan as they approached the helicopter. Before climbing onboard, Roy turned, looking toward the Shaheen residence. Behind the living room window, Oksana stood with her arm around Victor, waving hesitantly. With a clenched jaw, he nodded, thinking he would rather take a bullet in the belly than return without Marina in one piece.

"How fast can this bird fly?" Roy asked the pilot as soon as the aircraft lifted off.

"Hundred thirty-five miles per hour," the pilot said. "With tailwind, a little faster."

"That should put us at Pebble Beach in an hour."

"Sounds about right."

"Step on it."

✒︎

AT 9:35 AM, FARZAD GLANCED AT HIS WATCH AS HE CASUALLY STROLLED on the beach. He was passing a few yards behind Marina and Roberto for the third time. The green and yellow Hawaiian shirt, the straw hat, and the sandals made him blend into the scenery. While he surveyed the area for anything that might threaten the operation, he whispered into his headset, "Call Fisherman."

"Come in, Boy Scout."

"The coast is clear. Slowly approach until you have a visual on me."

Agent Norm Tavish placed his binoculars on the empty lounge-chair next to him and reached inside the beach-bag searching for his cell phone. He flipped it open. "Shit! No juice." Suddenly anxious, he rummaged around the bottom of the bag, found the extra battery, and replaced the dead one. Then he dialed his voice mail to retrieve his messages. There were 18 waiting for him. *This is unusual,* he thought.

The first one was from his wife; he skipped it. The second message was from his boss, Roy Sullivan.

"Goddamn it, Norm, pick up! Marina is in danger. They've come after her. Call me or the Dispatch as soon as you get this message."

Norm didn't listen to the remaining 16 and nervously dialed Roy.

"Where in the burning hell have you been, Agent Tavish? I must have called your dumb ass at least a hundred times."

"Right here on the beach, boss. Sorry, my cell was dead."

"Listen, where's Marina?"

Looking through the binoculars, he said, "Fifty yards away. I'm looking at her."

"Get over there this minute and escort her inside. Then stand guard, with your weapon drawn, till I get there."

"Are you on your way here?"

"Yes. I'll be there in fifteen, twenty minutes."

"What's going on, boss?"

Not fond of long explanations, Roy barked orders at Norm, punctuated by profanities.

"Hey, check it out," Roberto said, pointing. "That boat is heading straight this way."

"Yeah, maybe they wanna take us out for a spin."

"Wouldn't that be cool?"

Farzad stood motionless a few yards behind Marina and Roberto. Looking through his binoculars at Mehdi and Bijan as their boat rapidly closed in, he whispered abbreviated instructions into the mouthpiece of his cell.

"Nice and easy. Come straight toward me. Slow down. You don't wanna get stuck in the sand."

"Who's the guy?" Mehdi said.

"Her boyfriend."

"He's pointing at us."

"Never mind him. I've got his ass covered. You just stay the course."

A number of scattered joggers and power-walkers had noticed the speedboat slicing through the waves and racing to the shore. They stared at it with puzzled amusement. Meanwhile, Norm Tavish listened to Roy Sullivan's rant.

"Wait a minute, boss. That's strange."

"What?"

"The boat. It's heading straight toward them."

"Toward who?"

"Marina and Roberto."

"It's them!" Roy shouted. "They're on the boat!"

Norm dropped the cell phone, emptied the beach bag on the sand, and retrieved his Glock-22. He rose and started to walk toward the shore. His determined eyes were fixed on the boat. As it loomed closer, he picked up the pace and began to run.

"She's gonna hit us, babe," Roberto said, as he stood, pulling Marina up with him. "Let's book—this bitch is crazy!"

Seconds away, Mehdi shouted into his mouthpiece, "Look out, Boy Scout. There's someone behind you with a gun."

Without any hesitation, Farzad reached under his shirt and retrieved his Colt. He swung around, knelt, and aimed his weapon at Norm as he rushed toward him. Before Farzad had a chance to squeeze the trigger, Norm dove on the sand, rolled over, and fired three rounds at Farzad. Only one of the bullets found its mark, shattering his left shoulder. Farzad coiled back but quickly regained his balance and fired back with a volley of bullets. The stray rounds kicked up a batch of sand, but one of the Hollow Point bullets struck Norm in the neck, bursting his jugular vein—blood squirted out like a geyser as he squirmed in pain.

Roberto and Marina were frozen in place. Shielding her from danger, he held her in a tight embrace. "Oh, God. Please help me!" she cried.

The bow of the boat carved into the sand and came to a sudden halt a few feet away from Roberto and Marina. The giant engines idly groaned, shooting water and sand up in the air.

"Let's run," Roberto yelled with terror. "Go as fast as you can."

Soaked in blood, Farzad fired two rounds into the sand in front of Roberto and grunted, "You move, you die."

Roberto and Marina stopped cold in their tracks, and then slowly turned to face Farzad. Marina was shaking.

Farzad struggled in vain to get up. He was bleeding profusely and felt an unbearable pain in his chest and shoulder. The bullet had sliced through his body, leaving a mammoth exit wound. Kneeling, he pointed his gun at Roberto and said, "Don't move."

Mehdi followed Bijan, jumping off the boat. Leaning against the vessel, Bijan stood watch in knee-high water holding an Uzi submachine gun at the ready. With a determined look, Mehdi walked toward Roberto, pointing a handgun at his head.

"There must be a mistake," Roberto said sheepishly, as he slowly raised his hands. "We haven't done anything,"

Mehdi shoved the barrel of his Colt into Roberto's nostril and, with clenched teeth, said, "If I pull this trigger, half of your brain would burst out of the back of your skull." Then he laughed. "Breakfast time! The seagulls would love me for it."

"Don't," Roberto pleaded. "I'll do anything you ask, Mister. Please don't shoot."

"It's your lucky day—" With a sudden motion, Mehdi hit Roberto in the forehead with the handle of his gun. Roberto fell to the ground, unconscious, blood oozing down his face. "I'm gonna let you live."

Marina started to scream hysterically, "Help! Someone, please help!"

"Shut up!" Mehdi lifted her over his shoulder. "You're coming with me." He headed back to the boat. Marina kept on howling and waving her arms and legs in the air. "Put me down! Put me down, you asshole." Mehdi kept walking as Marina continued to plead, "Help! Someone please help me!"

Bijan ran toward Farzad to help him up. He had lost a lot of blood and was too weak to walk on his own. Bijan grabbed his right arm, threw it over his own shoulder, and together they started toward the speedboat.

A few bystanders had found the courage to approach the mayhem. But unarmed, they were impotent to do anything. From a safe distance, a young man shouted, "Hey! Put her down," which was the extent of his bravado.

As she continued to kick and scream, Mehdi threw Marina into the boat and climbed in behind her. Fed up, he backhanded her and yelled, "You'd better be quiet if you want to stay alive, bitch!" Marina fell to the floor of the boat and curled up in a corner, shaking and quietly weeping.

Bijan lifted Farzad as Mehdi pulled him inside the boat. He slumped into a chair, holding his left arm in agony. Bijan paused to scan the beach before climbing aboard.

"Go!" Bijan shouted. "Let's go!"

Mehdi pushed the throttle into reverse and gunned the engines. They bellowed with a deafening sound, pulling the boat out to the ocean. Seconds later, he turned the wheel, shifted into forward, and sped away. Soon, they vanished into the horizon as the seagulls returned to hover above the beach.

JUDGING BY THE SIZE AND THE FORMATION OF THE CROWD, ROY Sullivan intuitively knew there was something awfully wrong on the beach. As his helicopter approached, he saw a half-dozen police cars, blue lights gleaming, parked randomly on the greens. A boxy ambulance was on the beach.

When the aircraft descended to land, every person in the crowd turned to stare. Inside the helicopter, time seemed to move ahead grudgingly. Roy felt as if he was watching a silent movie in slow motion. "What in the hell is going on?" he wondered aloud.

The chopper landed the length of a football field away from the onlookers. Roy jumped out and started to run toward the crowd. Without a clue what he would find in the epicenter of the swarm of people, he forged ahead. Quietly, he prayed that it wouldn't be Marina.

"FBI. Let me through," he said repeatedly, as he made his way through the curious bystanders. Agents Konarski and Morgan caught up with him and plunged through the crowd. It took a while, but eventually they made it to the middle. Medics had strapped someone to a gurney, covered head-to-toe in a yellow blanket, and were struggling through the sand to carry him off.

"Hold it!" Roy shouted as he approached. Noticing the machinegun-toting FBI Agents, the medics put the gurney down and stepped back. Roy walked over and, with a swift motion, removed the cover revealing the victim's face. It was Agent Norm Tavish—lifeless and blood-soaked. Roy's heart sank. The crowd gasped and then became totally silent. Roy stood quietly for a minute, his face grave. He seemed to be carrying the weight of the moment on his shoulders. Thinking of Norm's six-year-old son, and how he could ever deal with his father's death, he whispered, "Oh, man…what a waste!" and, slowly, covered him back up.

"Did anyone see what happened here?" Roy shouted. "Any witnesses?"

A few people raised their hands. Agents Konarski and Morgan called them over to record their accounts.

Roy noticed a young man sitting in the back of the ambulance holding an icepack on his forehead. He was being attended to by a medic. He walked over and said, "What's your name, son?"

"Roberto Marquez."

"Did you see what happened?"

"Yes, sir." He looked up, and said tearfully, "I saw everything." Then he started to cry. "They took her. I couldn't help her. The bastards took her."

Dreading the answer, Roy asked, "Took who?"

"Marina. Marina Shaheen."

Suddenly feeling his own heartbeat, Roy asked, "Which way did they go?"

Pointing toward the ocean, Roberto said, "I was knocked out. But they took her in a boat."

"What kind of a boat?"

"A blue and white speedboat—twenty-five, maybe thirty feet long."

"How long ago?"

"Thirty, forty minutes or so."

Roy ran toward Agent Konarski, who was interviewing one of the witnesses. "Broom, you and Morgan get back on the bird and fly south. Go as fast as you can, and look for a white and blue speedboat that seems like it's in a hurry. They've got Marina."

"Got it, boss."

Roy clicked on the transmit button of his hand-held radio, calling out to the FBI's Airborne SWAT team, which was on its way. "SWAT-1, come in. Come in, SWAT-1."

"SWAT-1, here."

"What's your position?"

"Thirty miles north of Pebble Beach."

"Listen. Get out to sea and start looking for a fast-moving boat going north. They've kidnapped our VIP. If you find them, stay with them."

"Ten-four."

31

A T THE TIP OF A MILE-LONG WAKE, THE SPEEDBOAT RUSHED NORTH while maintaining a safe distance from the shore. Squeezing the wheel with both hands, his jet-black hair blowing back, Mehdi was so focused on steering that he looked as if he were in a trance.

Farzad was in the cabin below and had passed out on the oval-shaped bed. All Bijan could do was cover him with blankets and pour whiskey down his throat.

Marina was kept out of sight, as Mustafa had instructed. Bound and gagged, she was stuffed in the red cooler, which had been modified with hundreds of small breathing holes.

"Farzad...Farzad," Bijan whispered into his ear, "wake up!" Gently shaking him, he said, "You've got to give me Mustafa's number." Then, a little louder, "How do we get in touch with him? You need a doctor... Real bad."

There was no response.

Bijan had a worried look as he emerged from the cabin. Clutching the handrail for balance, he approached Mehdi at the helm. The sound of the wind combined with the roar of the engines was deafening. Once within Mehdi's earshot, Bijan yelled, "What should we do with Farzad?"

"How is he?" Mehdi shouted, looking straight ahead.

"Unconscious...He's lost a lot of blood."

"We can't worry about him now." Mehdi glanced at the GPS device on his wrist. "We'll figure something out when we get back to the warehouse."

To drown out the noise, Bijan yelled, "We have to contact Mustafa." Standing close to Mehdi, he added, "He'll know what to do."

"Only Farzad knows how to get a hold of him."

"That's the problem…Farzad's lights are out."

"Then, we'll just execute the plan, with or without Farzad."

"Without a doctor, he'll die. We should—"

Mehdi interrupted, *"Beh darak; bezar bemeereh*—To hell with him; let him die."

Bijan paused for a minute, and then said, "How much longer?"

"We're almost there." Mehdi glanced at his GPS device. "About three miles out."

Bijan used a pair of powerful binoculars to make a 360-degree inspection of the horizon. "We're all clear."

Mehdi drove the boat toward the shore until the warehouse was in sight. As they closed in, he pressed a button on a remote control device, which was taped to the front panel. The sea-gate groaned open.

The sun was nearing its zenith when the speedboat docked inside the warehouse. Bijan jumped ashore to secure the vessel with a yellow mooring rope. Mehdi used the remote to close the gate behind them. In the dark, he instructed Bijan, "Get the flashlight." But before he had a chance to oblige, the florescent lights came on.

From the far side of the warehouse, a well-dressed man, wearing a French beret, strolled toward them. Mehdi quickly grabbed his gun, aiming at the stranger.

"Put the gun away, idiot." The man's voice sounded confident as he calmly approached the boat. "It's me, Mustafa."

"How do I know that?" Mehdi said.

"You wouldn't." He lit up a cigarette. "Where's Farzad?"

Mehdi glanced at Bijan, who nodded approvingly. Holstering his gun, Mehdi said, "He is down below."

Mustafa climbed aboard as Mehdi stepped off. Face to face, Mehdi tried to be nonchalant. "He's been shot."

"Shot?" Mustafa reacted with dismay. "How did it happen?"

"We were ambushed," Bijan volunteered. "But that can wait. Let's do something about Farzad."

"Did you get the girl?"

"Yes, sir," Mehdi said proudly.

Mustafa disappeared into the cabin. After a few minutes, he emerged—oddly unperturbed. Pointing to the suite of rundown rooms, he said, "Take the girl to the office."

Once Mehdi and Bijan approached, he added, "We have a long wait before midnight. Keep her inside; let her stretch out. And make damn sure she doesn't see my face."

"What about Farzad?" Mehdi asked.

"I'll take care of him."

"God bless you."

Mehdi followed Bijan into the cabin. They hauled the red cooler out on deck, and then onto the concrete floor. As they carried the container away, Mustafa reached inside his jacket and quietly drew his gun. Then he withdrew a silencer from his pocket and calmly screwed it onto the barrel.

When Mehdi and Bijan disappeared into the office, Mustafa entered the cabin and stood a few feet from where Farzad lay on the bed. He was now conscious, moaning in pain. His eyes locking onto Mustafa's. "Mustafa, is that you?" he grunted.

"Yes."

"Help me…Please."

Pointing the gun at his chest, Mustafa whispered, "I wish I could." Then he squeezed the trigger three times. With each muffled sound of the gunfire, Farzad's body flinched.

Strolling toward his shiny black BMW, Mustafa returned his gun to its holster and dropped the warm silencer into his coat pocket. From a distance, using a remote key, he popped the trunk door open. He retrieved a black gym bag and a sack of groceries and headed toward the office.

Inside, Mehdi was pacing the floor smoking, his hands shaking from nerves. Bijan was slumped in a rundown chair staring at the ceiling.

"Here's some food," Mustafa said, placing the groceries on a desk. Then he threw the gym bag in front of Mehdi. "Take this to the girl. There are warm clothes inside."

"I don't know," Mehdi said, grinning. "She looks mighty delicious in that bathing suit."

"You better keep your mind off of her!" Mustafa snapped. Stepping closer, he brought his lips within inches of Mehdi's ear. In a low, menacing voice, he said, "If anything happens to that girl, if you touch her, or even think about it, I'll put a couple of bullets into your eyeballs, one each—I promise!"

Mehdi froze.

Using his hand, Mustafa mimed a handgun pointing at Mehdi's eyes. "You got that, Casanova?"

Mehdi wiped the grin off his face, picked up the bag sheepishly, and walked toward the adjacent room.

"What about Farzad?" Bijan said impatiently.

"He's dead."

"Dead?" Bijan was surprised. "Are you sure?"

"Positive." Mustafa took a drag from the cigarette, which he held between his thumb and index finger. "He'd lost too much blood. Besides, even if he were alive, we couldn't quite wheel him into San Francisco General. Could we?"

"What a waste." Shaking his head, Bijan lamented, "He was very talented…Too young to die."

"Oh, well," Mehdi said, as he opened the door to the adjacent office. "It is what it is."

"What do we do with the body?" Bijan asked.

"It'll go down with the boat tonight."

"You mean you're going to sink *that* boat?"

"Absolutely. Too many people have seen it, and the FBI will be looking for it everywhere."

"I can't believe they were waiting for us," Bijan said. "How the hell did they know we were coming?"

"How many were there?" Mustafa inquired.

"Just one. And Farzad dispatched him to hell."

"If the operation had been compromised, there would have been fifty men waiting for you, not just one. He must have been an off-duty policeman, or maybe her bodyguard." Mustafa took a long drag on his cigarette. "No. They didn't know you were coming." Exhaling a cloud of smoke, he continued. "But, somehow, the FBI has wised up to us this morning."

Entering the room, Mehdi said, "This morning? The FBI? What do you mean?"

"Shit must have hit the fan after you guys left," Mustafa explained. "When our clean-up crew went to the Miller house to sanitize the place and remove the equipment, they saw an army of FBI agents running around. There was even a helicopter parked in the middle of the street."

"I'll be damned!" Mehdi growled. "They've got our equipment? With that, they can certainly track us down."

"Probably," Mustafa said. "And that's why you two will have to leave town as soon as possible."

"And go where?" Mehdi demanded.

"You'll go to the safe house, lay low, and provide additional security. I'll arrange to get you guys back into Canada in a week or so."

"That's all we need," Bijan grumbled, "another endless house-sitting mission."

"In the meantime," Mehdi peeked into the brown bag, "what's for lunch?"

THE MIDNIGHT SKY WAS MOONLESS. DRIVING THE GREEN CALIFORNIA Fish and Wildlife van, Mehdi turned onto Venice Boulevard heading toward the beach. Bijan was in the passenger seat nervously looking at the side view mirror for anything out of the ordinary.

Neither one spoke. The oversized red cooler rested against the sidewall in the back of the van. Bound and gagged, Marina Shaheen lay inside the container in a fetal position, shaking and quietly weeping.

Earlier that evening, after scuttling the boat and sending Farzad to his watery grave, Mustafa had returned to San Francisco, leaving his crew to finish the job. They were to hand over their precious cargo to their cohorts, Jaffar and Emad, for transfer to the safe house in Northern California.

The van rolled to a stop at the far corner of a deserted parking lot on the edge of the sandy beach. Mehdi turned off the engine, stepped out, and lit up a cigarette. So did Bijan. They circled the van, checking their surroundings. Except for the rhythmic sound of the waves washing ashore, the beach was quiet. The two slowly walked toward a secluded bench a short distance away and sat in the dark, restlessly waiting.

Before long, a Pacific Community Police car entered the parking lot, circled the area, and stopped a dozen yards away from the van. Its spotlight came on, scanning the beach.

"Oh shit!" Mehdi whispered. "That's all we need."

Cloaked by darkness, Bijan quietly moved behind the bench and drew his gun. Mehdi joined him with his Colt, already out, pointing at the police car.

"If they touch the van," Mehdi whispered, "we'll blow them into the ocean."

"Agreed."

After inspecting the beach, the spotlight turned to the van and stopped. A beefy policeman, holding an oversized flashlight, emerged from the car and started toward the van.

Careful not to make a sound, Mehdi slowly loaded the chamber of his weapon.

A second cop, this one skinny, joined the first as he circled the van, peering inside the cabin with his flashlight. "What are these environmental bozos doing here at this late hour?"

"I don't know," said the skinny cop. "Maybe catching turtles or transporting some exotic crabs."

"The bastards cost me a ton of money last year."

"How so?" the skinny policeman asked, as he continued his visual inspection of the vehicle.

"There's this shallow creek at the back of my house," the fat policeman said, turning to face his partner. "When it rains, the damn thing floods my basement. I wanted to dredge it, or make it deeper or something. But, no!" He gestured wildly. "That would endanger some microscopic snail that lives in my creek."

"So, what did you do?"

"Nothing. The wild life fascists stopped me."

"That's funny," the skinny cop said, laughing. "So the creek is still flooding?"

"Yup, like clockwork, every time it rains."

"I guess they got their job to do, and we've got ours."

"I guess."

"What's that big-ass cooler for?" the skinny cop said, focusing the beam of his light on the inside.

"I can't tell from here…wanna take a closer look?"

Bijan and Mehdi had the policemen in their gunsights, ready to fire. Mehdi whispered, "I'll take the fat one."

As the portly officer reached for the door handle of the rear hatch, a voice crackled over the police radio, "Units three and five, respond to a brawl at the Mermaid Lounge on Elm Street. Repeat, there's a brawl at the Mermaid. Units three and five, respond."

At once, the policemen turned off their flashlights, ran to the squad car, and drove away—blue lights flashing.

"That was close," Bijan gasped. "Real close."

"Our boys are late," Mehdi said impatiently, as he returned to the bench. "Where the hell are they?"

"They'll be here."

JAFFAR AND EMAD LEFT THE FISHERMAN'S WHARF AROUND TEN o'clock but had underestimated the time it would take to reach Venice Beach. It was half past midnight when Jaffar, driving the white Avalon, entered the lot. Slowly approaching the van, he parked beside it and promptly cut off the engine. Emad was in the passenger seat. They waited several minutes before leaving the vehicle.

Mustafa's instructions didn't allow any contact between the two teams in public—even after midnight in a desolate parking lot. This way, if one team was ambushed, the other could either get away or assist. So Bijan and Mehdi watched from a distance as Jaffar and Emad climbed aboard the van.

Once inside, Emad opened the glove compartment, retrieved an envelope, and handed it over to Jaffar—these were Mustafa's latest instructions.

Take the patient to the hospital, Mustafa had written, referring to Marina and the safe house. *M & B will join you shortly. I will arrange for their safe passage as soon as I can. Wait for further instructions directly from home.*

"Get the bags, Emad," Jaffar said, as he stepped into the back of the van. Flashlight in hand, he cautiously approached the red cooler and slowly opened the lid.

Inside, Marina started to shake uncontrollably. The odor of sweat mixed with the stench of urine was ghastly. Disheveled hair covered most of her face; what little remained exposed was bright red from the heat.

The moment Jaffar looked at Marina, somehow, she reminded him of his own daughters. Looking at her petite body crammed into the cooler in such a wretched condition made him feel ashamed.

This is so unnecessary, he thought.

Emad opened the rear door of the van and started to load their luggage and gear, including the metal trunk containing their secret communication equipment.

"What are you doing?" Emad asked.

"What does it look like? I'm letting her out."

"But…Mustafa—"

"To hell with Mustafa," the burly Jaffar barked, as he tenderly pulled Marina out of the container. "I'm calling the shots here…Understand?"

Emad stared as Jaffar continued. "We'll complete the job, as planned." He placed Marina on the floor. "But there's no reason to behave like animals."

Emad climbed inside and quickly closed the door behind them. Marina seemed to be in pain. Jaffar gently seated her next to the cooler, leaning her against the wall. He gazed into her eyes and said, "Listen. I will not hurt you. But if you make a sound, I'll have to put you back into the cooler. Do you understand?"

Marina nodded.

"Are you hungry?"

She shook her head.

"Thirsty?"

"Yes."

"Emad, get me some water," Jaffar said.

Emad quickly retrieved a bottle of water from one of the bags and handed it to him.

"If I get rid of this gag," Jaffar whispered, "will you be quiet?"

Marina moved her head up and down.

Hesitantly, Jaffar removed the strip of cloth covering her mouth.

She remained quiet. He smiled and held the bottle to her mouth as she drank eagerly.

"I can't untie your hands or legs," Jaffar said, "not yet, anyway."

Marina muttered, "What do you want from me?"

"Nothing from you," Jaffar said, attempting to be reassuring. "Don't be afraid, sister. No one's going to hurt you."

After a silent nod of thanks, Marina looked away, tears streaming down her cheeks.

"Well then, go to sleep," Jaffar said, as he slumped into the driver's seat. "We have a long road ahead of us."

A minute later, they drove away, disappearing into the darkness.

Following them in the Avalon, Mehdi and Bijan stopped at a Waffle House to allow a couple hours of distance between themselves and the van. To celebrate the successful execution of FOXHUNT, they chased their omelets with multiple servings of pecan pie topped with ice cream.

32

THE BEIGE, ORANGE, AND SEA GREEN MOTIF IN THE BANQUET HALL of the French Embassy in Moscow understated its ornate opulence. Intricate tapestries and priceless paintings from the Renaissance period adorned the walls, while Napoleonic furniture reproductions, richly upholstered with maroon and gold fabrics, dotted the hardwood floors.

Earlier, the new French Ambassador had presented his credentials to the President of the Russian Federation. The dinner reception was meant to mark the occasion, while, simultaneously, introducing the new envoy to the diplomatic corps.

Following the sumptuous cuisine, standing in front of a massive fireplace, General Viktor Pugachov was engaged in quiet conversation with the new Ambassador and his deputy chief of mission. Above the mantle, a giant oil painting of King Louis IV looked on.

"My dear Minister," the Ambassador said, with tortured politeness, "many French businessmen are somewhat reluctant to invest in Russia." Shrugging in characteristic French manner, he added, "Frankly, they are...how should I say? Even afraid of traveling to your great country."

"And why is that?" Pugachov said, with a feeble attempt at humor. "They don't like our weather? Our vodka? Or, are they concerned they might be enchanted by Russian women?"

Faking laughter, the Ambassador said, "I wish it was that simple." Then, in a somber tone, he added, "But, honestly, they fear for their safety."

"Nonsense! Moscow is as safe as Paris."

"But not for wealthy businessmen." The Ambassador waved his

hands in frustration. "You know how it is…they have to pay protection money to the Mafia for permission to do business here."

"All that talk about the Russian Mafia is grossly exaggerated—western propaganda."

"What about Pierre La Perch?" the deputy chief of mission cut in. "He was in Moscow for the grand opening of his hotel when he was found dead in the subway—with his eyeballs gouged out. Rumor has it that he had refused to pay off the Mafia."

With a cold stare, the French Ambassador signaled his displeasure to his deputy. Diplomatic protocol precluded even the mention of specific criminal cases in the presence of such a high-ranking official, let alone discussion of the gruesome details.

"That was an unfortunate mugging," Pugachov said sternly. "It had nothing to do with organized crime."

The Ambassador continued the conversation in a more diplomatic tone. "That could very well have been the case, honorable Minster. However, I am certain your Excellency would grant that there might be a problem with the Mafia in Russia vis-à-vis foreign businessmen."

"And you find that unacceptable?"

"Well, with all due respect, yes. We have nothing of the sort in France and our investors, aside from fearing for their lives, believe the payoffs to be an extra business tax, which reduces their profits."

"Mr. Ambassador, I am certain you will agree that one's conduct can only be judged in the context of the underlying culture." Pugachov took a sip of Cognac from the crystal glass he was holding and continued to philosophize. "What's virtuous in one culture may be sinful in another. And what's deemed criminal in your world is only *modus operandi* in ours."

"But, my dear Minister—"

Suddenly, Pugachov's chief of security approached, interrupting the Ambassador with "Excuse me, comrade General." He whispered something in Pugachov's ear.

"If you would pardon me, Mr. Ambassador, I have an urgent phone call."

"You can take it in the parlor, if you wish. You'll have privacy there."

Pugachov politely declined the offer, knowing full well that the French as well as the Russian intelligence services recorded all phone calls in and out of the embassy. "The call is waiting for me in the limousine."

"Certainly."

"I might as well bid you goodnight." Pugachov shook the Ambassador's hand. "Thank you for your kind hospitality."

"You honored us with your presence, General Pugachov."

At a determined pace, the chief of security led the way through the assembled crowd. General Pugachov barely acknowledged the nods of respect from the distinguished guests as he passed them.

Under the portico, an armor-plated ZIL limousine waited with its engine running. Pugachov climbed inside. His security chief closed the door and sprinted to one of the two SUVs parked in front. Two other sedans waited behind the limousine. All five spotlessly polished vehicles were black, with tinted glass. The ZIL flew two small Russian Federation flags at each side of the hood, while the SUVs were equipped with flashing blue lights.

Even though the younger officials and the new rich of Russia preferred Mercedes or BMW limousines, Pugachov favored the ZIL. While dated, it had a mysteriously austere aura. Besides, it was a Russian car, and for him, it remained an expression of a great and proud nation.

As soon as the convoy started to move, Pugachov pressed a green button on the instrument panel labeled *VIBRIOROVAT*—VIBRATE.

To ward off foreign spies from using invisible laser microphones to listen in on conversations inside official limousines, the Russian counter espionage service had installed hundreds of micro-motors throughout each vehicle. Once activated, these specialized devices caused the limousine's metal skin, along with all windowpanes, to silently vibrate. The high-frequency random patterns effectively frustrate would-be eavesdroppers.

Pugachov lifted the secure phone to his ear, and in his low baritone voice said, *"Da!"*

"Papa, eto ya—" Oksana whimpered, "Papa, it's me."

Instantly noticing the agony in her voice, Pugachov said, "What's the matter?"

Choking with emotions, she paused, and then in a barely audible voice said, "They've kidnapped Marina."

"Kidnapped?" A cold chill rushed down Pugachov's spine. "Who's responsible? What do they want?" he demanded.

With great pain, Oksana recounted the events of the previous twenty-four hours, conveying what little Roy Sullivan had disclosed about Marina's disappearance. Alternating between despondency and anger, she added that all fingers were pointing to the Iranian intelligence, MOIS. And she further explained how the kidnapping could be a ploy to pressure Ross, who had also disappeared.

General Pugachov was stunned and at a loss for words. After an awkward moment, he grumbled, "I knew this trip to Iran was an act of lunacy."

"It's too late for that, Papa. What are we going to do about Marina?"

"Does the FBI have any leads? Any suspects?"

"No. Not really."

"The CIA?"

"I have not heard anything from the CIA."

Gritting his teeth, Pugachov said, "You *will* hear from them—you will."

"Can you help find her, Papa?"

"Yes my dear…And I certainly will."

"How?"

"I cannot explain over your open line. But rest assured I will do everything in my power."

"Thank you, Papa."

Pugachov somberly returned the phone to its cradle. Then, using the intercom, he ordered his driver to take him to the Kremlin, and fast. His meaty face tense, he pressed his neck into the velvet headrest and closed his eyes. *What a catastrophe!* The muscles beneath his right eye started to twitch randomly. *Hang in there, my sweet Marina. We'll find you—hang in there.*

After a few moments of reflection, Pugachov lifted the phone, pausing for the special operator to come on line. Then, with rapid-fire commands, he summoned the heads of FSB and GRU to his office. He also sent word to the Russian Ambassador in Tehran to return to the Embassy, along with the FSB Station Chief, for a secure phone call.

Pugachov retrieved a crystal bottle tucked into the side panel of the limousine and poured himself a glass of brandy. As the convoy whisked through the *Bolchaia Iakimanka* Boulevard, he retrieved a little black book from his jacket pocket, looked up a number, and dialed it. It took a while for the call to go through.

"This is Mira Cordoba. How may I help you?"

"Get me Colonel Nash!"

HALF A WORLD AWAY, DEEP BENEATH THE UNSUSPECTING COUNTRYSIDE of Natanz, Ross endured his captivity. He had long thought of Hell as a place without sounds or sunshine. Now, ironically, he found himself in the middle of it. Over a hundred feet of dirt and concrete separated him from daylight, while the utter silence in the bunker was only broken by the sporadic sound of footsteps in the hallways. He wasn't treated as a prisoner, but in the confinement of Amir's private suite, in the belly of the sprawling subterranean facility, he felt as if he were.

It was day three. He spent it as he had the previous ones: studying the detailed blueprints of the bomb and the schematics of the enrichment plant stored in Amir's personal computer. By committing as much detail to memory as was humanly possible, Ross kept himself occupied. What is more, the mental exercise masked the agony of his detention and numbed the recurring feelings of despair. Recalling that the CIA-issued Berkeley ring on his right middle finger contained a powerful suicide pill gave him pause more than once. He would tell himself, *Don't be stupid, Ross!*

Amir's PC proved to be a treasure trove of information. Ross couldn't believe he was given ready access to it. *Is it disinformation?* he often wondered. *Or, is Amir so certain that I will never leave this place alive that he sees no harm in such disclosure?* The questions swirled in Ross' head. *Maybe he's just bragging.* It didn't matter. Ross was not under any delusions. At the moment, he was a pawn in Amir's clutches.

The wall clock displayed noontime when the door flung open. Amir, flanked by Kazem and a thuggish-looking uniformed guard, entered the suite.

Startled, Ross swiveled in his chair, facing the three. "Welcome to my prison cell."

"You're not a prisoner," Amir said, fingering his prayer beads. "You can leave anytime you wish. But—" he stepped forward and sat on the edge of the desk, "you *know* what you have to do first."

"Don't you ever give up?" Ross snapped. "We've been over that before. I've told you a hundred times that I can't access the Scorpion from here…and I wouldn't even if I could."

Prepared for this answer, Amir reached into his jacket pocket and pulled out a white envelope, which was stamped *SERRIE*—SECRET in large red letters. His blistering stare fixed on Ross, he tapped the sealed envelope over his knee a few times and then, unceremoniously, tossed it on the desk. "Maybe this will change your mind."

Ross picked up the envelope. *What the hell is this?* he thought, as he swiftly ripped the side open. There were two postcard-size photographs inside. He slowly removed them, looking once at Amir before glancing at the top picture.

It was Marina.

As he looked closer, he recoiled in disbelief. Her face appeared beet red, her hair was disheveled, and her bloodshot eyes were filled with fear. Ross' breath quickened. He could hear his own heartbeat. He examined the second picture. She was handcuffed to a metal chair in the middle of a sparse room as if she were an inmate awaiting electrocution.

Oh my God!

The blood drained from Ross' face. For a few seconds, he felt dizzy. Nauseous. Then, came rage—slowly building, as the gravity of the situation set in.

Silence lingered.

Suddenly, like a volcanic eruption, he lunged for Amir. *"Ey maadar sagg!*—You son of a bitch!" Ross grabbed him by the collar and pulled him onto the floor, raining punches upon him. He stopped only long enough to move his hands to Amir's neck. Squeezing, Ross screamed, "What have you done to my daughter?" He shook Amir violently. "Where is she?" Landing a right hook onto his face, he shouted, "I'll kill you!"

Kazem and the security man rushed to break up the struggle. The guard grabbed Ross from behind, peeling him off Amir. As Ross was being dragged away, he continued to kick and shout, "Leave me alone! I'll kill that scumbag!" One powerful thrust of his leg caught Amir in the nose.

Amir moaned, blood gushing out of his nostrils. Kazem knelt on the floor, trying to shield Amir from the blows. "You're all animals!" Ross kicked Kazem in the back of his head as the guard struggled to keep them apart. "She's just a kid!"

The guard placed Ross in a chokehold, struggling to keep him under control. Kazem stepped forward and shoved his knee into Ross' groin as hard as he could. Ross doubled over. After dragging him to an armchair, the guard produced a pair of handcuffs and latched Ross' wrists to the chair. Amir stumbled out of the room as Kazem slumped onto the couch breathing heavily.

The next few minutes passed quietly.

Unlike his anxiety level, Ross' breathing had returned to normal. Handcuffed to the chair, in the surreal confines of the mammoth bunker, he felt completely alone. *Please, God—keep her safe.* He prayed as hard as he could. Then, staring into the kaleidoscope of his memories, he saw Marina.

It was her birthday—sweet sixteen.

Ross had conspired with Oksana to keep the special present they had picked out for the occasion a total secret. They had gone as far as to purchase a decoy gift to throw her off. After a small group of her friends gathered around the kitchen table, cheering as she blew out the candles, Ross announced, "Now for the big surprise. Everyone, follow me."

"What is it, Dad?"

Outside, a shiny, yellow MINI Cooper was parked in the driveway with a giant red bow on top. Roy, who had become part of the conspiracy by hiding the car in his garage, was capturing the moment on his video camera.

At first glance, Marina froze in astonishment. Then she let out a loud scream, ran to the car, circling it, and then sprinted back to Ross. She stopped in front of him, tearfully looking into his eyes, and then hugged him tight. "You're the best, Daddy."

33

At the Kremlin, General Viktor Pugachov was in rare form. Throughout the years, he had dealt with countless crises. From the Cold War to the breakup of the USSR, and from the debacle in Afghanistan to the Chechen war, he had seen them all. This crisis, however, was different.

It was personal.

Someone had attacked his flesh and blood. His granddaughter had been kidnapped. Her life was in peril. Gone was the cold, impervious persona; he was angry beyond measure and made no attempts at hiding it.

With his tie loosened and his patience taxed, Pugachov briefed the heads of the elite Russian intelligence agencies that had assembled in his office. He meant business. In a steely voice that sliced through the tension in the room, he let it be known that he was determined to find Marina—no matter what price, in treasure and blood, would be necessary.

"Nikolai," Pugachov said, addressing the FSB chief, "what assets do we have inside Iran's security apparatus?"

General Nikolai Kurnakov, a fearsome figure with an elegant mustache, and an old friend of Pugachov, said calmly, "We have many informants in MOIS."

"How high up the command structure?"

Admiral Zinkewich, an ambitious middle-aged bureaucrat who had recently left the Navy to head the GRU, cut in. "We have one high-ranking source inside the J2 unit—Iran's military intelligence. If anyone knows what's going on, it would be him."

Kurnakov gave Zinkewich a knowing look and continued. "Of course, we have significant signal intelligence capabilities. We even have their President's office bugged."

"With all this capability, how could we not have advance knowledge of this plot?"

The men looked down, avoiding Pugachov's glare.

"Do you think this is a government sanctioned operation or the work of some rogue faction?" Pugachov asked.

"Their military depends on us for hardware, technical assistance, and satellite imagery," Admiral Zinkewich said. "We can practically put them out of business. Or, delay the delivery of the air-defense missile systems they just purchased. They have much to lose with a stunt like this and little to gain." He paused. "I have trouble believing that the Iranian military would be involved."

General Kurnakov opined, "The clerics keep the government highly compartmentalized. The right hand is usually ignorant of what the left hand is doing. But MOIS, they would know. They are the only agency in Iran with such a global reach."

"Well, then…" Pugachov rose and started to pace, clasping his hands behind his back, "activate your networks. Send word to all intelligence assets in Iran that the Kremlin wants every scrap of information they can dig up regarding Dr. Shaheen and his whereabouts. What docs MOIS want from him? What schemes do they have for his family in America? I want to know everything." He stopped and fixed his gaze on the Generals. "And above all, I want to know where they are keeping my Marina." He resumed pacing. "Or, at a minimum, the name of someone who knows where she is."

Pugachov's personal secretary walked in. "The Ambassador is on the secure line."

"Put him through."

For the next hour, Pugachov and the assembled intelligence chiefs reviewed the crisis with the Russian Ambassador in Tehran. Like the Generals, he was stunned by the news of Marina's kidnapping. He was, however, aware of Ross' whereabouts—Reza, the driver, had promptly filed a report with the FSB station chief. But the Ambassador didn't have any first-hand information about Ross' condition in the underground facility.

The Ambassador asked Pugachov, "Do you want me to file a formal complaint with the Foreign Ministry?"

"No. No. We should not draw any attention to ourselves," Pugachov said. "We must operate in the shadows."

"As you wish, General."

"But, you may convey a private message to the top man at MOIS that I hold him personally responsible for the safety of my granddaughter and Dr. Shaheen."

"I will do so first thing in the morning."

"No. Do it now."

"Certainly, Comrade General."

It was approaching midnight when the spy chiefs left the Kremlin to attend to their urgent assignments.

Pugachov was alone in his vast, dimly lit office. Parting the heavy curtains, he stared into the Moscow night, despondent. His towering figure slightly stooped, he closed his eyes, thinking, *God! I haven't prayed to you for a lifetime. I don't even know if you exist. But, if you are there, please keep her safe...I beg you.*

His personal secretary entered, interrupting his thoughts. "General, you must be exhausted. May I call your driver?"

"Yes."

As she turned to leave, Pugachov said, "Contact Dimitry Veloshin. Have him meet me at my dacha immediately."

"Tonight?"

"Yes, without delay."

Amir Meshkin staggered into his office suite holding an ice pack against his left cheek. What was visible of his face was swollen and bruised. His light blue suit, which had once been neat and well pressed, was now crumpled and bloodstained. Two extra guards walked in behind him.

In pain, he slid an armchair in front of Ross and slumped into it. Then he looked at one of the guards. *"Tasbeehe mano peyda kon—Find my prayer beads."*

Ross stared at him. An awkward silence hung in the air, and then Amir broke it. "You remind me of your late brother, Dr. Shaheen. He also had a temper."

How would he know Sohrab and his temper? Ross thought.

Seeing Ross' bewildered expression, Amir explained. "You see, I was an interrogator at the Evin prison when your brother was brought in."

One of the guards approached, handing the prayer beads to Amir. He took it and started to finger them, smiling, like a child with his security blanket.

"Yes…I remember Sohrab as if it were yesterday," Amir said. "What we wanted was his signature on an apology letter. That's all. But he wouldn't do it. He was stubborn—like you—and a fireball of rage."

Ross listened, transfixed.

"The guards beat him mercilessly. 'Just say you're sorry,' I would plead. 'Sign the damn letter!' He wouldn't budge. This went on for days. Toward the end, his face was so swollen that I couldn't make out his features. He wouldn't listen. Finally," Amir lowered the icepack from his face and, leaning closer to Ross, whispered, "I got tired of him. I had unfinished business with hundreds of other prisoners. So, one morning, I put him out of his misery. I shot him in the back of his head."

Recalling the image of Sohrab's desolate gravesite, Ross felt nauseous. At long last, he'd discovered what had become of his brother—how, and why, he had died. What's more, he was now face to face with Sohrab's murderer.

Amir was not through. "Do you know what happens when you get shot in the back of your head, Dr. Shaheen?"

Although his blood was boiling with rage, Ross remained quiet. Stone faced. Amir illustrated by cupping his hand over his face. "Your whole face blows out…It's an ugly scene."

This is psychological torture, Ross thought. *He's trying to break my will. I won't give him the satisfaction.*

"That was twenty-five years ago," Ross said, squeezing the armrests. "Why are you telling me this?"

"I want you to know what I'm capable of doing."

"You want to shoot me in the back of my head? Go right ahead. I'm not afraid of you. Or death."

"No, no, no. You won't get off that easy, Dr. Shaheen. I will not lay a hand on you. But, your daughter…That's an entirely different story." Once again, Amir came closer, whispering, "As God is my witness, I will have her chopped into tiny little pieces and ship the parts to her mother. And I will have the whole thing filmed for you to watch."

Ross' instinctive impulse was to lunge for Amir again. And had it not been for the handcuffs, he would have torn him limb from limb.

"You leave her alone!"

"I will if you would just go to that computer and feed our designs to the Blind Scorpion. That's all. Then you and your daughter will go free…It's that simple."

"How do I know you'll let her go?"

"We can ill afford to add Russia to our long list of enemies," Amir said. "Once we have what we want, hurting you or your daughter will not be in our self-interest. We are well aware of your connection with Viktor Pugachov."

Ross dropped his head, thinking, *Amir holds all the cards—Marina and me. I have no choice. So, what if I test their bomb with the Scorpion? What difference would it make? They have built the damn thing anyway. It just provides them with deniability. Nuclear ambiguity—a strategic fig leaf. It's not as if I'm helping them build a bomb. It's the end of the road, and I've got to save Marina. If anything happens to her because of something I did or refused to do, I'd never be able to live with myself.*

He looked up and whispered, "Okay, Amir."

Flashing his gold tooth, Amir smirked knowingly.

"You win." Ross struggled with the words. "I'll do it."

THREE KNOCKS. "ROSS?" ANOTHER TWO. "ROSS! ARE YOU IN THERE?" Leila Conner placed her ear to the door.

No answer.

It was her fifth attempt at contacting Ross Shaheen since the last time they had been together. The front desk did not know, or would not say, where he had gone. They would only disclose that he was still a registered guest at the hotel and had not checked out. But, mysteriously, Leila's messages went unanswered.

Frustrated, Leila produced a sheet of paper from her purse and started to scribble a note.

Dear Ross,

Where are you? I've been trying to reach you for the past three days with no luck. I hope you're not mad at me. Anyway, I have scored a big interview—Amir Meshkin. Do you know him? He is a big shot at the AEOI. I believe he's the No. 2 guy. I'm supposed to meet him in Natanz, and he has promised me a tour of the facility! Can you believe it? I'll be the first journalist to go into the bunker.

I need to get together with you and pick your brain about what all to ask him. I don't want to sound like the rest of the blowhards who report on Iran's nukes. And you're my secret weapon.

I'm in room 713. You can drop by if you want. Or call me if that's more convenient. And the front desk will connect you. I promise! I'm not as big a VIP as you are, with "authorized callers list" and all.

I'm only joking. Don't get excited.

Anyway, call me ASAP. I'm leaving for Natanz tomorrow afternoon.

Hugs, Leila.

She read over the note, folded it, and slid it under the door. She straightened up and stood with her hand on the door for a minute thinking, *I hope he's okay.*

SPETSNAZ, THE RUSSIAN ARMY SPECIAL FORCES, WERE THE MOST elite and the best-trained units of the Russian military. Unlike the Special Forces of the United States, the Spetsnaz were not organized as independent brigades and boasted no official names. Instead, they were typically integrated into the ranks of other military units and wore the uniforms of their hosts in order to blend in and protect their identities.

Controlled by the GRU, the Spetsnaz soldiers had a license to kill anyone at will in the interest of accomplishing the objectives set before them. Despite the shroud of secrecy, the Spetsnaz had developed a reputation as one of the most ferocious Special Forces in the world.

Their stealth, ruthless tactics, and the very harsh standards of their five-year training were legendary.

During the Cold War, these units were deployed in Eastern Europe to carry out reconnaissance and sabotage missions against the NATO forces in the event of a war. Subsequently, they were mostly assigned to counter terrorism and black-ops missions. Few details were actually known about their operations, but it was generally accepted that the Spetsnaz were heavily involved in the conflict in Chechnya.

And that's where Dimitry Veloshin, one of the finest soldiers Spetsnaz ever produced, had polished his skills. Participating in counter-insurgence operations, he had twice foregone rotation back to Moscow in order to stay and attend to his duties, which, among other things, included tracking, capturing, and interrogating enemy leadership. Above all, he relished his specialty—assassinations.

Slender and handsome, with his blond buzz cut and piercing green eyes, Veloshin was a man of few words. His raspy voice sounded more like a whisper, leaving most listeners with a haunting impression. The ever-present turtleneck hid the deep scar that ran from his left ear to the base of his throat—a "souvenir" from Chechnya. At thirty-two, he was at the peak of his physical strength. A loner by choice, Veloshin was a complete stranger to regrets.

He was motivated by an uncommon mixture of patriotism and the dark pleasure he took in his work. As such, Dimitry Veloshin was singularly an indispensable asset, a tool that Viktor Pugachov used like an artisan would a fine chisel. For the previous two years, Veloshin was on loan to the Russian Mafia, where he obediently advanced the aims of the criminal enterprise, which, as a rule, were in lockstep with those of the Kremlin.

2:05 AM.

General Pugachov tenderly stroked the chest of a white homing pigeon, which was gently cupped in his right hand. The spacious aviary, built behind his palatial dacha, was home to hundreds of rare pigeons from around the world. One of the few escapes Pugachov allowed himself was training the birds to fly away, come back circling in the air, and then return to their coop. The aviary was his mental refuge.

A whisper broke the silence. "You sent for me?"

"Yes," Pugachov said, without turning to look at his visitor.

"I'm here."

"The French Ambassador is not pleased with what was done to Pierre La Perche."

"The pig wouldn't pay."

Pugachov placed the bird in its cage. Then he turned, facing the man. "Was gouging out his eyeballs necessary?"

"It was a warning to others."

"And, I suppose, you savored the moment."

"My work is not without its thrills."

"Let us tone it down for a while."

"Is that why you sent for me?"

"No." Pugachov walked toward the rear entrance of his dacha. "Come inside, Dimitry."

⌒∿⌒

THE RUSSIAN WORD *DACHA* GENERALLY REFERRED TO A MODEST cottage in the Russian countryside. The more affluent city dwellers often procured dachas to use as getaways on summer weekends. However, official dachas, reserved for the top government leaders, were in a class by themselves. These were huge, barricaded resort compounds with numerous large buildings and a full-time staff to cater to the leader's every need. Viktor Pugachov's dacha was second only to the one used by the President of the Russian Federation.

Sitting in adjacent leather chairs in front of a giant fireplace, Pugachov glanced at Veloshin and said, "Take a look at this file." An overly stuffed red folder lay on the coffee table. Veloshin cracked it open and started to read. Within seconds, his expression changed. He seemed angry. Pugachov quietly watched as Veloshin thumbed through the intelligence briefs, photos of Marina and Ross, maps of Iran, and transcripts of intercepts. After nearly half an hour of careful review, he closed the dossier.

"They are foolish," Veloshin said, as he placed the folder on the coffee table. "Do they think they can get away with this?"

"For the past thirty years, the Iranians have gotten away with all sorts of crazy schemes without repercussions...Why stop now?"

Veloshin nodded.

"Aeroflot has a daily flight to Tehran." Pugachov leaned forward. "It leaves at 10:15 in the morning. They are holding a seat for you."

"What is my mission?"

"To find the mastermind behind this travesty. To discover where Marina is kept."

"And then?"

"To go after her."

"What about Dr. Shaheen?"

"He is beyond your reach. The underground facility in Natanz is impenetrable. We have a few assets there, but I can't jeopardize them for his rescue."

"I will need local assets to get around."

"The Embassy will provide whatever you require."

Veloshin rose. "I better get some sleep."

"Dimitry…" Pugachov looked up. "Find my Marina."

Exuding the quiet confidence of a military man who had never failed to accomplish his mission, Veloshin looked at Pugachov, paused, and said, "Rest assured, General. If she is alive…I will find her."

"And as you look for her, the fewer the witnesses you leave behind the better."

Veloshin whispered, "I will enjoy this," as he turned to leave.

34

Roy Sullivan emptied the rest of the Coke down his throat, crumpled the can, and aimed for the wastebasket across the room. He nailed it. Then he swiveled in his chair, staring at the gray STU-3 telephone. He took another look at his watch. Waiting.

In the four days since Marina's abduction, time stretched on endlessly. Roy could not banish Marina from his head even for a moment. Unable to sleep or eat, he felt responsible for what had befallen her. The memory of saying farewell to Ross, assuring him that his family would be safe, was painfully vivid. Roy felt as if he had let his friend down.

The FBI had issued an all-points bulletin seeking the suspicious Iranians who had been holed up for months across the street from the Shaheens. Fortunately, one of the neighbors had snapped a photograph of the three, which was now enhanced and being used in the FBI alert. Described as "armed and dangerous," every law enforcement agency along the western seaboard was on the lookout for the three Iranians.

At two minutes after 8:00 AM, the STU-3 rang. Roy grabbed the receiver. "Agent Sullivan."

"Go secure," Colonel Nash said.

Roy inserted the red crypto-ignition key into the phone and pressed the oval button.

After a few seconds, Colonel Nash said, "What's the latest?"

Roy proceeded to brief the Deputy Director of the CIA about the FBI's investigation. That the cigarette butts they had found at the parking lot matched the ones left in the Miller's house—"A DNA bull's eye." This was the basis for the FBI's belief that Venice Beach must have been the transfer point. And a couple of cops on patrol had reported seeing a green California Fish and Wildlife van parked there on the night of the kidnapping.

"Have you found the van?" Nash inquired.

"Nope. It seems to have vanished…Like the rest of them."

"What else?"

Roy continued with his report. The FBI had found the Iranians' SUV abandoned in an underground parking garage in Half Moon Bay, and it had not provided any clues.

"They know their shit, don't they?"

"Yup." Roy sighed. "The surveillance, the fleet of cars, and the speedboat—it was a well planned operation all right."

"This must have been in the works for a long time, maybe a year," Nash said. "Don't you think?"

"With two months of it in my own damn neighborhood." Now upset, Roy growled, "Right under my frigging nose!"

"Don't beat yourself up, Sullivan," Nash said. "It doesn't help anything."

"How about the CIA?" Roy asked. "You guys have anything?"

Colonel Nash revealed as much as he could. That he had just received a call from General Pugachov, and how he had tore him "a new diplomatic asshole."

"I figured he'd be pissed," Roy said.

"You have no idea. It was real ugly. After all the yelling and cussing, he wanted to know if we were making any progress and if the investigation was getting high enough of a priority from the FBI. I assured him it was."

"You're damn right it's priority," Roy said indignantly. "She's like my own daughter, for God's sake. I'll find her come hell or high water, and you can promise Pugachov plenty of both."

Colonel Nash informed Roy that he had sent the photo of the Iranians to all the CIA's liaison intelligence services, and the Canadian CSIS had identified one of them: "The younger man, the clean-shaven one, his name is Farzad Ibrahimi—an engineer and a known MOIS agent."

"So that nails it," Roy said. "The Iranian intelligence is behind this whole thing."

"Yes. It's all falling in place."

"Can Washington do something about it?"

"Like what?"

"I don't know…Use diplomatic channels to protest. Warn the Iranians. Maybe fire a dozen cruise missiles up their ass. Or anything else you can think of."

"Our options are quite limited. We have sent word through the Swiss. But I'm certain the mullahs will play their usual game of denial and belligerence."

"The bastards!"

"I just left the White House. The President has instructed that we use any and all means at our disposal to rescue Ross. We figure if he's out of Iran, they would have no use for Marina and might let her go."

"Can you rescue Ross?" Roy sounded astonished. "Is that even possible?"

"It's possible…Not probable. But we'll give it all we've got, which isn't much."

"What about the Mossad? Can they help?"

Thinking about his appointment with Commander Rafael in the afternoon, Colonel Nash said, "We've asked them…Time will tell."

"Surely they've got assets in Iran."

Colonel Nash changed the subject. "How's Oksana holding up?"

"She's not…and who can blame her?"

"I owe her a phone call."

"She'll be glad to hear from you."

"Let me know if anything new turns up, Sullivan—anything at all."

"You'll be my first call."

By bringing to mind the pitiful image of Marina handcuffed to the chair, Ross kept his ambivalence in check. He had to save his daughter, no matter what the cost. And the only option was to give Amir Meshkin what he wanted—to test Amir's nuclear creation using the awesome powers of the Blind Scorpion. *I must do it or else Marina dies.* Ross kept repeating it to himself.

But giving into Amir's demands was easier said than done.

The Blind Scorpion was burrowed inside a dedicated supercomputer at the NERSC—National Energy Research Scientific Computing Center—back in Oakland. A recent upgrade to the fastest supercomputer in the world, the IBM's Blue Gene, with its mind numbing 1,400 teraflops of computing power, had cut down Blind Scorpion's run time by a factor of twelve. With the new system, a typical nuclear simulation required only two hours of number crunching compared to nearly 24 hours on the old machine.

All it took was to upload the DFX files of the bomb design, stored in Amir's PC, to the Blue Gene computer, then to launch the Blind Scorpion software and set a few parameters specifying the purity of the uranium and other materials used. And then wait. A couple of hours later, the monster machine would spit out a string of numbers denoting the probability of a successful explosion followed by the expected yield of the nuclear device in kilotons.

Numerous rings of security, however, surrounded the Blind Scorpion. And Ross was intimately aware of every layer. After all, they were mostly his creation; his way of ensuring that would-be hackers were stopped cold. In fact, the most effective defense against intruders was in place: the Blue Gene was a standalone supercomputer; it was not connected to the Internet. The small community of authorized users mostly lived around the Berkeley Lab and accessed the Blind Scorpion using workstations that were hardwired to the Blue Gene. And the few remote users always connected to the machine via dedicated fiber channels or secure, encrypted VPNs—Virtual Private Networks.

How can I access the damn thing from here? Ross searched his mind for the answer over and over again.

Standing in front of him, while fingering the long strand of agate prayer beads, Amir interrupted Ross' thoughts. "You've made the right decision, Dr. Shaheen. Now, time is short. Let's get started."

Ross looked at Kazem and the guards scattered around the room. "Get these people out of here. I need some peace and quiet to figure out a way to access the computer from here."

"Figure out?" Amir said, surprised. He approached his desk and, lifting the phone receiver, rapidly dialed a number. "This is Meshkin... put my workstation on-line."

Then he turned to Ross. "In a few minutes, you'll have a high-speed connection to the net. It's a gigabit pipeline." He continued sarcastically, "What's there to 'figure out?' Have you forgotten your password? Getting old?"

Shaking his head, Ross gave Amir a disdainful look. "With all due respect, Amir, you don't have a clue what the hell you're talking about."

Amir frowned, looking puzzled.

"The Blind Scorpion runs on a supercomputer that's not on-line. It's not connected to the Internet. I have no way of accessing it from here."

"That's a lie!"

"No. It's the truth."

"I know for a fact that physicists all around the Berkeley Lab use it for research."

"They're all fibered to the machine—every one of them."

"What about the special users in England. How do they get access?"

"They use secure VPNs to connect."

"Are you telling me that the fastest computer in the world doesn't have a single connection to the Internet?"

"Not one."

Amir looked at his PC for a minute and then slumped in his chair, quietly processing what he had just learned. *This changes everything.*

Ross continued. "You've hatched this damned scheme for nothing, Amir. I cannot give you what you want. It's physically impossible."

"Well, you'd better figure something out quickly," Amir snapped. "I shouldn't have to remind you what's at stake...Or, should I?"

"I'm trying...I need to think...Now, will you get these idiots out of this room so I can concentrate?"

Amir snapped twice. "Everyone, out!"

The guards obediently filed out of the room. The last one stopped at the door and inquired if Amir felt safe being left alone with Ross. "He is violent, sir."

"I'll be fine," Amir said. "But stay in the hallway just in case."

Motioning him out, Ross said, "You, too, Kazem."

Once he and Amir were alone, Ross said, "What time is it?"

"Ten till eleven."

"Day or night? It's hard to tell down here."

"Morning."

"Is it Monday?"

"Yes."

"That makes it about midnight Sunday in Berkeley."

"So?"

"I need to call my secretary...In about eight hours from now."

Taken aback, Amir said, "Are you out of your mind?"

"She's my only hope of accessing the system."

"Can she do it?"

"It'll be difficult. But with my help, I believe she can."

"Is she reliable?"

"Yes. Very."

Fingering his prayer beads, Amir stared at Ross intently, thinking. After a minute, he said, "Whatever you're planning...it better work."

Ross didn't answer.

"I'll be back in the afternoon to arrange the call," Amir said, walking toward the door. "Ironically, I have to prepare for an interview with a CNN reporter."

"Who's that?"

"Leila Conner," Amir said, as he turned the doorknob. "Another Iranian turncoat, like you."

Ross shook his head in disbelief, smiling faintly. "Will you let me out of these handcuffs?" he asked.

"I'll think about it."

THE TEHRAN–ISFAHAN HIGHWAY SNAKED AROUND THE EDGE OF THE Dasht-e-Kevir desert. The sun loomed hot in the midsummer morning as the white Volkswagen van, emblazoned with an oversized CNN logo, made its way south toward Natanz.

The air-conditioner was shot.

In the passenger seat, Leila Conner had rolled down the window for some relief. But the cloudless skies and the rush of warm air did little to abate the oppressive heat. Her white cotton shirt and khaki pants, drenched in sweat, were stuck to her skin. She felt helpless. *I'd give a month's pay for a cold shower.*

Her driver, Eskandar—Persian name for Alexander—a handsome, British-educated Iranian, said little. He also doubled as her security guard, and, recently, Leila had "promoted" him to the position of lover as well. It was a fleeting relationship of convenience, which despite Eskandar's desire to the contrary, he knew would not lead anywhere.

In the backseat, her producer and cameraman whined mercilessly about the heat.

"Guys!" Leila said impatiently, as they approached the city of Qum, marking the halfway point in the six-hour trek, "There's nothing we can do about the heat or the air-conditioner. So will you please cut the crap?"

Their silence lasted less than two minutes.

Before entering the city, Eskandar told Leila to cover up. Disgusted, she grabbed her *chador* and placed it over her head, covering her entire body.

"I'll suffocate under this damn thing."

"We're in Qum," the driver said. "This is Iran's holiest city and a major theological center. To Shiite Muslims, Qum is second only to Najaf in importance. The people around here are quite fanatic. If they find a woman without proper *hijab*, they'll probably stone her to death."

"It seems I'm going to die either from a heatstroke or stoning. It's not much of a choice. Is it?"

"You won't die under that *chador*," her producer chimed in from the backseat. "I assure you."

"That's easy for you to say…Let's just blaze through the city as fast as we can. This place has too many mosques and mullahs. And I am sick of both."

Despite the suspicious stares of the bystanders, the drive through Qum was uneventful. Peering from underneath her *chador*, Leila grudgingly admired the majesty of the sprawling mosques adorned with enormous golden domes and towering minarets.

After Qum, as the sun continued rising to its zenith, the journey to Natanz became increasingly painful. The passengers were so exhausted from the heat that they could not even complain, let alone carry on a normal conversation. Even sleeping was impossible. At last, nearly an hour past noon, they arrived in the dusty and desolate city.

The modest, two-story inn was as welcome as a lush desert oasis would have been to a lost caravan. The CNN crew quickly checked in. Their rooms were clustered together at the end of a narrow hallway on the second floor. Leila's interview with Amir Meshkin was less than two hours away, giving her enough time to clean herself up.

As she took delight in the cold shower, she also felt her anxiety level rising. Soon she would enter Natanz uranium enrichment plant, the epicenter of the world's greatest nightmare. Where the next American—or Israeli—military conquest would probably start. As Iran's indispensable gateway to its nuclear ambitions, Natanz would be the highest value target in any air strike.

It was 3:15 PM when Amir Meshkin, the deputy director of AEOI—Atomic Energy Organization of Iran—sat down for his first on-camera interview with an American journalist. The setting was the lobby of the administrative building at the center of the sprawling facility, with an oversized image of the Supreme Leader as backdrop.

For the next two hours, Amir and Leila engaged in a bizarre intellectual swordfight. In response to her observation that international crises do not usually result from one dramatic event, but rather as a result of a series of missteps, Amir said, "Tell that to your president... *He* is the king of missteps. You will find no such thing in Iran."

Amir's tone was at times terse and often condescending, while Leila maintained her calm demeanor. She knew the camera well and how negatively it would portray Amir and his rhetoric. However, Amir, a master of diversion, successfully blunted Leila's persistent attempts at uncovering the truth behind Iran's atomic energy program. At the end, there were no new revelations.

Once the spotlights were turned off and as the cameras were being loaded into their metal containers, Leila thanked Amir for granting the interview and said, "By the way, do you know Dr. Ross Shaheen?"

"Of course I do."

"Do you know where he might be? It seems he has vanished."

"He lectured at the NRC in Karaj last week. That's where I saw him last."

"That's about when I spoke with him also. But I haven't been able to contact him since."

"He was supposed to go to Shiraz for the rest of his stay in Iran. Maybe he is there now."

"Maybe so…"

"We'll tour the plant tomorrow, Ms. Conner."

"I'm looking forward to it."

A hundred feet below, handcuffed to an armchair, Dr. Ross Shaheen sat. Waiting. And worried sick about his daughter.

⟋⟋⟋

TALL AND BLOND, CLAD IN BLACK HEAD-TO-TOE, WITH HIS GREEN eyes hidden behind dark sunglasses, Dimitry Veloshin stood out conspicuously in the Tehran Mehrabad Airport. Oblivious to the hustle and bustle of the chaotic terminal, he calmly strolled toward the passport control area.

Behind the station reserved for diplomats, an undercover FSB agent was waiting to expedite his entry. As Veloshin placed his green, gold-embossed passport on the counter, the FSB agent approached and whispered something to the immigration officer. Looking at Veloshin, the officer nodded subtly and waived him through without stamping the document.

With few words exchanged, the FSB agent whisked Veloshin away in a sleek black Lexus with a Russian Embassy license plate.

It was early afternoon.

The embassy of the Russian Federation in the capital city of the Islamic Republic of Iran was a sprawling compound that spanned an entire city block. Sandwiched between Ferdowsi Street and Hafez Avenue, major thoroughfares named after two of Iran's greatest poets, the place looked more like a medieval fortress than a modern day embassy. Brick walls, twelve feet high and topped with razor wires, surrounded the compound.

Ironically, during the peak of the Islamic Revolution in 1979, when the American Embassy was overrun and the British legation endured violent protests on a daily basis, the Russian Embassy remained untouched and its diplomats were treated with respect. They remained unmolested not because of the formidable walls that protected their embassy but largely because the Iranian revolutionaries knew too well that, unlike the Americans or the Brits, their neighbors to the north would not tolerate such nonsense.

The Lexus entered the compound through heavily guarded iron gates and pulled up in front of a low rise, modern guesthouse.

"Let me show you to your room, comrade Veloshin."

"That can wait. I have urgent business to attend to."

"As you wish…The station chief is waiting."

In a windowless, concrete building, topped with a jumble of antennae and satellite dishes, the FSB Chief received Dimitry Veloshin with respectful disdain. Kremlin had instructed him, in no uncertain terms, to extend every consideration to Veloshin. But the top spy in Iran did not like the idea of a loose cannon on his turf. Besides, he had spent the last decade in Iran building a vast network of informants and spies. He knew the country well and took the sending of a special envoy from Moscow to deal with the crisis as a personal insult.

The FSB Chief walked Veloshin through the available information in painstaking detail. The Russian intelligence knew of Ross' whereabouts; their mole at Natanz had confirmed that he was alive and well. But information about Marina and her abduction were sketchy. The FSB spies could not pinpoint the agency that was running the operation, or who had authorized it. The GRU had traced it to MOIS, which in turn had denied knowledge and pointed the finger at elements within the Revolutionary Guards. Nothing was certain; anyone asked denied knowledge with the intent to place as much possible distance between themselves and the kidnapping. It seemed no one wanted the hot potato.

"I get it." Veloshin calmly assessed the situation. "We have nothing on Marina."

The FSB Chief said, "Not yet."

"Where should I start?" Veloshin whispered. "What's the shortest path to the bottom line?"

"Sergey Saidayev," the Station Chief said, as he handed a thick dossier to Veloshin. "He's one of our own scientists working in their nuclear weapons program…He would be my first stop."

"Where do I find him?"

"I'll arrange for a local agent to take you to him."

"I work alone."

"You need an Iranian with you," the Chief said. "Trust me on this."

"Is he reliable?"

"As reliable as they come. His name is Reza...He's a proven asset and well-wired into the Tehran underworld."

"Tell him to be here at midnight."

Unaccustomed to taking orders from a junior officer, the Station Chief gritted his teeth and said, "He'll be ready."

Staring at the first page of the folder, Veloshin carefully studied Sergey's photograph and profile. Then, in a low voice, he said, "Another Chechen dog...Certainly a good place to start."

35

IT WAS JUST ANOTHER MORNING FOR PAM CARLISLE, DR. SHAHEEN'S secretary. To her, Mondays were as merry as Fridays and rain showers as delightful as sunshine. However, since Ross' trip to Iran and the bizarre disappearance of Marina, her cheerful demeanor had lost its luster.

After the kidnapping, Pam had phoned Oksana every morning to offer moral support and inquire if there was any break in the investigation, only to find out there had been none. Feeling Oksana's pain, she sympathized with her over the phone and frequently in person.

She had worked for Ross for over ten years. Being single and away from her own family, the Shaheens had practically adopted her. What's more, the children adored her earthy nature and free spirit. Pam and the Shaheens were very close.

Pam was sipping a concoction of hot apple cider mixed with ginger tea when she was startled by the ringing of her phone. With Ross out of the country, few people called, especially that early on a Monday morning. Thinking it might be another eager reporter fishing for tidbits on Marina, she ignored the call, letting it roll over to voice mail. But it rang again, and again.

"Dr. Shaheen's office," she finally answered.

"Pam..." a hushed voice said. "It's me, Ross."

"Oh my God," Pam screamed. "Ross. Is that you? Are you okay? Where are—"

"I'm okay. I don't have any time for questions. You must do exactly as I say."

"Sure! Anything."

Ross spoke slowly. "Put me on hold, go to my desk, and pick up the phone from there."

"Hang on."

Pam rushed to the door to Ross' office and inserted her magnetic badge into the slot. It cracked open. She ran to his desk and sat down. Then she pressed the HANDSFREE button on the telephone. "Ross, I'm here at your desk."

"Listen. Stay calm. Take a deep breath. I'll walk you through the steps."

"What steps?"

"No questions! Remember?"

"All right. All right. Tell me what to do."

"Turn on both of my PCs."

Pam powered up Ross' unsecured computer first. Once the flat-screen monitor on the left side of the desk came up, she said, "What's your password?"

"Which PC?"

"The one you use for your regular stuff…The one on the left."

"SOHRAB+233"

"Your brother's name?"

"Yes."

After a few seconds she said, "It's up." Then she proceeded with the secure PC on the right side of his desk.

"What's the password for the other one?"

The line was silent.

"Ross? Are you still there?"

Pam heard a click.

Amir Meshkin had just loaded the chamber of the gun he was pointing at Ross' head. "It's too late for any hesitation, Dr. Shaheen."

From the phone: "Ross? Are you there? Please say something!"

"I'm here, Pam." Ross glanced at Amir, who was listening to the conversation with a headset, and wiped the sweat off his brow. He spoke into the phone again. "We have to be very careful with that computer, Pam."

"I know. This one has a camera…It won't recognize me."

"Don't worry, we can trick the camera."

"How?"

"Take the camera out of its cradle."

"What?"

"Just lift it up; it separates from the monitor."

"Aha. Got it, it's off."

"Do you see the framed picture of me and Oksana on the side table?"

"Yes."

"Place it next to you."

"Okay." Shuffle. "It's here."

"Listen carefully, Pam. Once you enter the password, the system will activate the camera to verify the identity of the person accessing the system."

"I know. I've seen it work."

"You'll recognize the camera is active when the little green light starts to blink. At that exact moment, you should point it to my face in the picture. Do you understand?"

"Yes, I do," Pam said nervously.

"You must hold the camera about five or six inches from the photo to fool it."

"I'll try."

"No! Trying isn't good enough, Pam. Get a grip. If you don't do as I say, the security system will be tripped."

Ross heard her take a deep breath.

"I know you can do it. Just stay cool," he said.

"All right. I'm fine."

"The main password is TRINITY#000—that's three zeros."

"Okay."

"Go ahead, type it in."

Ross could hear the keys clicking as she entered the password. *I hope to God she doesn't screw up...*

"Do you have the green light?" he asked.

"Yes."

He imagined her pointing the camera to the photo, the faint green laser beam painting a box around his image. His mouth dry, he said, "Has the green light stopped flashing?"

"No. It's still flashing, what does it mean?"

"It's not recognizing the image. We only have twenty seconds."

"What should I do? Please tell me, Ross!"

"Is your hand shaking?"

"I don't know. Maybe."

"Hold the camera with both hands. It must be steady."

"I'm trying. I'm trying."

"Concentrate," Ross said. "You can do it."

Amir moved the gun away from Ross' head. "What if the camera doesn't recognize your image?"

Covering the mouthpiece, Ross said, "The fiber channel between my PC and the Blue Gene will automatically shut down, and two security guards will be dispatched to my office within five minutes."

"Then what?"

"Game over. The FBI will be alerted, and there will be no other way to access the Blind Scorpion."

"Then I hope your scheme works, Dr. Shaheen…For Marina's sake."

Looking down, Ross swallowed hard.

REZA ROLLED TO A STOP IN FRONT OF A CHARMING HOUSE IN A DARK, shadowed alley. Lit only by moonlight, the sleepy neighborhood, a few kilometers north of Karaj, was deserted at 1:35 AM. The only sounds were the chirping of crickets and an occasional cat's meow.

Musing over how peculiar his passenger was, Reza said, "This is the house."

Veloshin leaned forward, looking up at the building. Whispering the only words he had spoken during the 90-minute ride, he said, "Does he live alone?"

"To my knowledge, yes."

Veloshin turned slowly, facing the driver. His displeasure at Reza's lack of certainty was palpable in his stare.

Reza corrected his response. "He lives alone."

"Drive away…" Veloshin carefully opened the door, so as not to make any sound. "Return in two hours."

He left the vehicle carrying a small satchel over his shoulder.

Freestanding houses in Iran are typically surrounded by small, lush gardens protected by high fences or brick walls. Aside from providing security, the fortress-like barriers reflect a culture of intense privacy. Yet, Iranians are keenly interested in discovering what goes on behind their neighbor's walls. The irony eludes them all. Thus, the rumors and gossip abound. A standard phrase in daily greetings is, *"Tazeh cheh khabar?"* Meaning, "What's the latest news or gossip?"

Sergey Saidayev had rented the elegant house from a retired Iranian couple living abroad. The two-story, four-bedroom residence was much more that he needed. He only used the kitchen, the living room, and the master bedroom upstairs. But the reclusive scientist welcomed the peace and quiet it afforded.

Veloshin scaled the brick wall with cat-like prowess. Jumping into the garden, he landed behind a large rosebush. In the faint moonlight, he looked around. All was quiet.

He sneaked around the perimeter of the house, gently testing the doors and windows for a way in. They were all locked. From his shoulder bag, he retrieved a pencil-size diamond cutter and a miniature suction cup. Using the tools, he cut a small, irregular circle in the glass pane of the rear entrance. A gentle tap broke it loose. He cautiously reached in and unlocked the door. Then he retrieved a set of night vision goggles from his satchel and strapped them to his forehead.

Looking like a creature from another planet, the Spetsnaz veteran entered the house. As he scanned the space, everything appeared in shades of gray and green through the goggles. The living room, sparsely furnished, was cluttered with piles of books and magazines. With great stealth, Veloshin searched the rest of the ground floor. As expected, the other rooms were completely bare.

He climbed the stairs to the second floor and found four doors opening into a small lobby. Three were closed shut while the fourth was slightly open. *That must be the dog's lair.*

Veloshin pulled a switchblade from his pocket and pressed the trigger. The seven-inch knife snapped open. Peering into the bedroom, he saw Sergey sleeping face down. The scientist was lying on the left side of a full-size bed, uncovered, hugging a large pillow. A ceiling fan spun slowly. Veloshin quietly opened the door just enough to enter. As he approached, he noticed the silhouette of a woman on the right side of the bed with her back to Sergey.

He hesitated. *She could complicate things.*

Veloshin crept closer. Sergey was snoring softly. Glancing at the shapely outline of the woman, Veloshin rehearsed his next moves in his head.

He passed the knife to his left hand. Then, suddenly, with his right hand, he clutched Sergey's neck and squeezed. Sergey woke up startled but could not move. Before he had a chance to scream, Veloshin bent over and whispered into his ear, *"Molchat chechenskaia sobaka*—Be quiet, Chechen dog...or die." As if any further emphasis was necessary, Veloshin squeezed Sergey's neck a notch further, pushing down.

Barely audible, with his face shoved into the pillow, Sergey moaned, *"Kto ti?*—Who are you?"

"Tvoj nochnoj koshmar—Satan's worst nightmare."

"Chto tebe nado?—What do you want?"

"Informatsiya—Information."

The bedroom was full of starlight. Sergey's brief jolt and their hushed exchange woke up his companion. Still appearing to be asleep, she muttered something and turned, facing Sergey and Veloshin. Gripping Sergey's neck, Veloshin stared at her through the night vision goggles. Seconds passed. Her eyes remained shut. Veloshin and Sergey were motionless. Then, unexpectedly, she opened her eyes.

At the sight of Veloshin's shadow, she bolted upright. "Sergey! Wake up! There's a thief in the house."

Veloshin instantly let go of Sergey's neck and grabbed the knife with his right hand. The woman, now sitting up and wide awake, opened her mouth to scream. With a rapid, sweeping motion of his arm, Veloshin crossed her neck with the blade, slitting her throat. At the same time, he pressed his right knee onto Sergey's back while clutching his neck.

The woman grabbed her throat with both hands frozen in place. Her windpipe severed, she made only wet, groaning sounds. She stared at Veloshin, paused, and slumped over. Motionless. Through the goggles, the expanding pool of blood seemed black.

Done with the woman, Veloshin let go of Sergey and said, "Turn around."

Veloshin flung his satchel on the bed, reached inside, and withdrew a Micro-Uzi automatic handgun with a silencer attached. Pointing the gun at Sergey's head, Veloshin walked backwards to the window. "Don't move a muscle," he said, as he closed the curtains.

Sergey remained still. He summoned all the courage he could muster and said, "Are you FSB?"

Veloshin turned on the nightlight, dropped the goggles on the floor, and said, "Spetsnaz."

"You said you w-wanted information," Sergey said, protecting his eyes from the glare of the light. "What information?"

"Get up." Veloshin grabbed Sergey by the hair, pulled him up, and made him obey. Shoving the silencer to the side of his neck, Veloshin said, "I ask the questions, Chechen dog...Understand?"

Sergey nodded. Veloshin stepped back. Then, all of a sudden, as if Sergey had remembered something, he turned and looked at his lifeless bedmate, her hands clutching her neck, her face soaked in blood.

Sergey glanced back at Veloshin with a sickened expression. "She was innocent...An ordinary housekeeper." His voice trembling, he said, "Why did you have to kill her?"

Veloshin whispered, "Instinct."

Sergey looked down at his own hands. They were shaking uncontrollably. The last time he had felt this fearful was when the bloodied bodies of his wife and son were dragged out from the rubble of his house, back in Grozny.

He swallowed, his eyes back on Veloshin. "Are you going to kill me?"

"Not yet."

Veloshin grabbed him by his arm and threw him in the direction of the door as if he were a rag doll. "Get downstairs!"

Sergey crawled toward the bedroom door and pulled himself up by the handle. Veloshin jabbed the gun into Sergey's back, prodding him. Halfway down the stairs, Veloshin shoved him to hurry him along. But he tumbled, landing on the bottom in a pathetic, quivering heap.

"Stop this torture," Sergey begged. "I'll tell you whatever you want."

Again, Veloshin grabbed him by the hair and pulled him to his feet. "Torture?" Veloshin chuckled. "Compared to what will come later, this is a walk in the park."

He turned the lights on and pushed Sergey into an armchair in the middle of the living room. While keeping the gun leveled at Sergey's head, he pulled two sets of handcuffs out of his satchel and threw them on the floor. "Put these on your wrists and ankles."

With a cowed look, Sergey complied. Veloshin tucked the gun in his belt and retrieved the blood-soaked switchblade from his pocket. He pulled up a chair and sat close to Sergey, facing him. Neither one spoke. Veloshin wiped the knife back and forth on Sergey's pajama bottoms, leaving bloodstained streaks. "Did you know that the American Indians skinned their enemies alive?"

The scientist's face went chalk white.

"It must have felt glorious to inflict such pain on someone they despised."

Trembling, Sergey blurted, "I'll tell you everything you want to know. Everything!"

Veloshin glanced at the switchblade and then slowly lifted his gaze to Sergey's terrified face. Then, in an instant, he covered Sergey's mouth with his left hand and sliced open a deep gash across his thigh.

Sergey let out a muffled scream.

Veloshin pressed his hand harder against Sergey's mouth and whispered, "Hush. You'll wake up the neighbors. We wouldn't want them talking about you, would we."

It took several minutes for Sergey to calm down and for the sting of his wound to subside. Veloshin shoved a piece of cloth in Sergey's mouth and secured it with duct tape. Then came another cut across Sergey's other thigh. He squirmed in pain. After a brief respite, there was another slice, and then another. The gruesome sport continued for about half an hour. There was blood everywhere. At one point, Sergey fainted. But Veloshin brought him back by pouring a pitcher of cold water on his head.

Finally, Veloshin started his interrogation. He removed the duct tape from Sergey's mouth. He began to wail. Then Veloshin pressed the REC button on a handheld recorder, placed it on the side table, and said, "Tell me about Dr. Shaheen. Why is he here?"

Sergey spoke with great difficulty through a red haze of pain. He had lost a lot of blood and was weak. Revealing every secret he knew, he spoke about Amir Meshkin and his henchman, Kazem. Sergey described the atomic bomb he had helped design for the Iranians and how they needed to ensure it would work without detonating it.

Breathing heavily, he spoke about the conspiracy to lure Dr. Shaheen to Iran to test their nuclear bomb with his computer system, the Blind Scorpion. And how Ross had refused Amir by resisting his overtures, bribes, and threats.

Finally, Sergey told Veloshin what he wanted to know the most. That it was Amir who had arranged the kidnapping of Dr. Shaheen's daughter in order to secure his cooperation.

Veloshin came in close. Placing his hand on Sergey's bleeding thigh, he pressed down, whispering, "Does Amir know where she is?"

"I don't know."

He pressed harder. Sergey squirmed. Veloshin demanded, "Who knows?"

In agony, Sergey blurted, "Kazem! He knows. He must know."

"Who is this Kazem?"

"He is our liaison with MOIS. They did the kidnapping."

"What is his full name?"

"Kazem Dowlat."

Veloshin stood. After a moment's pause, he turned the recorder off and packed his equipment into his satchel. Sergey's moans and uncontrollable contortions spoke of his agony.

Veloshin stepped into the kitchen. He washed the bloody knife and his hands in the sink. Looking inside the refrigerator, he reached for a plate of *Piroshki*—small Russian meat pies—and devoured two. Then he returned to the living room holding a third pie in his left hand and stood a few yards away from Sergey.

Veloshin aimed the Mini-Uzi at the hapless scientist. He closed his eyes. Eating the third *Piroshki*, Veloshin squeezed the trigger and held it for two seconds. Thirty-five rounds of .38 caliber bullets tore Sergey's body into shreds.

It was approaching 3:30 AM when Veloshin emerged from the house. Reza was waiting in the car.

"How did it go?" Reza asked, as he drove them away.

Licking the *Piroshki* crumbs off his fingers, Veloshin said, "Delicious."

"Back to the Embassy?"

"No."

"Where to?"

"Do you know someone named Kazem Dowlat?"

"Yes. I know him well. I'm one of his drivers." Reza added, "He is the one who lured Dr. Shaheen to Iran."

Staring into the dark of the night, Veloshin whispered, "Take me to him."

36

I T STOPPED BLINKING!" PAM CARLISLE SAID. "THE GREEN LIGHT IS solid!"

On the other end of the line, seven thousand miles to the east of Berkeley, Ross breathed a sigh of relief. "That's good, Pam. You're doing great."

"It's asking more questions. The system wants to know your pet's name."

"That's part of the authentication procedure. Just type in ROMEO."

After a brief pause, Pam said, "I'm in. It says WELCOME TO THE BLIND SCORPION."

"Now," Ross said, "pay attention. I'll e-mail a file to my public PC. You will have to copy it to a flash memory card and transfer it to the Scorpion...Understand?"

"Where do I get a flash memory card?"

"There's one in my pencil drawer."

"Okay...Send it."

Ross looked at Amir for approval. He nodded. Ross proceeded to transmit the DFX file containing the bomb schematic to his own e-mail address.

After clicking SEND, an agonizing silence lingered at both ends of the open phone line. Amir fingered his prayer beads while Ross nervously wrung his hands together. And with quiet unease, Pam stared at the computer screen.

"It's here," Pam said. "I've got the file."

"Copy it over."

The DFX file was large. It took Pam several minutes to download it into the flash memory card and then upload it to the Blind Scorpion. The wait was unbearable. Finally, she said, "It's ready."

Ross methodically instructed her to enter the necessary commands to launch the Blind Scorpion. Pam followed the steps meticulously. The last parameter was the degree of purity of the uranium core. Ross looked at Amir. Waiting.

Amir hesitated. He was about to reveal Iran's most closely held state secret. For many years, the Islamic Republic had claimed that it was only enriching uranium to the allowable five percent to fuel its nuclear power plant. It was time for truth. He had to stop the lies.

"Ninety-three percent."

Ross repeated the number, and Pam typed it in.

"It says PROCESSING."

"Good. Leave it alone."

"How long will it take?"

"About two hours…I want you to sit there and not move."

"Okay."

"I'll call you back in two hours."

"Ross…What is this Blind Scorpion? What are we doing?"

"As I said earlier, no questions."

Amir seemed pleased. As Ross hung up the phone, Kazem entered the room and said, "Amir, the chopper is leaving and if it's all right with you, I'll return to Tehran." Then he added sheepishly, "Domestic problems."

"Dr. Shaheen is making good progress," Amir said, smiling as he twirled his prayer beads around his fingers. "Go ahead. I'll see you in the morning."

⌒⅍⌒

REZA SPED OUT OF THE STYLISH NEIGHBORHOOD WITH KAZEM IN THE backseat of the official car. The gated community was located in Niavaran—a posh, leafy suburb north of Tehran, nestled in the foothills of the picturesque Damavand Mountain.

It was early morning. Eager to catch the air shuttle to Natanz,

Kazem quietly read the newspaper, frequently looking at his watch. Reza skillfully threaded the Mercedes through the narrow alleyways. He felt apprehensive and rolled his window down to breath in the fresh mountain air.

The traffic was still manageable, and there were no bystanders in sight. Reza abruptly stopped at an intersection. The tires screeched, jolting Kazem forward. "What the hell are you doing?" he barked. "Why are we stopping here?"

From nowhere, Dimitry Veloshin opened the rear door opposite where Kazem was sitting and entered the car. Pointing the Mini-Uzi at Kazem, he closed the door and said, "Go! Go!"

"What is this?" Kazem demanded.

The cold stare from Veloshin's green eyes and the thrust of the silencer against Kazem's jugular silently answered the question.

Reza drove on inconspicuously. Thirty long and wordless minutes later, the uniformed guards waived the vehicle through the gates of the Russian Embassy.

Kazem was not a stranger in the compound. As a high-ranking officer in the Ministry of Mining and Metals, he had participated in many official meetings with the Russian delegation. Not to mention the countless social events and Embassy receptions he had attended. So, his demeanor quickly changed from horror to anxious puzzlement.

As they drove slowly through the tree-lined streets of the sprawling compound, Kazem turned to Veloshin and said, "Why would you bring me to such friendly grounds at gunpoint?"

"I'm not a friend," Veloshin said, in his raspy voice.

"I must protest," Kazem blurted. "I want to see the Ambassador immediately."

"Be quiet," Veloshin said.

"This is highly irregular! Do you know who I am?"

Tired of his rants, with one swift blow, Veloshin struck Kazem in his forehead with the handle of the gun. Kazem slumped against the window, instantly unconscious.

Reza rolled to a stop at the rear of the FSB building, where a solitary metal door was propped open with a broken brick. Veloshin left the vehicle and walked around the car to let Kazem out. When he opened the door, Kazem nearly fell out onto the gravel road. Reza came running to assist. Together they dragged Kazem's limp body toward the metal door, his feet carving trails in the gravel.

The door opened to a steep flight of stairs leading to a dark, underground cell. Veloshin heaved the husky Kazem over his shoulder and disappeared beneath the windowless, concrete building.

Reza closed the metal door and drove away.

WHEN KAZEM CAME TO, HE FOUND HIMSELF SITTING ON A CHAIR IN the middle of a poorly lit, cold, and damp room. A bare light bulb at the center of a metal cone hung from the ceiling, flickering. The moldy smell made the place feel like a forgotten crypt. Still dizzy, he could barely make out the outlines of aging filing cabinets against the walls. A handful of wooden crates overflowing with folders and dossiers dotted the floors.

As his head became clearer, Kazem felt a sharp sting. Originating in his left hand, the pain was soon shooting up his arm. Before long he realized that it was not his hand that was hurting; it was his pinkie. The throbbing pain was so excruciating that he felt nauseous. Trying to lift his arm, he noticed that his hands were duct taped to the armrests. As were his ankles to the front legs. He bent over, squinting at his left hand.

"Goddamn!" he screamed. "You son-of-a-bitch!"

From the shadows, Veloshin stepped into the light and whispered, "Anything wrong?"

"My finger is gone!" Kazem howled. "Oh my God! How did this happen?"

Veloshin lifted a bloody wire cutter from a small metal table, waived it before Kazem, and said, "One of my specialties."

"You did this?" Kazem moaned. "But why?" He squirmed. "Are you a sadist?"

Veloshin approached Kazem, smiling. "Yes, I am." He grabbed Kazem's middle finger with the wire cutter and said, in a low voice, "And I am looking forward to snipping this one off while you watch."

"No! Don't!" Kazem pleaded. "What do you want?"

"Marina." Veloshin placed his portable voice recorder on the metal table, pressed the REC button, and said, "Marina Shaheen."

"What about her?"

"Where is she?"

"America."

Veloshin squeezed the handles of the wire cutter slightly and said, "I know all about her kidnapping…"

Kazem screamed in pain.

"I was with Sergey last night." Veloshin pressed a little more. "He told me everything…Now it's your turn."

Kazem thrashed about.

"I will ask you one last time." Veloshin demanded, "Where is Marina?"

"I don't know."

Without further warning, Veloshin squeezed the handles of the wire cutter. Crunch. Kazem's middle finger separated from his hand, falling into a pan on the floor. Blood squirted out of the stump.

Kazem threw his head back with his mouth wide open, ready to scream. At first, no sound came out. Then he shrieked uncontrollably.

"Oh God!" he pleaded, crying. "Please help me!"

Clutching Kazem's hair, Veloshin pulled his head back and whispered, "Down here, I am God. But not in a helping mood…" Veloshin grabbed Kazem's thumb with the wire cutter and said, "Unless you tell me where she is."

"Okay! Stop! I'll tell you what I know."

Veloshin reached inside a plastic bucket nearby, grabbed a handful of ice chips, and dumped it on Kazem's blood-soaked fingers.

"Start talking," Veloshin said.

"Mustafa. His name is Mustafa," Kazem said, with great difficulty. "He is the MOIS man in charge."

"Where?"

"San Francisco."

"What is his last name?"

"I don't know," Kazem said, wailing.

"How do I find him?"

"I have been to his flat." Kazem breathed heavily. "I can't stand this pain much longer. Can you do something? Please!"

"I can cut off your thumb if you want."

"No!" Kazem mumbled. "I beg you!"

"What is his address?" Veloshin inquired calmly.

"Let me think." Kazem moaned again. "It's on the top floor of a seven-story building. The corner of Van Ness and Jackson."

"Is Marina at this place?"

"No. She is kept at a safe house." Kazem continued to writhe in pain. "Somewhere north, in the middle of the woods."

"Where is the safe house?" Veloshin squeezed the handless of the wire cutter again, partially slicing Kazem's thumb.

Horrified, Kazem yelled, "Not again! Please don't!"

"Where?"

"I don't know! I swear I don't! But Mustafa…He knows."

Veloshin threw the wire cutter on the metal table. Then he stepped behind Kazem, whispering in his ear, "I am going upstairs to verify your story about this Mustafa. If you're lying to me, I will cut off every one of your fingers—one by one. Then I'll move to your toes. Understand?"

"Trust me," Kazem wept. "I'm telling you the truth, I promise."

"I will return," Veloshin said.

"Will you let me go if what I told you checks out?"

"If you're telling the truth, you will be rewarded."

Veloshin climbed the staircase, skipping every other step. Inside the FSB communications room, he stood behind an operator as he transmitted a coded message to the Russian consulate in San Francisco urgently requesting verification of Kazem's story. Specifically, Veloshin wanted to know if there was someone named "Mustafa" living in San Francisco where Kazem had pointed.

Awaiting their response, Veloshin slumped on a couch and promptly fell asleep. He had been up all night.

Three hours later, an FSB agent woke him. There was a reply from the San Francisco station chief, which was being deciphered.

Veloshin sat up straight, rubbing his eyes. He felt anxious but didn't show it. A decade of gruesome work with the Spetsnaz paramilitary forces had hardened him. By now, he was a complete stranger to emotional displays.

Moments later, he returned to the cellar. Kazem's chair faced away. Scaling down the steps, Veloshin said, "My comrades in San Francisco say that there is a Mustafa living where you said and that he is an MOIS agent."

"See? I told you the truth."

Again, Veloshin grabbed Kazem's hair, pulling his head back. "You will die anyway," he whispered in Kazem's ear. "But I give you one last chance to make sure you are telling me everything you know about Marina."

"Please don't kill me." Kazem started to weep. "I have told you the truth...I swear it!"

"Listen!" Veloshin let go of Kazem's hair and came around to face him. "If Mustafa does not have Marina, or if she is harmed in any way, I will return here and kill both of your wives. Then I will burn their houses down with your children in them."

Kazem looked down, sobbing.

"Do you want me to do that?"

Kazem shook his head from side to side.

"Is there anything else you have forgotten to tell me about Mustafa or Marina?"

Kazem mumbled, "No. I have told you everything."

Veloshin walked to the metal table, picked up the Mini-Uzi, and pointed the gun at Kazem.

"Here is your reward," he whispered.

THE LONG, EVENTFUL DAY IN THE SECLUSION OF AMIR'S OFFICE WAS coming to a close. And the excruciating two-hour wait for the Blind Scorpion to spit out the results was almost over.

Now free of his handcuffs, Ross nervously paced the room as Amir looked on from the couch. With his feet propped on top of the coffee table, he sipped tea while taking comfort in his prayer beads.

After Amir gets his answer, Ross thought, *he will have no further use for me. What then? Is he going to kill me? Or continue to hold me? What about Marina?*

"Amir," Ross said, "in a few minutes you'll have your results. I want your word of honor that you'll let Marina go—if not for honor then for old time's sake."

"She will not be harmed. I assure you."

"And me?"

"We'll cross that bridge when we come to it."

Ross understood. He had seen too much of Iran's so-called peaceful nuclear program. Amir would never let him leave the bunker alive. It would be impossible. Yet, Ross didn't care. All that mattered to him was Marina's safety.

After another glance at his watch, Amir stood and said, "It's time." He smiled in excitement. "Let's call your office."

PAM CARLISLE ANSWERED ON THE FIRST RING. "I'M HERE."

"Do you have the results?"

"No."

"What does the screen say?"

"EVENT: SUPER CRITICAL. CALCULATING YIELD."

Ross glanced at Amir as he listened in. Even though he was unfamiliar with the Blind Scorpion's jargon, SUPER CRITICAL and YIELD gave him the good news he had been eagerly anticipating. His bomb design was a success. It would detonate, restoring Iran to her past glory. When Iran flexed its muscles, all nations in the Middle East, Southeast Asia, and Western Europe would quake as they had two millennia before. The Persian Empire would be restored, and America wouldn't dare attack it. The nukes would guarantee the survival of the Islamic Republic.

With eyes gleaming, Amir flashed a big smile, his gold tooth glinting. "How long before it gives the yield?"

Speaking into the mouthpiece, Ross said, "There's a timer in the lower right corner of the screen. What does it say?"

"It's been counting down from 20 minutes. There's less than a minute to go."

Amir stared at his watch. Waiting.

Ross held a pencil at the ready over a yellow notepad.

Time crawled.

"It's finished," Pam finally said.

"What does the screen show?"

"A bunch of numbers."

"Read them to me."

"Forty-eight KT, slash, ninety-eight percent, slash, four H."

Ross scribbled down the results: 48 KT / 98% / 4H.

He double-checked them with Pam. They were correct. Then he verified them for the third time.

"Pam, you've done a fantastic job. I am indebted to you."

"What now?"

"Sign off, and don't speak a word of this to anyone."

"When are you coming back?"

CLICK.

Amir hung up the phone. He said impatiently, "What do the numbers mean?"

"Isn't it obvious? The Scorpion estimates your device to have a yield of 48 kilotons—it's a monster bomb."

"What does the rest mean?"

"98% is the degree of certainty."

Amir looked puzzled.

"It means the Scorpion is 98% sure of the 48 kiloton estimate."

"What does the 4H stand for?"

Ross sighed, then said, "Four times Hiroshima."

37

Armed with promising clues as to the whereabouts of Marina Shaheen, Veloshin quickly made his way to Tehran's international airport where a private jet, courtesy of his benefactor, Viktor Pugachov, awaited him.

The gleaming Gulfstream 500, personal property of some Russian tycoon, had a range of 5,800 miles and could cruise at 460 miles per hour. This would be the quickest way to travel from Tehran to San Francisco, and it afforded Veloshin flexibility and stealth. He could swiftly go where the evidence pointed, without having to explain his gadgets and arsenal to airport screeners.

Before takeoff, the pilot briefed Veloshin that the flight plan would take them non-stop from Tehran to New York City, where they would refuel. And the next stop would be San Francisco. With any luck and weather permitting, they would reach their destination in about eighteen hours.

The sun was setting behind the gloomy silhouettes of skyscrapers when the jet soared above the cloudless skies of Tehran.

Veloshin sat quietly in a luxurious leather chair in the midsection of the cabin, looking out of the porthole. Considering what lay ahead, he thought, *Will I get my hands on Mustafa in time to save Marina? Is she still alive?* The answers would have to wait till the next day—an eternity.

A blond, leggy stewardess in a tight blue uniform with a short skirt was strapped in her chair at the back of the aircraft. She was waiting for the plane to level off. The remaining twelve seats were empty.

This was Veloshin's first trip to America, and the idea that the watchful eyes of the FBI might follow his every move concerned him. As he gazed at the sunset, he thought, *I must remain unnoticed for at least twenty-four hours.* Then he reassured himself. *The General would surely see to that. He's probably on the phone right now making the necessary arrangements. How can I ever face the General if I fail this mission?*

Veloshin had met Oksana and her family a few years before during an informal function at General Pugachov's dacha. Remembering the occasion, he wondered if she would recognize him.

The plane was at the cruising altitude when the stewardess approached and, with a pleasant smile, said, "What will you drink, Mr. Veloshin?"

"Vodka."

"Smirnoff, Stoli, or Absolut?"

"Smirnoff."

"When would you like to have dinner?"

"Now."

After a few shots of Vodka and a lavish meal, Veloshin dimmed the lights as he reclined his chair. He was exhausted.

The young flight attendant sat down in the adjacent seat and attempted to start a conversation. Not knowing that Veloshin was a stranger to small talk, she persisted. She seemed fascinated by his air of mystery. The secrecy, the fewness of words, the undeniable importance, and his powerful persona were an irresistible combination. She gave up after a few minutes and said, "You seem tired, Mr. Veloshin. Is there anything else you need before I let you sleep?"

Veloshin looked up, revealing a rare smile. Painting her with a seductive stare, he whispered, "Of course there is."

She beamed.

Gently squeezing his right hand, she said, "Come with me. There is a comfortable couch in the back."

Amir Meshkin was overjoyed with the results. He relished the words, "Four times Hiroshima," as if God Himself had whispered them into his ears. The Iranian Oppenheimer had at last succeeded in fathering the Shiite nuclear bomb. And thanks to the Blind Scorpion, the regime had gained full confidence about its membership in the nuclear club. Following in Israel's footsteps, they had achieved their strategic objective while maintaining nuclear ambiguity.

Amir was grinning from ear to ear. Gleefully fingering his prayer beads, he stood and said, "Praise be God! The Persian Empire shall rise again in her ancient glory. America and Israel, the Great Satan and the Little Satan, better beware." He jabbed his fist into the air, clutching the beads. "We will defeat you! We will crush you! Islam will erase the Zionist state off the face of the earth!"

"And start World War three?"

"Yes! If that's what it takes to bring the End of Times, the Armageddon, if you will, when the promised twelfth Imam shall return and establish peace and justice on earth, then why not?"

Ross shook his head in disbelief, thinking, *What is it about my people? They can create such modern technology, construct an underground enrichment facility, build a nuclear bomb, all under international sanctions, and yet believe in such superstition at the same time. Why is it that they are capable of so much love and, at the same time, so much hate, yet unable to find anything in between? This great civilization is doomed.*

"I must inform the Supreme Leader at once," Amir said. "He has been waiting for this glorious day for the past fifteen years."

"What about my daughter?" Ross demanded. "You must let her go immediately!"

"When I meet the Supreme Leader, I will ask for his permission."

"But that was our bargain. I gave you the Blind Scorpion in exchange for her freedom."

"The Supreme Leader is a humanitarian," Amir said, in a reassuring voice. "He wants nothing but the good of the world. He would not wish any harm on your daughter."

Is he serious? Ross thought. *The Supreme Leader is "a humanitarian?" In what twilight zone do these people live? Every terrorist group, from Hezbollah to Hamas and from the Mahdi Army to the Badr Brigade, takes their orders from his office. Every proxy war, every chaos in the Middle East is somehow connected to the Supreme Leader. And he's a "humanitarian?"* Ross changed the subject to make sure his expression did not reveal his aversion. "And what about me?"

"What about you?"

"Now that you have what you were after, will you let me leave?"

"I will ask His Excellency," Amir said, as he left the room. "Your fate is in his hands."

⚜

IT WAS HALF PAST MIDNIGHT. IN THE SMALL BEDROOM ADJACENT TO Amir's office, Ross laid on the narrow bed staring at the ceiling. A thousand thoughts crowded his mind: *Will they let Marina go? She's of no further use to them unless they want something else from me. I doubt if I can pull off another Scorpion test. The Lab has probably discovered the ruse by now and plugged the hole. I hope they don't give Pam any trouble. How can I get the hell out of here? There must be a way...*

Deep in thought, he heard the door creep open and then quietly shut. He lifted his head, looking into the darkness. A silhouette slowly approached. Ross felt nervous. *Is this my executioner?* he thought. His heart was pounding in his chest when the intruder stepped out of the shadows into the dimly lit bedroom.

It was a woman.

Wearing a black *hejab*—a headscarf covering a woman's hair— and a long gray coat called a *monteau* over blue jeans, she walked over and confidently sat at the edge of the bed. She demonstrated that she was not bound by the false modesty gripping Iranian women when she removed her *hejab*, revealing her short, jet-black hair. After a brief pause, she looked at Ross and, in fluent English, said, "Colonel Nash sends his regards."

Ross bolted upright. He recognized her. She was one of the "students" attending his lectures in Karaj. She had pressed him on America's foreign policy. *"Colonel Nash sends his regards."* Ross replayed her words in his mind. He was speechless. *Is she CIA? Or, is she a plant by Amir? Isn't this room bugged? Surely, it must be. So, she's definitely playing games.*

"Colonel Nash?" Ross said dismissively. "I don't know who you're talking about."

The woman grinned, pointed to the CIA-issued Berkeley ring on Ross' finger, and then held up a similar one on her hand. "We're on the same side, Dr. Shaheen." She squeezed Ross' hand. "My name is Parvin. I attended your lectures at Karaj…Remember? You can trust me."

"So you graduated from Cornell…" Unconvinced, Ross probed further. "What's that supposed to prove?"

"Do you want to see the poison pill under the ring stone?"

The penny dropped. Ross knew she was CIA.

"Are there any bugs in this room?" he whispered.

"I turned them off before coming in."

"What's in store for me?"

"They're going to kill you."

It took a while for her words to sink in. Ross swallowed hard. "When?"

"Probably tomorrow."

"Can you get me out of here?"

"It's very difficult. This place is built as an underground fortress."

"More like an underground prison."

She nodded. "But I have some ideas."

Roy Sullivan was fuming. Colonel Nash had called at 5:00 am to inform him that Pugachov was sending an operative—a specialist— to San Francisco with actionable intelligence about Marina. And the FBI was expected to cooperate fully. Nash had dismissed Roy's protests regarding jurisdiction, telling him, "Take your turf and shove it up your ass, Sullivan! You *will* assist the Russian. You *will* extend every possible courtesy. And you *will* do so with a smile." Nash had concluded the secure call with, "Need I remind you that Marina's relation to Pugachov makes this a national security matter?"

Roy slammed down the phone. He had a lot to do. Aside from security considerations, transportation, and devising a cover story, he had to come up with a safe house where Veloshin could stay out of sight. And his plane was only two hours away.

Hurriedly changing into his field clothes, Roy thought, *What the hell could the Russians possibly know about the case? They're way over there while we're here in the middle of it. They don't have shit! And if they did, wouldn't it be easier to give us the intel so that we could act on it? Why send an agent? "A specialist," my ass! The bastards! They want the glory, not the girl.*

Their initial encounter was cold yet professional. With a firm handshake, Roy introduced himself as the FBI Special Agent in charge of the investigation. Veloshin just gave his name.

Driving away from the jet, Roy proceeded with briefing the Russian about the evidence and what the FBI had been able to piece together. Veloshin listened intently, asking questions in heavily accented English. He made no effort to hide his sarcasm. "So, three Iranian men, total strangers, somewhat suspicious, move across the street from General Pugachov's daughter and no one at the FBI asks any questions?"

"This is not Russia," Roy retorted. "We have laws."

"As do we, Mr. Sullivan," Veloshin said calmly. "But we also have common sense."

Roy ignored the put down. They were over the Golden Gate Bridge when he completed his briefing. An uncomfortable silence filled the SUV. Roy expected professional courtesy and reciprocity. *What did the Russian know? What was his plan?* But, to his dismay, no information was forthcoming.

When they pulled into the driveway of the Shaheens' house, Roy stopped the car, turned to Veloshin, and broke the silence. "Now, listen up. I don't give a rat's ass who you are and who you know. You're now playing in my sandbox. One wrong move, one mistake, and I'll throw your ass in jail faster than you can count to three. Understand?"

Veloshin listened, nodded, and left the vehicle. As they walked toward the front door, he whispered, "If Marina is still alive, Mr. Sullivan, I will find her...with or without your assistance."

To his delight, Oksana remembered Veloshin and warmly invited him and Roy inside. Natasha was cordial and seemed pleased to meet Veloshin.

Roy sat on the ottoman in the corner of the living room and observed as the Russians carried on for what seemed like an eternity. He felt as if he were watching a foreign movie without subtitles. At first, Romeo added noise to the gibberish but soon he climbed onto Oksana's lap and became quiet.

After about an hour, Oksana turned to Roy. "My father sent Dimitry to Tehran to pick up Marina's trail." Hugging Romeo, she continued, sounding excited. "And he has discovered who the ringleader is and where he lives."

Roy was skeptical. "If that's true, then what are we waiting for?" He looked at Veloshin. "Let's go pick his ass up."

Natasha interjected. "The problem is, Mr. Sullivan, we have very little time. Maybe hours. Even less."

Roy looked puzzled. "Why?"

Veloshin said, "I had to use special methods to extract this information. Before long, the Iranians will discover...how should I say, the 'mess' I have left behind, and may order Marina's—" Veloshin glanced at Oksana and didn't complete his sentence.

Oksana closed her eyes.

Roy stood up. "Then let's go."

"I have to do this alone, Mr. Sullivan."

"Why?"

"Because we cannot arrest him and hope he cooperates. No. We must make him speak...Now."

"By special methods?"

Veloshin nodded.

"That's cool," Roy said confidently. "But I'll have to go with you anyway...You don't know your way around."

"Like I said, I work alone."

Addressing Veloshin, Oksana ended the argument. "Dimitry...Roy goes with you."

Veloshin's face tensed. He stood before Roy and said, "As you wish. However, if you find my methods unacceptable, you should just turn and walk away."

"If your methods work, I'll hold the son-of-a-bitch down for you."

ROSS AND THE CIA OPERATIVE PARVIN PORED OVER THE BLUEPRINTS of the underground facility stored in Amir's computer. Exploring various exits and possible escape routes, she quietly explained that during the graveyard shift, the number of guards would be at a minimum. In fact, all together, there were fewer than twenty people in the bunker at that hour.

Ross listened carefully as Parvin outlined her escape plan. She wanted to scale one of the ventilation shafts to safety. Ross dismissed her idea as impossible. "That's over a hundred feet of vertical climb, without any steps or ropes." Then she presented her backup plan, which was to disguise Ross as a janitor and simply walk out. Ross didn't like that either—too many guards and checkpoints. After several such trial balloons, Ross described his own escape plan to Parvin. "I've been thinking about this for days. I believe, with your help, it'll work." Ross pointed to Parvin. "You're the missing link."

"It's risky." Parvin hesitated after listening to Ross' plan. "But I don't have a better idea, and staying here is far more dangerous."

"Staying might be dangerous for you," Ross said bluntly. "But it's fatal for me."

"Then, let's do it."

Ross removed his class ring and placed it on the desk. Parvin followed suit. He retrieved a small screwdriver from Amir's desk drawer and pried the stones out of both rings. As each stone fell on the desk, an aspirin-size red tablet, marked with the letter X, dropped out of the cavity.

"What time is it?" Parvin asked.

"Two forty-five."

"We don't have much time," Parvin said, as she carefully slid the pills into a small paper pouch she had made from a sheet of paper. "This is so lethal that it would make you sick if it even touched your skin."

"I wonder what it is."

"My 'handler' told me about these pills. That they're fifty-thousand times more lethal than cyanide," Parvin said. "But its exact chemical composition is TOP SECRET."

"If it does the job, who cares."

She placed the pouch into her pocket. "Exactly."

Ross whispered, "Good luck."

"Thanks. I'm going to need it." As she tiptoed toward the door, she said, "I'll be back soon."

Walking down the deserted corridor, Parvin felt anxious. She knew that if caught, she would be killed. No questions asked. Even worse, she would probably be tortured for months, eventually begging for death.

At the end of the long hallway, she turned right and then left. After a few more steps, she entered a large break room.

Brightly lit, most of the area was filled with round tables and matching chairs capable of seating nearly 200 people. To the right, a dozen or more vending machines of all stripes lined the wall. On the left, there was a long countertop with a sundry of kitchen equipment—a few microwave ovens, several toasters, and two coffee makers. At the end of the counter stood an oversized samovar crowned with a large metal teapot. Blowing off steam, the samovar made the hissing sound as water boiled inside its stainless steel belly.

Parvin was aware of the security camera above the entrance. So she approached the samovar as casually as she could. She removed a glass teacup from one of the drawers beneath the samovar and placed it on the counter. Using a towel, she lifted the hot teapot resting on top of the samovar and filled her glass one-third full of the strong tea. She carefully positioned herself to block the camera. Then she opened the pouch and dropped the X-pills into the teapot. After returning the vessel to its cradle, she proceeded to dilute the tea by filling the cup with hot water from the small faucet attached to the belly of the samovar.

The ancient Iranian tea ritual was complete. She proceeded to one of the tables and sat down, perusing a newspaper that someone had left behind. As she took a small sip, she noticed her hands were moist with sweat and lightly trembling.

A few minutes after 3:00 AM, a young steward entered the break room pushing a metal cart, its wheels quietly squeaking. He acknowledged Parvin respectfully and asked if she would like more tea. She declined politely.

The steward continued the small talk as he placed two-dozen glass cups on top of the cart in neat rows. He proceeded to fill each one with a perfect combination of concentrated tea from the pot and hot water from the samovar. Then he filled a bowl with a good measure of sugar cubes, refreshed the supply of small spoons, and gently pushed the cart toward Parvin.

As he approached, she noticed her hands were now visibly trembling.

She clasped them under the table, thinking, *What does he want?* With a big smile, he placed a teacup in front of her and said, *"Chaie tazeh befarmayeed*—Have some fresh tea." Then he pushed the cart away.

The squeaking of the wheels combined with the clanking of the teacups were familiar sounds. Parvin had heard the symphony hundreds of times before, as the polite young man would serve her during the wee hours of the morning.

As he left the break room, Parvin felt a lump in her throat.

38

2:30 PM. THE TRAFFIC WAS BUMPER-TO-BUMPER ON US-101. Veloshin rode in the passenger seat, his red satchel laying flat on the floor mat. Natasha was in the backseat occasionally speaking in Russian. He listened and gave short responses now and then.

Driving the SUV, Roy ignored them both. He was concerned about going on a risky mission without proper backup. *What if all hell breaks loose?* he thought. *What if there's a shootout and some civilian bastard gets caught in the crossfire? It'll be my ass!* And to make matters worse, he had two foreign agents along for the ride, which violated more FBI protocols than he cared to tally.

It's all for Marina... So, who gives a damn?

Inching south for the better part of an hour, Roy finally crossed the Golden Gate Bridge and turned right onto Van Ness. The traffic was lighter in the city, and Jackson Street was only a few blocks away.

Roy turned right onto Jackson and then a sharp left into the ramp leading to the building's garage. He parked at an angle, blocking the entrance. As he climbed out and walked toward the front door, he pressed a button on his car key. The familiar sound of a double-chirp indicated that his vehicle was locked. Veloshin, toting his satchel, followed alongside Natasha a few steps behind.

In the far corner of the lobby, an old man was sitting in an armchair reading a newspaper. He looked up, staring suspiciously at the three. But after a long pause, he returned to the paper and turned the page.

Roy Sullivan entered the elevator; the Russians followed. Veloshin pressed the seventh floor button. No one spoke. They all knew their parts.

Seventh floor.

Natasha walked toward the door marked 7-D. The nameplate read, "Mustafa A." Veloshin and Roy stood against the wall, one on each side of the door.

Natasha rang the bell. At first, there was no response. She rang it a second time. After an uneasy moment, a voice with a Middle Eastern accent said, "Who is it?"

Natasha could tell that someone was staring at her through the peephole. Looking back indifferently, she said, "I have an important message for Mr. Mustafa."

"Message? From whom?"

"The Russian Consul in San Francisco."

"Slide it under the door."

"It is not a written message. My instructions are to deliver it in person."

Another silent moment crept by before Mustafa cracked the door open until the chain grabbed. He looked up and down at Natasha and then closed the door to release the chain. When it was free, he opened the door wide, inviting her in.

With a swift motion, Roy pushed Natasha aside and barged inside, pointing his Glock at Mustafa's face. "Freeze!"

Mustafa was stunned. He raised his hands and sheepishly stepped backwards. Roy walked toward him cautiously, with the Glock trained at his head. Veloshin and Natasha followed Roy inside the apartment; she locked the door.

"What do you want?" Mustafa asked, tripping over the words.

Roy pointed to an armchair in the middle of the room. "Sit your ass down."

"I don't keep anything of value here," Mustafa said nervously.

Roy handed his gun to Natasha and said, "Shoot this sack of shit if he makes a move." Then he stepped toward Mustafa, grabbed him by the collar, and punched him in the face. Hard. Mustafa fell on the floor.

Roy said, "I'm no thief…Scumbag!"

Mustafa looked up, his nose bleeding. "Who are you?"

"I am with the FBI. These two are Russian agents."

"What do you want from me?"

Roy grabbed Mustafa and pushed him onto the armchair. Walking behind him, Roy leaned forward and whispered, "I'm gonna ask you once...Where is Marina?"

Mustafa used his sleeve to wipe the blood off his face. After a brief pause, he said, "I want to see my lawyer."

Roy grabbed him in a chokehold and growled, "Didn't I tell you? *I* am your lawyer." Squeezing hard, he added, "Now, tell your lawyer—where's Marina?"

Mustafa mumbled, "She is safe...I c-can't breathe."

Roy released him. Mustafa was gasping for air.

Veloshin dragged a coffee table close to the armchair. Then, without saying a word, he reached inside the red satchel and retrieved a small leather bundle. He placed it on the coffee table and rolled it open, revealing what seemed to be a set of shiny surgical instruments. Neatly organized in small pockets were scissors, hooks, scalpels, and a miniature hacksaw.

Mustafa looked wide-eyed at Veloshin. Roy came around facing Mustafa and said, "Listen! You better start singing like a bird or I'll have Doctor Mengele here go Nazi on your ass."

"What do you want to know?"

"Right now, all I care about is Marina...Where are you keeping her?"

"If I talk, I'll be a dead man."

"You are already a dead man," Veloshin whispered, with a cold stare.

"She is kept in a safe house."

"Where?"

"Someplace near Eureka."

Veloshin grabbed a large roll of duct tape, threw it at Roy, and said, "Tie him up." Then he pulled out a hook-like instrument from the surgical set. "I will start with his eyeballs."

Roy unwound the tape and started to tie Mustafa to the armchair. Mustafa held his hands up and cried, "Stop! That will not be necessary... We are all professionals here. Let's be civilized."

Roy said, "Then quit playing games with us, asshole...'Someplace near Eureka,' ain't the answer I'm looking for." Roy came closer, shoving his face into Mustafa's. "I'll ask you again...Where is Marina *exactly?*"

"She is in a safe house near Eureka," Mustafa said. "I don't have an address, but I can draw you a map."

"Screw your map." Roy grabbed Mustafa by the color and pulled him up. "You're taking us there."

"How far is this Eureka place?" Veloshin asked.

"About five hours drive," said Roy.

"We can fly there."

"Good idea."

Roy yanked a pair of handcuffs from his belt and snapped them on Mustafa. "Seems like you're gonna fly the friendly skies courtesy of our Russian pals." He shoved Mustafa toward the door. "Just don't give me an excuse to throw your worthless ass into the Pacific from thirty thousand feet up."

PARVIN SNEAKED INTO THE OFFICE TO FIND ROSS PACING BACK AND forth. On her way, per Ross's instructions, she had stopped in the wire integration room to sever the fiber cables that carried all communications with the outside world.

"How did it go?"

"So far so good," Parvin said anxiously. "But God help us if someone doesn't feel like sipping tea this morning."

"In that case, we need guns," Ross said matter-of-factly.

"The guard stations are full of them."

"Let's go," Ross said, stepping toward the door.

Parvin followed as he walked cautiously down the hallway toward the staff cubicles. As they approached, Ross noticed a man stooped over his computer. An empty teacup lay sideways on the floor. Foaming at the mouth, his vacant eyes stared at nothing.

"Don't look," Ross said. But it was too late.

Parvin sighed. "Oh my God...That's Hussein. We went to graduate school together."

"He probably didn't feel a thing," Ross said, as he gently nudged her away.

The control room looked chaotic. Three men and one woman were motionless, lying in different positions. One was on the floor with his left leg caught in his chair. Two were hunched over their desks, while the third was sitting on the floor, leaning against a filing cabinet with a telephone receiver dangling over his shoulder.

Ross and Parvin cautiously entered the all-white lobby where a guard station was normally manned around the clock. But it looked empty. Ross approached the window and peered inside. A uniformed man lay motionless on the floor in a fetal position, foaming at the mouth.

Parvin tested the door of the guard station. "It's unlocked."

Ross entered the small room and came out with two guns. Handing one to Parvin, he said, "Strange looking things."

"These are nine millimeter Makarovs, Russian semi-automatics. Be careful. It will fire all ten rounds if you squeeze the trigger and hold it."

Ross holstered the gun in his belt as he approached the elevator. "Do you have authorization to go down below?" he asked.

"Yes. But aren't we going up?"

"Not yet, not this way."

"There's no time," Parvin said, urgently tapping at her watch. "If we want to make a run for it, it's now or never."

"We'd be better off using the freight elevator from the basement. I doubt anyone would notice it operating at this hour." Pointing to the floor, Ross said, "Besides, I have unfinished business down there."

Parvin froze. Staring at him gravely for a few seconds, she read his thoughts…and acquiesced.

Inside the passenger elevator, Parvin used a brass key to turn the access control knob to the left. After sliding a magnetic card through the reader, the hand scanner swiveled open. She wiped the sweat off her palm against her clothes and then placed her hand on the scanner. A green light signaled authentication. The elevator groaned to life and started its descent.

Parvin nervously paced the floor as the cabin crept down. Calmly leaning against the wall, Ross thought, *If we pull this off, it'll make history.*

After about a minute, the elevator jerked to a stop. Parvin quit pacing and faced Ross as the doors slid open. "I hate coming down here," she said, breaking the silence. "It's always cold and damp."

"Not for long," Ross said under his breath.

Ross remembered which of the three doors Amir had led him

through during the VIP tour and headed straight for it. He stopped short of the entrance, turned to Parvin, and said, "Give me a hand, will you?"

Again, Parvin wiped her palm dry and placed it on the scanner. The door snapped open.

"Would anyone work here at this hour?" Ross asked.

"I doubt it."

"But you're not certain?"

Parvin shook her head no.

Ross entered the mammoth plant and started down the same path that Amir had taken him before. Passing the long row of machinery, he walked at a determined pace toward the glass double doors at the other end. Pistol in hand, Parvin followed, nervously looking in different directions.

The sliding doors automatically swooshed open. He waited at the threshold for Parvin to catch up. They entered the bomb assembly area together. The place was faintly lit and seemed deserted.

Ross whispered, "Can you turn on the lights?"

Parvin nodded and quietly walked to where the switches were located. "Now what?"

Ross pointed to the freezer-like stainless steel door against the wall and said, "I need to get inside that."

"What's in there?" Parvin asked.

"You don't know?"

She shook her head.

"A live nuke."

Parvin looked pale. "I knew they were working on it. Have they managed to assemble one?"

"Yes. And not only have I seen the damn thing, I know it works."

"God help us all." Parvin frowned as she walked toward the metal door. "I don't have security authorization to enter this."

"I do."

Ross stepped toward the work area where another half-assembled nuclear device was laid bare on the table. Using a power tool, he started to unscrew the round metal plate from one end of the device. Parvin approached nervously and said, "Do you know what you're doing?"

Ross only glanced at her. He continued taking the screws out as fast as he could, dropping them on the floor one after the other. Soon the disc fell out, revealing the shaped Semtex explosives.

"Get me a knife," Ross said.

Parvin ran to one of the tool boxes and started opening and closing the trays. "Knife...Knife...Knife." She slammed the last tray shut. "There's no knife."

Ross pointed to a work table. "You see that box cutter?"

"Yes," she said, as she rushed to get it.

Ross pried open the casing of the box cutter with a screwdriver and revealed a long blade. He carefully placed the sharp edge on the cream-colored mass of plastic explosives and made a deep, two-inch slice with surgical precision. Then he made a similar cut parallel to the first one but two inches to the right. He repeated this on the top and bottom, connecting the lines. Using the knife, he gently pried out a square chuck of the Semtex and started to knead it as if it were playdough.

Parvin swallowed. "Are you trying to kill us?"

"Don't worry; it's totally inert. Now, all we need is a detonator."

"Where do we get one?"

"There are dozens buried inside the device, but those are hard to reach," Ross said, looking at Parvin for help.

"Sorry. I can't think of anything."

"Is there a big flashlight around here?"

Parvin moved toward the tool box. "I think I saw one earlier."

She returned with the flashlight and turned it on as she handed it to Ross. Ross screwed open the top of the flashlight. Using his front teeth, he stripped the insulation from a long piece of wire. He cautiously tied the bare ends of the wire to the electrical contacts where the light bulb rested and then secured them in place with a piece of electrical tape. He unspooled about fifty feet of the cable and cut it. Then, at the other end, he wrapped each wire around a one-inch screw. Again, he secured each connection with electrical tape.

"We now have a detonator," he proudly announced.

"I'm impressed."

Ross approached the stainless steel door and kneeled in front of its massive locking mechanism. He positioned the explosive on the lock and squeezed it in place. He checked the flashlight switch, ensuring it was in the off position. Then, ever so gingerly, he inserted the two screws into the Semtex, where they were barely touching each other. He secured the cable against the giant handle with more electrical tape and started to step backward, unspooling the wire.

They entered the small conference room and crawled under the table. Ross looked at Parvin and said, "Did I ever thank you?"

"No, you haven't."

"Then, thank you." Ross said, as he pressed the ON button on the flashlight.

The shockwave blew the conference room door open, knocking some of the chairs on their sides. The smoke alarms went off as Ross and Parvin emerged from the room. The shop area looked as if a hurricane had hit it. Tools, furniture, and debris were scattered everywhere. A thick cloud of dust and smoke filled the space.

Ross headed for the stainless steel door. There was a two-feet-wide hole where the locking mechanism had stood before. Ross reached to open the door but immediately yanked his fingers away from the hot metal.

Parvin came over holding a crumpled lab coat. "Here, use this."

Grabbing the jagged edge of the hole with the cloth, Ross pulled the metal door open and stepped inside. He found the light switch and turned it on.

There it was.

The fairest fruit of Iran's age-old xenophobia; the answer to its hopes for an empire and fears of foreign occupation—a fully assembled nuclear bomb lying on a wooden cradle, as a coffin would lie in a morgue.

Looking at the nuclear device, Ross whispered, "Four times Hiroshima."

39

THE RUSSIAN PILOTS WERE HOLED UP AT THE SAN FRANCISCAN HOTEL. They were dead to the world, their phones off the hook. It took the better part of the afternoon for Veloshin to track them down and drag them out of bed for the unscheduled flight to Eureka. Exhausted from the long intercontinental flight, they were not too keen on flying again, but they saluted and rushed to the airport anyway.

Mustafa, handcuffed and shackled, was parked on the couch at the back of the plane. Roy was sitting next to him, peppering him with questions about MOIS and its operations in North America. Veloshin observed the interrogation as he played with his switchblade knife, flicking the blade open and then releasing it to close. The silent message was not lost on Mustafa. Resigned to his fate and visibly scared, he chattered nervously. Natasha was napping in one of the chairs in the midsection.

The sun was setting over the ocean when the jet taxied to a remote hanger in the far corner of the Eureka airport. A black, unmarked van with opaque windows was parked at an angle out front. Inside the giant hanger, Agent Konarski and a small contingent of the FBI's rapid response team, on full-ready standby, were staying out of sight. Two unmarked FBI helicopters had ferried the team to Eureka earlier.

Roy came down the stairs with Mustafa in tow. Immediately behind him, Veloshin was clutching Mustafa's collar so tightly he could hardly breathe. Natasha was last.

Agent Konarski met the party where the van was parked. Veloshin shoved Mustafa into the van and signaled Natasha to stand watch over him. Konarski opened the back hatch and started to itemize the equipment as Roy looked on.

"Here are the Kevlar jackets you asked for," Konarsky said. "And there's the guns and ammo…Night vision goggles are in that box; explosives are in this container."

"That's my boy," Roy said. "We've got enough here to invade China."

"You can never have enough firepower," said Konarski, as he slammed the hatch shut.

"All right, let's review the drill," Roy said in a hushed voice. Veloshin and Konarski gathered close to listen. "The safe house is about a forty-five minute drive from here. We'll wait until midnight before we make our move."

"How many men are inside?" Konarski asked.

"Scumbag says four," Roy said, pointing to Mustafa. "I believe him."

"I don't like the sound of that," Konarski said. "It's three of you on the outside versus four of them on the inside. They have the advantage. You should take a couple of my guys with you."

Veloshin shook his head. "No. The fewer people the better."

Roy nodded. "He's right. We have the element of surprise. What I need you to do is to stay up at three thousand feet and circle the house five miles out. If we need you, I'll call on you to bring in the cavalry."

"Are you sure, boss?"

Roy looked at him in amusement. "You bet your ass I'm sure."

THE ISLAMIC REPUBLIC OF IRAN CONSIDERS SECRECY AND DECEPTION as useful tools for effective governance. The office of the elected president has limited executive authority over domestic issues and none over foreign policy and national security matters. Real authority rests with a nameless council of unelected clerics, headed by the Supreme Leader, whose informal deliberations are never recorded, let alone published. Their consensus is whispered into the ears of elected front men or appointed military commanders. This, of course, is not a novel approach to governance. Throughout its long history, the Persian rulers have always operated in a secretive manner. In fact, a universally understood norm in the Persian culture is that anything of importance must be done quietly and in the shadows.

After a long audience with the Supreme Leader that had dragged on past midnight, Amir Meshkin was at home in bed.

During his one-on-one meeting with the top cleric, Amir had gleefully reported the successful testing of his nuclear device using the Blind Scorpion. He had meticulously detailed the events of the past few days, and had concluded by explaining how their nuke would explode with the ferocity of four Hiroshima bombs.

The Supreme Leader was so thrilled that he rose to embrace Amir with warmth and affection, as a proud father would his son. Then he gave his own prayer beads to Amir as a token of gratitude. The gesture brought tears to Amir's eyes.

Before leaving, Amir inquired about the fate of Dr. Shaheen and his daughter. As usual, the Supreme Leader responded opaquely. "We are not in the business of harming little girls any more than we are interested in letting the Great Satan discover our secrets."

Amir had known exactly what the Leader meant: Kill Ross, but let his daughter go.

THE RINGING OF THE SECURE, RED PHONE ON AMIR'S NIGHTSTAND WAS loud...too loud. He jumped and yanked up the receiver. The call was from the head of MOIS. Amir sat up on the edge of the bed and turned on the reading light as the MOIS chief began speaking. He explained that they had found the mutilated body of Sergey at his house and that of Kazem's hidden in the bushes at a remote corner of the Jamsheed Park.

Amir's wife was awake now, wondering what was going on. He motioned for her to be quiet, the words of the MOIS chief fading into incoherence. *Who could have done such a thing?* Amir thought. *What a horrible end to such stellar careers.* The MOIS spook continued by explaining that the men had been savagely tortured before being executed and that he had no doubt the murders had been committed by the same person...Or team.

"Who do you think is behind this?"

"It looks like the handiwork of the CIA. But I cannot be sure at this time."

"Why would they do this?"

"Are you dense? Think! They are after Dr. Shaheen."

"I don't buy it."

"Why not? It makes perfect sense."

"Surely the CIA knows where Dr. Shaheen is…Both of us are aware that they have moles in our organization."

"Then how do you explain these murders? And torture?"

"Americans aren't this ruthless. They're soft. They don't have the stomach for this kind of operation," Amir said. "This has Moscow written all over it."

"Pugachov?"

"Yes, Pugachov," Amir said. "He's looking for his granddaughter."

"Makes sense. Now that you mention it, a private Russian jet arrived two days ago and abruptly left yesterday afternoon."

"Who was onboard?" Amir said.

"They said a high-ranking GRU officer. It doesn't matter," the MOIS Chief said. "What do we do now?"

"Get a message to your boys to evacuate the safe house."

"What about the girl?"

"Release her in the woods."

"*Release* her? Are you mad? She can identify my men. How can we possibly release her?"

"The Supreme Leader has ordered not to harm the girl."

"Well, maybe she'll get lost in the woods. Or, be attacked by a bear."

Amir paused, looked at the handset, and then placed it on its cradle. He buried his face in his hands thinking, *It's time for Dr. Shaheen to have an accident. There will be an international outcry. We will offer our condolences and soon the whole thing will be forgotten. Americans have short memories.*

He picked up the phone again and rapidly punched a string of numbers. After a few seconds he said, "Have a driver pick me up in an hour and order the helicopter ready. I must go to Natanz immediately."

THE RANDOM CALL OF OWLS BROKE THE QUIET AS A GENTLE BREEZE chilled the mountain air. A drizzle started to settle in. Keeping watch, the MOIS musclemen, Mehdi and Bijan, huddled at the edge of the veranda, taking long drags off cigarettes. Jaffar, the senior officer, and his gofer, Emad, were sound asleep inside the safe house. So was Marina, chained to a cold metal bed in the cellar.

"What time is it?" Mehdi asked, staring into the darkness.

"Quarter past one," Bijan replied, as he lifted his lapels. "It's too damn late, and too damn cold."

"I hate night watch."

"Ditto that."

Mehdi took another drag, inhaling hungrily. Then, after holding the smoke in his lungs for a long time, he exhaled, saying, "You know what would stick to my ribs right now?"

"A hot cup of tea?"

Mehdi coughed. "No."

"What?"

"The girl...her soft, warm body against mine." Mehdi grinned.

"You're an idiot," Bijan snapped. "Didn't Jaffar teach you a lesson the other night when you tried this crap? Have you already forgotten the bloody nose? Broken tooth?"

"No. I have not forgotten," Mehdi said with contempt. "Who made him the boss anyway?"

"Mustafa made him the boss. Any more questions?"

"Ah, the hell with both of them," Mehdi growled. Looking into the dark abyss, he paused and then whispered, "Besides, Jaffar is probably in a deep sleep anyway."

"For God's sake," Bijan said. "Can you please get her out of your mind?"

"I'm going inside."

"No!"

Mehdi flicked his cigarette over the handrails and headed toward the French doors. Bijan followed in a huff. As soon as they entered the living room, Mehdi slipped his shoes off and began to tiptoe toward the door leading down to the cellar. Bijan slumped into a large armchair near the fireplace, glaring at Mehdi.

Mehdi grabbed the doorknob and turned it slowly. He could hear

Jaffar snoring in the loft. Once the latch released, he cracked the door and gradually pulled it open. Then he disappeared into the stairway and quietly closed the door behind him.

Bijan stared at the fake fire logs glowing on top of the gas flames. *All hell will break loose if Jaffar wakes up,* he thought.

Mehdi crept down the stairs in the dark. He stood in front of the cellar door for a minute to collect his thoughts. He felt his heart racing. He unlocked the door ever so quietly and stepped inside. The faint glow of starlight poring through the tiny window illuminated the room. He crept closer to the stainless steel bed and stood there, staring at Marina as she slept in a fetal position. A few seconds passed. As he slowly reached over to cover her mouth, the sound of a loud beep followed by a long whistle broke through the quiet. It was coming from the living room.

Mehdi quickly turned and left the cellar. He hurried up the stairs and entered the den. He almost bumped into Bijan, who was heading toward him. Mehdi noticed that the source of the sound was the large metal suitcase, parked on the floor next to the fireplace.

"What's that sound?" Mehdi whispered anxiously.

"We have a message from Tehran," Bijan said quietly. "Jaffar will come down any moment."

"Shit."

"You're lucky he didn't catch you downstairs. This time he would have killed you."

Mehdi and Bijan walked toward the fireplace, pretending to warm their hands. Soon, Jaffar came down from the loft rubbing his eyes. Emad was a few steps behind.

Jaffar looked at Bijan. "Do we have any tea?"

"Yes sir. I'll get you a cup."

Jaffar slowly shuffled over and looked inside the suitcase. Talking to himself, he mumbled, "It's about time we got some instructions." He retrieved the laminated card containing the ciphers from his wallet. Cross-referencing the day of the month with the day of the week, he typed the resulting code into the laptop. Almost immediately, the plain text communication appeared on the screen. Jaffar started to read the cryptic message, carefully whispering each word.

YOUR POSITION COMPROMISED STOP
EVACUATE HOSPITAL AT ONCE STOP
TERMINATE PATIENT STOP
HEAD UP NORTH STOP
END

Jaffar's face turned grim. He hunched over the suitcase to read the message again. And, then, once more.

"What does it say?" Bijan asked.

Silence.

"Is it bad news?" Emad said.

Jaffar slumped in the armchair, paused, and said, "The Americans are coming. Tehran says we should evacuate the safe house and run to Canada."

"What about the girl?" Mehdi said. "We can't take her with us."

Jaffar became quiet.

"Are we supposed to release her?" Bijan said.

"That would be stupid," Mehdi said. "She could identify all of us."

The three men stared at Jaffar, wondering. An uncomfortable silence filled the air. After a moment, Jaffar said, "Tehran wants us to terminate her."

"What?" Bijan said. "She is just a kid."

"I know," Jaffar said. "It's not an easy task."

"I have no trouble doing it," Mehdi said. "Why don't you guys start packing? I'll take her into the woods and take care of her."

Jaffar looked up.

Mehdi continued, grinning. "Yeah...I can't wait to carry out *this* assignment."

Jaffar stared at Mehdi with disdain.

"I'm serious, boss."

Without warning, Jaffar lurched out of the armchair, lunging at Mehdi. "You are scum," he hissed, punching Mehdi in the face. Mehdi collapsed. "I will not let you touch that child," Jaffar said, as he held Mehdi down, punching him right and left. "Son-of-a-bitch...I'll kill you!"

Emad rushed in to break up the fight. "Forgive his ignorance, sir. He is stupid." Bijan came over, lending a hand.

"Get me my gun," Jaffar yelled. "I'm going to kill this bastard first."

"Please sir," Emad said, pulling Jaffar off Mehdi. "Calm down. We have important work to do."

Mehdi's face was covered with blood. He crawled to a corner and sat up against the wall, wiping the blood off his face.

Emad and Bijan held Jaffar down in the armchair as he screamed obscenities at Mehdi.

40

ONCE THE FAINT LIGHTS OF THE CABIN APPEARED IN THE DISTANCE, Roy rolled the van to a quiet stop. They were about a quarter of a mile downhill from the safe house. Wearing high-resolution, infrared night-vision goggles, he had been driving with the headlights off.

After carefully surveying their surroundings, Roy turned and faced Mustafa in the backseat. "You're sure this is the house?"

Mustafa could only nod. His mouth was sealed with duct tape.

Looking at Natasha in the passenger seat, Roy said, "We shouldn't be long. If he moves, just blow his brains out."

Natasha pointed her Glock at Mustafa and said, "Good luck comrades."

"Luck has nothing to do with it," Veloshin whispered from the backseat. Facing Natasha, he added, "If you have to shoot him, aim for his stomach. It is more painful."

Natasha cocked her gun.

With that, Roy and Veloshin left the vehicle and gently closed the doors behind them. Roy walked around to the back of the van, opened the hatch, and began to remove weapons and equipment. First, he donned a black Kevlar vest. Then he picked up an XM8 Lightweight Assault Rifle—especially designed for NATO forces—and flung it over his shoulder. Two extra magazines, an Army knife, and two small contraptions filled with plastic explosives completed his arsenal.

Veloshin reached into the red satchel and retrieved his mini-Uzi, two loaded cartridges, and a belt stuffed with grenades. "Let's go," he said.

Roy pointed to a Kevlar vest. "Put this on."

"Not necessary."

"Come on, don't be a fool," Roy said. "They may have snipers waiting for us."

Veloshin looked at Roy, paused, and reluctantly grabbed the vest. Then he started walking toward the safe house.

Roy followed.

The closer they got to the house, the slower they moved. Every step was taken with great stealth. They traversed the last hundred feet hunched over, using the woods for cover, and communicating with each other through hand signals.

Twenty feet away from the cabin, Roy raised his head above the brush and looked inside. There were four men...They seemed to be arguing. One was seated in an armchair, while two others were standing in front of him, speaking excitedly. The fourth man was across the room, leaning against the wall.

Signaling Veloshin, Roy pointed to the electrical meter on the side of the cabin and then crossed his own neck with his index finger. Veloshin nodded, removed the grenade belt, and gestured to the front door. Roy understood, giving him a thumbs up.

Roy crawled to the left side of the house where the electric meter was affixed to the building. He retrieved one of the explosive devices from his pocket and pressed it on the meter. It stuck in place. Then he pushed a button on top of the device, activating a three-minute timer. The red digits started the countdown.

With the charge in place, Roy crept along the wall, around the rear of the house, and onto the porch. Now he could hear the argument inside but could not understand the words. He could also see the men standing in the middle of the room. One had a sidearm. There were several assault rifles leaning against the wall.

Roy pointed his XM8 rifle at the men and waited.

Holding his mini-Uzi at the ready, Veloshin tiptoed toward the front door. He took off the grenade belt from around his shoulder and quietly hung it on the door handle. Then he sneaked backward, pointing his weapon at the door, until he backed into a tree. He quickly hid behind it.

The timer displayed 1:35 as the countdown continued.

Roy noticed that the man sitting in the armchair rose. He stepped toward the men standing in the middle of the room. He seemed to be issuing instructions. After a brief moment, he reached for one of the assault rifles and cocked it into ready. Then he disappeared from Roy's line of sight.

Pumped with adrenaline, Roy could hear his own heartbeat but willed himself to remain calm. *What would this guy want with a gun at this hour?* he thought. *Where is he going? Where are they keeping Marina?*

The timer displayed twenty-five seconds.

Roy lowered the night vision device into position.

Veloshin raised his mini-Uzi and aimed for the grenade belt.

The timer displayed five, four, three, two, and one. With a deafening sound, a small explosion eviscerated the electrical meter, taking a bite out of the sidewall.

The entire house shook as the lights went out.

Without flinching, Veloshin squeezed the trigger. The burst of bullets struck the grenades, setting them off in rapid succession. The explosions gutted the front side of the cabin. Where the front door stood was now a hole large enough to drive a small truck through.

Veloshin ran to the house, slowing and taking the last steps through a cloud of smoke and dust. Glancing in several directions, he saw a man on the floor crawling toward an assault rifle. Veloshin squeezed the trigger. The man shook violently as the bullets shredded his torso.

As soon as the lights went out, Roy stepped onto the veranda. He aimed at the two men standing in the middle of the room and opened fire. The torrent of bullets shattered the glass doors and cut the men down.

Roy cautiously entered the carnage. Stepping over the bodies, he was on the lookout for the fourth man. Veloshin walked into the living room from the opposite side. Roy pointed to the loft and signaled Veloshin to check it out. Veloshin obliged and started to ascend the stairs, the muzzle of his weapon leading the way.

Roy pressed his body against the wall and started to slide toward the first door. With great care, he turned the knob and cracked the door open. Then, with a sudden move, he kicked the door in. He quickly scanned the room from right to left. It was empty.

He continued to slide toward the next door. Now he was joined by

Veloshin. Again, he carefully turned the door handle. Veloshin kicked it wide open. It led to a stairwell leading down.

He glanced at Veloshin. The Russian stared back. With night-vision gear on their heads, dressed in black and brimming with weapons, the two men looked like characters in a science fiction movie.

Roy started down the steps. Veloshin watchfully followed. There were no signs of Marina or the fourth man. A metal door stood at the bottom of the stairs.

Standing to the side, Roy pounded on the metal and said, "Listen up! Come out with your hands on top of your head."

Silence.

"You're surrounded," Roy shouted. "There's no way out. Give us the girl, and we'll let you live."

Roy heard a faint whimper. *That must be Marina!* he thought, as he gave thumbs up to Veloshin.

"As sure as I'm standing here," Roy said, "if I have to bust this door down, you'll die. Be smart, man!"

"What guarantees do I have?" an accented voice said from inside the cellar.

"This is the FBI. I cannot shoot an unarmed man. Throw down your weapon, put your hands over your head, and I guarantee your safety."

"I do not guarantee anything," Veloshin whispered. "I will kill him."

"If he surrenders, no one dies!" Roy replied through clenched teeth. "Understand?"

"I have my orders. They all must die."

"Then you have to shoot me first," Roy said quietly.

Veloshin did not respond.

"What's it gonna be?" Roy said, facing the metal door. "My partner is getting restless here. And he's trigger happy."

"You guys better stay calm," the voice said. "There's an AK-47 pointing at the girl's head. You bust in, she'll be as good as dead."

"We're cool man. You be cool, too."

A tense minute or two eked by. Roy and Veloshin stood there, patiently coaxing the man into peaceful surrender. At last, they heard someone inside unlocking the door.

Roy and Veloshin pulled back. The Russian trained his gun at the door. Roy reached over, grabbed the nozzle, and gently pointed it downward.

At first Veloshin stared at him, disgusted, but at last he obliged.

The door cracked open, revealing a faint light.

Roy said, "Stay smart. Easy. Put your hands over your head and come out."

Slowly, the door opened wider, allowing Roy and Veloshin a better view of the room. Inside, they saw a scruffy man wearing a white undershirt. His hands were raised over his head. Behind him, covered under a blanket with only her face showing, was Marina, sitting on the edge of a metal bed.

"Uncle Roy," she cried. "Is that you?"

"Yes, darling, you're gonna be fine. Just stay where you are."

Roy handed a set of manacles to Veloshin and said, "Cuff him."

Veloshin approached the man, yanked his hands behind his back, and restrained him. Then he shoved him onto the ground face down.

Roy rushed to Marina and sat next to her. Gently holding her in his arms, he said, "It's all over. You're safe. And we're going home, pumpkin."

"Don't hurt him, Uncle Roy," Marina said softy, pointing to the man on the floor. "His name is Jaffar. He's been nice to me." She paused, sniffling. "If it wasn't for him...I hate to think what would have happened to me."

She began to sob.

From where he lay, Jaffar looked up at Marina with thankful eyes.

Roy hugged her closer, "It's okay, honey. Nobody's going to hurt anyone."

Speaking into a small microphone clipped to his shoulder, he said, "Broom...Are you there?"

"Yes, boss," Agent Konarski's voice crackled over the micro speaker.

"We've got Marina. She's all right. Set the birds down on the front lawn."

"Copy that."

WITHIN THE HOUR, ROY, VELOSHIN, NATASHA, AND MARINA WERE airborne heading toward San Francisco. One of the FBI helicopters had promptly ferried them back to the Eureka airport where they had boarded Veloshin's airplane for the hour-long flight.

En route, Veloshin passed the good news to General Pugachov by calling in a coded message into an FSB voicemail.

Midway to San Francisco, after informing Oksana that Marina was safe and allowing the mother and daughter to speak with each other, Roy decided to place a call to Colonel Nash.

"Sorry to wake you, Colonel. But I thought you might want to hear the good news."

"I'm already up, and I already know. Congratulations."

Son of a bitch! Roy thought. *How the hell did he find out?* "I'm afraid to ask how you got the word so quickly."

"Then don't."

"I know you can't talk on this line, but any word from our mutual friend?"

"We're working on it."

"Please keep me informed."

"Will do."

"What next?"

"Debrief the girl as quickly as you can and then put mother, daughter, son, and the dog on that plane and send them all to their grandpa. He wants them out of sight for a while."

"Understood."

⌒᷍ℳ⌒

HANDCUFFED AND SHACKLED, MUSTAFA AND JAFFAR WERE IN THE other helicopter heading for the FBI Division Office in downtown San Francisco.

41

IT WAS COLD AND EERILY QUIET IN THE SECRET CHAMBER ON THE bottom floor of the Natanz facility. The nuclear device, which lay on a stand in the middle of the softly lit room, seemed deceptively harmless. The hunk of shiny metal could easily pass for a refrigerator or some industrial equipment. But Ross knew better. "Four times Hiroshima" meant exactly that.

Hiroshima conjures up images of Hell. No other manmade event in history has killed more people and caused more destruction in an instant than the detonation of the nuclear bomb, coldly named "Little Boy," over the sleepy town of Hiroshima, Japan, at 8:15 AM on August 6, 1945. All told, "Little Boy," yielding 13 kilotons of TNT, incinerated nearly 100,000 inhabitants and leveled several square miles.

Ross was staring at four times the destructive power of "Little Boy" before him. For a moment, he couldn't believe what he was seeing. It all seemed surreal.

Parvin broke the silence as she cautiously approached the bomb. "Is this really a live nuke?"

Ross nodded.

"They finally built it?"

"You didn't know?"

Parvin shook her head. "What's its yield?"

Ross stood next to the bomb and faced her. "Over forty kilotons."

Parvin's eyes widened. "Wow."

Ross nodded.

"It's a monster," Parvin said.

"That it is."

"What are you thinking?"

"I'm thinking that a nuclear explosion might be the only way to end this nightmare. It would destroy this plant, set Iran's nuclear program ten years back, and maybe prevent an all out war in the Middle East."

"Yeah," Parvin said. "Sooner or later, all hell will break loose around here."

"But if this place just blew up mysteriously, then, that's a different story. People might think it was an accident."

"Can you make this explode?"

"Yes," Ross said. "I've been studying its fire control mechanism—it's quite primitive."

"What about the city? Will there be any fallout?"

"I doubt it."

"But you're not sure?"

"Underground nuclear tests are usually conducted at depths of more than 200 meters. We're not that deep, but all the layers of concrete should help contain the explosion. I doubt if anything will reach the surface. This whole place would just implode. Shockwaves will reach the city, but they will not cause any major damage."

"But you're not sure?"

Ross shook his head.

"You're not talking about a suicide mission...are you?"

"*Hell*, no!" Ross said.

"Then let's go to work. We don't have much time."

"I need the power screwdriver, a set of hand tools, wires, soldering gun, and electrical tape."

As Parvin ran out to fetch the tools, Ross climbed on top of a folding chair and brought down a wall clock—the old fashioned kind with hands—and placed it on the chair. Then he turned and slowly approached the nuclear device. A torrent of emotions raced through him as he walked around the bomb. He ran his hand along the edge of its case, recalling something he had heard in a speech. *"Courage is not about what you've done before; it's not about what you plan to do tomorrow; it's all about what you're prepared to do today—here and now."* Then he thought about his brother, recalling the image of his grave: *I'll do this for you, Sohrab.*

Parvin entered the room carrying a plastic bucket. She placed it on the floor before Ross. "Here is your stuff."

Ross pointed to the wall clock laying flat on the chair. "See if you can remove the glass cover. Make sure you don't damage the hands."

Using the power tool, Ross started to take out the screws that held the top plate in place. Within minutes, the metal sheet was loose. He pushed it away, letting it clatter to the floor. She flinched, and then continued with what she was doing.

Ross set out to examine the device. He had studied the blueprints before, but touching the actual gadget with his own two hands was altogether a different experience.

Inside the casing, the hourglass-shaped bomb was secured in place, fitted with wooden blocks on all sides. The wide ends of the apparatus, stuffed with Semtex explosives, narrowed into the fission chamber in the middle where the highly enriched uranium disks were kept a few inches apart. The fire control panel was located above the middle chamber. It consisted of an electronic ignition mechanism with an attached numeric keypad and built-in circuitry that recognized preprogrammed authentication codes. Once activated, it would close the power loop, sending simultaneous electrical surges to the Semtex masses at both ends of the bomb. The resulting explosion would in turn smash the two uranium disks together, causing a violent chain reaction.

Ross slowly removed the cover of the control panel, revealing an electronic circuit board stuffed with banks of microchips. He carefully popped a microprocessor out of its socket with a small screwdriver, and then another. He paused to wipe the sweat off his hands and forehead. Then he took a deep breath and proceeded to snip a pair of red and black wires coming out of the panel, stripping the insulation from their tips.

"Is the clock ready?"

"I'm just about done. Give me a minute."

"We don't have a minute...hurry up!"

"Okay, okay, here it is."

Ross gently placed the clock on top of the deactivated control panel. Using the soldering gun, he attached a cut of wire to the tip of the long hand. Then he fixed another piece of wire to the face of the timer at the twelve o'clock position. He manually turned the long hand to the top to ensure a good connection would be made between the wires. It was perfect. He then proceeded to connect the clock, the bomb's power source, and the loose wires so that once the long hand reached the top of the clock the electrical circuit would be closed, causing the nuclear device to detonate.

He took a deep breath and then nudged the long hand to the one o'clock mark. "Fifty-five minutes to Armageddon," he said under his breath. Then he glanced at his watch: 5:02 AM. "We need to get the hell out of here."

"I'm ready."

With Parvin in tow, Ross led the way out of the secret chamber, into the bomb assembly area, and then toward the automatic sliding glass doors. They passed the doors and rushed toward the giant freight elevator. Ross pushed the call button repeatedly. Nothing happened. Parvin stepped forward and slid her red magnetic card into a slot to the right of the call button and then glanced at him, smiling.

The elevator groaned to life. Ross and Parvin stood in the hallway staring at the stainless steel doors as the hydraulics moaned in the background. Ross kept looking at his watch, waiting for the elevator to arrive.

All of a sudden, a voice called out from afar. "Who's there? What are you doing?"

Ross turned to Parvin. She whispered, "I guess someone missed the tea cart."

Ross tiptoed to a large machine and hid behind it. She shouted, "It's me, Parvin…Parvin Esmatt."

"What is going on?" A uniformed guard stepped forward, holding a machinegun at his side. It was pointing down. "Have you seen all the dead bodies?"

"Dead bodies?" Parvin acted surprised. "What dead bodies?"

The giant doors parted open.

"Why are you using the freight elevator?"

"I was down here studying a manual," Parvin said, "and for some reason, the lobby elevator wouldn't recognize my handprint." She held up her right palm. "So, I thought I would try this one."

"Something isn't right." The guard stepped closer. "Everyone is dead, the phones are cut off, and you are not where you're supposed to be at this hour."

"I don't know what you're talking about. I told you—"

"Hands up!" The guard pointed his weapon at Parvin. "You're under arrest."

"But you're making a huge mistake."

Ross sneaked out of hiding, aimed his gun at the back of the man's head, and squeezed the trigger. The semi-automatic Makarov fired five rounds in a burst. The guard collapsed in a heap, twitching.

Ross said, "Let's go."

Parvin walked into the spacious freight elevator and pushed the UP button. Stuffing the Makarov into his jacket pocket, Ross walked in as the steel doors closed behind them.

THE MI-28 HIND STREAKED ACROSS THE DESERT SKY TOWARD NATANZ in the dead of night. Aboard the Russian-made helicopter, Amir Meshkin sat in a window seat staring into the abyss, fretfully thumbing his prayer beads.

He had reasons to be anxious. Two of his close lieutenants, Kazem and Sergey, had been savagely murdered; his repeated phone calls to the underground bunker would mysteriously ring busy; and to top it all, he had to deal with the nuisance of terminating Dr. Shaheen and making it look like an accident.

Something is seriously wrong, he thought, as he glanced at his watch. 5:08 AM. *We have never had any problems with the communication systems. Now, all of a sudden, even the backup circuits are not working. What could it be?* His thoughts were suddenly interrupted by the voice of the pilot crackling in his headset. "We will arrive in twenty minutes, sir."

The first faint rays of the dawn could be seen over the horizon.

THE MASSIVE ELEVATOR DOORS SLID OPEN. ROSS STUCK HIS HEAD OUT, looking in every direction. Other than a handful of semi-trucks and fuel tankers parked neatly to the right, the area was deserted. Pistol in hand, he cautiously stepped out with Parvin closely behind him.

"Where are we?"

"This is the loading area," Parvin said, and then pointed to the opening of a large tunnel opposite the elevator. "That tube leads to the entrance plaza where my car is parked."

Ross looked at this watch. 5:15 AM. "We have forty minutes left."

"Let's run for it," Parvin said.

The tunnel was wide enough to accommodate two eighteen-wheelers passing each other. The dimly lit passageway sloped upward, stretching the length of a football field.

With a healthy measure of bravado, Ross started running on the right shoulder. Parvin tried to keep up with the running enthusiast but couldn't. Every once in a while, Ross would stop, allowing her to catch up. Within a few minutes, they reached the mouth of the tunnel.

Ross breathed the fresh morning air deep into his lunges. *Delicious!* He had been underground for over a week. *Thank you, God!*

Again, he looked out, his eyes scanning their surroundings. It was deathly quiet. The access road was sandwiched by vast and mostly empty parking lots. He recognized the administrative building where his VIP tour had started. The distant silhouette of a large watchtower stood conspicuously against the backdrop of the faintly glowing horizon.

"Where's your car?"

"It's the white Toyota. Out there." Parvin pointed. "Don't run, just walk by my side."

Ross stuffed the gun in his jacket pocket. Trying their best to appear calm and businesslike, the two approached Parvin's vehicle at a determined pace. Ross darted his eyes in every direction without turning his head. There were a few people, mostly security guards, nonchalantly milling about near the perimeter fence. Time and again, Ross glanced at the menacing watchtower.

He whispered, "I wonder if someone up there has us in his crosshairs."

"Probably."

They reached the white Toyota. Parvin took the wheel as Ross climbed into the passenger seat. Driving out of the parking lot, Parvin said, "Put your head back and hold your chest in agony. You're having a heart attack."

Ross checked the time. 5:25 AM.

He pressed his neck into the headrest, worrying about the unknown that lay ahead. What would he do next? How would he leave the country? All the while, he felt pity for the people that worked at Natanz. After a week of living among them, it was no longer an abstract sympathy; it was up close and personal. He had come into contact with these living, breathing human beings. The butler who tended his needs, the technicians doing their jobs, and the stiff security guards waving him through as long as he stayed in the vicinity of Amir's office. These were innocent victims. The lucky ones were already dead.

Then he thought about Marina as he grabbed his chest.

Parvin rolled the Toyota to a gentle stop before the main gate. A uniformed guard with a machine gun flung over his shoulder stepped out of a small building and walked toward them. She took her hands off the wheel and wiped the sweat on her dress.

"ID please."

Parvin handed a plastic badge to the man.

"Why are you leaving during lockdown?"

"This gentleman is a special consultant and a friend of Mr. Meshkin. He is having severe chest pains; it could be a heart attack. I am taking him to the emergency room."

"Does Director Meshkin know this?"

"I couldn't reach him. Something is wrong with the phones."

"Stay here. I'll try to call him."

Parvin nervously glanced at Ross as the guard disappeared into the small building.

"How much time do we have?" she whispered.

"Twenty-five minutes."

"How far should we be from here to be safe?"

"Five kilometers…At least."

A minute went by. Parvin couldn't take the wait any longer. She left the vehicle and started toward the small building. Ross held his chest and dropped his head while spying on Parvin. As soon as she reached the entrance, the guard stepped out.

"I couldn't reach Director Meshkin, but he's on his way here. He should arrive shortly…Just wait in your car until his helicopter lands."

Parvin turned up her volume. "This man may die in the next five minutes! As I told you before, he's a very important scientist and a close friend of Mr. Meshkin." She then lowered her voice. "Are you going to tell the Director that you let his honored guest die here on your watch?"

The guard hesitated. "Let me try to reach Director Meshkin one more time."

Parvin turned and glanced at Ross as she followed the guard inside. The guard leaned his machine gun against the wall, sat behind a small desk, and spoke into a microphone. "Director Meshkin, come in please. Director Meshkin, can you hear me?"

A faint voice crackled. "This is Meshk—" and was soon lost in the noise.

"We don't have time for this!" Parvin said.

"Sit down, sister." The guard pointed to a folding chair. "A minute isn't going to make any difference."

"Director Meshkin, can you hear me?"

"Yes," the voice responded. "What's the matter?"

Parvin froze; her heart racing.

"We have a medical emergency," the guard said. "Your guest has had a heart attack, and someone wants to take him out during lockdown."

"No!" the voice crackled. "Stop them—"

The guard jumped out of his chair and reached for his weapon. Before he could pick it up, there was a gunshot. The guard collapsed in a heap. Parvin turned to look at the shooter. Ross was standing at the entrance pointing his Makarov at the guard.

After a few awkward seconds, Ross said, "We better get the hell out of here."

Parvin couldn't move.

"Come on! Let's go."

Parvin rose and said, "I think this button opens the gate." She pressed it. The gate opened.

Parvin and Ross returned to the vehicle, walking slowly. As she sped through the checkpoint, her hands started to tremble.

Ross rolled down the window to take in the fresh air. But for the faint sound of a helicopter whipping in the distance, the road leading to the city was very quiet. He looked up into the dark blue sky for the source of the whipping sound but could not see anything.

Parvin nervously looked into the rearview mirror.

"Are we being followed?" Ross said.

"No. Not that I can see."

"Where are we going?"

"Your driver is waiting at my house."

"You mean Reza?"

"Yes."

"This guy is incredible! I haven't figured out whose side he is on."

"The side that pays the most."

"I hope that's our side."

A minute of silence passed. Parvin said, "Can you describe the explosion and what will happen down there?"

"It's really fast. It only takes one millisecond for the entire energy to be released. Shockwaves will be felt miles away, and seismographs all over the world will pick up the event as if it were an earthquake." Ross leaned his head out of the window, inhaling deep. Then he continued. "The explosion vaporizes everything—rock, concrete, and steel—creating a huge underground spherical chamber filled with superheated radioactive gas. The initial temperature exceeds that of the surface of the sun. As the chamber cools, a pool of molten rock collects at the bottom. A few minutes later, the pressure starts to fall, and the chamber collapses in on itself, causing total destruction at the surface. What you'll wind up with is a giant crater."

Parvin did not ask any more questions.

Speeding eastbound through the dusty main street, Ross suddenly noticed the white CNN van parked in front of a small motel.

"Stop! Turn around!"

"What are you talking about?"

"I said, turn the damn car around! I need to see someone at that hotel."

Parvin slammed the breaks. The Toyota screeched to a halt in a cloud of dust. "You must be out of your mind," she said under her breath, as she turned around and headed for the motel.

She parked at an angle next to the CNN van. Ross opened the door and said, "Keep the engine running, I'll only be a minute."

"Hurry up!"

He ran inside and walked straight to the counter. A bored-looking, middle-aged man was sitting on a folding chair reading a newspaper, his feet propped up on a wooden box. Once Ross reached the counter, the man looked up. "What do you want?"

"Is Leila Conner staying here?"

"We cannot give out that information."

Ross pointed his gun at the man's head. "Do you want your brain splattered all over that wall?"

"She is upstairs." He pointed to a narrow staircase. "Third room on the left."

Ross reached over the counter, picked up the phone console, and yanked it out of its socket. Then he threw it across the small lobby. "You won't need this for a while." Then he rushed up the stairs.

Third room to the left, he pounded on the door. "Leila!" A few seconds later, he pounded again. "Leila! Are you there?"

"Yes," a faint voice responded. "Who is this?"

"Ross…Ross Shaheen. Open the door. It's urgent!"

"Hang on."

Ross stared at the doorknob for a few long seconds. Finally it turned; the door cracked open, revealing Leila wearing a long, white nightgown. She stepped into the hallway, closed the door behind her, and hugged Ross eagerly. "Where the hell have you been? I thought you were dead."

"I don't have time to explain." Ross gently pushed her back to face her. "Can I come in?"

"I'm not alone."

"Oh…then, just listen. Your room faces the mountain. Get your camera man to set up at your window and film the plant. It'll blow up in fifteen minutes."

"Blow up?"

"Yes."

"How?"

"I said there's no time to explain. This will be the story of the century, and a great finale for your documentary. Understand?"

"Is it safe here?"

"Yes. Things will shake up a bit, but you won't be harmed. If you see gasses or dust venting from the site, make sure you're not down wind."

"Is it nuclear?"

"Yes…but it's deep underground."

"Then what?"

"Then, get your crew, grab your tapes, and go to the closest airport. I believe that would be Isfahan, and get the hell out of here—fast."

"What about you?"

"I'll be fine."

Leila hugged him again. "Will I ever see you again?"

"Probably not, and, please…we never met. Okay?"

Leila nodded.

THE HELICOPTER LANDED. THIS TIME, INSTEAD OF THE GOLF CART, AN open jeep waited at the landing zone. Amir Meshkin climbed aboard and said, "Step on it."

Amir ran inside the administrative building, heading straight for the elevator. During the overnight lockdown, only he and a handful of other senior officers could enter or exit the underground facility.

The stainless steel doors started to close as Amir, staring at the giant portrait of the Supreme Leader hanging in the lobby, swirled his prayer beads around his index finger.

AT THE EASTERN EDGE OF THE DUSTY TOWN, PARVIN PULLED THE Toyota into a side alley and stopped in front of a small, two-story house. In front of the building, the all too familiar Reza was standing next to an Iranian-made pickup truck loaded with wooden crates. As soon as he saw them, he entered the truck and started the engine.

"He will get you out of the country," Parvin said.

"What about you?"

"I'm heading north to Tehran. And, from there, I'll go where Langley sends me."

Ross looked at his watch. "We better get going; we have about six minutes left."

"Good luck, Ross."

Ross looked at Parvin, squeezed her hand, and nodded approvingly. He regretted that he could find no words to properly convey his gratitude.

As soon as he left her car, she took off in a cloud of dust. Seconds later, Reza turned the truck around and headed in the opposite direction, with Ross in the passenger seat.

"Good to have you back, Dr. Shaheen."

"Good to be back. Which way are we going?"

"West toward Iraq…We'll cross the border at Shalamcha, and, God willing, we'll be in Basra before sundown."

"We can't go west. That's where the plant is. Go south for about ten kilometers first and then turn west."

"Why?"

"You'll find out soon enough."

LEILA CONNER STOOD NEXT TO HER CAMERAMAN AS HE HURRIEDLY placed the CNN-emblazoned video equipment on top of a hefty tripod and trained its telephoto lens out of the window.

"All is set."

"Got enough tape?"

"Two hours worth."

"Keep it rolling."

The image came alive on a small TV monitor. He zoomed in on the sprawling Natanz facility perched conspicuously on the slope of the mountain.

"Zoom in," Leila said. "Make it a little tighter."

Seconds felts like minutes and minutes like hours. The rest of her crew was busily packing their bags and loading the rest of their equipment into the CNN van.

AMIR MESHKIN KNEW SOMETHING WAS AFOUL AS SOON AS HE ENTERED the operation center. Corpses were scattered everywhere. His first stop was his office. Ross was gone. *Damn!* He hurried to the elevator. At the bottom floor, he started running toward the bomb assembly area. The place was in ruins. The steel door to the bomb chamber had been blown to bits. He ran inside and looked at the device. Its top cover had been removed. Puzzled, he approached cautiously. Once he saw the clock with wires sticking out of it, the penny dropped. He screamed, "No!" as he lunged toward the bomb. "Damn you, Ross! Damn you!"

Suddenly, for a fraction of a second, he saw his Armageddon.

AT THE MOTEL, THE ROOM STARTED TO SHAKE AS IF THERE WAS AN earthquake. Leila Conner fell on the floor but quickly stood up. "Are you filming this?"

"Yes," the cameraman said, with exuberance. "This is incredible."

The earth around the facility began to swell into the shape of a shallow dome and then receded, radiating concentric waves of rock and dirt. As one wave fell, a new one followed. The ground continued to tremble underneath their feet. Then the roar of the explosion arrived. Coming from several miles away, it was still deafening. Leila was transfixed, staring at the small TV monitor. Once the rolling waves stopped, a cloud of dust kicked up in the air, obscuring the view. Soon, all that was left of the sprawling Natanz uranium enrichment facility was a gigantic crater on the side of the mountain.

"You'll get the DuPont Award for this," the cameraman said, as he peered through the eyepiece.

"Let's get out of here alive. We'll worry about the DuPont later."

THE SHOCKWAVES MADE PARVIN SWERVE OFF THE ROAD. SHE ROLLED to a stop on the shoulder and came out of the Toyota looking south. All that was left of the plant was an enormous crater beneath a huge cloud of dust. The ground continued to tremble gently. Awestruck, she thought, *And these idiots were thinking of dropping this on Tel Aviv? What fools! Israel would retaliate with fifty such bombs and throw Iran back to the Stone Age.* She started her Toyota, heading north. *It's better this way.*

REZA STOPPED HIS NOISY TRUCK IN THE MIDDLE OF THE ROAD TO HAVE a better view. Mesmerized by the scale of the explosion, he stared but didn't ask any questions. He could imagine what must have transpired. He gave Ross a knowing look and continued west toward Isfahan, and then onward to the Iraqi border.

Thirty minutes after the explosion, Ross reached into the inside pocket of his jacket and retrieved his CIA-issued cell phone. It had some juice left. He dialed a number and pressed the phone to his ear.

"I'll be damned!" Colonel Nash said exuberantly. "You made it out alive?"

"Sorry to disappoint you, Colonel."

"I haven't seen the satellite photos yet, but I know something big has blown up in Natanz. What is it?"

"Let me put it to you this way: all that's left of the Natanz enrichment plant is a giant crater...You won't have to worry about the mullahs getting their hands on any nukes for a long time to come."

"Great news! I'll brief the President."

"Wait until you hear the whole story. The program was much bigger than we thought...I have a lot to tell you."

"I see you're heading west." Nash looked at the computer monitor on his desk showing the location and trajectory of the signal Ross's cell was transmitting. "There will be a chopper ready at the border to pick you up and deliver you to the Green Zone. I'll leave for Baghdad as soon as I can. I want to hear your story first-hand."

Ross was afraid to ask, but he had to. His heart started to pound in his chest. He took a deep breath and said, "Any news from Marina?"

"Relax. She's safe."

Ross closed his eyes and exhaled. Blood rushed to his head, giving him a sense of euphoria. He looked up. *Thank you!*

Colonel Nash continued. "With a little help from our Russian friends, we found her location and then Roy and his boys went out and grabbed her. She's shook up, but she'll be fine."

"Where is she now?"

"As we speak, your entire family is on its way to Moscow. General Pugachov thought it would be best that they stayed with him for a while, until things settle down."

"Can you arrange a lift for me to join them?"

"Sure thing," Nash said. "And with you out of sight, the Iranians will assume that you died in the bunker. It's better to let them think that."

"How is that?"

"If they know you're alive, they won't rest until they kill you. It's that simple. You've seen too much."

Ross listened.

"Besides, they might blame you for the explosion. You didn't have anything to do with it, did you?"

"My hands may be dirty, Colonel," Ross paused for effect, "but my conscious is clear."

"All the same, you should vanish."

"So, we pretend I'm dead?"

"Yes, or else, you will be."

"For how long?"

"For as long as it takes...until there's a regime change. Or, until we can establish a new identity for you."

"What about the Lab, my job?"

"Forget about the Lab for now. Until things cool off, you'll be a nuclear science advisor to the Agency. And we always take care of our own."

Ross nodded. "I guess that's an offer I can't refuse."

"So, it's settled."

"Let me make it to the border alive and to the Green Zone in one piece—then we'll discuss my future career."

"After what you've been through, that's a walk in the park. But before I let you go, I've been dying to ask you a question."

"Shoot."

"Why did you name your system, *The Blind Scorpion?*"

"It started as a joke." Ross smiled. "I thought the flash of light from a nuclear explosion in some remote desert would blind all the scorpions."

"Only a mad scientist would think of that."

"I guess that's what I was back then."

"And now?"

"Now, I'm a ghost."

THE FALL WEATHER IN THE MOSCOW COUNTRYSIDE WAS TOO COLD for Ross's comfort. After living in the perfect climate of the Bay Area for over two decades, he dreaded the approaching winter.

Following his harrowing escape from the jaws of death at Natanz, he had been living, along with his family, in a comfortable cottage inside the sprawling, barricaded compound of Viktor Pugachov's dacha. News agencies the world over had pronounced him dead—victim of a strange nuclear accident in the underground enrichment facility. Even his colleagues at the Berkeley Lab had held a memorial service in his honor. Aside from Colonel Timothy Nash and a few senior officers in the U.S. Government, only Roy Sullivan was in on the secret. In fact, Roy had made a clandestine trip to Moscow to pay his old pal a private visit.

Lounging on a comfortable sofa, Ross and Oksana were ready to watch the long anticipated documentary—*Mushroom in the Sand*. The two-hour special was billed as the most comprehensive review of Iran's secret nuclear program. It was supposed to end with the exclusive footage of the famous "incident" at Natanz. Even before the official broadcast of the documentary, the reporter, Leila Conner, had become a news superstar. She was nominated for every award and recognition in television journalism.

Marina and Victor joined their parents a few minutes into the broadcast. The entire family watched the program with great interest. At times, they would press the pause button on the DVR to stop the show and pepper Ross with questions.

In the closing scene, Leila Conner appeared on screen with a huge still photo of the Natanz explosion as backdrop. The black and white picture showed the crater that was once Natanz beneath an enormous dust ball—eerily resembling a mushroom cloud.

"What you just witnessed has an unseen and unsung hero—a renowned physicist, and a dear friend. If it weren't for his generous contributions and assistance, this program would not have been possible. And if it weren't for his final act of heroism, this historic footage, documenting the annihilation of Iran's notorious uranium enrichment plant at Natanz, would not have been recorded. I cannot identify our hero, but wherever he might be, if you're watching, I dedicate this program to you."

Oksana turned and stared at Ross. "Is she talking about you?"

"No dear. I've never met Leila Conner." Ross stood and started toward the kitchen. "Besides, nowadays, in Iran, physicists are a dime a dozen."

Back in Mill Valley, Roy and Alice Sullivan watched the much-hyped CNN documentary from the comfort of their den. As Leila Conner signed off the program with a tribute to some mystery physicist, Roy glanced at her autographed photo, now framed and placed on the mantle; he then turned to a picture of him and Ross taken in their backyard and shook his head, grinning.

"Son of a bitch!" he whispered.

THE END.

www.ingramcontent.com/pod-product-compliance
Lightning Source LLC
Chambersburg PA
CBHW031144050726
47495CB00018B/629